D0944400

THE WORLD'S CLASSICS

599

CHEKHOV
SELECTED STORIES

Oxford University Press, Ely House, London W. 1

GLASGOW NEW YORK TORONTO MELBOURNE WELLINGTON
CAPE TOWN SALISBURY IBADAN NAIROBI LUSAKA ADDIS ABABA
BOMBAY CALCUTTA MADRAS KARACHI LAHORE DACCA
KUALA LUMPUR HONG KONG

ANTON CHEKHOV

SELECTED STORIES

Translated
with an Introduction
by
JESSIE COULSON

LONDON
OXFORD UNIVERSITY PRESS
NEW YORK TORONTO

ANTON CHEKHOV

Born: Taganrog, 1860
Died: Badenweiler, 1904

The stories in this volume, first published between 1887 and 1902, have been newly translated from the edition of Chekhov's Collected Works *published in Moscow in 1956. This translation was first published in* The World's Classics *in 1963 and reprinted in 1966*

PRINTED IN GREAT BRITAIN

CONTENTS

Introduction	vii
The Boys	1
Miss N's Story	9
The Siren	14
The Beauties	21
The Butterfly	32
The Black Monk	64
The Student	105
An Anna round his Neck	110
The House with a Mezzanine	127
The Peasants	151
The Cart	193
A Visit to Friends	204
On Love	228
From a Case-book	240
The Darling	254
The Lady with the Little Dog	270
In the Ravine	292
The Bishop	345

INTRODUCTION

CHEKHOV loved people. He crammed his life with them, as he crammed his stories and plays. Wherever he went he knew everybody, talked to everybody, listened to everybody, liked everybody. There is such abundance and variety of people in the world of his creation that if they could all be spilled out on to the pavements and into the houses, they would supply the population of a small town. Probably it would be a provincial town, perhaps the capital of a Province, with its Governor and his wife representing the highest social circles, officials and clerks of the various Ministries jostling for rank in the service and decorations to wear in their button-holes or hang round their necks, bishops and priests and monks, rich merchants, small shopkeepers, doctors, lawyers, actors, schoolmasters, painters, writers, students, police, school caretakers, house-porters, engineers, work-people, servants, craftsmen, and their wives and sisters and aunts and children: Chekhov knew and understood children well, and wrote both for and about them with great success, as he does in one of the stories in the present selection, *The Boys*, where everybody and everything is seen through the eyes of Volodya's sisters, in the little girls in *The Peasants*, the small schoolboy in *The Darling*, and the bishop's niece in *The Bishop*. Then there would be the gentlefolk living on the estates round about, and the villages with the workers in their mills and factories, their innkeepers, stationmasters, rural policemen, postmasters, and, above all, peasants. What is more, with the exception of a few grotesques and stock characters in some of the one-act farces and the early stories written for the comic journals, none of these people is a lay figure; they are all intensely real and alive, and what they do is a part of what they are. Again and again we experience the little shock of recognition that says, 'Yes, that is right, that is exactly what happened, although it seems so unexpected'. We have the feeling that Chekhov was personally acquainted with all these people, and even when he tells us nothing about their appearance we are sure that if he wished he could describe their features and the clothes they wore with great accuracy; and because he both loves and likes most of them, reserving his dislike for those who are false to their own natures and betray their humanity, he knows them from the inside.

These figures, so clear and so individual, are not seen in isolation but as part of the great closely interwoven web of human lives; a small portion is lifted near to our eyes so that we can see the detail, but it is not cut off; the unbroken threads run on out of our sight, but we feel that Chekhov knows both the course that has brought them to this point and the way they will contribute to the further development of the pattern. The pattern in the Russia of Chekhov's day was particularly complicated and rapidly changing. The span of his short life (1860–1904) covered a period of far-reaching social and political development. The year after his birth, 1861, saw the first of the 'great reforms', the abolition of serfdom, and the year after his death, 1905, the 'First Revolution'; in 1881, a year after his first story was published, the assassination of the tsar Alexander II led to the destruction of the 'Party of the People's Will', the heirs of the nihilists and populists, and to ten years of black repression and reaction. Throughout the period industry and commerce expanded and ramified, bankers and merchants grew in numbers and importance, railways multiplied, mills and factories sprang up, largely in the country, where cheap labour was available, and the social structure was modified and shaken by the emergence or unprecedented growth of the proletariat, the petty *bourgeoisie*, and the intelligentsia.

All these developments are reflected in Chekhov's short stories, and several of those in this volume, although they were all selected on the basis of personal preference, illustrate the wide variety and the profundity of his knowledge and understanding of different social settings and situations.

The emancipation of the serfs had proved in many ways a disappointment. It set free millions of peasants, to whom land was distributed through the *mir* or village commune, but in many regions the land was poor, producing barely enough for subsistence even in good years, and to the state and provincial taxes which already put a heavy burden on the peasants were now added the instalments of the redemption payment that must be made to compensate the former owners for the loss of their land. The sombre picture of the poverty, bleakness, and crudity of village life in *The Peasants* did not seem exaggerated to Chekhov's contemporaries, and it is not surprising that some former serfs thought they had been happier and more secure under the old masters. The workers in the factories, mines, and mills and on the railways were hardly better off, and their life in the kind of conditions described in *From a Case-book* must have been even harsher and meaner. In the country the only prosperity, except for some of the landowners and a few professional people like the railway engineers, was found among the factory-owners and managers, village innkeepers, and small traders who form the subject of *In the Ravine*.

These last were often as boorish as the peasants among whom they lived. The intelligentsia, on the other hand, to whom Chekhov belonged and among whom he found perhaps the greater part of his subjects, were civilized, intelligent, and highly educated. They were largely the product of the high-school and university education made available by the educational reforms of the sixties to many young people who would have had no chance of it before, and they supplied the majority of the professional men and women who seized the increasing opportunities for lawyers in the reformed courts, teachers in the new high schools and the universities, doctors in the hospitals opened by the *zemstvos*, the elected local administrative bodies which also owed their existence to the 'great reforms' of the sixties, and so on. For the most part they were idealists and crusaders, at least in their youth, with a strong sense of their duty to the community and a determination to fulfil it, and especially to work and struggle to relieve the poverty and wretchedness of the enormous mass of the people. The fact that by the very nature of their zealous and enthusiastic spirit they so often became frustrated, restless, bored, and indifferent accounts for much of the mood of waste, futility, and vague sorrow that to many people seems to be the main and characteristic ingredient of the Chekhovian atmosphere. It is a mistake, however, to think of Chekhov as a gloomy or hopeless writer, and he himself protested vigorously against this estimate, often referring to his favourite story, *The Student*, as proof of its injustice. It is true that he was sensitive to the sadness of young lives wasted, friends and lovers lost, bright dreams fading, but he was never hopeless or melancholy, either in his work or in his life. Of all his favourite words the most characteristic and most frequently occurring is 'happiness', and the single idea that seems to recur most often in plays and stories alike is the faith that, whatever the difficulties of the present, however much has been lost in the past, happiness will come to everybody in the future. 'Yes, life is difficult . . . And yet you must admit that it is gradually getting easier and brighter, and it's clear that the time isn't far off when the light will spread everywhere.'[1] 'I'm young, and I'm still a student, but I've suffered so much already . . . And yet, always, every moment of the day and night my soul has been filled with such marvellous hopes and visions. I can see happiness, Anya, I can see it coming . . . It's coming nearer and nearer, I seem to hear its footsteps.'[2] Again, in the same play, 'Humanity is advancing towards the highest truth, the greatest happiness that it is possible to achieve on earth, and I am in the van!'[3] Sometimes the happy future is only just round the corner, sometimes it is twenty or thirty years away, sometimes two hundred, and most often it is conceived as arriving at some indefinite but comparatively remote date, but come it will, that is sure. It would be easy to find other examples of this belief; those given here all happen to have been written when Chekhov was already experiencing the rich and abundant personal happiness of his love for Olga Knipper, whom he married a little over three years before his death. But it cannot be said that to him happiness came as a consolation for past suffering and unhappiness; it was a crowning joy added to the great store he already possessed, for in spite of the inevitable trouble, pain, and disappointment of life, in spite of his sensitiveness to all sorrow and distress and his

[1] *Three Sisters*, II (1900). This and other quotations from the plays are taken from the translations by Elizaveta Fen, Penguin Classics, 1951.

[2] *The Cherry Orchard*, II (1903).

[3] Ibid. IV.

capacity for sharing the feelings of all who were sad, there can be no doubt that Chekhov was a happy man.

Anton Pavlovich Chekhov was born at Taganrog on the Sea of Azov on 17 January (o.s.) 1860, the youngest but one of a family of four brothers and a sister. His grandfather had been a serf on a large estate in the Province of Voronezh, who managed to acquire enough money to purchase his own and his family's freedom when his son Pavel, Chekhov's father, was nine years old. When Pavel Egorovich went to Taganrog, the old man remained in Voronezh, and some of Anton Pavlovich's memories of his visits to his grandfather can be found in the first part of *The Beauties*. His father opened a grocer's shop in Taganrog, but his heart was in more artistic pursuits: he was interested in painting and became quite a respectable iconographer, he taught himself to play the violin, and his favourite occupation was singing church services and hymns with his family. In later life Chekhov became, like most of the intelligentsia, an agnostic, but perhaps this early knowledge of the Church and his parents' deep and simple-hearted piety helped to give him the insight and sympathy displayed in his portrait of Bishop Peter in *The Bishop*.

He began very young to lead the laborious, hard-working life that continued until his death: as schoolboys he and his brother had to spend their spare time working in the shop and singing church music; later, when the building of a railway took trade away from Taganrog to nearby Rostov-on-Don and the grocer's shop went bankrupt, the rest of the family moved away to Moscow, leaving Anton to finish his high-school course, and he helped to keep himself by acting as a tutor to other boys. In 1879 he joined his family in Moscow and entered the university as a student in the Faculty of Medicine. He took his degree in 1884, but meanwhile he had become established as a frequent and successful contributor to the comic papers. He had begun to write for them almost as soon as he reached Moscow, in order to supplement his family's income. His father earned very little, and his two elder brothers wasted their not inconsiderable talents as writer and artist by addiction to drink, and it was not long before he found himself almost the sole support of the family. Living, as he continued to do until his death, with his parents and sister, and working hard and conscientiously at his medical studies, he yet found time to write an enormous number of short humorous stories, sketches, and studies. Many of the stories still seem very funny and are often reprinted even today, but although they contain much that is characteristic and could hardly have been written by anybody else, they are not in what we now think of as the true Chekhov style and spirit, which begins to manifest itself roughly in the years 1886–7. By this time he had published two collected volumes of his work, which had had considerable success with the public; the second had also attracted the attention of Suvorin, editor of the most important newspaper of the day, the *New Times*, who was sufficiently impressed to invite its author to contribute regularly to his paper. Chekhov's literary position was now firmly established, he was able both to write at greater length and to write what he chose, and he almost completely dropped his purely comic anecdotes; of the few written after 1886, *The Siren* is a delightful example. From this time, too, his financial position steadily improved, and at the beginning of 1892 he was able to buy a small estate at Melikhovo, some eighty versts south of Moscow, where he lived with his parents, younger brother, and sister for six years.

At Babkino, close to Moscow, where they had rented a *dacha* and spent every summer for several years, Chekhov had already grown to know country life and country people very well, and had practised as a doctor. In Melikhovo he plunged with enthusiasm into restoring his almost derelict estate to its former neat and attractive condition, and into all kinds of local activity. He took an active part in all the doings of the *zemstvo*, attending the meetings, building schools (at his own expense), helping with medical services, and acting as head of a sanitary district during the cholera epidemic of 1892–3. In the autumn of 1897 he was forced to leave Melikhovo; by that time it had become impossible to ignore that he was ill with tuberculosis and must live in a warmer climate and avoid overwork. He spent the autumn and winter in Nice; when he returned it was to the Crimea, and he spent the greater part of the next few years between the south of Russia and various health resorts in France and Germany, but mostly in Yalta, where he built a villa for himself; in June 1904 he was sent to the Black Forest resort of Badenweiler, and there on 2 July (O.S.) he died.

Chekhov's connexion with the theatre had begun as far back as 1887, when his first play, *Ivanov*, was produced in Moscow. The same play was given a production in St. Petersburg a year later, and it was followed by several successful and popular but unimportant one-act comedies. His next full-length play, *The Seagull*, was a catastrophic failure when it was produced in St. Petersburg in 1896, by a cast which did not understand it and acted it badly. Chekhov vowed he would never write another play but, luckily for lovers of the theatre, in 1898 the Moscow Art Theatre (newly founded by Stanislavsky and the dramatist Nemirovich-Danchenko) persuaded him to let them have *The Seagull* for one of their first productions and, with an excellent production, many rehearsals, and actors who understood what they were doing, the play retrieved its first failure with a success so great that the Art Theatre has used a seagull as its emblem ever since. Chekhov, who was in Yalta, could not himself attend the fateful performance, but he had seen one rehearsal. He had attended a rehearsal also of a play by Alexis Tolstoy, at which he met for the first time the actress who played one of the leading roles, Olga Knipper. After the success of *The Seagull*, all Chekhov's plays were performed by the Art Theatre, and *Three Sisters* and *The Cherry Orchard* were written specially for the theatre company and Olga Knipper. It was a great pleasure for him when the Art Theatre had a summer season in the Crimea in 1900 and he was able to see their productions of *Uncle Vanya* and *The Seagull* for the first time. At the beginning of 1901 he married Olga Knipper.

The only difficulty in the choice of stories for this volume has been that of deciding what to leave out. All the stories included were selected because they were personal favourites of my own, but it would have been perfectly possible to omit all of them and still fill all the space available with stories which qualify on that basis. Some of those included, notably *The Peasants* and *In the Ravine*, are among Chekhov's acknowledged masterpieces, but there are a number of others that are, I think, unlikely to be familiar to the majority of English readers, including two, *A Visit to Friends* and *The Black Monk*, which certainly deserve to be better known. As English critics of Chekhov's work usually refer to the stories by the titles given them by Constance Garnett, I ought to mention that in several instances I have preferred a different title; the stories I call *The Butterfly*, *The House with a Mezzanine*, *The Cart*, and *From a Case-book* are Mrs. Garnett's *Grasshopper*, *An Artist's Story*, *The Schoolmistress*, and *A Doctor's Visit*.

As always, I am grateful to Mrs. T. Tchernavina for the kindness and skill with which she has explained the Russian background of various words and phrases, so that a translation might be sought which would produce the right kind of association for the English reader.

JESSIE COULSON

THE BOYS

1887

'VOLODYA's come!' somebody shouted from the courtyard.

'Volodichka's come!' clamoured Natalya, running into the dining-room. 'Oh Lord, Lord!'

The whole Korolev family, who had been expecting their Volodya from moment to moment, rushed to the windows. By the gate stood a wide, roomy sledge, a cloud of steam rising from its troika of white horses. The sledge was empty, because Volodya was already standing in the hall, unwinding his hood with frozen red fingers. His school overcoat, his cap, his galoshes, and the hair on his temples were all covered with hoar-frost, and from head to foot he gave off such a hearty smell of frost that just to look at him made you want to shiver and say 'B-r-r-r!' His mother and aunt ran to hug and kiss him, Natalya plumped down at his feet and began pulling off his felt boots, his sisters raised a squeal, doors squeaked and slammed, and Volodya's father, in his shirt-sleeves and with a pair of scissors in his hand, rushed into the hall with a startled shout.

'We were expecting you yesterday! Did you get here all right? Quite safely? Heavens above, let him say hello to his father! I am his father, aren't I?'

'Wuff, wuff!' barked Milord in a loud bass. He was an enormous black dog, and his tail banged against the walls and furniture.

The whole blended into one prolonged joyful uproar that lasted a couple of minutes. When the first outburst of rejoicing was over, the Korolevs saw that besides Volodya there was another small person in the hall, muffled in scarves and shawls and hoods and covered with hoar-frost; he stood motionless in a corner, in the shadow thrown by a big fox-fur coat.

'Who's this, Volodichka?' asked his mother in a whisper.

'Oh!' Volodya recollected himself. 'Allow me to introduce my friend Chechevitsyn; he's in the second form . . . I've brought him to stay with us.'

'That's very nice, we are honoured!' said his father cheerfully. 'Excuse my homely shirt-sleeves . . . You are welcome! Natalya, help Mr. Cherepitsyn to take off his things. Heavens above! Put that dog out! It's torture!'

A little later Volodya and his friend Chechevitsyn, still stunned by their noisy reception and rosy with the cold, sat at the table having tea. The pale winter sun, striking through the snow and frost patterns on the window-panes, flickered on the samovar and dipped its clear rays in the slop-basin. It was warm in the room, and in their frozen bodies the boys could feel the tingling warmth and the frost, neither willing to yield to the other.

'Well, Christmas will soon be here,' drawled Volodya's father, rolling a cigarette of dark-brown tobacco. 'And it doesn't seem long, does it, since the summer, when your mother cried as she saw you off? And here you are back again . . . Time goes quickly, my boy! Before you have time to turn round, old age is upon you! Mr. Chibisov, please help yourself, don't be shy! We don't stand on ceremony.'

Volodya's three sisters, Katya, Sonya, and Masha—the oldest of them was only eleven—sat at the table, never taking their eyes off their new acquaintance. Chechevitsyn was the same age and height as Volodya, but not so plump and fair-skinned; he was thin, dark, and covered with freckles. His hair was bristly, his eyes small, his lips thick, and altogether he was extremely plain and, if he had not been wearing school uniform, might have been taken from his appearance for the cook's little boy. He seemed glum, had not a word to say for himself, and never once smiled. The little girls, watching him, at once concluded that he must be a very clever and learned person. He was thinking about something all the time, and so engrossed in his thoughts that when he was asked a question he started, shook his head, and asked for it to be repeated.

The little girls noticed that Volodya, who was always cheerful and talkative, had little to say this time, and did not smile at all or even seem glad to be at home. While they sat at tea he addressed his sisters only once, and even then what he said was very odd. He pointed his finger at the samovar and said,

'In California they drink gin instead of tea.'

He also was engrossed in his own thoughts, and to judge by the looks he exchanged from time to time with his friend Chechevitsyn, both boys were thinking about the same thing.

After tea they all went into the nursery. The little girls and their father sat down at the table and resumed the work the arrival of the boys had interrupted. They were making coloured paper flowers and chains for the Christmas tree. It was engrossing and noisy work. Every newly completed flower was greeted by the little girls with cries of delight and even awe, as though it had fallen from the skies; their papa was equally enraptured, and occasionally flung the scissors down on the table, annoyed with them for being blunt. Once or twice Mama hurried into the room with a harassed expression and asked.

'Who's taken my scissors? Ivan Nikolaich, have you taken my scissors again?'

'Good heavens above, I can't even borrow the scissors!' Ivan Nikolaich would answer plaintively, flinging himself back in his chair and adopting the pose of an injured man, but in another moment he was full of excitement again.

On previous occasions when he came home, Volodya also had busied himself with preparing Christmas decorations, or gone running into the yard to watch the coachman and the shepherd making a snow mountain, but now he and Chechevitsyn paid no attention to the coloured paper, and did not go out, even to the stables, but sat down by the window and began whispering together; then they opened an atlas and began to look at one of the maps.

'First to Perm . . .' said Chechevitsyn softly, 'from there to Tyumen . . . then Tomsk, . . . then . . . then . . . to Kamchatka . . . From there the Samoyedes take you in their boats across the Bering Straits . . . And there you are, that's America . . . There are lots of fur-bearing animals there.'

'And what about California?' asked Volodya.

'California is lower down . . . Once you get to America it isn't far to California. You can keep yourself by hunting and robbery.'

Chechevitsyn kept away from the little girls all day and looked at them askance. In the evening after tea he happened to be left alone with them for about five minutes. It was awkward not to say anything. He coughed harshly, rubbed his left hand with the palm of his right, looked glumly at Katya and said,

'Have you read Mayne Reid?'

'No, I haven't . . . Listen, can you skate?'

Deep in his own thoughts, Chechevitsyn did not answer this question, only inflated his cheeks and puffed out his breath as though he felt very hot. He looked at Katya again and said,

'When a herd of bison stampedes over the prairie, the earth shakes and the frightened mustangs neigh and kick.'

He smiled gloomily and added, 'Indians attack the trains, too. But worst of all are the mosquitoes and termites.'

'What are they?'

'Like ants, only with wings. They bite very hard. Do you know who I am?'

'Mr. Chechevitsyn.'

'No, I'm Montigomo the Hawk's Claw, Chief of the Unconquerables.'

Chechevitsyn's completely incomprehensible words and the fact that he was always whispering to Volodya, while Volodya would not play and was always thinking about something—all this was strange and puzzling. And the two older girls, Katya and Sonya, began to keep a sharp watch on the boys. In the evenings, when the boys had gone to bed, the little girls crept to their door and listened to their talk. And what did they hear? That the boys were planning to run away to America to look for gold; they had even got everything ready for the journey: a pistol, two knives, biscuits, a magnifying glass for making fires, a compass, and four roubles. They learnt that the boys would have to travel thousands of versts on foot, fighting on the way with tigers and savages, then they would acquire gold and ivory, kill all their enemies, become pirates, drink gin, and finally marry beautiful maidens and cultivate plantations. As they talked, Volodya and Chechevitsyn interrupted one another in their enthusiasm. Chechevitsyn in these conversations called himself 'Montigomo the Hawk's Claw' and Volodya 'my paleface brother'.

'Mind you don't tell mama,' said Katya to Sonya, as they went back to bed. 'Volodya will bring us back some gold and ivory from America, but if you tell mama, they won't let him go.'

On the day before Christmas Eve, Chechevitsyn spent all day studying the map of Asia and making notes, but Volodya, languid and puffy as though he had been stung by a bee, wandered gloomily about the house and would not eat. And once, in the nursery, he even stopped in front of the icon, crossed himself and said,

'Lord forgive me, miserable sinner! Oh Lord, preserve my poor unhappy mama!'

Towards evening he burst into tears. When he went to bed he lingered a long time over kissing his mother, father, and sisters good night. Katya and Sonya knew what was the matter, but the youngest, Masha, could not understand it at all.

Early in the morning of Christmas Eve, Katya and Sonya got up quietly and went to see the boys run away to America. They crept close to the door.

'So you're not going to come?' Chechevitsyn was asking angrily. 'Go on, say it: you're not going to come!'

'Oh Lord!' wept Volodya softly. 'How can I go? I'm too sorry for mama!'

'My paleface brother, do let's go, I beg you! You swore you were going, it was you who persuaded me, and now when it's time to go, you funk it.'

'I . . . I'm not funking, but I'm . . . I'm sorry for mama.'

'Tell me, are you coming or not?'

'I'm going, only . . . only wait a bit. I want to stay at home for a little while.'

'In that case I'll go by myself!' said Chechevitsyn resolutely. 'I can get on without you. And you wanted to hunt tigers and fight! If that's the way it is, give me back the caps for my pistol!'

Volodya was crying so bitterly that his sisters could not bear it and themselves began to cry softly. Silence fell.

'So you're not coming?' asked Chechevitsyn again.

'Yes, I'll c-come.'

'Get dressed, then.'

And, to encourage Volodya, Chechevitsyn praised America, roared like a tiger, described a steam-boat, scolded, and promised to give him all the ivory and the lion and tiger skins.

This thin, dark, freckle-faced boy seemed to the little girls extraordinary and wonderful. He was a hero, dauntlessly resolute, and when he roared it was really possible, standing outside the door, to believe that it was a lion or a tiger.

The little girls went back to their own room and got dressed, and Katya, with her eyes full of tears, said, 'Oh, I'm so frightened.'

Until two o'clock, when they sat down to dinner, everything was quiet, but at dinner it suddenly became clear that the boys were not at home. They sent to the servants' quarters, the stables, the steward's office in the lodge—the boys were not there. They sent into the village—they were not there either. They had tea, too, without the boys, and when they sat down to supper, mama was very worried and even cried. At night they went into the village again, and searched all the way down to the river with lanterns. Lord, what a commotion there was!

The next day a policeman came, and some sort of form was filled in in the dining-room.

But then there was the big sledge, and it stopped at the porch, steam rising from the troika of white horses.

'Volodya's come!' somebody shouted from the courtyard.

'Volodichka's come!' clamoured Natalya, running into the dining-room.

Milord barked gruffly, 'Wuff, wuff!' It appeared that the boys had been stopped in the shopping arcade in the town, where they had been going about asking where they could buy gunpowder. As soon as he got into the hall, Volodya burst into sobs and flung himself on his mother's neck. The frightened little girls, trembling to think what would happen now, heard papa take the boys into his study and talk to them there for a long time; mama was talking too, and crying.

'Is that the way to behave?' papa said earnestly. 'God forbid the school should get to know about it, or you would be expelled. And you ought to be ashamed of yourself, Mr. Chechevitsyn! It was very naughty! You were the ringleader, and I hope your parents will punish you. Is that the way to behave? Where did you spend the night?'

'At the railway station!' answered Chechevitsyn proudly.

Then Volodya went to lie down, with a towel steeped in vinegar on his head. A telegram was sent somewhere, and the next day a lady, Chechevitsyn's mother, arrived and took her son away.

When Chechevitsyn left his face was stern and proud, and he did not say a single word as he parted from the little girls; but he took Katya's exercise book from her and wrote in it, to remember him by, 'Montigomo the Hawk's Claw'.

MISS N's STORY

1887

ABOUT eight years ago, at hay-time, I had ridden in the late afternoon to the station for letters with Peter Sergeich, who was an examining magistrate.

The weather had been magnificent, but on the way back we heard peals of thunder and saw an angry black cloud advancing straight towards us. It was coming to meet us, and we were riding to meet it.

Against this background our house and the church showed white, and the tall poplars looked silvery. There was a smell of rain and new-mown hay. My companion was in high spirits. He was laughing and talking all kinds of nonsense. He said it wouldn't be a bad thing to come suddenly on some medieval castle, with its battlemented towers, its moss, and its screech-owls, so that we could take shelter from the rain and be killed at last by the lightning . . .

But now the first wave ran over the rye and the oat-field, a wind sprang up and spirals of dust rose in the air. Peter Sergeich laughed and set spurs to his horse.

'Splendid!' he exclaimed. 'Really splendid!'

Infected by his gaiety, I too began to laugh at the thought that I was going to get wet through and might be killed by lightning.

Such swift and impetuous motion as ours, with the wind taking one's breath away, stirs and pleasurably excites the breast. When we rode into the courtyard the wind had died and great drops of rain were pounding on the lawn and roofs. There was not a soul near the stables.

Peter Sergeich himself unbridled the horses and led them to their stalls. Waiting for him to finish, I stood on the threshold and watched the driving bands of rain; the sweet exciting smell of the hay was stronger here than in the fields; the clouds and the rain made it quite dark.

'There's a peal for you!' said Peter Sergeich, coming up to me after one particularly long and heavy roll of thunder, when the sky seemed to split in two. 'What do you think of it?'

He stood by my side on the threshold, out of breath from our gallop, and looked at me; I could see that he admired me.

'Natalya Vladimirovna,' he said, 'I would give anything just to go on standing here and looking at you. You are beautiful today.'

His eyes were full of delight and entreaty, his face was pale, drops of rain sparkled in his beard and whiskers, and they too seemed to look lovingly at me.

'I love you,' he said. 'I love you, and it makes me happy to look at you. I know you cannot be my wife, but I want nothing, I need nothing. Only know that I love you. Don't say anything, don't answer me, take no notice, only know that you are dear to me, and permit me to look at you.'

His enchantment communicated itself to me too. I saw the inspiration in his face. I heard his voice mingle with the sound of the rain and, like somebody under a spell, I could not stir.

'You are silent—and that is right!' said Peter Sergeich. 'Do not speak.'

I was content. I laughed with pleasure and ran through the downpour to the house; he followed me, laughing and leaping.

Noisily, like a pair of children, wet and out of breath,

we clattered up the steps and dashed into the rooms. My father and brother, unused to seeing me laughing and joyful, looked at me in surprise and began to laugh too.

The storm-clouds vanished, the thunder died, but raindrops still glittered in Peter Sergeich's beard. All the evening until supper-time he sang and whistled, played noisy games with the dog, chased it from room to room and almost swept off his feet the footman carrying the samovar. At supper he ate a great deal and talked a lot of nonsense, swearing that when you eat fresh cucumbers in winter your mouth tastes of the spring.

When I went to bed I lit a candle and threw my window wide open, and an indefinable emotion possessed my heart. I remembered that I was free, healthy, rich, and distinguished, that I was loved, but chiefly that I was rich and distinguished—rich and distinguished—heavens, how good that was! . . . Then, shrinking as I lay in bed from the slight chill that penetrated from the garden with the dew, I tried to decide whether I loved Peter Sergeich or not . . . And without deciding anything I fell asleep.

In the morning when I saw the patches of sunlight quivering on my bed, and the shadows of the lime-tree branches, the previous day sprang vividly to life in my mind. Life seemed rich to me, full of variety and enchantment. I hummed as I dressed swiftly and hurried into the garden.

What happened next?—Nothing. In the winter, when we lived in the town, Peter Sergeich occasionally came to see us. Country friends are charming only in the country and in summer; in town in winter they lose half their charm. When you give them tea in town, they seem to be wearing somebody else's clothes and to go on stirring their tea too long. Even in town Peter Sergeich sometimes spoke of love, but it sounded quite different from in the country. In town we were more strongly aware of the wall that divided us: I was rich and distinguished and he was poor, not even a gentleman, only a deacon's son and an examining magistrate; we both—I because of my youth, and he God knows why—considered this wall to be very high and thick, and when he called on us in the town, he wore a strained smile and criticized high society or, if there was anybody else in the drawing-room, sat glumly silent. There is no such thing as a barrier which cannot be broken down, but the heroes of our contemporary novels, so far as I am aware, are too timid, languid, lazy, and distrustful, and too easily reconciled to the idea that they are failures and frustrated in their private lives; instead of showing fight they merely criticize, calling society vulgar and forgetting that their criticism itself gradually turns into vulgarity.

I was loved, happiness was not far away, and indeed seemed to be standing close by my side; I lived in easy contentment, without trying to understand myself, or knowing what I expected or wished from life; and time went on—and on. People and their love passed before me, the bright days and warm nights flickered past, the nightingales sang, the air smelt of new-mown hay—and all this, dear and wonderful in remembrance to me, as to all men, passed swiftly, without leaving a trace, unvalued, and disappeared like a cloud . . . Where is it now?

My father is dead, I have grown old; all that was pleasant, and full of tenderness and hope—the sound of rain, the pealing of thunder, the thought of happiness, the talk of love—all has become only a memory, and I see before me the featureless, empty distance; there is not a living soul in the desert waste, and over there, on the horizon, all is dark and terrible . . .

There was the door-bell . . . It was Peter Sergeich. When I see the trees in winter and remember how green they were for me in the summer, I whisper,

'Oh, my dear ones!'

And when I see the people with whom I passed my springtime, I feel warm and sad and whisper the same words again.

It is a long time since, through my father's influence, he was transferred to the town. He has grown a little older, a little thinner. Long ago he ceased to declare his love, he no longer talks nonsense, he does not care for his profession, he suffers from some illness, he is somewhat disillusioned, looks on life with indifference, and lives without desire. There he sat by the hearth, looking silently into the fire. Not knowing what to say, I asked,

'Well, how is everything? How are you getting on?'

'All right,' he answered.

Silence again. The red light of the fire played over his sad face.

I remembered the past, and suddenly my shoulders began to shake, and I bent my head and broke into bitter weeping. I was unbearably sorry for him and for myself, and passionately longed for what had once been, which life now denied us. And now I no longer thought of being rich and distinguished.

I sobbed aloud, pressing my temples, and murmured, 'Oh God, oh God, my life is in ruins . . .'

And he sat there in silence and did not say 'Don't cry'. He understood that tears are necessary, and that the time for them had come. I saw pity for me in his eyes, and I both pitied and was angry with this timid failure, who had been unable to organize either my life or his own.

When I saw him out, he seemed purposely to take a long time putting on his coat. He kissed my hand, silently, two or three times, and gazed up into my tear-stained face for a long time. I think he was remembering the thunder-storm, the slanting lines of rain, our laughter, the way I looked then. He wanted to say something, he would have been happy to say it, but he said nothing, only shook his head and pressed my hand. God be with him!

When he had gone I returned to the study and again sat down on the carpet in front of the fire. The red coals were covered with ash and had begun to die. The frost crackled still more ominously outside, and the wind had begun to howl in the chimney.

The housemaid came in and, thinking I was asleep, called me by name . . .

THE SIREN

1887

AFTER one of the sittings of the monthly sessions at N. the justices had gathered in the conference room to take off their uniforms and rest for a moment before going home to dinner. The chairman, a very imposing gentleman with bushy whiskers, who in one of the cases they had just discussed had persisted in holding a 'dissentient view', was sitting at the table making a quick note of his opinion. The district magistrate Milkin, a young man with a face of languid melancholy, reputed to be a philosopher dissatisfied with his environment and looking for an aim in life, stood by the window gazing dismally out. A second district magistrate and one of the others had already left. Another, a flabby man, fat and scant of breath, sat with the assistant public prosecutor, who was an adenoidal young German, on a sofa and waited for the chairman to finish writing so that they might all go to dinner together. The Clerk of the Court, Zhilin, a little man with short side-whiskers and a sweet expression, was standing in front of them, looking at the fat man with a honeyed smile, and talking in an undertone.

'We are all ready for a meal at this moment, because we are tired and it is four o'clock, but, my dear Gregory Savvich, that is not real appetite. A really ravenous appetite, when you feel as if you could eat your own father, only comes after physical exercise, like coursing with hounds, for example, or galloping a hundred versts or so without stopping. Imagination counts for a lot, too. Suppose you are coming home from hunting and you want to dine with a good appetite, you must never think of anything intellectual; anything clever or learned always spoils the appetite. You know yourself, philosophers and scholars are the last people in the world as far as food is concerned, and not even pigs, excuse me, eat worse than they do. On the way home you must try not to let your mind dwell on anything but the decanter and the hors-d'œuvre. Once, on my way home, I shut my eyes and imagined a sucking-pig with horse-radish until appetite drove me hysterical. Then, when you are driving into your own premises, there must be a smell from the kitchen at that moment of, you know . . .'

'There is nothing to beat roast goose for smell,' said the fat magistrate, panting heavily.

'Don't you believe it, my dear Gregory Savvich, a duck

or a snipe can give a goose ten points and a beating. The bouquet of a goose has neither tenderness nor delicacy. The headiest aroma of all is a young onion when, you know, it is just beginning to fry, and the rascal sizzles, if you know what I mean, all over the house. Well then, when you get into the house, the table ought to be already laid, and when you sit down, you tuck your napkin under your collar at once and stretch out your hand, not hurrying, for the decanter of vodka. But don't pour such precious stuff into a wineglass, but into some antediluvian silver cup of your grandfather's, or one of those fat-bellied ones with an inscription, "Even monks take this medicine", and don't drink it straight away, but take a deep breath first, rub your hands, look up carelessly at the ceiling and then, still without hurry, lift it, the vodka I mean, to your lips and—your belly sends sparks all over your body . . .'

The clerk's sweet face wore an expression of bliss.

'Sparks . . .' he repeated, with half-closed eyes. 'As soon as you've drunk it, you must eat something at once.'

'Listen,' said the chairman, looking up at him, 'talk a little more quietly! This is the second sheet you have made me spoil.'

'Oh, I'm sorry, Peter Nikolaich! I'll be quiet,' said the clerk, and went on in a half whisper, 'Well, but my dear Gregory Savvich, there again you must know what you're doing. You must know what to eat. The very best hors d'œuvre, if you want to know, is a herring. You should eat a small piece, with mustard sauce and a little onion, my dear sir, at once, while you can still feel the sparks in your stomach, then eat some caviare by itself or, if you like, with a little lemon, then a radish with salt, then some more herring, but the very best of all, my friend, is those brownish salted mushrooms, if they are cut up as small as caviare and, you know, dressed with onion and olive oil . . . delicious! But eel-pout livers are a tragedy!'

'M-yes . . .' agreed the fat magistrate, narrowing his eyes. 'Another thing that is good for hors d'œuvre is . . . white mushrooms in sour cream.'

'Yes, yes, yes . . . with onion, you know, and a bay leaf, and spices. When you take the lid off the saucepan, the steam, the smell of the mushrooms . . . it even makes your eyes water sometimes! Well then, as soon as the pasty is brought in from the kitchen, you must drink another glass at once, without waiting a moment.'

'Ivan Guryich,' said the chairman tearfully. 'Now you've made me spoil the third sheet!'

'Be damned to him, he thinks about nothing but eating!' grumbled the philosopher Milkin, pulling a scornful face. 'Isn't there anything in life but mushrooms and pasties?'

'Well, a drink before the pasty,' went on the clerk, in an undertone; he was by now so carried away that, like a nightingale in song, he heard nothing but his own voice. 'The pasty must be savoury, and shameless in all its seductive nakedness. You wink at it and cut yourself a good big piece, and your fingers flutter over it with excess of emotion. When you begin to eat it, the fat runs out like tears, and the filling is rich and succulent, with eggs and giblets and onion . . .'

The secretary rolled his eyes and smiled from ear to ear. The magistrate cleared his throat and his fingers fluttered, as he apparently pictured the pasty to himself.

'This is the very devil,' muttered the district magistrate, moving away to the other window.

'You eat two pieces and save another for the soup,' continued the clerk, inspired. 'As soon as you have finished with the pasty, you must order the cabbage soup to be served at once, so that your appetite does not get blunted . . . The soup must be boiling hot. But best of all, my dear sir, is a Ukrainian *borshch* made of beetroot, with ham and tiny little sausages. It is served with sour cream and chopped parsley and fennel. Kidney soup is magnificent, too, made with giblets and young kidneys, and if you like a clear soup, then the very best is one with vegetables in it—carrots and asparagus and cauliflower and all that sort of jurisprudence.'

'Yes, that is magnificent . . .' sighed the chairman, raising his eyes from his paper, but he recollected himself at once and groaned, 'Have a bit of mercy! If this goes on I shan't get my opinion written by night. That's the fourth sheet!'

'I won't do it again! I'm sorry, sir!' the clerk apologized, and went on in a whisper, 'The minute you finish your *borshch* or whatever soup it is, order the fish to be served immediately, my dear sir. The very best of dumb fish is crucian carp baked in cream; only, so that it shan't smell of mud and be coarse eating, it must be kept alive in milk for twenty-four hours.'

'Sterlet is good, too, with its tail in its mouth,' said the fat magistrate, closing his eyes. Then, quite unexpectedly, he pulled himself to his feet, made a wolfish grimace and roared at the chairman,

'Peter Nikolaich, will you be ready soon? I can't wait any longer. No, I can't wait!'

'Let me finish!'

'Well, I'll go by myself, then, devil take you!'

With a sweep of his arm the fat man seized his hat and hurried from the room without saying good-bye. The clerk sighed and, stooping to the assistant prosecutor's ear, went on softly,

'Bass and carp are tasty, too, with a sauce of mushrooms and tomatoes. But you mustn't eat too much fish, Stepan Franzich, it's not an essential part of the meal. The chief thing is neither the fish nor the sauce, but the roast. Which bird do you adore most?'

The assistant prosecutor pulled a sour face and said with a sigh, 'Unfortunately, I can't share your feelings: I have catarrh of the stomach.'

'Don't say that, sir! Catarrh of the stomach is something the doctors have invented! It is an illness due mainly to free thinking and pride. Don't pay any attention to it. Suppose you have no appetite or feel sick, take no notice, have something to eat. If, let us suppose, the roast is a brace of snipe, and if there is a partridge as well, or a pair of nice fat quail, you'll forget all about your catarrh, I give you my word of honour as a gentleman. Or what about a roast turkey-hen? White and plump and juicy, like a nymph . . .'

'Yes, that's certainly very good,' said the prosecutor with a wistful smile. 'Perhaps I might eat turkey.'

'Lord, yes! Or what about a duck? If you take a duck so young it has only just seen the thin ice of the first frosts, and broil it on a girdle with potatoes, the potatoes cut thin and nicely browned and basted with the duck fat, and . . .'

The philosopher Milkin made a wolfish grimace and was apparently about to say something, but suddenly he smacked his lips, probably at the thought of roast duck, and without a word, impelled by some unknown force, seized his hat and ran out.

'Yes, I might perhaps eat duck, too . . .' sighed the assistant prosecutor.

The chairman got up, walked a few steps, and sat down again.

'After the roast a man feels full and falls into a blissful eclipse,' the clerk continued. 'At that moment his body is comfortable and his soul is full of sweet content. Now if you want a treat you may drink two or three glasses of cherry brandy.'

With a sharp exclamation the chairman crossed out the whole page.

'That's the sixth sheet of paper spoilt,' he said angrily. 'It's too bad!'

'Write, write, my dear sir!' whispered the clerk. 'I won't disturb you again. I'll be as quiet as quiet. Honestly, Stepan Franzich,' he continued in a barely audible whisper, 'home-made cherry brandy is better than any sort of champagne. Your whole soul is enveloped in its aroma, like a mirage, and you feel as though you were not in your own armchair at home, but somewhere in Australia, on the softest of ostriches . . .'

'Oh, let's go, Peter Nikolaich,' said the prosecutor, restlessly tapping his foot.

'Yes, sir,' went on the clerk. 'While you drink your brandy it is nice to smoke a cigar and blow smoke-rings, and then such wonderful dreams come into your head, such as being a generalissimo, or married to the most beautiful woman in the world, and this woman swims before your eyes all day in a pool among gold-fish. And while she swims, you say to her, "My darling, come and kiss me!" '

'Peter Nikolaich!' groaned the assistant prosecutor.

'Yes, sir,' went on the clerk again. 'When you have finished your smoke, you pick up the skirts of your dressing-gown, and off to your bed! There you lie on your back, stomach up, and take the newspaper in your hands. When your eyes are heavy and your whole body drowsy, it is pleasant to read about politics; here you see that things are in a bad way in Austria, there that France has displeased someone or other, there again that the Pope of Rome has been making himself awkward—and it makes agreeable reading.'

The chairman sprang to his feet, flung aside his pen and seized his hat with both hands. The assistant prosecutor, his catarrh forgotten, and faint with impatience, also jumped up.

'Let's go!' he exclaimed.

'Peter Nikolaich, what about your opinion?' said the alarmed clerk. 'When will you write it, my dear, good sir? You have to travel to town at six o'clock, you know!'

The chairman, hurrying to the door, carelessly waved his arm. The assistant prosecutor also waved his arm, seized his portfolio, and disappeared with the chairman. The clerk sighed, looking reproachfully after them, and began to gather up the papers.

THE BEAUTIES

1888

I

I REMEMBER, when I was a schoolboy in the fifth or sixth form, travelling with my grandfather from the village of Bolshaya Krepkaya, in the Don Province, to Rostov-on-Don. It was a sultry August day, oppressive and tiring. The heat and the dry burning wind that drove clouds of dust into our faces made the eyelids stick together and parched the mouth; I had no desire to look or speak or think, and when the drowsy Ukrainian coachman, Karpo, flourishing the whip, flicked my cap with it, I did not protest or utter a sound, but only roused from my half sleep and looked for a dispirited moment into the distance, to see whether a village was visible through the dust. We stopped to feed the horse in the big Armenian village of Bakhchi-Saly, at the house of a rich Armenian acquaintance of my grandfather's. I have never in my whole life seen anything more like a caricature than this Armenian. Picture a small shaven head with thick drooping eyebrows, a beak-like nose, long grey moustaches, and a wide mouth from which projected a long cherry-wood cigar-holder; the little head was awkwardly attached to a lean, hunch-backed body dressed in a fantastic costume: a very short red jacket and voluminous light-blue Turkish trousers; this figure moved, shuffling his slippered feet, on legs wide apart, talked without removing the cigar-holder from his mouth, and behaved with true Armenian dignity, staring with unsmiling goggle eyes and paying as little attention to his guests as possible.

The Armenian's rooms were out of the wind and dust, but just as unpleasantly stuffy and wearisome as the road and the steppe. I remember sitting on a green chest in a corner, exhausted with heat and covered with dust. The unpainted wooden walls, furniture, and ochre-stained floors exhaled a smell of dry wood scorched by the sun. Wherever you looked—flies, flies, flies . . . My grandfather and the Armenian were talking in low voices about pasture and manure and sheep . . . I knew the samovar would be kept going a good hour and that grandfather, after spending an hour over drinking tea, would then lie down for a nap of two or three hours, so that a quarter of my day would have been spent in waiting; and after that would come the blazing heat again, the dust and the jolting roads. I listened to the murmur of the two voices and began to feel that I had been gazing at the Armenian, the china cupboard, the flies, and the window through which the hot sun beat down; for a long, long time and would cease to see them only in the very distant future, and I was full of hatred for the steppe, the sun, and the flies . . .

A Ukrainian woman wearing a kerchief on her head carried in a tray of tea-cups and then the samovar, and the Armenian waddled into the passage and shouted,

'Mashya! Come and pour out tea! Where are you? Mashya!'

There was a sound of hurrying footsteps, and into the room came a girl of about sixteen, in a simple cotton dress and a white head-scarf. As she rinsed the cups and poured out the tea she had her back to me, and I noticed only that she was slender-waisted and bare-footed and that the legs of her long loose trousers came low enough to cover her little bare heels.

Our host invited me to have some tea. Sitting down at the table I glanced into the face of the girl as she handed me a glass of tea, and suddenly felt as though a breeze had blown through my spirit and swept away all the impressions of the day with its dusty tedium. I saw the enchanting face of the most beautiful person I had ever met in real life or imagined in my dreams. Before me stood a real beauty, and I recognized this at once, as one recognizes lightning.

I am prepared to swear that Masha or, as her father called her, Mashya, was a true beauty, but I cannot prove it. Sometimes it happens that a formless mass of clouds piles up on the horizon, and the sun, hidden behind them, stains them and the sky with every conceivable colour—crimson, orange, gold, purple, muddy pink; one cloud looks like a monk, another like a fish, another like a Turk in a turban. The red glow envelops a third of the sky, blazes on the church cross and the windows of the big house, is reflected in the water of the river and the ponds, and trembles on the trees; far away against the background of the sunset a flock of wild ducks flies home to roost . . . The boy driving home the herd, the surveyor crossing the dam in his britzka, the ladies and gentlemen out for a walk—all look at the sunset and find it beautiful, but nobody knows or can tell where its beauty lies.

I was not the only one who found the Armenian girl beautiful. My grandfather, an old man of eighty, austerely indifferent to women and the beauties of nature, gazed tenderly at Masha for the space of a minute and asked,

'Is this your daughter, Avet Nazarych?'

'Yes, she's my daughter . . .' answered our host.

'A pretty young lady,' said my grandfather approvingly.

The beauty of the young Armenian was what an artist would call severely classical. It was exactly the type of beauty which inspires one, God knows how, with the conviction that one is seeing the perfection of regularity and that the hair, eyes, nose, mouth, neck, breast, and every movement of the young body are blended into a harmonious chord in which nature has not struck one false note. Somehow it seemed that ideal feminine beauty must include just such a nose as Masha's, straight and very slightly aquiline, and just such large dark eyes, long lashes, and languid gaze, and that her black eyebrows and curly hair were as becoming to the delicate whiteness of her forehead and neck as green rushes to a tranquil stream; Masha's white neck and young breast were not yet fully developed, but a sculptor would require enormous creative talent to produce anything like them. Gazing at her, you were gradually filled with a desire to say something heart-felt, sincere, and beautiful, as beautiful as she was herself.

I felt shamed and offended because Masha kept her eyes cast down and took no notice of me; she seemed separated from me by her own special atmosphere of joy and pride, which jealously warded off my glances. 'It is because I am all dusty and sunburnt,' I thought, 'and because I am still only a boy.'

But then I gradually forgot about myself and gave myself up to the experience of beauty. I no longer remembered the tedium of the dusty steppe. I did not hear the buzzing of the flies or taste the tea; I only felt that a beautiful girl was standing on the other side of the table.

There was something strange in this experience of beauty. Masha aroused in me neither desire nor rapturous delight, but a heavy, though pleasant, melancholy. It was a melancholy as vague and confused as a dream. I felt a kind of pity for myself, my grandfather, the Armenian, and even the girl herself; it was as though we had all lost something important and vital and would never find it again. My grandfather seemed sad, too. He no longer talked of pasturage and sheep, but watched Masha in thoughtful silence.

After tea, my grandfather lay down for a nap and I went outside and sat on the steps. The house, like all those in Bakhchi-Saly, stood in the full glare of the sun: there were no trees, no awnings, no kind of shade. The large courtyard, overgrown with pig-weed and mallow, was full of cheerful bustle, in spite of the scorching heat.

Beyond one of the low hurdles which intersected the yard here and there, threshing was going on. Round a post driven into the very centre of the threshing-floor, harnessed side by side so that they formed a long radius, twelve horses were running. A Ukrainian in a long waistcoat and wide loose trousers walked beside them, cracking a whip and shouting in derisive tones, as though trying to parade his power over the horses,

'Ay-ay-ay, you damned brutes! Ay-ay-ay, devil take you! What are you frightened of?'

The horses, bay, white, and piebald, could not understand why they were being made to run round in circles trampling wheat straw, ran reluctantly, as though the effort was too great, and twitched their tails in an offended way. The wind raised clouds of golden chaff from under their hooves and carried it away over the fence. Near the high fresh stacks carts moved slowly and women bustled about with rakes, and beyond the stacks, in the next yard, another dozen horses ran round a post and another Ukrainian cracked his whip and jeered at them.

The steps on which I sat were hot to the touch; on the thin handrail and the window-frames the resin had exuded in places with the heat; little red beetles crowded into the strips of shade under the steps and the window-shutters. The sun scorched my head and breast and back, but I did not notice it and was conscious only of the sound of bare feet on the wooden floors of the rooms and passage behind me. When she had cleared away the tea things, Mashya ran down the steps, wafting a breeze over me and flitting like a bird towards a small sooty outbuilding, probably the kitchen, from which came a smell of roasting mutton and the sound of angry Armenian voices. She disappeared into the dark doorway and in her place there appeared on the threshold a bent old Armenian woman with a red face, wearing green trousers. She was scolding furiously. Soon Mashya again appeared on the threshold, flushed with the heat of the kitchen, and with an enormous loaf of black bread on her shoulder; swaying gracefully under the weight of the bread, she ran across the yard to the threshing floor, darted over the hurdle and, enveloped in a cloud of golden dust, vanished behind the carts. The Ukrainian driving the horses lowered his whip and stopped shouting at them, stared silently towards the carts for a moment and then, when the girl again darted past the horses and over the hurdle, followed her with his eyes and began shouting again, in the tone of a man with a grievance,

'Oh, to hell with you, you brutes!'

After that I could hear the sound of her bare feet all the time and see her hurrying about the yard with a serious, preoccupied expression. Now she ran past me up the steps, bringing a breeze with her, now she darted into the kitchen, now to the threshing-floor and now out of the gates, and I could scarcely turn my head fast enough to follow her movements.

The more often she flitted past me in all her beauty, the deeper grew my melancholy. I felt sad for myself, for her, and for the Ukrainian mournfully following her with his eyes every time she hurried through the clouds of chaff to the carts. Whether the cause was jealousy of her beauty, or sorrow that this girl was not and never could be mine and that I was a stranger to her, or a confused feeling that her rare beauty was accidental, superfluous and, like everything on this earth, transitory—or whether my sadness was perhaps the special emotion evoked by the sight of true beauty, God knows!

The three hours of waiting passed unnoticed. I had not had time, it seemed, to gaze my fill at Masha before Karpo had taken our horse down to the river, bathed him, and begun harnessing him. The wet horse was snorting with pleasure and clattering its hooves against the shafts. Karpo shouted 'Whoa back!' My grandfather woke up. Mashya opened the creaking gates for us, and we climbed in and drove out of the yard. We drove in silence, as though we were angry with one another.

When Rostov and Nakhichevan appeared in the distance two or three hours later Karpo, who had not spoken all the way, suddenly looked round and said,

'That's a fine lass of the Armenian's!'

He whipped up the horse.

II

On another occasion, when I was a student, I was travelling south by train. It was May. At one small station, between Belgorod and Kharkov, I think, I got out of the carriage to stretch my legs on the platform.

The shadows of evening already lay on the little station garden, the platform, and the fields; the station buildings screened the setting sun from us, but from the tip of the plume of smoke from the engine, which was stained a tender pink, it was evident that it had not yet entirely sunk.

As I strolled along the platform I saw that the majority of the passengers were walking or standing near one second-class carriage, with the sort of expressions that suggested somebody famous was sitting in it. Among the inquisitive groups near this carriage was an artillery officer who was travelling with me, and who, like everybody whose acquaintance we make on a journey, by chance and for a short time, was an intelligent, friendly, and attractive young man.

'What are you looking at?' I asked.

He said nothing, only made a sign with his eyes towards a feminine figure. This was a young girl of about seventeen or eighteen, dressed in Russian costume, with an uncovered head and a small shawl thrown carelessly over one shoulder, not a passenger but probably the stationmaster's daughter or sister. She was standing near the carriage window talking to an elderly woman passenger. Before I had time to realize what I saw, I was seized by the same emotion that I had once felt in the Armenian village.

The girl was strikingly beautiful, as neither I nor any of the others who were watching her had any doubt.

If one were to describe her appearance feature by feature, in the accepted manner, her single claim to real beauty would be the luxuriant flowing waves of fair hair, confined only by a ribbon round her head; all the rest was either irregular or very ordinary. Her eyes were screwed up, either from a peculiar form of coquetry or from short-sightedness, her nose was uncertainly tip-tilted, her mouth small, her profile weakly and uncertainly drawn, her shoulders too narrow for her age; the impression she produced, nevertheless, was of true beauty, and watching her I became convinced that the Russian face does not need strictly regular features in order to seem beautiful; more, that if this girl had been given a straight, regular and sculpturally faultless nose like the Armenian's in place of her turned-up one, her face would probably have lost all its charm.

As she stood chatting by the window, shrinking slightly from the evening damp, the girl looked round at us from time to time, put her hands on her hips, raised them to her head to smooth her hair, talked, laughed, twisted her features into expressions of astonishment or horror; I cannot remember an instant when her face and body were at rest. The whole secret and magic of her beauty resided precisely in those small, infinitely graceful movements, her smile, the play of her features, her swift glances at us, the combination of the slender grace of those movements with her youth, her freshness, the purity of heart echoing in her voice and laugh, and the fragility we so love in children, birds, fawns, and young trees.

Hers was the butterfly beauty that is so well suited to waltzing, flitting about the garden, laughter and gaiety, and so unsuited to serious thoughts, melancholy, and repose; it seemed that it would be enough for a stiff breeze to blow along the platform or a few drops of rain to fall, for the frail body to wilt and the fleeting beauty be scattered like the pollen of a flower.

'Ah, ye-s-s,' murmured the officer with a sigh as the second bell rang and we returned towards our own carriage.

But what that 'ah yes' meant, I could not undertake to say.

Perhaps he felt sad and reluctant to leave the beautiful young girl and the spring evening for the stuffy railway carriage, or perhaps, like me, he felt unaccountably sorry for the girl, himself, me, and all the passengers who were making their way listlessly and unwillingly back to their carriages. As we passed the station window behind which the pale, red-haired telegraph clerk, his curls piled high above his faded face with its prominent cheek-bones, sat by his apparatus, the officer sighed and said,

'I'll wager the telegraph clerk is in love with that pretty

little girl. To live in the country under the same roof as that ethereal creature and not fall in love with her is beyond the power of any man. And what a disaster, my friend, what a joke, to be round-shouldered, shaggy, commonplace, respectable and not unintelligent, and fall in love with that pretty silly girl who won't take the slightest notice of you! Or even worse: suppose the clerk is in love and yet is already married to a wife as round-shouldered, unkempt, and respectable as himself . . . Torture!'

Near our carriage, leaning against the railing of the platform at the end of the coach, stood the guard, looking towards the place where the beauty still stood, and his exhausted, wrinkled, unpleasantly self-indulgent face, weary with sleepless nights and jolting train journeys, wore an expression of tenderness and the profoundest melancholy, as if in the girl he saw his own youth and happiness, his sobriety, purity, his wife and children; as if he were penitent and his whole being was moved because this girl was not his and because he, with his premature old age, his uncouthness, and his fat face was as far from ordinary, human, railway passengers' happiness as from heaven itself.

The third bell rang, whistles blew, the train moved lazily forward. Past our carriage windows slipped first the guard and the stationmaster, then the garden, then the beautiful girl with her marvellous, childlike, subtle smile . . .

I leaned out of the window and looked back, and saw her following the train with her eyes, turning to walk along the platform past the window where the telegraph clerk sat, smoothing her hair, and then running into the garden.

The buildings no longer hid the sunset, open fields lay

all around, but the sun had already disappeared, and black puffs of smoke spread over the velvety green of the winter wheat. The spring air, the darkening sky, and the railway carriage, were full of melancholy.

The guard's familiar figure entered the carriage, and he began to light the candles.

THE BUTTERFLY

1892

I

ALL Olga Ivanovna's friends and acquaintances came to her wedding.

'Look at him: don't you agree there is *something* about him?' she said to her friends, nodding towards her husband and apparently trying to explain why she had married this simple, ordinary, in no way remarkable man.

Her husband, Osip Stepanych Dymov, was a doctor and had reached the rank of Titular Councillor. He worked in two hospitals, in one as supernumerary house-surgeon, in the other as dissector. Every day from nine till twelve he saw patients and worked in the ward, and in the afternoon he went by horse-tram to his other hospital and did post-mortem examinations. His private practice was negligible, bringing him in about five hundred roubles a year. And that was all. What else was there to say about him? Olga Ivanovna and her friends and acquaintances, on the other hand, were not altogether ordinary people. Every one of them was remarkable in one way or another and enjoyed a little fame, had made a name and considered himself a celebrity or, although not yet celebrated, showed brilliant promise. There was an actor whose great talent had long been recognized, a clever and modest man and an excellent reciter, who taught Olga Ivanovna to recite; a fat, warm-hearted opera singer who had assured Olga Ivanovna with a sigh that she was wasting herself: if she were not so lazy and would take herself diligently in hand, she would make a wonderful singer; then several artists, headed by the landscape, animal, and genre painter Ryabovsky, a very handsome fair-haired young man of about twenty-five, who had had great success at exhibitions and had sold his latest picture for five hundred roubles: he corrected the faults in Olga Ivanovna's sketches and said that something might perhaps be made of her; then there was a violoncellist, who could make his instrument weep, and who openly acknowledged that of all the women he knew only Olga Ivanovna could accompany him; then a man of letters, young but already famous, who had written short stories, novels, and plays. Who besides? Well, there was Vasili Vasilyevich besides, a gentleman, a landowner, amateur illustrator and vignettist, extremely sensitive to the old Russian epic-ballad style: on paper, porcelain, and smoked dinner-plates, he produced literally miracles. Among this free, artistic society, so pampered by fate, who were admittedly considerate and unassuming, but who remembered the existence of doctors only when they fell ill, and for whom the name Dymov meant no more than Sidorov or Tarasov—in this society Dymov seemed out of his element, in the way and, in spite of his height and broad shoulders, small. He seemed to be wearing somebody else's frock-coat and a beard like a shop assistant's. If he had been a writer or an artist, though, his beard would have reminded people of Zola.

The artist told Olga Ivanovna that with her flaxen hair and in her wedding dress she looked like a graceful young cherry-tree in the spring, when it is covered with tender white blossom.

'No, but listen,' said Olga Ivanovna, seizing his arm. 'What made me do this all of a sudden? Listen, listen . . . I must tell you that my father worked in the same hospital as Dymov. When poor dear father fell ill, Dymov kept watch by his bed for days and nights together. What self-sacrifice! Listen, Ryabovsky . . . And you listen too, you're a writer, and this is very interesting. Come a little closer. How much self-sacrifice and genuine sympathy! I could not sleep at night, and I too used to sit up with my father—and all of a sudden, I had made a conquest of the good young man! My Dymov had fallen head over heels in love. Really, fate plays such odd tricks! Well, after my father's death he came to see me sometimes, or we met in the street, and suddenly, one fine day—there we were—he proposed to me . . . out of a clear sky . . . I cried all night, and fell desperately in love. And so, as you see, I have become a wife. Don't you agree there is something strong, powerful, bearlike, in him? Just now we see him three-quarter face, and the lighting is bad, but when he turns round, look at his forehead. Ryabovsky, what will you say to that forehead? Dymov, we are talking about you,' she called to her husband. 'Come here. Stretch out your honest hand to Ryabovsky . . . That's right. I want you to be friends.'

Dymov held out his hand with a naïve and good-natured smile and said,

'Delighted! There was a Ryabovsky who graduated at the same time as me. Is he any relation?'

II

Olga Ivanovna was twenty-two years old, Dymov thirty-one. They set up house very successfully after their marriage. Olga Ivanovna hung all the walls of her drawing-room with her own and other people's sketches, framed and unframed, and round the furniture and the grand piano arranged a handsome profusion of Japanese sunshades, easels, multicoloured draperies, Eastern daggers, busts, and photographs . . . She pasted crude popular woodcuts round the dining-room, hung up bast shoes and sickles, placed a rake and a scythe in one corner—and the result was a dining-room in the Russian taste. In the bedroom, to produce the effect of a cave, she draped the walls and ceiling with dark hangings, hung a Venetian lamp over the beds, and set a figure with a halberd near the door. And everybody thought the young couple had a very nice little home.

Every day, rising at about eleven o'clock, Olga Ivanovna played the piano or, if it was sunny, did some painting in oils. Later, about one o'clock, she went to her dressmaker's. She and Dymov had very little money, only just enough, and simply to ensure that she frequently appeared in a new dress and that her *toilettes* were striking demanded much cunning contrivance, both hers and her dressmaker's. Very often, from an old dress dyed a different colour and a few scraps of tulle, lace, velvet, and silk costing practically nothing at all, something simply miraculous, not a dress but a vision, emerged. From the dressmaker's Olga Ivanovna usually went on to see some actress she knew, to hear the latest theatrical news and put in a timely word for tickets for the first night of a new play or a benefit performance. From the actress's she would have to go on to a painter's studio or an exhibition, and then visit one of her celebrated friends, to issue an invitation, return a call or simply talk. And everywhere she received a friendly welcome and was assured that she was pretty, charming, and unusual . . . The people she called great and famous accepted her on an equal footing, as one of themselves, and prophesied with one voice that with her talents, taste, and intelligence, if she did not squander her gifts, she could become something great. She sang, played the piano, painted, modelled in clay, took part in amateur theatricals, and all this not in a haphazard fashion but with talent; whether she made little lanterns for an illumination, dressed herself up, or tied somebody's tie, everything she did was unusually artistic, graceful, and charming. But in nothing were her talents so clearly revealed as in her ability to become rapidly acquainted with celebrated people and make intimate friends of them. It sufficed for anybody to become even a little known and talked about, and she had already met him, become friends on the spot, and invited him to come and see her. Every new acquaintanceship made a red-letter day for her. She idolized celebrities, was proud of knowing them, and dreamed of them every night. She thirsted for them with a thirst that nothing could assuage. The old ones left and were forgotten, new ones came to take their place, but she soon got used to these or disillusioned with them and began to look for other great people, and still others, found them and began to search again. To what end?

At five o'clock she dined at home with her husband. His simplicity, common sense, and kindness filled her with delight and tender emotion. Every now and then she would jump up, throw her arms impetuously round his head and smother him with kisses.

'Dymov, you are a wise and noble person,' she would say, 'but you have one grave failing. You are not in the least interested in art. You reject both music and painting.'

'I don't understand them,' he would say mildly. 'I have been busy with medicine and natural science all my life, and have had no time to interest myself in the arts.'

'But that is really terrible, Dymov!'

'Why? Your friends know nothing about natural science or medicine, yet you don't reproach them for that. To each his own. I don't understand landscapes and operas, but what I think is this: if some clever people devote their whole lives to them, and other clever people pay them huge sums of money for doing so, it means they are necessary. I don't understand them, but not understanding does not mean rejecting.'

'Let me press your honest hand!'

After dinner, Olga Ivanovna went to see friends and then to the theatre or a concert, returning home after midnight. Every day was the same.

On Wednesdays she held an at-home. On these evenings the hostess and her guests did not dance or play cards, but entertained themselves with various arts. The actor read aloud, the opera singer sang, the painters sketched in the albums of which Olga Ivanovna had a large supply, the 'cellist played; and their hostess also drew, modelled, sang, and accompanied. In the intervals between reciting, playing, and singing they talked and argued about literature, the theatre, and painting. There were no ladies, because Olga Ivanovna considered all ladies, except actresses and her dressmaker, boring and commonplace. Not one of these evenings passed without the hostess giving a start at every ring and saying with an expression of triumph, 'There he is!', meaning by 'he' some new celebrity. Dymov was never in the drawing-room and nobody remembered his existence. But at exactly half-past eleven the doors leading into the dining-room opened and Dymov appeared with his mild, good-natured smile, rubbing his hands and saying,

'Gentlemen, please come to supper.'

Everybody went into the dining-room and every time they saw on the table exactly the same things: a dish of oysters, a piece of ham or veal, sardines, cheese, caviare, mushrooms, vodka, and two decanters of wine.

'My own dear *maître d'hôtel*!' said Olga Ivanovna, clasping her hands with delight. 'You are simply enchanting. Gentlemen, look at his forehead. Dymov, turn your profile. Look, gentlemen, the head of a Bengal tiger, but the good, kind expression of a stag. You darling!'

The guests ate and thought, as they looked at Dymov, 'A splendid young fellow, indeed,' but they soon forgot about him and went on talking about the theatre, music, and painting.

The young couple were happy and their life ran on well-oiled wheels. The third week of their honeymoon, however, was not entirely blissful, in fact it was quite gloomy. Dymov caught erysipelas in the hospital, was in bed for a week, and had to shave off all his beautiful black hair. Olga Ivanovna sat by his bed weeping bitterly, but when he was a little better she draped a white handkerchief over his shaven head and began to make a drawing of him as a Bedouin. It kept both of them amused. About three days afterwards, when he returned to the hospital quite cured, he suffered a new mishap.

'I have no luck, mama,' he said one day at dinner. 'I had four autopsies to do today and gashed two of my fingers with one cut. I didn't notice it until I got home.'

Olga Ivanovna was frightened. He smiled and said it was nothing, and that he often cut his hands during autopsies.

'I get carried away, mama, and don't notice what I'm doing.'

Olga Ivanovna waited anxiously for blood-poisoning to set in, and said prayers at night, but everything turned out well. Once more life flowed peacefully and happily, without alarms or sorrows. The present was wonderful; spring was already advancing, smiling from afar with the promise of a thousand future joys. Happiness would be everlasting! In April, May, and June a cottage deep in the country, walks, sketching, fishing, and nightingales, and then, from July until autumn, the artists' trip down the Volga, in which, as an essential member of their society, Olga Ivanovna would take part. She had already had two gingham travelling costumes made and bought colours, brushes, canvases, and a new palette. Almost every day Ryabovsky called to see what progress she was making with her painting. When she showed him the picture she was working on, he thrust his hands deep into his pockets, compressed his lips, snorted, and said,

'Hm-m . . . That cloud of yours shrieks; that is not evening light on it. Your foreground is a bit chewed up and there's something, you know, not quite right about it . . . That hut looks squashed and is wailing dismally . . . that corner ought to be made darker. But on the whole, not bad at all . . . I like it.'

And the more incomprehensibly he talked, the more easily Olga Ivanovna understood him.

III

On Whit Monday, after dinner, Dymov bought hors d'œuvre and sweets and went off to see his wife in the country. He had not seen her for two weeks, which he had found immensely boring. Sitting in the train and afterwards searching for the *dacha* in the big grove of trees, he felt hungry and weary, and dreamed of having supper with his wife, and afterwards falling into bed. And he contemplated with satisfaction the parcel into which were packed caviare, cheese, and smoked Volga white salmon.

By the time he had found his own *dacha* the sun was setting. The old servant said the mistress was not at home, but ought soon to be back. In the wretched-looking cottage with its low ceilings covered with sheets of cheap white paper and its cracked, uneven floors, there were only three rooms. In one stood a bed, in the next the window-sills and chairs were littered with canvases, brushes, dirty paper, and men's coats and hats, and in the third Dymov found three strange men. Two were dark-haired and bearded, the third clean-shaven and fat, evidently an actor. A samovar hissed on the table.

'What do you want?' asked the actor in a bass voice, examining Dymov with an unfriendly eye. 'Are you looking for Olga Ivanovna? Just wait, she will be here presently.'

Dymov sat down and waited. One of the dark men, eyeing him languidly and sleepily, poured himself tea and asked,

'Perhaps you would like some tea?'

Dymov was both thirsty and hungry, but refused the tea so as not to spoil his appetite. Soon footsteps and the familiar laugh were audible; a door banged and Olga Ivanovna, in a wide-brimmed hat and with a box in her hand darted into the room, followed by the cheerful, red-faced Ryabovsky, who carried a large umbrella and a folding stool.

'Dymov!' exclaimed Olga Ivanovna, flushing with pleasure. 'Dymov!' she repeated, laying her head and hands on his breast. 'It's you! Why were you so long in coming? Why? Why?'

'How could I come, mama? I am always busy, and when I am free, it always happens that the railway time-table doesn't fit.'

'But how glad I am to see you! I dreamed of you every bit of last night, and I was afraid you were ill. Oh, if you only knew how nice you are to have come at exactly the right moment! You will be my salvation. You are the only one that can save me! Tomorrow there is going to be a wedding here, most original,' she went on, laughing and tying her husband's tie. 'The young telegraph clerk at the station, Mr. Chikeldeev, is getting married. A handsome young man, quite intelligent, and he has something in his face, you know, strong . . . like a bear . . . One might use him as a model for a young Viking. We, all the summer visitors, take an interest in him, and we have given him our word to be at the wedding . . . He is poor, lonely, and shy, and of course it would be a shame to refuse to take part. Imagine it: after the mass, the wedding ceremony, then everybody goes on foot from the church to the bride's home . . . You know, the wood, the birds singing, patches of sunlight on the grass, and all of us making bright-coloured patches on a bright-green background—very original, in the French Impressionist style. But, Dymov, what am I to go to church in?' said Olga Ivanovna, pulling a mournful face. 'I have nothing here, literally nothing! Neither a dress, nor flowers, nor gloves . . . You must come to my rescue. Your arrival means you have been sent by fate to save me. Take the keys, my dear, go home and get my pink dress from the wardrobe. You remember it, it is hanging in the front . . . Then in the box-room you will see two cardboard boxes on the floor on the right-hand side. If you open the top one, it is all tulle, tulle, tulle, and various pieces, and flowers underneath. Take out all the flowers carefully, and darling, try not to crumple them, and I will choose which I want afterwards . . . And buy some gloves.'

'Very well,' said Dymov. 'I will go tomorrow and send them to you.'

'Tomorrow?' asked Olga Ivanovna, looking at him with astonishment. 'When will there be time tomorrow? The first train leaves at nine o'clock, and the wedding is at eleven. No, darling, you must go today, it absolutely must be today! If you can't come tomorrow, send them by messenger. Well, go now . . . The passenger train must be due. Don't be late, darling.'

'Very well.'

'Oh, how sorry I am to let you go!' said Olga Ivanovna, tears starting to her eyes. 'Why did I promise the telegraph clerk, fool that I was?'

Dymov hastily drank a glass of tea, took a cracknel and, smiling meekly, went off to the station. The caviare, cheese, and fish were eaten by the two dark-haired men and the fat actor.

IV

One quiet moonlight night in July, Olga Ivanovna stood on the deck of a Volga steamer and looked now at the water, now at the beautiful banks. Beside her stood Ryabovsky, telling her that the black shadows in the water were not shadows but a dream, and that here, confronted by that magical water with its strange glitter, those infinite deeps of sky, those melancholy, pensive banks, which all spoke of the vanity of this life and the existence of something higher, eternal, blessed, it would be good to lose oneself, to die and become no more than a memory. The past was flat and without interest, the future was empty, and this miraculous, unique night would soon be over, would merge with eternity—why then go on living?

But Olga Ivanovna, listening now to the voice of Ryabovsky, now to the silence of the night, thought that she was immortal and would never die. The turquoise colour of the water, like no water she had ever seen before, the sky, the banks, the black shadows, and the unaccountable joy that filled her heart, told her that she would become a great artist and that somewhere beyond the horizon, beyond the moonlight night, there awaited her in the boundless expanse of the future success, fame, the love of the people . . . When she gazed long and unblinkingly into the distance, she could imagine crowds of people, lights, solemn sounds of music, cries of delight, herself in a white dress, and flowers raining on her from all sides. She thought also that here, leaning on the rail by her side, there was a really great man, a genius, one chosen by God . . . Everything he had created until then was beautiful, new and unusual, and what he would create in the future, as maturity strengthened his rare talent, would be striking and immeasurably great; all this could be seen in his face, in his way of expressing himself, and his attitude to nature. He spoke of the shadows, the colours of evening, the moonlight, in a special way, in his own language, so that one involuntarily felt the fascination of his power over nature. He was very handsome and original, and his life, free and independent, to which everything commonplace was foreign, was like the life of a bird.

'It is getting chilly,' said Olga Ivanovna, shivering.

Ryabovsky wrapped her in his cloak and said gloomily,

'I feel that I am in your power. I am a slave. Why are you so enchanting today?'

His gaze was fixed immovably on her, and his eyes were terrible; she was afraid to look at him.

'I love you madly,' he whispered, his breath fanning her cheek. 'Say one word, and I will cease to live, I will abandon my art, . . .' he murmured, violently agitated. 'Love me, love me . . .'

'Don't talk like that,' said Olga Ivanovna, closing her eyes. 'This is terrible. What about Dymov?'

'What of Dymov? Why Dymov? What have I to do with Dymov? The Volga, the moon, beauty, my love, my ecstasy—Dymov does not exist . . . I know nothing . . . I don't want the past, give me one moment . . . one instant.'

Olga Ivanovna's heart was beating violently. She wanted to think of her husband, but all the past, with her marriage, Dymov, and her at-homes, seemed to her petty, trivial, dim, futile, and far, far away . . . What indeed of Dymov? Why Dymov? What had she to do with Dymov? Did he in fact exist, or was he only a dream?

'The happiness he has already had is enough for a simple, ordinary person like him,' she thought, covering her face with her hands. 'Let them condemn me *there*, let them curse me, I will defy them all and perish, defy them and perish . . . One must experience the whole of life. Oh God, how painful, and how splendid!'

'Well? Well?' murmured the painter, taking her in his arms and greedily kissing the hands with which she feebly tried to fend him off. 'Do you love me? Do you? Do you? Oh, what a night! A marvellous night!'

'Yes, what a night!' she whispered, looking at him through eyes shining with tears; then, glancing swiftly round, she put her arms round him and passionately kissed him on the lips.

'We are coming to Kineshma,' said somebody on the other side of the deck.

There was the sound of heavy steps. It was a waiter from the bar going past.

'Here!' said Olga Ivanovna, laughing and crying with happiness. 'Bring us some wine.'

The artist, pale with emotion, sat down on the seat, looked at Olga Ivanovna with grateful, worshipping eyes, then closed them and said with a weary smile,

'I'm tired.'

And he leaned his head against the side.

V

The second of September was warm and still, but overcast. Early in the morning a light mist drifted over the surface of the Volga, and after nine o'clock a few drops of rain began to fall. There was no hope that the sky would clear. At breakfast Ryabovsky told Olga Ivanovna that painting was the most thankless and boring of the arts, that he was no artist, and that only fools thought he had talent, then suddenly seized a knife and with it scraped off his best study. After breakfast he sat by the window and stared gloomily at the Volga. The Volga was no longer shining but dingy, lustreless, and cold-looking. Everything spoke of the approach of sullen, melancholy autumn. It was as if the luxurious green carpets of the banks, the diamond sparkle of the light, the blue transparent distance, and all the elegance and parade of nature had been stripped off the Volga and packed away until the spring, and the ravens flying over the river mocked its nakedness: 'Bald! Bald!' Ryabovsky listened to their croaking and thought that he was already played out, and had lost his talent, that everything in this world was relative, conditional, and stupid, and that he ought not to have got entangled with this woman . . . In short, he was out of spirits and out of sorts . . .

Olga Ivanovna sat on the bed on the other side of the partition, running her fingers through her lovely flaxen hair and imagining herself now in her own drawing-room, now in her bedroom, now in her husband's study; her imagination carried her to the theatre, her dressmaker's, the homes of her famous friends. What were they doing now? Did they remember her? The season had begun and it was time to think of at-homes. And what of Dymov? Dear Dymov! How meekly and with what childlike plaintiveness his letters begged her to come home! Every month he sent her seventy-five roubles, and when she wrote to tell him that she owed the artists a hundred roubles, he sent those as well. How kind and magnanimous he was! Olga Ivanovna was weary of travelling and wanted to get away as soon as possible from the dreary peasants and the damp river smells, and be rid of the feeling of physical dirtiness she experienced all the time she was living in peasant huts and wandering from village to village. If Ryabovsky had not promised to stay with the other artists until the twentieth of September, they might have left that very day. And how wonderful that would have been!

'My God!' groaned Ryabovsky. 'Will the sun never come out? I can't go on with my sunlit landscape without the sun! . . .'

'You have the sketch with a cloudy sky,' said Olga

Ivanovna, coming from behind the partition. 'You remember, with a wood on the right and a herd of cows and some geese on the left. You could finish that now.'

'Huh!' frowned the artist. 'Finish it! Do you think I'm too idiotic to know what I ought to do?'

'How you have changed towards me!' sighed Olga Ivanovna.

'And a good thing too!'

Olga Ivanovna's face quivered, she moved away towards the stove and burst into tears.

'Yes, all we needed was tears! Stop it! I have thousands of reasons for tears, and I'm not crying.'

'Thousands of reasons!' sniffed Olga Ivanovna. 'The most important is that you find me a burden already. Yes!' she said, sobbing. 'If the truth must be told, you are ashamed of our love. You are always trying to prevent the other artists from noticing anything, although it can't be hidden and they knew all about it long ago.'

'Olga, one thing I beg of you,' said the artist in imploring tones, laying his hand on his heart, 'one thing: don't nag me! I can't stand any more from you!'

'But swear you still love me!'

'This is torture!' said the artist through clenched teeth, jumping up. 'It will end with my throwing myself into the Volga or going out of my mind! Leave me alone!'

'Then kill me, kill me!' shrieked Olga Ivanovna. 'Kill me!'

She began to sob again, and retreated behind the partition. The rain rustled on the thatched roof of the hut. Ryabovsky clutched his head and stalked from corner to corner, then with a resolute expression, as though trying to prove something, put on his cap, threw a gun across his shoulder and went out.

When he had gone, Olga Ivanovna lay crying on the

bed for a long time. At first she thought what a good idea it would be to poison herself, so that when Ryabovsky returned he would find her dead; then her thoughts carried her into her drawing-room and her husband's study, and she imagined herself sitting quietly by Dymov's side, enjoying the relaxation and cleanness of her body, or at the theatre in the evening hearing Masini sing. A longing for civilization, the noises of the town, and the people she knew gnawed at her heart. A peasant woman came into the hut and began leisurely stoking the stove to cook dinner. There was a smell of burning and the air was blue with smoke. The artists came in, their high boots muddy and their faces wet with the rain, looked over their sketches and tried to console themselves by saying that the Volga had a charm of its own even in bad weather. The cheap clock on the wall ticked away . . . Flies drowsy with the cold buzzed in the corner near the icons, and cockroaches could be heard scurrying in the fat portfolios under the benches . . .

Ryabovsky came back when the sun was setting. Pale and exhausted, his boots covered with mud, he threw his cap on the table, lowered himself on to a bench and closed his eyes.

'I'm tired,' he said, and his brows twitched with the effort he made to raise his eyelids.

In order to be nice to him and show she was not angry, Olga Ivanovna went up to him, kissed him silently, and tenderly drew a comb through his fair hair. She wanted to comb it for him.

'What's that?' he asked, starting up as though he had felt the touch of something cold, and opening his eyes. 'What is it? Leave me alone, I beg you.'

He warded her off with his hands and walked away, and it seemed to her that his face expressed annoyance and disgust. At that moment the peasant woman carefully carried over to him in both hands a plateful of cabbage soup, and Olga Ivanovna saw that she had her thumbs in it. The dirty woman with her distended belly, the soup, which Ryabovsky had begun to eat greedily, the hut, and everything about this life that she had at first liked so much for its simplicity and artistic disorder now seemed to her horrible. She felt a sudden sense of outrage and said coldly,

'We must part for a time, or else sheer boredom may drive us into a serious quarrel. I am tired of all this, I shall leave today.'

'How? On a broomstick?'

'Today is Thursday; that means a boat will be here at half past nine.'

'Oh? Oh yes . . . Very well, then go . . .' said Ryabovsky mildly, wiping his lips with a towel instead of a napkin. 'It is dull for you here, you have nothing to do, and I should be very selfish to want to keep you. Go, and we will meet again after the twentieth.'

Olga Ivanovna packed in a cheerful mood, and her cheeks were flushed with pleasure. Could it really be true, she asked herself, that soon she would be writing letters in a drawing-room, sleeping in a bedroom, and dining off a table-cloth? Her heart was light and she no longer felt annoyed with the artist.

'I will leave my paints and brushes with you, Ryabusha,' she said. 'Bring what is left back with you . . . Mind you don't let yourself get lazy and depressed when I'm not here, but work. You really are a dear, Ryabusha.'

Ryabovsky kissed her good-bye at nine o'clock, in order not to have to do it on the steamer in front of the others, she thought, and took her to the landing stage. Soon the boat came along and carried her away.

It took her two and a half days to reach home. Without taking off her hat or waterproof, she walked into the drawing-room and then into the dining-room, breathless with excitement. Dymov, in his shirt-sleeves and with his waistcoat unbuttoned, was sitting at the table, whetting the carving-knife on the fork; a woodcock lay before him on a plate. When Olga Ivanovna entered the flat, she did so with the conviction that it was essential to conceal everything from her husband and that she was capable of doing it and possessed the necessary strength, but now, when she saw his wide, gentle, happy smile and his eyes shining with joy, she felt that it was as base, infamous, and impossible to deceive this man as to calumniate, rob, or murder him, and she instantly made up her mind to tell him all that had happened. After she had let him embrace and kiss her, she sank to her knees before him and covered her face with her hands.

'What is it, mama, what is it?' he asked tenderly. 'Didn't you enjoy it?'

She raised her face, red with shame, and looked at him with imploring, guilty eyes, but fear and shame prevented her from speaking the truth.

'It's nothing,' she said. 'I only . . .'

'Sit down,' said he, lifting her up and seating her at the table. 'That's right . . . Have some woodcock. You are hungry, poor little thing.'

Greedily she absorbed the familiar atmosphere and ate her woodcock, and he watched her tenderly and laughed with joy.

VI

About the middle of winter it became clear that Dymov had begun to suspect he was being deceived. As though it was he who had a guilty conscience, he could no longer look his wife directly in the face or greet her with a joyful smile, and he often brought his friend Korostelev back to dinner, so as to be less often alone with her. Korostelev was a little fellow with cropped hair and a wrinkled face, who was so embarrassed when he talked to Olga Ivanovna that he would first undo all the buttons of his jacket, then do them up again, then begin to pluck at the left-hand side of his moustache with his right hand. At dinner the two doctors would tell each other that a high position of the diaphragm sometimes caused irregularity in the heart-beat, or that multiple neuritis had been observed very frequently of late, or that the previous day Dymov had found carcinoma of the pancreas during a post-mortem examination, when the diagnosis had been pernicious anaemia. They seemed to be conversing on medical topics simply in order to give Olga Ivanovna the opportunity of remaining silent, that is, of not lying. After dinner Korostelev would sit down at the piano and Dymov would sigh and say,

'Ah, brother! Well, such is life! Play something sad.'

Raising his shoulders and spreading his fingers wide, Korostelev would strike a few chords and begin to sing in his tenor voice, 'Oh show me the place where no sound of the people's distress can be heard!' and Dymov would sigh again, propping his head pensively on his fist. Recently Olga Ivanovna had been acting most indiscreetly. Every morning she woke up in the blackest of moods and with the idea that she no longer loved Ryabovsky, thank God, and that it was all over. By the time she had finished her coffee, however, she was thinking that she had lost her husband through Ryabovsky and was now left without either of them; then she would remember that her friends told her Ryabovsky was painting something very striking for an exhibition, part landscape and part genre picture, in the manner of Polenov, which threw everybody who visited his studio into raptures; after all, she thought, it had been created under her influence, and altogether he had been greatly changed for the better by her influence. Her influence was so real and beneficial that if she deserted him he might perhaps be utterly finished. She remembered too that the last time he came to see her he wore a sprigged grey frock-coat and a new tie and asked her in a languishing voice, 'Do I look nice?' He really had looked handsome with his elegance, his long curls, and his blue eyes (or perhaps she only imagined so), and he had been very affectionate.

Remembering and pondering over many things, Olga Ivanovna dressed and went to Ryabovsky's studio full of excitement. She found him in high spirits and delighted with his picture, which really was magnificent; he pranced about, played the fool, and answered serious questions with a joke. Olga Ivanovna was jealous of the picture and hated it, but out of politeness stood silently in front of it for five minutes, sighed as people sigh before a shrine, and said quietly,

'Yes, you have never painted anything like it. You know, it is even awe-inspiring.'

Then she would begin to implore him to love her, not to abandon her, to take pity on her, poor and unhappy as she was. She wept, kissed his hands, insisted that he should swear he loved her, tried to prove that without her good influence he would lose his way and come to grief. Then, having destroyed his good mood, she would go off, feeling humiliated, to her dressmaker's or to an actress friend's to ask for tickets.

If she did not find him at his studio, she would leave

a note swearing to poison herself unless he came to see her that very day. He would be alarmed, go and see her, and stay to dinner; her husband's presence did not prevent him from saying offensive things to her, and she replied in kind. Each was conscious of being an encumbrance, a tyrant and an enemy to the other, they were furiously angry, and in their fury they did not notice how disgracefully they were behaving, and that even Korostelev knew all about them. After dinner Ryabovsky was always in a hurry to take his leave and be gone.

'Where are you going?' Olga Ivanovna would ask in the hall, with detestation in her eyes.

Frowning, he would name some lady whom they both knew, and it was evident that he was mocking at her jealousy and wanted to annoy her. She would go into her bedroom and lie down on the bed; she would bite her pillow with jealousy, annoyance, humiliation, and shame, and begin to sob aloud. Dymov would leave Korostelev in the drawing-room, go into the bedroom, troubled and embarrassed, and say quietly,

'Don't cry so loud, mama . . . What good is it? You must keep quiet about it . . . You must not show anything . . . You know, what can't be cured must be endured.'

Not knowing how to assuage the painful jealousy that made her temples ache, and thinking she could still mend matters, she would wash and powder her tear-stained face and rush off to the lady Ryabovsky had named . . . Not finding him there, she would go on to another, and then a third . . . At first she was ashamed of doing this, then she got used to it, and sometimes she went round in one evening to all the women she knew, looking for Ryabovsky, as everybody was aware.

Once, speaking of her husband, she said to him,

'That man persecutes me with his generosity!'

This phrase so pleased her that when she met any of the artists who had known of her affair with Ryabovsky, she always said, with an emphatic gesture,

'That man persecutes me with his generosity!'

Their lives followed the same course as in the previous year. On Wednesday evenings she was at home. The actor recited, the artists sketched, the violoncellist played, the opera singer sang, and invariably at half past eleven the doors leading to the dining-room opened and Dymov said, smiling,

'Gentlemen, please come to supper.'

As before, Olga Ivanovna sought out celebrities, found them and, dissatisfied, looked for more. As before, she returned home late every evening, but now Dymov would not be asleep, as in the previous year, but sitting working in his study. He went to bed about three o'clock and rose at eight.

One evening when she was getting ready to go to the theatre, Dymov, wearing a frock coat and a white tie, came into the bedroom where she was standing before her looking-glass. He was smiling meekly, and he looked joyfully into his wife's eyes in his old way.

'I have just been defending my thesis,' he said, sitting down and smoothing his knees.

'Were you successful?' asked Olga Ivanovna.

'Aha!' he laughed, stretching his neck to see his wife's face in the glass as she continued to stand with her back to him, arranging her hair. 'Aha!' he repeated. 'You know, it's quite possible I shall be offered a readership in general pathology. It looks like it.'

It was plain from his beatific, beaming face that if Olga Ivanovna had been willing to share his joy and triumph, he would have forgiven her everything, present and future alike, and all would have been forgotten, but she did not know what he meant by a readership or general pathology, and besides she was afraid of being late for the theatre, and so she said nothing.

He continued to sit there for a minute or two, smiled apologetically, and went out.

VII

It was a most disastrous day.

Dymov had a violent headache; he had no breakfast in the morning and did not go to the hospital, but lay all the time on the Turkish divan in his study. Olga Ivanovna went out at about one o'clock as usual, to see Ryabovsky and show him a still life, and to ask him why he had not come the day before. She did not think her still life was any good and had only painted it to have another pretext for going to see him.

She walked straight in without ringing the bell, and while she was taking off her galoshes in the hall she thought she could hear a soft scurrying in the studio and the rustle of feminine garments, but when she hurried to the studio door all she saw was a momentary glimpse of the hem of a brown skirt whisking past and vanishing behind an easel holding a big picture and covered down to the floor with a sheet of black cotton. It was impossible to doubt that a woman was hidden there. How often Olga Ivanovna herself had taken refuge behind that picture! Ryabovsky, clearly very much out of countenance, looked astonished at her arrival and held out both hands to her with a strained smile.

'A-a-ah! I'm very glad to see you. What good news do you bring?'

Olga Ivanovna's eyes filled with tears. She felt bitterly

ashamed, and would not for a million roubles have consented to talk in the presence of the stranger, her rival, the false woman standing behind the picture and probably tittering with malicious glee.

'I've brought you my sketch . . .' she said in a thin, timid little voice, 'a still life.'

'O-o-oh . . . a sketch?'

The artist took the sketch in his hands and, as he looked at it, walked as if mechanically into the next room.

Olga Ivanovna meekly followed him.

'*Nature morte*—the best sort,' he muttered, picking up a rhythm, 'resort . . . port . . . sport . . .'

From the studio came the sound of hurrying steps, the rustle of a dress. That meant *she* had gone. Olga Ivanovna wanted to scream, strike the artist on the head with something heavy, and go, but she was blinded by tears and crushed with shame, and no longer felt like Olga Ivanovna and an artist, but like some kind of small insect.

'I'm tired,' said the artist languidly, looking at the sketch and shaking his head to combat his drowsiness. 'This is nice, of course, but it's a sketch, and it was a sketch last year, and in a month's time it will be another sketch . . . Don't you get bored? In your place I should drop painting and take up music or something seriously. After all, you're a musician, not a painter. But you know, I'm so tired! I'll order some tea at once, shall I?'

He left the room and Olga Ivanovna heard him giving some order to his servant. To avoid farewells and a scene, but chiefly so as not to burst into sobs, she hurried into the hall before Ryabovsky could return, put on her galoshes and went out into the street. Once there, she uttered a light sigh, and felt free for ever from Ryabovsky, from painting and from the oppressive shame which had crushed her in the studio. It was all over!

She drove to her dressmaker's, then to see the German actor Barnay, who had arrived only the day before, and from him to a music shop, and all the time she was thinking of how she would write Ryabovsky a cold, cruel letter, full of proper pride, and in the spring or summer go away to the Crimea with Dymov, to shake off the past for good and begin a new life.

Late that night, as soon as she got home, she sat down in the drawing-room, without taking off her things, to write her letter. Ryabovsky had told her that she was not a painter, and in revenge she would tell him now that he always painted the same things every year, and always said the same things every day, that he had become stereotyped and that he would never be anything more than he already was. She meant to say also that he owed a great deal to her good influence and that if he was behaving badly now it was because her influence was nullified by various two-faced creatures like the one who had hidden behind the picture this morning.

'Mama!' called Dymov from his study, without opening the door. 'Mama!'

'What is it?'

'Don't come in here, mama, just come close to the door. It's this . . . The day before yesterday I picked up a diphtheria germ at the hospital, and now . . . I feel bad. Send for Korostelev as quickly as you can.'

Olga Ivanovna always called her husband by his surname, not his Christian name, as indeed she did all the men she knew; she did not like his name, which was Osip, because it reminded her of Gogol's character of the same name and because it lent itself to puns. Now, though, she exclaimed,

'Oh no, Osip, it's impossible!'

'Send for him. I feel bad . . .' said Dymov from behind the door, and she could hear him crossing the room and lying down. 'Send for him!' came his stifled voice.

'What is all this?' thought Olga Ivanovna, cold with fright. 'It may be dangerous!'

Aimlessly she took up a candle and went into her bedroom and there, while she stood wondering what to do, her own reflection in the long mirror caught her eye. With her pale, terrified face, her short jacket with its puffed sleeves, the yellow frills at her breast, and the unusual pattern of stripes on her skirt, she looked to herself terrible and repulsive. She felt a sudden painful pity for Dymov, his boundless love for her, his young life, and even the lonely bed in which he had not slept for so long, and she remembered his usual mild, resigned smile. She burst into bitter tears, and wrote Korostelev an imploring note. It was two o'clock in the morning.

VIII

When Olga Ivanovna came out of her bedroom at eight o'clock next morning, her head heavy from a sleepless night, her hair uncombed, looking plain and conscience-stricken, a gentleman with a black beard, evidently a doctor, passed her in the hall. There was a smell of medicines. By the study door stood Korostelev, twisting the left side of his moustache with his right hand.

'I'm sorry, I can't let you go to him,' he said sternly. 'You might catch it yourself. And what good would it do anyhow? He's delirious.'

'Has he really got diphtheria?' asked Olga Ivanovna in a whisper.

'People who run unnecessary risks ought to be hanged,'

grumbled Korostelev, without answering Olga Ivanovna's question. 'Do you know how he got the infection? Sucking the diphtheria pellicles out of a little boy's throat on Tuesday. And for what? Stupid . . . A stupid thing to do . . .'

'Is there danger? Great danger?' asked Olga Ivanovna.

'Yes, they say it's the virulent form. We ought really to send for Schreck.'

There arrived a little red-headed man with a long nose and a Jewish accent, then a tall, stoop-shouldered shaggy one, who looked like an archdeacon, then one who was young and very fat, with a red face and spectacles. These were doctors who had come to watch by their colleague's bedside. When Korostelev had finished his turn he did not go home but stayed and wandered all over the place like a shadow. The servant made tea for the doctor on duty and ran errands to the chemist's, and there was nobody to clean up the rooms. It was quiet and melancholy.

Olga Ivanovna sat in her room and thought that God was punishing her for deceiving her husband. A silent, resigned, incomprehensible being, impersonal in his mildness, characterless and weak from excess of goodness, was dumbly suffering there somewhere on his divan, without complaining. If he had complained, even in his delirium, the doctors who sat with him would have known that not only diphtheria was to blame here. They might have asked Korostelev: he knew everything, and it was not without reason that he looked at his friend's wife with eyes that seemed to say that she was the true, the most important culprit, and the diphtheria was only her accomplice. She no longer remembered the moonlight night on the Volga, the declarations of love or the poetry of life in a peasant's hut, but only that out of empty caprice, like a spoilt child, she had smeared herself all over from head to foot with something filthy and clinging that could never be washed away again . . .

'Oh, what horrible lies I told!' she thought, remembering the uneasy love between herself and Ryabovsky. 'Damnation take it all!'

At four o'clock she dined with Korostelev. He ate nothing, only scowled and drank red wine. She ate nothing either. Now she prayed silently, vowing that if Dymov got well she would love him again and be a faithful wife. Now, forgetting herself for a moment, she looked at Korostelev and thought, 'Surely it must be dull to be a simple, undistinguished, unknown person, with a face so worn and furrowed, and bad manners.' Now she thought that God would destroy her that instant for being so afraid of infection that she still had not once gone into her husband's study. But her general feeling was of dull depression and a conviction that her life was spoilt and there was no way of mending matters . . .

Dusk had come by the time they finished dinner. When Olga Ivanovna went into the drawing-room Korostelev was asleep on the sofa, with a gold-embroidered silk cushion under his head. 'Whee-pooah . . .' he snored, 'whee-pooah . . .'

The doctors, coming to take their turns on duty and going away again, did not notice the disorder. The stranger asleep and snoring in the drawing-room, the sketches hanging on the walls, the fantastic furniture, the unkempt hair and slovenly dress of the mistress of the house—all this now aroused not the slightest interest. One of the doctors laughed unexpectedly, and his laughter sounded strange and timid, and was even distressing.

When Olga Ivanovna returned to the drawing-room

for the second time, Korostelev was not asleep, but sat smoking.

'He has diphtheria of the nasal cavities,' he said in an undertone. 'His heart is not standing it too well, either. In fact, things are pretty bad.'

'Why don't you send for Schreck?' asked Olga Ivanovna.

'He's already been. It was he who discovered that the diphtheria had attacked the nose. Besides, who is Schreck? Really, Schreck is nobody. He's Schreck, I'm Korostelev—that's all.'

The time dragged with unbearable slowness. Olga Ivanovna lay down on the unmade bed without undressing and dozed. She dreamed that the whole house was filled with an enormous mass of iron from floor to ceiling, and that this need only be taken away for everybody to feel cheerful and happy. When she awoke, she remembered that it was not iron but Dymov's illness.

'*Nature morte*, port . . .' she thought, drifting off again into a doze, 'sport . . . resort . . . What about Schreck? Schreck, speck, fleck, check. Where are my friends now? Do they know that we are in trouble? Oh Lord, save us . . . Deliver us. Schreck, check . . .'

The iron again. The time dragged interminably, yet the clock on the floor below struck frequently. Now and then the bell rang; the doctors had come . . . The maid came in with an empty glass on a tray and asked,

'Shall I make the bed, madam?'

Receiving no answer, she went out. The clock struck below, she dreamed of the rain on the Volga, and again somebody came into the room, a stranger, she thought. Olga Ivanovna started up and recognized Korostelev.

'What time is it?' she asked.

'About three.'

'Well, what is it?'

'What is it? I have come to tell you: it is the end . . .'

He sobbed, sat down on the bed beside her and wiped the tears away with his sleeve. She did not immediately understand, but went cold all over and began slowly crossing herself.

'It's the end,' he repeated in a shrill voice, and sobbed again. 'He is dying, because he sacrificed himself . . . What a loss to science!' he said bitterly. 'Compared with all the rest of us he was a great man, an extraordinary man! What gifts! What hope he gave us all!' continued Korostelev, wringing his hands. 'God in heaven, he would have been a scientist the like of whom we shall never see now. Oska Dymov, Oska Dymov, what have you done? O-o-oh God!'

Korostelev covered his face with both hands and rocked his head in despair.

'And what moral strength!' he went on, getting more and more angry with somebody. 'A good, pure, loving spirit—not a man but a sheet of clear glass! He served science and he died for science. He worked like a horse, day and night, nobody spared him, and the young scientist, the future professor, had to go looking for patients and do translations at night to pay for these . . . trumpery rags here!'

Korostelev looked at Olga Ivanovna with hatred in his eyes, seized the sheet in both hands and tugged angrily at it as though it were to blame.

'He did not spare himself, and nobody else spared him. Oh, what's the use?'

'Yes, a rare person!' said a bass voice in the drawing-room.

Olga Ivanovna remembered all her life with him, from beginning to end, in all its detail, and suddenly realized that he had indeed been a rare, unusual and, compared with everybody she knew, a great man. Remembering her father's attitude to him, and that of all his medical colleagues, she understood that they had all seen in him a future celebrity. The walls, the ceiling, the lamp, and the carpet all seemed to wink at her in mockery, as though trying to say, 'You let him slip, you let him slip!' She rushed wailing out of the bedroom, through the drawing-room, past some unknown man, and into the study to her husband. He lay motionless on the Turkish divan, with a blanket covering him to the waist. His face was terribly sunken and wasted, of a greyish-yellow colour that is never seen in the living; and only the forehead, the black eyebrows, and the familiar smile were recognizable as Dymov's. Olga Ivanovna hastily felt his forehead, his hands, and his breast. His breast was still warm, but his hands and forehead were unpleasantly cold. The half-open eyes were looking not at Olga Ivanovna but at the blanket.

'Dymov!' she called aloud. 'Dymov!'

She wanted to explain that it had all been a mistake, that all was not yet lost, that life could still be splendid and happy, that he was a great, rare, and unusual person and that all her life she would worship him, pray and feel holy awe . . .

'Dymov!' she called, shaking him by the shoulder and unable to believe that he would never wake again. 'Dymov, Dymov!'

In the drawing-room Korostelev was saying to the maid,

'What need is there to ask? Go to the church and ask where you can find the almswomen. They will wash the body and clean up—they will do all that is necessary.'

THE BLACK MONK

1894

I

ANDREY VASILYICH KOVRIN, a postgraduate student, was overstrained and nervy. He was not receiving treatment for his complaint, but he had mentioned it casually over a bottle of wine to a friend who was a doctor, and who advised him to spend the spring and summer in the country. Just at that moment there arrived a long letter from Tanya Pesotskaya, in which she asked him to go down and stay with them at Borisovka. He decided that he really must go away.

First of all—this was in April—he went to his own family estate of Kovrinka, where he spent three weeks in solitude; then, having waited for the fine weather, he travelled by road to visit his former guardian, Pesotsky, well known in Russia as a horticulturist, who had brought him up. From Kovrinka to Borisovka, where the Pesotskys lived, was not reckoned to be more than seventy versts, and travelling in a comfortable, well-sprung carriage along roads softened by the spring thaw was a real pleasure.

The Pesotskys' was an enormous house, with columns, peeling plaster lions, and a frock-coated manservant at the front door. The ancient park, grim and severe, laid out in the English style, stretched for nearly a verst from the house to the river, where it ended abruptly in a steep earthen bank on which grew pine-trees whose exposed roots looked like hairy paws; below, the water had an inhospitable gleam, snipe drifted past with a melancholy cry and at all times the mood of the place might well have prompted one to sit down and write a woeful ballad. Near the house, on the other hand, in the courtyard and the orchard, which, with the nurseries, covered about eighty acres, it was bright and cheerful even in bad weather. Kovrin had never seen anywhere else such marvellous roses, lilies, camellias, tulips of every conceivable colour from pure white to soot black, and altogether such a wealth of flowers, as at the Pesotskys'. Spring was as yet only beginning and the real peak of magnificence of the flower gardens still lay concealed in the greenhouses, but what was already in bloom along the walks and here and there in the beds was enough to make one feel, strolling about the garden, that one was in a kingdom of delicate colour, especially in the early hours when the dew sparkled on every petal.

This, the ornamental part of the garden, which Pesotsky himself scornfully called a lot of nonsense, had produced on Kovrin at one time in his childhood the effect of a fairy-tale. Such flights of fancy, such elegant monstrosities and mockeries of nature! There were espaliered fruit-trees, a pear in the shape of a Lombardy poplar, spherical oaks and limes, an umbrella made from an apple-tree, arches, monograms, candelabra and even the figures 1862—the date when Pesotsky first took up horticulture—in plum-trees. There were handsome, well-shaped little trees, too, with trunks as strong and straight as a palm-tree's, and it was only if you looked closely that you would recognize gooseberry or currant bushes in these small trees. But the most heartening thing in the garden, and what gave it its look of animation, was its constant bustle. From early morning until evening people swarmed like ants round the trees and shrubs, in the walks and about the flower-beds, with wheelbarrows, hoes, and watering-cans . . .

Kovrin reached the Pesotskys' in the evening, between nine and ten o'clock. He found Tanya and her father, Egor Semenych, very worried. The clear, starry sky and the thermometer both presaged frost before morning, and the head gardener, Ivan Karlych, had gone to the town, so that there was nobody they could rely on. At supper the talk was all of the early frost, and it was decided that Tanya would not go to bed, but soon after midnight would walk through the garden to see whether all was in order, and Egor Semenych would get up at three o'clock or even earlier.

Kovrin sat with Tanya all the evening and soon after midnight went out with her into the garden. It was cold. Outside there was already a strong smell of burning. In the big orchard, which was called the Money-maker and brought Egor Semenych a few thousand roubles clear profit every year, thick black acrid smoke lay along the ground and enveloped the trees, preserving those thousands from the frost. The trees here stood in a chess-board pattern, their rows as straight and regular as ranks of soldiers, and this pedantically strict correctness and the fact that all the trees were the same size and had identical crowns and trunks produced a scene of monotony and indeed dullness. Kovrin and Tanya walked along the rows, where fires of dung, straw, and all kinds of refuse smouldered, now and then meeting workmen wandering through the smoke like shadows. Only the cherries, plums, and some sorts of apples were in flower, but the whole orchard was drowned in smoke and it was only near the nurseries that Kovrin could fill his lungs with air.

'When I was a child the smoke here used to make me

sneeze,' he said, shrugging his shoulders, 'but to this day I don't understand how smoke can be a protection against the frost.'

'The smoke replaces the clouds when there aren't any,' answered Tanya.

'And why are clouds necessary?'

'There are no early morning frosts in dull and cloudy weather.'

'So that's it!'

He laughed and took her arm. Her broad, intensely serious face, pinched with cold, her thin black eyebrows, the turned-up collar of her coat which prevented the free movement of her head, her whole slim graceful figure, and her dress tucked up to avoid the dew, all moved him.

'Good Lord, she is grown-up already!' he said. 'When I left here last time, about five years ago, you were still quite a child. You were so scraggy and long-legged, with your head bare and a short little frock, and I used to call you the heron . . . What time does!'

'Yes, it is five years!' sighed Tanya. 'A lot of water has flowed under the bridges since then. Tell me, Andryusha, honestly,' she hurried on, looking into his face, 'have you grown away from us? But need I ask? You are a man, you live your own interesting life, you amount to something . . . Some estrangement is so natural! But whatever happens, Andryusha, I want you to think of us as your own family. We have a right to that.'

'I do, Tanya.'

'Word of honour?'

'Word of honour.'

'You were surprised today that we have so many photographs of you. But you know my father adores you. I sometimes think he loves you more than me. He is proud of you. You are a scholar, a distinguished man, you have made a brilliant career for yourself, and he believes that you have turned out the way you have because he brought you up. I don't try to stop him thinking so. Let him.'

Dawn was already approaching, and this was particularly noticeable in the distinctness with which the puffs of smoke and the tree tops were beginning to stand out in the air. Nightingales were singing, and the piping of quails was borne in from the fields.

'It's time for bed,' said Tanya. 'And it is cold.' She took his arm. 'Thank you for coming, Andryusha. The people we know are uninteresting, and there are not many even of them. With us everything is garden, garden, garden—and nothing else. Standards, half-standards,' she laughed, 'pippins, rennets, russets, budding, whip-grafts . . . . Everything, the whole of our lives, has gone into the garden; I don't even dream of anything but apples and pears. Of course it's very good, it's useful, but sometimes I can't help wishing for something else for a change. I remember when you used to come here for the holidays, or just for a visit, the house seemed somehow fresher and lighter, as though we had taken the covers off the furniture and chandeliers. I was only a little girl then, but I understood.'

She went on talking for a long time, with great feeling. For some reason it suddenly came into his head that during the summer he might become attached to this frail little chatterbox, be attracted, fall in love—in their situation it was so possible and so natural! The idea touched and amused him; he bent his head towards the dear worried face and began to sing softly,

'Onegin, there is no concealing
That I love Tatyana madly . . .'

When they reached the house, Egor Semenych was already up. Kovrin was not sleepy, and he chatted to the old man and returned with him to the garden. Egor Semenych was tall, broad-shouldered, and big-bellied, and he suffered from asthma, but he always walked so fast that it was difficult to keep up with him. He wore an extremely worried look and was always hurrying, with an expression that seemed to say that if he delayed even for one minute, all would be lost!

'Now here is an odd thing, my dear chap . . .' he began, stopping to get his breath. 'On the surface of the ground, as you can see, there is frost, but take a stick and lift the thermometer about fifteen feet above the ground, and it is warm there . . . Why is that?'

'Really, I don't know,' said Kovrin, laughing.

'Hm . . . Of course, nobody can know everything . . . However capacious a mind may be, it can't find room for everything. I suppose philosophy would be much more in your line?'

'Yes. I am reading psychology, but I study philosophy in general.'

'And doesn't it bore you?'

'On the contrary, it's all I live for.'

'Well, please God . . .' said Egor Semenych, thoughtfully stroking his grey whiskers. 'Please God . . . I'm very glad for you . . . glad, my dear . . .'

Suddenly he pricked up his ears and, with a terrible grimace, ran off to one side and disappeared behind the trees in clouds of smoke.

'Who has tied a horse to the apple-tree?' he cried in a desperate, heart-rending shriek. 'What ruffianly scoundrel has dared to tie a horse to the tree? My God, my God! Spoilt, frozen, destroyed, ruined! The garden's finished! The garden's done for! My God!'

When he returned to Kovrin his face was outraged and worn with emotion.

'What are you to do with these damnable people?' he said in a complaining voice, waving his arms. 'During the night Stepka brought a load of dung and tied his horse to an apple-tree! The wretch twisted the reins round as tight as he could, so that the bark got rubbed in three places. A fine thing! I speak to him, but he's a stupid blockhead and only stands and blinks! Hanging's too good for him!'

When he had calmed down, he embraced Kovrin and kissed him on the cheek.

'Well, please God . . . please God . . .' he murmured. 'I am very glad you have come. Unspeakably glad . . . Thank you.'

Then with the same quick gait and worried expression he walked all round the garden and showed his former ward all the orangeries and hot-houses and his two apiaries, which he called the marvels of our age.

While they talked the sun came up and shone brightly on the garden. It grew warm. Anticipating a long, fine, cheerful day, Kovrin remembered that it was still only the beginning of May and that the whole summer was still to come, just as long, fine and cheerful, and suddenly the joyful, youthful feeling he had known when he ran about this garden as a child stirred again in his breast. And in his turn he embraced the old man and kissed him tenderly. Both much affected, they returned to the house and sat down to drink tea from antique porcelain cups, with cream and rich, satisfying cracknels—and these little things again reminded Kovrin of his childhood and youth. The wonderful present and the newly awakened memories of the past within it merged together, crowding in upon the mind, but bringing a feeling of well-being.

He waited until Tanya woke up, and drank a great deal of coffee with her, took a stroll and then went to his own room and sat down to work. He read carefully, making notes, occasionally raising his eyes to look at the open windows or the fresh flowers, still wet with dew, that stood in vases on the table, and lowering them again to his book; and every nerve seemed to leap and quiver with pleasure.

II

He continued to lead exactly the same strained and restless life in the country as in the town. He wrote and read a great deal, studied Italian and, when he went for a walk, took pleasure in the thought that he would soon be sitting down to work again. He slept so little that everybody was amazed; if he chanced to doze for half an hour during the day he did not sleep at all the following night, and felt as well and in as good spirits after his sleepless night as if nothing had happened.

He talked a lot, drank wine, and smoked expensive cigars. Frequently, indeed almost every day, young ladies from the neighbouring houses drove over to the Pesotskys', and Tanya sang and played the piano with them; sometimes another neighbour, a young man who played the fiddle very well, came as well. Kovrin listened so avidly to the music and singing that he was exhausted by it, an exhaustion expressed physically by closed eyes and a head sunk on one side.

One evening he was sitting on the balcony after tea, reading. In the drawing-room Tanya, who was a soprano, and one of the young ladies, a contralto, were practising Braga's well-known *Serenade* with the young violinist. Kovrin listened to the words—they were in

Russian—without being able to grasp their sense. At last, abandoning his book and giving all his attention to the song, he understood that a young girl, morbidly imaginative, has heard in the garden at night sounds so beautiful and so strange that she must recognize that their harmony is heavenly and not to be understood by us mortals, and that it therefore mounts again to the skies. Kovrin's eyelids grew heavy. He rose and walked wearily through the drawing-room and into the big ballroom. When the singing ceased he took Tanya's arm and walked out on to the balcony with her.

'I have been thinking about a certain legend ever since this morning,' he said. 'I don't remember whether I read it somewhere or was told about it, but it is rather strange and completely absurd. To begin with, it is not notable for clarity. A thousand years ago a monk, dressed in black, was walking in the desert, somewhere in Syria or Arabia . . . Some miles away from where he was walking some fishermen saw another black monk moving slowly over the surface of a lake. This second monk was a mirage. Now forget all the laws of optics, which the legend apparently does not acknowledge, and listen further. From the mirage arose a second mirage, and from the second a third, so that the image of the black monk began to be transmitted endlessly from one layer of the atmosphere to another. He was seen now in Africa, now in Spain, now in India, now in the Far North . . . Finally, he left the limits of the earth's atmosphere and is now wandering all through the universe, and has still not encountered the conditions which would allow him to disappear. Perhaps he can now be seen somewhere on Mars or on one of the stars of the Southern Cross. But, my dear, the essence, the whole kernel, of the legend is that exactly a thousand years after the monk walked in the desert, the mirage will again fall into the earth's atmosphere and appear to men. And it seems that the thousand years have almost run out . . . According to the idea of the legend we may expect to see the black monk any day now.'

'A strange sort of mirage,' said Tanya, who did not like the legend.

'But the oddest thing,' laughed Kovrin, 'is that I simply can't remember where I got the legend into my head from. Did I read it somewhere? Was I told it? Or perhaps I dreamed of the black monk? I solemnly swear that I don't remember. But the legend engrosses me. I have been thinking about it all day.'

Allowing Tanya to go back to her guests, he left the house and walked thoughtfully among the flower-beds. The flowers, because they had just been watered, gave out a damp and disturbing scent. The singing had begun again in the house, and from a distance the violin produced the effect of a human voice. Kovrin, still racking his brains to remember where he had heard or read the legend, wandered slowly into the park and came by degrees as far as the river.

By a footpath that ran down the steep bank among the exposed tree-roots he descended to the level of the water, disturbing the snipe and frightening two ducks. Here and there on the sombre pines the last rays of the setting sun still shone, but on the level of the river it was already evening. Kovrin crossed to the other side by a footbridge. Before him lay a wide field, covered with young rye not yet in flower. The distance held neither a human dwelling nor a living soul, and it seemed that if one followed the path it would lead one to that same mysterious and unknown place where the sun had just sunk and where the sunset now glowed with such imposing grandeur.

'How spacious and free and peaceful it is here!' thought Kovrin, walking along the path. 'It seems as though the whole world were watching me, keeping quiet, and waiting for me to understand it . . .'

But now ripples ran over the rye and a faint evening breeze lightly touched his uncovered head. A minute later there was another gust of wind, but stronger—the rye rustled and the dull murmur of the pines sounded from far behind him. Kovrin stood still in astonishment. On the horizon, like a tornado or a cyclone, a tall black pillar rose from earth to heaven. Its outlines were indistinct, but in the first moment it was possible to make out that it was not standing still but moving with terrible speed, moving straight towards Kovrin, and the closer it moved, the smaller and clearer it became. Kovrin flung himself to one side, among the rye, to make way for it, and he was only just in time . . .

Past him sped a black-robed monk, with a grey head and black brows, his arms crossed on his breast . . . His bare feet did not touch the ground. His progress had carried him some yards past when he looked round at Kovrin, nodded his head and smiled graciously and at the same time slyly. But how pale, terribly pale and thin the face was! Once more increasing in stature, he skimmed across the river, noiselessly struck against the clayey bank and the pines and, passing right through them, disappeared like smoke.

'Well, do you see that?' muttered Kovrin. 'That means there is truth in the legend.'

Without trying to explain the strange apparition to himself, satisfied merely to have seen so close and so distinctly not only the black robe but even the monk's face and eyes, and pleasurably excited, he returned to the house.

In the park and the garden people were moving quietly about, in the house somebody was playing—that meant that only he had seen the monk. He very much wanted to tell Tanya and Egor Semenych all about it, but he reflected that they would probably think he was raving and be frightened; it was better to say nothing. He laughed aloud, sang, danced a mazurka; he was in high spirits, and everybody, Tanya and her guests alike, found something special, radiant, and inspired in his face, and thought him very interesting.

III

After supper, when the visitors had gone, he went to his room and lay down on the sofa: he wanted to think about the monk. But a minute later Tanya came in.

'Here, Andryusha, have a look at father's articles,' she said, handing him a packet of pamphlets and offprints. 'Wonderful articles. He writes excellently.'

'Oh yes, excellently!' said Egor Semenych, coming in after her and laughing constrainedly; he felt embarrassed. 'Please don't listen to her, don't read them! However, if you want to send yourself to sleep you might perhaps read them: they are an excellent way of inducing sleep.'

'I think they are magnificent articles,' said Tanya with profound conviction. 'You read them, Andryusha, and persuade papa to write more often. He could write a whole course of horticulture.'

Egor Semenych guffawed awkwardly, blushed, and began to make the kind of remark usually produced by bashful authors. At length he yielded.

'In that case read Gauchet's article first, and these Russian articles,' he muttered, sorting through the pamphlets with shaking hands, 'or you won't be able to understand. Before reading my replies, you must know what I am replying to. Still, they're only bits of nonsense . . . very dull. Besides, I think it's bedtime.'

Tanya went out. Egor Semenych sat down beside Kovrin on his sofa and sighed deeply.

'Yes, my dear boy . . .' he began after a silence. 'Yes, indeed, my dear young scholar. Here I am writing articles, and exhibiting at shows, and getting medals . . . Pesotsky's apples, they say, are as big as your head, and Pesotsky, they say, has made a fortune out of his garden. In short, rich and famous is Kochubey the Magician. But the question arises: what's it all for? The garden really is marvellous, a showpiece . . . It is not a garden so much as a complete institution, and it possesses immense importance for the State, because it is, so to speak, a step towards the new era of Russian agriculture and Russian industry. But what's it for? What's the object of it all?'

'It speaks for itself.'

'That's not what I mean. I want to know what is going to happen to the garden when I die. In the form you see it in at present it won't last for more than a month without me. The whole secret of my success is not that the garden is very big and employs a lot of workmen, but that I love the thing—do you know what I mean?—I love it perhaps more than myself. Look at me—I do everything myself, I work from morning till night. I do all the grafting, all the pruning, all the planting—the whole lot. When anybody helps me I get jealous and irritated and shout at them. The whole secret is love, the master's sharp eye, that is, and the master's hand, and the feeling, when you go out somewhere for a short time, that you may sit there, but your heart isn't in it, you are preoccupied, afraid all the time something has happened in the garden. And when I die, who will look after it? Who will do the work? The head gardener? The workmen? Will they? I can tell you one thing, my very dear friend: the principal enemy in our line of business is not hares, nor insect pests, nor frost, but the indifferent stranger.'

'What about Tanya?' asked Kovrin laughing. 'She can't possibly do more damage than a hare. She loves gardening and understands it.'

'Yes, she loves it and understands it. If she gets the garden after I'm dead and runs it herself, of course I could want nothing better. Well, but if, God forbid, she got married?' whispered Egor Semenych, looking at Kovrin with an expression of alarm. 'That's the point! She will get married, children will come along, and then there won't be time to think of the garden. What I am most afraid of is that she will marry some young spark who will be greedy and let the garden to market-women, and the whole place will go to the devil in the very first year. In our business women are the scourge of God!'

Egor Semenych sighed and sat silent for a moment.

'Perhaps it is selfish, but I tell you plainly I don't want Tanya to get married. I'm afraid of it! There is one young fop who comes here and saws away on his violin; I know Tanya would never marry him, I'm quite sure of it, but I can't bear to see him! Altogether, my dear boy, I'm a very odd sort of person, I confess.'

Egor Semenych got up and walked restlessly about the room, and it was plain that he wanted to say something very important, but could not bring himself to do so.

At last he made up his mind. 'I am very fond of you, and I will speak plainly,' he said, thrusting his hands into his pockets. 'I take a very simple line with certain ticklish subjects and say straight out what I think; I can't bear so-called mental reservations. I tell you plainly you are the only man I would not be afraid to let my daughter marry. You have a brain and a heart, and you wouldn't let my beloved work go to rack and ruin. But the main reason is that I love you like my own son . . . and I am proud of you. If you and Tanya came to some sort of understanding—well, I should be very pleased and happy. I tell you so straight out, without mincing matters, like an honest man.'

Kovrin smiled. Egor Semenych opened the door and paused on the threshold.

'If you and Tanya had a son, I'd make a gardener of him,' he said thoughtfully. 'But that's all idle dreaming . . . Good night.'

Left alone, Kovrin made himself more comfortable and began turning over the articles. One was entitled *Catch-crops*; another *Remarks on Mr. Z's Observations on Double Trenching the Soil of a New Garden*; a third, *Further Considerations on Grafting with Dormant Buds*—and there were more of the same kind. But what a harsh and discordant style, what passionate, almost morbid, feeling! Here was one article with what seemed a most unprovocative title and impersonal subject: it dealt with the golden rennet apple. But Egor Semenych had begun with the words '*Audi alteram partem*' and ended with '*Sapienti sat*', and in between these two sayings there was an absolute spate of envenomed expressions to the address of the 'learned ignorance of our professorial horticultural experts, observing nature from their distant academic heights' or 'M. Gauchet, whose success has been created by amateurs and ignoramuses', followed by out-of-place, forced, and insincere regrets that it was no longer possible to have peasants flogged for stealing fruit and breaking the trees.

'Gardening is a decorative, good-humoured, and healthy pursuit,' thought Kovrin, 'but even here we find passions and warfare. It must be because everywhere and in every calling, intellectuals are creatures of nerves and remarkable for heightened sensitivity. It is probably inevitable.'

He thought of Tanya, who was so pleased with Egor Semenych's articles. Short, pale, so thin that her collar-bones showed; the eyes wide open, dark, intelligent, always gazing somewhere, seeking something; steps short and quick, like her father's. She talked a great deal, loved to argue and, when she did so, underlined every phrase, however insignificant, with gesture and facial expression. She must be in the highest degree a creature of nerves.

Kovrin resumed his reading but found it impossible to follow the thread, and abandoned it. The same enjoyable excitement with which he had recently listened to the music and danced the mazurka now possessed him again and evoked a multiplicity of ideas. He got up and began to walk about the room, thinking about the black monk. It came into his mind that if he alone had seen that strange, supernatural monk it must mean that he was sick and had already reached the stage of hallucination. This consideration frightened him, but not for long.

'But after all I feel all right, and I do nobody any harm; that means there is nothing bad in my hallucinations,' he thought, feeling reassured.

He sat down on the sofa and wound his arms round his head, as if to keep in check the incomprehensible joy that filled his whole being, then again walked about the room for a time before sitting down to work. But the ideas he found in his book did not satisfy him. He wanted something vast, immense, stupendous. Towards morning he undressed and went reluctantly to bed: after all, he must sleep!

When he heard the steps of Egor Semenych going into the garden, Kovrin rang and ordered the servant to bring him some wine. He drank several glasses of claret with enjoyment, then covered up his head; his consciousness grew cloudy and he fell asleep.

IV

Egor Semenych and Tanya often quarrelled and exchanged unpleasant remarks.

One morning they had both lost their tempers. Tanya burst into tears and went into her own room. She did not emerge either for dinner or for tea. At first Egor Semenych went about with a pompous, sullen air, as though wishing it to be understood that for him the interests of truth and order ranked above everything else on earth, but he was unable to keep this up for long and soon lost heart. He wandered glumly about the park, sighing constantly, 'Ah, dear God, dear God!'—and at dinner did not eat a morsel. At last, with a guilty and conscience-stricken look, he knocked at the locked door and called timidly,

'Tanya! Tanya!'

From the other side of the door a voice, weak and faint with crying, but resolute, answered,

'Leave me alone, I implore you.'

The master's trouble was reflected all over the house and even among the people working in the garden. Kovrin was engrossed in the interest of his work, but towards the last even he began to feel bored and uncomfortable. In order to disperse the general ill-humour, he made up his mind to intervene and late in the afternoon knocked at Tanya's door and was admitted.

'Oh, oh, how disgraceful!' he began playfully, gazing with astonishment at Tanya's woebegone face, tear-stained and covered with red blotches. 'Is it so serious? Oh, oh!'

'If you knew how he makes me suffer!' she said, and copious bitter tears rained from her big eyes. 'He tortures me!' she went on, wringing her hands. 'I didn't say anything to him . . . nothing . . . I only said there was no need to keep . . . unnecessary workers on, when . . . when we can get day labourers if we want them. After all . . . after all, the workmen have been doing nothing for a whole week . . . I . . . I only said that, and he began to shout and say a lot . . . of hurtful, terribly insulting things to me. Why?'

'Stop it, stop it,' said Kovrin, smoothing her hair. 'You've quarrelled, you've had your cry, that's enough. You mustn't go on being angry, it's not nice . . . especially as he loves you very, very dearly.'

'He's spoilt . . . spoilt my whole life,' Tanya sobbed. 'I hear nothing but taunts and . . . and insults from him. He thinks I am in the way in his house. Well, what about it? He's right. I'll leave tomorrow, I'll get work as a telegraph clerk . . . Let him . . .'

'Come, come, come . . . Don't cry, Tanya. You mustn't, my dear . . . You are both hot-tempered and easily upset, and you are both in the wrong. Come along, I'll make it up between you.'

Kovrin spoke gently and persuasively, but she went on crying, her shoulders shaking and her hands clenched, as though she really had suffered a terrible misfortune. He was all the more sorry for her because her grievance was not serious, although her suffering was profound.

What little things were sufficient to make her unhappy for a whole day and, it might well be, for all her life! While he tried to comfort Tanya, Kovrin was thinking that besides this young girl and her father there were no others to be found in the whole world who loved him like one of themselves, as one of the family; he had lost his mother and father in early childhood and so might never, if it had not been for these two people, have known what sincere affection was, or that simple-hearted uncritical love which is lavished only on near kindred. And he felt that his own ravelled, half-sick nerves responded to the nerves of this quivering weeping girl like iron to a magnet. He could never have loved a strong healthy rosy cheeked woman, but the pale weak unhappy Tanya appealed to him.

Willingly he continued to stroke her hair and shoulders, pressed her hand and wiped away her tears . . . At length she stopped crying. She still went on for a long time complaining of her father and her intolerably difficult life in that house, and begging Kovrin to enter into her situation, then little by little she began to smile and sigh over the fact that God had given her such a bad disposition, and at last, with a loud laugh, called herself a wicked girl and ran out of the room.

When Kovrin went out into the garden a little later, Egor Semenych and Tanya were walking side by side along one of the paths as though nothing had happened, and eating rye-bread and salt as if they were both hungry.

V

Pleased that he had been so successful in the role of peacemaker, Kovrin went into the park. Sitting contemplatively on a bench, he heard carriage wheels and women's voices; visitors were arriving. When the evening shadows fell across the garden, the faint sounds of a violin and of voices singing came to his ears and reminded him of the black monk. Where, through what country, over what planet, was that optical illusion now in motion?

Hardly had he recalled the legend and pictured in his imagination the sombre vision he had seen in the rye-field than from beyond the pines directly opposite there emerged silently, without the slightest rustle, a man of medium height with an uncovered grey head, dressed all in black and with bare feet like a beggar, and on his pale deathly face the black brows stood out sharply. With a nod of greeting the beggar or pilgrim noiselessly approached the bench and sat down, and Kovrin recognized the black monk. For a moment they looked at one another, Kovrin with astonishment, the monk amiably and, as before, somewhat slyly, with the expression of a cunning old fox.

'But you're a mirage, you know,' said Kovrin. 'How is it that you are here, and sitting still in one place? It doesn't fit in with the legend.'

'That does not matter,' answered the monk softly, after a short pause, turning his face towards him. 'The legend, the mirage, and I myself are all products of your excited imagination. I am an illusion.'

'Then you don't exist?' asked Kovrin.

'Think what you choose,' said the monk, smiling faintly. 'I exist in your imagination, and your imagination is part of nature, which means that I exist in nature, too.'

'You have a very old, intelligent, and remarkably expressive face, as though you really had lived a thousand years,' said Kovrin. 'I didn't know my imagination was capable of creating such phenomena. But why do you look at me so delightedly? Are you pleased with me?'

'Yes. You are one of the few who are rightly called God's elect. You serve eternal truth. Your thoughts and purposes, your astonishing scholarship and your whole life bear a divine, a heavenly stamp, since they are dedicated to reason and beauty, that is to what is eternal.'

'You say eternal truth . . . But is eternal truth attainable by or necessary to men, if there is not eternal life?'

'There is eternal life,' said the monk.

'You believe in human immortality?'

'Yes, of course. A great and brilliant future awaits mankind. And the more people there are on earth like you, the sooner that future will come into being. Without you, the servants of the high First Cause, living consciously and freely, humanity would be null; in the natural course of development it would have to wait a long time for the end of its earthly history. But you will lead it several thousand years in advance into the realm of eternal truth—and in this lies your high desert. You are the embodiment of the blessing of God which rests on mankind.'

'What is the object of eternal life?' asked Kovrin.

'Like that of all life, delight. True delight is in knowledge; and eternal life presents uncountable and inexhaustible sources of knowledge, and this is the sense in which it is written, "In my Father's house are many mansions".'

'If you knew what a pleasure it is to listen to you!' said Kovrin, rubbing his hands with enjoyment.

'I am very glad.'

'But I know that when you go away I shall be worried by the question of your reality. You are an illusion, an hallucination. Does that mean that I am sick in mind, not normal?'

'Even if that is so, why be troubled? You are ill because you are overworked and have exhausted your strength, and that means that you have sacrificed your health to the Idea, and the time is near when you will give it your very life. What could be better? This is the end to which all noble natures, gifted from on high, aspire.'

'If I know that I am mentally ill, can I have faith in myself?'

'And how do you know that the men of genius in whom the whole world has faith did not see visions too? Scientists now say that genius is akin to madness. My friend, only the commonplace, the herd, are healthy and normal. Ideas about this being an age of nerves, degeneracy, overwork, and so on can seriously disturb only those for whom the present is the object of life, that is the herd.'

'The Romans said: *mens sana in corpore sano*.'

'Not everything the Greeks or Romans said is true. Exaltation, excitement, ecstasy—everything that distinguishes prophets, poets, and martyrs of the Idea from ordinary people, is antagonistic to the animal side of man, that is to his physical health. I repeat: if you want to be healthy and normal, join the herd.'

'It is strange—you say the same things as have often come into my own mind,' said Kovrin. 'It's as if you had spied and eavesdropped on my secret thoughts. But don't let us talk about me. What do you understand by eternal truth?'

The monk did not answer. Kovrin looked at him and could not distinguish his face: his features had grown fluid and hazy. Then the monk's head and hands began to disappear; his body merged into the bench and the twilight, and he vanished completely.

'The hallucination is over!' said Kovrin, and he laughed. 'A pity!'

He went back to the house cheerful and happy. The little that the black monk had said to him flattered not his vanity but his whole soul, his whole being. To be one of the elect, to serve eternal truth, to stand in the ranks of those who were trying to make mankind worthy of the kingdom of God several thousand years in advance, that is to spare them several thousand years of strife, sin, and suffering, to sacrifice everything to the Idea—youth, strength, health—to be ready to die for the common good—what an exalted and happy fate! His past, pure, virtuous, laborious, rose before his memory, he remembered what he had learnt and what he had taught to others, and decided that there was no exaggeration in the monk's words.

Tanya was walking towards him through the park. She had already changed her clothes.

'So this is where you are!' she said. 'We have been looking for you everywhere . . . But what is the matter with you?' she wondered, looking at his radiant excited face and eyes full of tears. 'How strange you seem, Andryusha!'

'I am content, Tanya,' said Kovrin, putting his hands on her shoulders. 'I am more than content, I am happy! Tanya, dear Tanya, you are an extraordinarily sympathetic person. Dear Tanya, I am so glad, so glad!'

He kissed both her hands warmly and went on,

'I have just experienced some bright, wonderful, celestial moments. But I can't tell you everything, because you will call me mad or not believe me. Let us talk about you. Dear, wonderful Tanya! I love you, and

I have grown used to loving you. It has become necessary to my heart to have you near and meet you a dozen times a day. I do not know how I can do without you when I go back home.'

'Well!' laughed Tanya. 'You will forget about us in two days. We are little people and you are a great man.'

'No, we must be serious!' he said. 'I will take you with me, Tanya. Shall I? You will come with me? You will be mine?'

'Well!' said Tanya, trying to laugh again, but the laugh would not come, and red patches appeared on her face.

She began to breathe fast and walked quicker and quicker, not towards the house, but further into the park.

'I did not think of this . . . I did not!' she said, clasping her hands as though in despair.

Kovrin went after her, saying with the same radiant, delighted face,

'I want a love which will possess me wholly, and that love only you can give me, Tanya. I am happy! Happy!'

She was stunned; she was stooping and shrunken as though she had aged ten years in a moment, but he thought her beautiful and expressed aloud his delight:

'How pretty she is!'

VI

When he learned from Kovrin that there not only was a romance afoot, but would even be a wedding, Egor Semenych spent a long time pacing from corner to corner, trying to hide his excitement. His hands began to shake, his neck swelled and went red, he ordered out his racing droshky and drove off somewhere. Tanya, seeing how he lashed the horse and how his cap was pulled down almost to his ears, understood his mood, shut herself up in her room and wept all day.

In the orangeries the peaches and plums were already ripe; the picking and dispatch to Moscow of this capricious and delicate freight demanded much care, labour, and trouble. Thanks to the hot dry summer, every tree had to be watered, which took much time and workers' effort; and a multitude of caterpillars made their appearance and, to Kovrin's disgust, the workmen and even Egor Semenych and Tanya crushed them with their bare fingers. With all this, it was necessary to take orders already for fruit and trees for the autumn, and conduct a big correspondence. And in the very busiest time, when nobody seemed to have a moment to spare, work in the fields began, taking away from the garden more than half of the labourers; Egor Semenych, deeply sunburnt, tired out, bad tempered, galloped from garden to field and shouted that he was being torn in pieces and would put a bullet through his head.

On top of this there was the bustle over the trousseau, to which the Pesotskys attached no small importance; the clashing of scissors, the noise of sewing machines, the fumes from the irons, and the whims of the dressmaker, a nervous and touchy lady, made the heads of everybody in the house swim. And as though on purpose to make matters worse, every day saw the arrival of visitors who had to be amused, fed, and even put up for the night. But all this drudgery passed unnoticed, as if in a dream. Tanya felt as though love and happiness had taken her unawares, although since the age of fourteen she had somehow been convinced that Kovrin was certain to marry her. She was stunned and bewildered, she could not believe it . . . Now she was visited by a sudden access of such joy that she wanted to fly above the clouds to give thanks to God, now she suddenly remembered that in August she would have to leave the nest and part from her father, or the idea would come from God knows where that she was worthless, trivial, and undeserving of the love of such a great man as Kovrin—and she would go off to her room, lock herself in, and weep bitterly for several hours. When there were visitors it would suddenly be borne in upon her that Kovrin was uncommonly handsome and that all the ladies were in love with him and jealous of her, and her heart would fill with pride and rapture, as though she had conquered the whole world, but it was enough for him to smile politely at some young lady for her to tremble with jealousy, go away to her room—and dissolve once more into tears. These new emotions took complete possession of her; she helped her father mechanically and noticed neither the peaches, nor the caterpillars, nor the workmen, nor how quickly the time fled.

Almost the same thing was happening with Egor Semenych. He worked from morning till night, was always hurrying off somewhere, losing his temper, getting beside himself with rage, but all in some enchanted half-dream. It was as if there were two people inside him: one was the real Egor Semenych who listened to the head gardener, Ivan Karlych, reporting that something had gone wrong, and waxed indignant or clutched his head in despair, the other an impostor, who seemed half drunk and would break off a business conversation in mid-sentence, clap the gardener on the shoulder and begin to mutter,

'Whatever you say, blood counts for a lot. His mother was a wonderful person, the best and cleverest of women. It was a pleasure to look at her kind, bright, pure face, like an angel's. She painted beautifully, wrote verses, spoke five foreign languages, sang . . . The poor thing, Heaven rest her soul, died of consumption.'

The false Egor Semenych sighed and, after a moment's silence, went on,

'When he was a boy and growing up in my house, he had the same angelic face, bright and good. His look, his movements, and his way of talking were gentle and elegant, like his mother's. And his mind? We were always struck by the quality of his mind. Indeed, he didn't get his master's degree for nothing! Not for nothing! You wait and see, Ivan Karlych, what he will be in ten years! There'll be no touching him!'

But here the true Egor Semenych, recollecting himself, pulled a terrible face, clutched his head and cried,

'Devils! Spoilt, destroyed, frozen! The garden's ruined! The garden's done for!'

Kovrin was working with all his former ardour and did not notice the turmoil. Love had only added fuel to his fires. After every interview with Tanya he returned, exalted and happy, to his room and took up a book or his manuscript with the same passion with which he had just been kissing and declaring his love for her. What the black monk had said about God's elect, eternal truth, the dazzling future of mankind, and so on, had given his work a special and extraordinary significance and filled his soul with pride and the consciousness of his own eminence. Once or twice every week, in the park or the house, he saw the black monk and held long conversations with him, but this did not frighten him, on the contrary it enraptured him, since he was firmly convinced that such visions appear only to the elect, to outstanding people who have dedicated themselves to the service of the Idea.

On one occasion the monk appeared during dinner and sat down by a window in the dining-room. Kovrin was delighted and adroitly led the conversation with Egor Semenych and Tanya to topics which might interest the monk; the black-robed visitor listened and nodded affably, and Egor Semenych also listened and smiled cheerfully, with no suspicion that Kovrin was talking not to them but to his hallucination.

The Feast of the Assumption arrived almost unnoticed, and soon after came the day of the wedding, which was celebrated, on Egor Semenych's insistence, 'with a splash', that is with senseless revelry that lasted for forty-eight hours. Something like three thousand people ate and drank, but what with the very bad hired orchestra, the noisy toasts, the hurrying servants, the din, and the crush, nobody could appreciate either the expensive wines or the marvellous food ordered from Moscow.

VII

During one of the long nights of winter Kovrin was lying in bed reading a French novel. Poor Tanya who, unused to town life, always had a headache in the evening, had long been asleep, and occasionally uttered some fragmentary, wandering phrases.

It struck three. Kovrin extinguished the candle and lay down, but he could not sleep because the room was very hot and Tanya was talking in her sleep. At half-past four he lit the candle again and saw as he did so the black monk sitting in an armchair near the bed.

'Good morning,' said the monk and after a moment's silence asked, 'What are you thinking about?'

'Fame,' answered Kovrin. 'The French novel I have just been reading depicts a man, a young scholar, who does stupid things and pines away out of longing for fame. It is a longing I cannot understand.'

'Because you are sensible. You treat fame with indifference, like a toy which does not interest you.'

'Yes, that's true.'

'Reputation does not attract you. What is there flattering, or entertaining, or edifying about having your name cut on a tombstone and the inscription with its gilding wiped away afterwards by the hand of time? Besides, there are luckily too many of you for a feeble human memory to be able to retain your names.'

'To be sure,' agreed Kovrin. 'Besides, why should they be remembered? But let us talk about something else. Happiness, for example. What is happiness?'

When the clock struck five he was sitting on the edge of the bed and saying to the monk.

'In antiquity a certain fortunate man grew at length afraid of his luck, it was so great, and in order to appease the gods he sacrificed his favourite ring to them. You remember? And I, like Polycrates, am beginning to be a little worried by my good fortune. It seems strange that I experience nothing from morning to night but gladness; it fills me completely and stifles all other feelings. I don't know what is meant by grief, sadness, or boredom. As you see, I don't sleep, I have insomnia, but I'm not bored. Seriously, it is beginning to worry me.'

'But why?' the monk wondered. 'Is joy an unnatural feeling? Should it not be a man's normal state? The higher a man's mental and moral development and the freer he is, the more pleasure does life give him. Socrates, Diogenes, and Marcus Aurelius experienced joy, not sorrow. And the apostle says, "Rejoice alway". Rejoice, then, and be happy.'

'And if the gods grow suddenly jealous?' asked Kovrin jestingly, with a laugh. 'If they take away my comforts and make me suffer cold and hunger, it will hardly be to my taste.'

Meanwhile Tanya had awakened and was watching her husband with amazement and terror. He was talking, addressing the armchair, gesticulating and laughing; his eyes glittered and there was something strange in his laugh.

'Andryusha, who are you talking to?' she asked, seizing the hand he had stretched towards the monk. 'Andryusha! Who is it?'

'What? Who to?' said Kovrin, disconcerted. 'To him . . . There he is, sitting there,' he went on, pointing to the black monk.

'There is nobody there . . . nobody! Andryusha, you are ill!'

Tanya put her arms round her husband, clinging to him as though shielding him from the apparition, and covered his eyes with her hand.

'You're ill,' she sobbed, her whole body shaking. 'Forgive me, my dear, but I have seen for a long time that your mind was disturbed . . . You are ill in mind, Andryusha . . .'

Her trembling communicated itself to him. He looked once more at the armchair, which was now empty, felt a sudden weakness in his arms and legs, and began to dress in alarm.

'It's nothing, Tanya, it's nothing,' he muttered, still shaking. 'I really am a little unwell . . . it is time I recognized it.'

'I noticed it long ago . . . and papa noticed,' she said, trying to restrain her sobs. 'You talk to yourself, you smile in a strange sort of way . . . you don't sleep. Oh God, God save us!' she said in terror. 'But don't be afraid, Andryusha, don't be afraid, for God's sake don't be afraid . . .'

She also began to dress. Only now, looking at her, did Kovrin understand the full danger of his position, the meaning of the black monk and his conversations with him. Now it was clear to him that he was mad.

Both, without knowing why, finished dressing and went into the drawing-room, she first, he following her. There, awakened by the sobbing, Egor Semenych, who was on a visit to them, stood in his dressing-gown and with a candle in his hand.

'Don't be afraid, Andryusha,' said Tanya, shaking as though with fever, 'don't be afraid . . . Papa, all this will pass . . . it will all pass . . .'

Kovrin could not speak for agitation. He tried to say to his father-in-law in a jesting tone, 'Congratulate me, it seems I've gone out of my mind,' but he could only move his lips and smile bitterly.

At nine o'clock in the morning they put on his overcoat and fur coat, wrapped him in a shawl, and took him in the carriage to his doctor's. He began to have treatment.

VIII

Summer had come again, and the doctor had ordered him to go into the country. Kovrin was already well again, he had ceased to see the black monk, and it only remained for him to regain his physical strength. Living with his father-in-law in the country he drank a great deal of milk, worked only two hours a day, and did not drink or smoke.

In the middle of July, on the eve of St. Elias's Day, an evening service was held in the house. When the clerk handed the priest the censer, the huge old ballroom began to smell like a cemetery, and Kovrin to feel restless.

He went out into the garden. Paying no attention to the rich profusion of flowers, he wandered round the garden, sat for a while on a bench, and then walked through the park; when he came to the river he went down the bank and stood there irresolutely, looking at the water. From the sombre pines with their mossy roots, which had seen him there the year before, so young, fit, and pleased with life, there now came not a whisper; they stood motionless and dumb, as though they did not know him. And indeed, his head had been cropped and the long, beautiful hair had gone, his movements were languid, and his face was fuller and paler than in the previous summer.

He crossed to the other side by the footbridge. There, where there had been rye the year before, the oats had been reaped and left lying in rows. The sun had gone down and a wide red sunset flared on the horizon, promising windy weather for the next day. It was quiet. Gazing in the direction from which the black monk had appeared the year before, Kovrin stood for about twenty minutes, until the red glow had begun to fade . . .

When he returned to the house, weary and dissatisfied, the service was over. Egor Semenych and Tanya were sitting on the terrace drinking tea. They were talking about something, but stopped abruptly when they saw him, and he concluded from their expressions that the conversation had been about him.

'I think it is time for your milk,' said Tanya to her husband.

'No, it's not,' he answered, sitting down on the lowest step. 'Drink it yourself. I won't.'

Tanya exchanged alarmed glances with her father and said apologetically,

'You say yourself that the milk is good for you.'

'Yes, very good!' Kovrin sneered. 'I congratulate you;

I have put on another pound since Friday.' Clutching his head tightly with his hands, he said in anguished tones, 'Why, oh why, did you try to cure me? Bromides, idleness, warm baths, constant watching, cowardly misgivings over every mouthful and every step—in the end it will all make a complete idiot of me. I was going out of my mind, I had delusions of grandeur, but on the other hand I was cheerful, vigorous, and even happy, I was interesting and original. Now I have become more reasonable and stable, but on the other hand I'm like everybody else: I'm a mediocrity, I'm bored with life . . . Oh, how cruel you have been to me! I did have hallucinations, but what harm did they do anybody? I ask you, what harm did they do anybody?'

'God knows what you are talking about!' sighed Egor Semenych. 'It's tiresome even to listen to you.'

'Then don't listen.'

The presence of other people, especially Egor Semenych, now irritated Kovrin; he answered him dryly, coldly, even rudely, sometimes without looking at him, as though he found him ridiculous or hateful, and Egor Semenych grew confused and coughed apologetically, although he did not feel guilty in any way. Not understanding why their pleasant, placid relations had changed so sharply, Tanya clung to her father and gazed anxiously into his eyes; she wanted to understand but she could not, and the only thing that was clear to her was that their relations grew worse and worse with every day, that her father had recently aged very much, and that her husband had grown moody, capricious, quarrelsome, and uninteresting. She could no longer laugh or sing, ate nothing at dinner, lay awake all night long waiting for something terrible to happen, and was so exhausted that sometimes she lay in a stupor from dinner-time until evening. During the service she had thought her father was crying, and now when they were all three sitting on the terrace she strove her utmost not to think about it.

'How lucky Buddha and Mahomet and Shakespeare were—they had no kind relatives and doctors to cure them of their ecstasies and inspirations!' said Kovrin. 'If Mahomet had taken potassium bromide for his nerves, worked only two hours a day, and drunk milk, as little would have remained of that remarkable man as of his dog. In the long run, the result of what the doctors and the kind relatives do will be that mankind will grow stupid, mediocrity will be considered genius, and civilization will perish. If you only knew how grateful I am to you!' said Kovrin, with venom.

He felt a rush of annoyance, and in order not to say more than he should, stood up quickly and went into the house. The night was still and the scent of tobacco-flowers and jalap was borne in through the open windows from the garden. In the great dark ballroom the moonlight lay in green patches on the floor and the grand piano. Kovrin was reminded of the delights of the previous summer, when the jalap was just as sweet-scented and the moon shone through the windows. In an attempt to bring back the mood of the past summer he hurried to his study, lit a strong cigar and ordered a servant to bring some wine. But the cigar made his mouth taste bitter and disgusting, and the wine did not seem to have the same savour as the year before. And what a difference the loss of habit made! The cigar and two mouthfuls of wine made his head begin to swim and his heart to pound, so that he had to take potassium bromide.

Before she went to bed, Tanya said to him,

'My father adores you. You are annoyed with him over

something, and it is killing him. Look, he is ageing not daily but hourly. I implore you, Andryusha, for God's sake, for the sake of your own dead father, for my peace of mind, be kind to him!'

'I can't and I won't.'

'But why not?' asked Tanya, her whole body beginning to tremble. 'Explain to me.'

'Because we are not in sympathy, that's all,' Kovrin answered with a careless shrug of the shoulders; 'but we won't talk about him, he is your father.'

'I can't understand, I can't!' said Tanya, clutching her temples and staring fixedly at one point. 'Something incomprehensible and horrible is happening in this house. You have changed, you are not like yourself . . . You, an exceptional and reasonable man, lose your temper over trifles and get involved in petty wrangles . . . Such little things upset you that sometimes we are left gaping and unable to believe this can really be you. Well, don't be angry, don't be angry,' she went on, frightened by her own words and kissing his hands. 'You are clever and good and noble. You will be fair to my father. He is so good!'

'He's not good, only good-natured. Stage uncles like your father, with well-fed, good-humoured faces and extraordinary hospitality and eccentricity, once used to touch and amuse me in books or music-hall sketches and in real life, but now I find them repulsive. They are egoists to the marrow of their bones. What I most dislike is their good living, and that visceral optimism, like a bull's or a wild boar's.'

Tanya sat down on the bed and laid her head on the pillow.

'This is torture,' she said, and her voice clearly showed that she was completely worn out and found it difficult to speak. 'Not one moment's peace since the winter! . . . My God, it is dreadful! I am in agony . . .'

'Yes, of course, I am Herod and you and your father are the Egyptian innocents. Of course!'

His face looked ugly and unpleasant to Tanya. Hatred and sneering did not suit him. Even earlier she had noticed that his face seemed to lack something, as though it too had lost something when his hair was cropped. She wanted to say something wounding, but the moment she detected a feeling of enmity in herself she took fright and went out of the bedroom.

IX

Kovrin had been given a university chair. His inaugural lecture was arranged for 2 December, and a notice announcing it hung in the university corridor. But on the appointed day he informed the supervisor of students by telegram that illness would prevent him from giving the lecture.

He was suffering from effusions of blood from the throat. He frequently spat blood, and once or twice a month it flowed copiously, and then he felt extremely weak and fell into a lethargic state. The illness did not particularly alarm him, since he knew that his mother had lived ten years or more with exactly the same condition, and the doctors assured him that it was not dangerous; they merely advised him not to get excited, to lead a regular life, and not to talk so much.

In January again the lecture did not take place, for the same reason, and in February it was already too late to start the course. It had to be postponed until the next academic year.

He was no longer living with Tanya, but with another

woman, two years older than himself, who looked after him like a child. His mood was peaceful and accommodating; he submitted willingly to everything, and when Varvara Nikolaevna—that was the name of his companion—proposed to take him to the Crimea, he consented, although he foresaw that no good would come of the journey.

They arrived in Sebastopol in the evening and stopped at a hotel to rest before going on the next day to Yalta. Both were weary with travelling. Varvara Nikolaevna had some tea, went to bed and was soon asleep. But Kovrin did not go to bed. At home, an hour before they left for the station, he had received a letter from Tanya, which he had felt unable to open, and now it lay in one of his pockets and the thought of it was unpleasantly exciting. In the depths of his heart he now sincerely believed that his marriage to Tanya had been a mistake, he was pleased to have broken finally with her, and the memory of this woman, who had in the end become a living, walking corpse, in which everything seemed to have died but the great, clever, staring eyes—her memory aroused only his pity and his anger against himself. The handwriting on the envelope reminded him that about two years ago he had been unjust and cruel, had avenged himself on innocent people for his spiritual emptiness, boredom, loneliness, and dissatisfaction with life. He remembered, too, how he had once torn into little pieces his thesis and all the articles he had written during his illness and thrown them out of the window, and how the pieces, carried on the wind, had lodged in the trees and on the flowers; in every line he had seen strange, unfounded pretensions, frivolous rage, insolence, and delusions of grandeur, and this had produced the same effect on him as reading an inventory of his own vices might have done; but when the last notebook had been torn up and vanished out of the window, he had felt suddenly vexed and bitter, and he had gone to his wife and assailed her with a flood of disagreeable remarks. God, how he had tormented her! Once, when he wished to cause her pain, he had told her that her father's part in their romance had been unsavoury, since he had asked him to marry her; Egor Semenych had chanced to overhear this, and had burst into the room, but desperation made him unable to utter a word and he could only stamp and produce a strange bellowing, as though his tongue had been torn out, while Tanya looked at her father, gave a heart-rending shriek, and fainted. It had been an ugly scene.

All this passed through his memory as he looked at the familiar handwriting. Kovrin went out on to the balcony; the weather was calm and warm and there was a smell of the sea. The glorious bay, reflecting the moon and the lights, had a colour to which it was difficult to put a name. It was a soft and tender mingling of blue and green; in places the water looked like blue copperas and in places it seemed as though the moonlight had thickened and now filled the bay instead of water; altogether, what a harmony of colours, what a mood of peace, exaltation, and tranquillity!

Below the balcony the windows of the floor beneath probably stood open, and the sound of laughter and women's voices could be clearly heard. Evidently a party was taking place there.

Kovrin made an effort, opened the letter and, going into the room, read:

'My father has just died. I am indebted to you for this, since it was you who killed him. Our garden is being ruined, it is already in the hands of strangers; that is to say that the very thing my poor father was so afraid of is happening. This also I owe to you. I hate you with my whole soul, and I hope you will soon perish. Oh, how I am suffering! My heart burns with unendurable pain . . . May you be accursed! I took you for an unusual being, a genius, I loved you, but you proved to be a madman . . .'

Kovrin could read no more, and he tore up the letter and threw it away. He was in the grip of an anxiety that was very like panic. Varvara Nikolaevna was asleep behind the screen and her breathing was audible; from the lower floor came the sound of women's voices and laughter, but he felt as though besides himself there was not a living soul in the hotel. Because the unhappy Tanya, overcome by grief, had cursed him in her letter and wished for his destruction, he was uneasy and glanced at the door as though afraid that the same unknown power that had brought such devastation into his life and the lives of those near to him would enter the hotel room and once again do as it pleased with him.

He knew by experience that when the nerves get out of control, the best remedy is work. He must sit down at his desk and force himself at whatever cost to concentrate his thoughts on one particular idea. From his red portfolio he took out a notebook in which he had sketched out the plan for a short piece of work he had thought of compiling, if he found the Crimea boring with nothing to do. He sat down and began to tackle this plan, and it seemed to him that his old peaceful, resigned, unconcerned, mood was returning. The notebook with its plan even led him to contemplate the vanities of this world. He thought of how much life takes from us in return for the trumpery or very mediocre benefits it is able to bestow. For example, to obtain a university chair, to be a very ordinary professor expounding very ordinary ideas that were not even his own, in lifeless, ponderous, and boring language, to attain, in short, the position of a second-rate scholar, he, Kovrin, had been obliged to study for fifteen years, to work day and night, to suffer from a serious psychological illness, and to commit a great number of such stupidities and wrongs as it would be pleasanter to forget. Kovrin now clearly recognized that he was a mediocrity, and had willingly reconciled himself to the fact, since in his opinion every human being ought to be satisfied with what he is.

His plan would have had complete success in soothing him, but that the torn letter lying on the floor prevented him from concentrating. He got up from the table, picked up the bits of paper and flung them out of the window, but a light breeze was blowing in from the sea and the paper scattered on the window-sill. Again an uneasiness that resembled fear took possession of him, and he began to feel as though except for himself there was not a soul in the whole hotel . . . He went out on to the balcony. The bay, like something alive, looked at him with a multitude of azure, dark blue, turquoise, and fiery-red eyes, and drew him towards itself. It was certainly hot and stuffy and it would not be a bad idea to bathe.

Suddenly a violin began to play on the lower floor, under the balcony, and two sweet women's voices began to sing. It was something familiar. The drawing-room ballad which was being sung down there was about a young girl with a sick imagination, listening in the garden at night to mysterious sounds and deciding that this was a sacred harmony, incomprehensible to mortals like us . . . Kovrin caught his breath, his heart contracted with sorrow, and yet a marvellous sweet joy, which he had long forgotten, quivered in his breast.

A tall black pillar, like a tornado or a typhoon, appeared

on the far shore of the bay. With terrible swiftness it moved across the bay towards the hotel, growing steadily darker and smaller, and Kovrin barely had time to move aside to give it passage . . . A monk with a grey uncovered head and black brows, barefooted, his arms crossed on his breast, swept past him and stopped in the middle of the room.

'Why did you not believe me?' he asked reproachfully, looking courteously at Kovrin. 'If you had believed me when I said that you were a genius you would not have spent two such sad and barren years.'

Kovrin already believed that he was one of God's elect and a genius, he vividly remembered all his former conversations with the black monk and would have spoken, but blood was flowing from his throat and down his breast; he passed his hands helplessly over his breast and his cuffs were wet with blood. He tried to summon Varvara Nikolaevna, sleeping behind the screen, made a great effort and said,

'Tanya!'

He fell to the floor and called again, raising himself on his hands,

'Tanya!'

He was invoking Tanya, invoking the great garden with its wealth of flowers sprinkled with dew, invoking the park, the pines with their mossy roots, the rye-field, his wonderful learning, his youth and fearlessness and his joy, invoking life itself, which had been so beautiful. On the floor near his head he could see a great pool of blood and he was so weak that now he could not speak a word, but a boundless, inexpressible happiness filled his whole being. Downstairs under the balcony they were playing the serenade, and the black monk was whispering to him that he was a genius, and that he was dying only because his weak mortal body had lost its equilibrium and could no longer serve as a sheath for his genius.

When Varvara Nikolaevna woke up and came out from behind the screen, Kovrin was dead, with a fixed smile of beatitude on his face.

THE STUDENT

1894

THE weather at first was mild and pleasant. The blackbirds sang and in the marshes near by some living creature made a plaintive hum, as if it was blowing into an empty bottle. A snipe called, and the shots fired at it sounded ragged and cheerful in the spring air. But when the wood began to grow dark, an unseasonably cold, biting wind sprang up from the east, and everything fell silent. Needles of ice crept over the surface of the pools and the wood was uncomfortably empty and deserted. There was a smell of winter in the air.

Ivan Velikopolsky, a theological student and the son of a parish clerk, on his way home from snipe shooting, was following a track through the water-meadows. His fingers were stiff with cold and his face burned with the wind. It seemed to him that the unexpected cold snap had destroyed all the harmony and order of things, that nature itself was uneasy, and that therefore the evening shadows had thickened too rapidly. All round him it seemed peculiarly dark and empty. Only in the Widows' Garden near the river was there a light shining, but everything more distant, including the village some four versts away, lay drowned in the cold evening mist. The student remembered how, when he left the house, his mother had been sitting barefooted on the floor of the passage cleaning the samovar, while his father lay coughing on top of the stove; because it was Good Friday no food had been cooked in the house, and he was painfully hungry. And now, as he shrank with the cold, he was thinking of how just such a wind had blown in the days of Rurik, and Ivan the Terrible, and Peter the Great, and there had been the same grinding poverty and hunger, too; the same holes in the thatched roofs, the same ignorance and frustration, the same empty wastes, the darkness, the feeling of persecution—all these horrors had always been, were now, and always would be, and so even when a thousand years had passed, life would be no better. He did not want to go home.

The market-garden was called the Widows' Garden because it was kept by two widows, a mother and daughter. The fire blazed hotly, crackling and lighting up the ploughed earth all round. The widow Vasilisa, a tall, stout old woman, wearing a man's overcoat, stood staring absently into the fire, and her daughter Lukerya, small and pock-marked, with a dull-witted face, was sitting on the ground washing out a cooking-pot and some spoons. Evidently they had only just finished supper. There was the sound of men's voices; it was the workmen watering the horses by the river.

'Well, here's winter come back again,' said the student, going up to the fire. 'Good evening.'

Vasilisa started, but recognized him immediately and smiled a welcome.

'God bless you, I didn't recognize you,' she said. 'That means you'll be rich.'

They began to talk. Vasilisa, a woman with some knowledge of the world, who had been a wet-nurse and then a children's nurse in gentlemen's houses, spoke in a refined way, and the gentle, quiet smile never left her face, but her daughter Lukerya, a real country peasant whose husband had beaten her stupid, simply squinted silently up at the student with a strange expression, like a deaf-mute's.

'The apostle Peter warmed his hands at a bonfire just like this one night,' said the student, stretching out his hands towards the blaze. 'That means it must have been cold then, too. Oh, what a terrible night that was, grandmother! A dreadfully long night, and dreadfully sad!'

He looked round at the darkness, jerked his head convulsively, and asked:

'I suppose you went to the Twelve Gospels yesterday?'

'Yes,' answered Vasilisa.

'If you remember, during the Last Supper Peter said to Jesus, "Lord, I am ready to go with thee, both into prison, and to death." And the Lord said to him, "I tell thee, Peter, the cock shall not crow this day, before that thou shalt thrice", that is three times, "deny that thou knowest me." After the supper, in the garden, the soul of Jesus was sorrowful unto death and he prayed, but poor Peter's heart was weary, he was weak and his eyes were heavy and he could not overcome his weariness. And he slept. Afterwards, as you heard, on that self-same night, Judas kissed Jesus and betrayed him to his enemies. They led him bound to the high priest, and smote him, and Peter, in an agony of distress and alarm, you understand? without having his sleep out, and full of foreboding that a fearful thing was about to happen here on earth at any moment, followed behind . . . He loved Jesus passionately, to distraction, and now he saw from afar how he was buffeted . . .'

Lukerya left her spoons and fixed an unblinking gaze on the student.

'They came to the high priest,' he went on. 'They began to question Jesus, and meanwhile the servants kindled a fire in the midst of the hall, because it was cold, and warmed themselves. Peter stood with them by the fire and also warmed himself, as I am doing now. One woman saw him and said, "This man was also with Jesus", meaning to say that he must also be taken for questioning. And all the servants who were round the fire must have looked at him grimly and suspiciously, because he was troubled and said, "Woman, I know him not." And after a little while another recognized him as one of the disciples and said, "Thou art also of them." But he denied it again. And for the third time one of them spoke to him: "Did I not see thee in the garden with him?" He denied him for the third time. And after this time, immediately the cock crew, and Peter, looking at Jesus from afar, called to mind the words he had said to him at the Supper . . . He remembered and roused himself and went out of the hall and shed bitter, bitter tears. The Gospel says, "And he went out, and wept bitterly." I imagine the garden, so very quiet and so very dark, and muffled sobbing scarcely heard in the stillness . . .'

The student sighed and stood musing. Still smiling, Vasilisa sobbed suddenly, large, abundant tears rolled down her cheeks, and she shielded her face from the fire with her sleeve, as though ashamed of her tears, while Lukerya, still gazing fixedly at the student, blushed and looked distressed and tense, like somebody trying to endure violent pain.

The labourers were returning from the river, and one

of them, astride a horse, was already near enough for the flickering light of the fire to play on him. The student bade the widows good night and walked on. The darkness came down again, and his hands felt cold. A cruel wind was blowing, winter had indeed returned, and it did not seem possible that the next day but one would be Easter.

Now the student was thinking of Vasilisa: if she had wept, that meant that what had happened to Peter on that terrible night had some relevance to her . . .

He looked round. The solitary fire twinkled peacefully in the darkness, and the people near it were no longer visible. The student thought again that if Vasilisa had wept, and her daughter showed embarrassment, what he had just been telling them about something that happened nineteen hundred years ago plainly had some relation to the present—to both women and probably to this isolated village, to himself personally and to all mankind. If the old woman cried, it was not because he knew how to touch her heart with a story, but because Peter was near to her and her whole being was concerned with what happened to Peter's soul.

Suddenly joy welled up in his heart, and he even stopped for a moment to catch his breath. The past, he thought, is linked with the present by an unbroken chain of events flowing one from the other. And it seemed to him that he had just seen the two ends of this chain: when he had touched one, the other had moved. While he was ferrying himself across the river, and afterwards as he climbed the hill, with his eyes on his native village and on the west where a narrow strip of sunset shone coldly red, he was thinking that the truth and beauty which had guided human life there, in the garden and the chief priest's palace, had continued without a break up to the present day and evidently constituted the most important thing in the lives of men and on the earth in general; and little by little he was filled with consciousness of health and strength and youth—he was only twenty-two—and the inexpressibly sweet expectation of happiness, a mysterious unknown happiness; and life seemed to him delightful, miraculous, and full of high significance.

AN ANNA ROUND HIS NECK

1895

I

AFTER the wedding there was not even a light meal; the bride and groom drank a glass of champagne, changed their clothes, and went off to the station. Instead of a cheerful wedding-ball and supper, instead of music and dancing, a pilgrimage to a monastery a hundred and fifty miles away. Many people approved of this, saying that Modest Alexeich was not young and had already attained a high position in the civil service, and that a noisy wedding might perhaps have seemed a little unsuitable; and besides, it is boring to listen to music when a fifty-two-year-old official marries a girl who is barely eighteen. They said also that Modest Alexeich, as a man of principle, had planned this pilgrimage on purpose to give his young wife to understand that even in marriage he gave first place to religion and morality.

The couple were seen off at the station. A crowd of colleagues and relatives stood with glasses in their hands, waiting to cheer as the train left, and Peter Leontyich, the bride's father, wearing a top hat and the tail-coat of his teacher's uniform, already drunk and very pale, kept stretching up his glass towards the window and saying in an imploring tone,

'Anyuta! Anya! Anya, just a word!'

Anna leaned out of the window towards him, and he whispered something to her, enveloping her in stale wine-fumes, blowing into her ear—it was impossible to understand what he was saying—and making the sign of the cross over her face and breast and hands, while his breath came unsteadily and tears glistened in his eyes. Anya's brothers, Petya and Andryusha, schoolboys, tugged at his coat from behind and whispered in embarrassment,

'Papa, stop it . . . Don't, papa . . .'

When the train moved Anna saw her father running a little way after it, staggering and splashing wine out of his glass, and saw how pathetic, kind, and guilty he looked.

'Hurrah!' he shouted.

The newly married pair remained alone. Modest Alexeich looked round the compartment, distributed their things on the racks, and sat down smiling opposite his young wife. He was an official of medium height, rather round and plump and very well nourished, with long whiskers but no moustache, and his round, shaven, sharply defined chin looked like a heel. The most characteristic thing about his face was the absence of a moustache, the freshly shaven bare place which gradually merged into fat cheeks quivering like a jelly. His demeanour was staid, his movements deliberate, his manners suave.

'I cannot help recalling just now a certain circumstance,' he said smiling. 'Five years ago, when Kosorotov was given the Order of St. Anne, second class, and called to thank the Governor, his Excellency expressed himself in these terms, "Well, now you have three Annas, one in your button-hole and two hanging round your neck." I must tell you that at the time Kosorotov's wife, a shrewish and trivial creature, whose name is Anna, had just returned to him. I hope that when I receive my Anna of the second class, his Excellency will not have occasion to say the same thing to me.'

He smiled with his little eyes. And she smiled too, agitated by the thought that at any moment this man might kiss her with his moist, full lips and that she no longer had the right to refuse him. The soft movements of his plump body frightened her; she felt both alarmed and revolted. He stood up and hurriedly removed the order he wore round his neck, took off his coat and waistcoat and put on his dressing-gown.

'There!' he said, sitting down beside Anya.

She was remembering how painful the wedding ceremony had been, when it had seemed to her that the priest, and the guests, and everybody in the church, had looked at her sadly: why, why was she, such a nice pretty girl, marrying that dull, elderly gentleman? This morning she had been delighted that everything was going so well for her, but during the ceremony and now in the railway carriage she felt guilty, cheated, and ridiculous. She had married a rich man, but all the same she had no money, her wedding clothes had not been paid for, and today, when her father and brothers were seeing her off, she could tell from their faces that they hadn't a single copeck. Would they have any supper tonight? And what about tomorrow? And for some reason she saw her father and the boys sitting at that moment without her, hungry and experiencing the same distress as on the first evening after her mother's funeral.

'Oh, how unhappy I am!' she thought. 'Why am I so unhappy?'

With the awkwardness of a solid citizen unaccustomed to dealing with women, Modest Alexeich touched her waist and patted her shoulder, while she thought of money, of her mother, and of her mother's death. When her mother died, her father, Peter Leontyich, a teacher of calligraphy and drawing in the high school, began to drink, and they felt the pinch; the boys had no boots or galoshes, their father was taken before the magistrate, the court bailiff came and made an inventory of the furniture . . . What shame! Anya had had to look after her drunken father, mend her brothers' stockings, go to market, and when she was complimented on her beauty, youth and elegant manners, she thought the whole world could see her cheap hat and the holes in her shoes smeared over with ink. And at night tears and the importunate, worrying thought that at any moment her father's weakness would get him dismissed from the school and that he would not be able to endure it, but would die like her mother. But now some of the ladies among their acquaintances bestirred themselves and began to look for a good husband for Anna. Before long they had found this same Modest Alexeich, not young or handsome, but well off. He had about a hundred thousand in the bank and a family estate which he let to tenants. He was a man of principle and stood well with his Excellency; it would cost him nothing, they told Anna, to get a note from his Excellency to the headmaster of the school, or even to the Director of Education, to prevent Peter Leontyich's dismissal . . .

As she recalled these details the sudden sound of music and voices was borne in through the window. The train had stopped at a halt. Among the crowd beyond the platform somebody was playing lively tunes on an accordion and a cheap, squeaky fiddle, and from behind the tall birches and poplars, and the summer villas flooded with moonlight, came the strains of a military band: evidently a dance was in progress. On the platform strolled summer visitors and people whom the fine weather had brought out from the town for a breath of fresh air. Artynov, who owned the whole summer colony, was there too, a rich, tall, heavily built, dark-haired man with protruding eyes, like an Armenian in the face, and oddly dressed. He was wearing a shirt open down the front, high boots with spurs, and a long black cloak hanging from his shoulders and trailing on the ground like a train. Two borzois were at his heels, their sharp muzzles lowered.

Anya's eyes still glistened with tears, but she had already forgotten all about her mother, and money, and her marriage, and was shaking hands with officers she knew and boys from the high school, smiling cheerfully and hurriedly saying,

'Good evening! How are you?'

She went out on to the platform at the end of the coach, in the moonlight, and stood so that everybody could see her in her magnificent new dress and hat.

'Why have we stopped?' she asked.

'This is a loop-line,' she was told, 'and they are waiting for the mail train.'

She saw that Artynov was watching her, and she coquettishly narrowed her eyes and began to speak French in a loud voice, and because her own voice sounded so splendid, because of the music, and the moon reflected in the pond, because Artynov, who was well known as a rake and Don Juan, was watching her with eager curiosity, and because everybody was cheerful, she felt suddenly gay, and when the train moved and her officer acquaintances saluted her by way of good-bye, she was humming the polka whose sound the military band, pounding away there behind the trees, sent in pursuit of her; and she returned to their compartment feeling as though something at the halt had convinced her that she could not fail to be happy, in spite of everything.

The couple spent two days in the monastery and then returned to the town. They lived in an official flat. When Modest Alexeich went to his office, Anya played the piano, or wept with boredom, or lay on the couch reading novels or looking through a fashion paper. At dinner Modest Alexeich ate a great deal and talked about politics, appointments, transfers, and awards, about the necessity for hard work, about how family life is not a pleasure but a duty, about how one must take care of the copecks and the roubles will take care of themselves, and about how he held religion and morals in higher esteem than anything else on earth. And holding his knife in his fist like a sword, he said:

'Every man ought to have his obligations.'

And Anya listened to him and was afraid, could not eat, and usually rose from the table hungry. After dinner her husband rested for a time, snoring loudly, and she went to see her family. Her father and the boys looked at her rather peculiarly, as though just before she came in they had been criticizing her for marrying for his money a dreary bore whom she did not love; her rustling dresses, bracelets, and general appearance of a lady embarrassed and offended them; in her presence they were a little confused and did not know what to talk to her about; but all the same they still loved her as much as before, and they had not yet got used to dining without her. She would sit down with them and eat cabbage soup, buckwheat porridge, and potatoes fried in mutton fat and smelling like tallow candles. Peter Leontyich poured out a glass of vodka with shaking hands and drank it off quickly, greedily and with aversion, then he drank a second, and a third . . . Petya and Andryusha, pale-faced thin little boys with big eyes, would take hold of the decanter and say worriedly,

'Don't, papa . . . That's enough, papa . . .'

Anya would be anxious also and beg him not to drink any more, and he would fly into a sudden rage and thump his fist on the table.

'I won't allow anybody to dictate to me!' he would shout. 'Brats! I'll turn the lot of you out!'

But his voice revealed his weakness and goodness and nobody was afraid of him. After dinner he usually dressed himself up; pale-faced, with cuts on his chin from shaving, he would stand a full half-hour craning his thin neck and smartening himself up in front of the mirror, combing his hair, twisting his black moustache, spraying himself with scent, knotting his tie; then he put on his gloves and top hat and went off to his private pupils. If it was a holiday he stayed at home and painted or played the wheezy, growling harmonium, trying to draw melodious sounds from it and humming an accompaniment, or growing angry with the boys:

'Wretches! Scoundrels! You've ruined the instrument!'

In the evenings Anya's husband played cards with the colleagues who lived in official quarters under the same roof with him. At such times the officials' wives, unattractive, tastelessly dressed, as coarse as kitchen maids, would call, and the flat was filled with gossip as ugly and tasteless as the women themselves. It sometimes happened that Modest Alexeich went to the theatre with Anya. In the intervals he did not allow her to stir a step away from him, but walked with her on his arm through the corridors and about the foyer.

After exchanging bows with anybody he would immediately whisper to Anya, 'He's high in the service, a State Councillor—on visiting terms with his Excellency', or 'Well-to-do . . . owns his house'. When they passed the buffet Anya would very much have liked something sweet; she loved chocolate and apple tarts, but she had no money and was too shy to ask her husband. He would take up a pear, squeeze it in his fingers and ask undecidedly,

'How much?'

'Twenty-five copecks.'

'Well, really!' he would say, putting the pear back; and because it was awkward to leave the buffet without buying anything, he would order seltzer-water and drink the whole bottle himself, making his eyes water; at such times Anya hated him.

Or, suddenly going red all over, he would say hurriedly, 'Bow to that old lady!'

'But I don't know her.'

'That doesn't matter. She is the wife of the Director of the Treasury Office. Bow, I tell you,' he would mutter insistently. 'Your head won't fall off.'

Anya bowed, and her head never did fall off, but she suffered torments. She did everything her husband wished, while she raged at herself for having been taken in by him like the silliest little ninny. She had married him only for money, and yet she had less now than before her marriage. At least then she had a few coins from her father, but now not a copeck. She could neither take any by stealth nor ask for it; she was afraid of her husband and trembled before him. It seemed to her that she had nursed her fear of this man in her heart for a very long time. At one time, when she was a child, the high-school headmaster had represented the most dread and awe-inspiring powers, looming like a thunder-cloud or advancing with crushing weight like a railway engine; another such power, always spoken of with fear in the house, was his Excellency; there were a dozen lesser powers, including the stern, implacable masters in the school, with their clean-shaven upper lips, and now, finally, there was Modest Alexeich, the man of principle, who resembled the headmaster even in looks. In Anya's imagination all these powers fused into one and advanced on the weak and erring, like her father, in the shape of a terrible, enormous white bear; and she was afraid to protest but met with a forced smile and an expression of feigned pleasure the coarse caresses and defiling embraces that filled her with horror.

Only once did Peter Leontyich dare to ask his son-in-law for a loan of fifty roubles to settle an unpleasant debt, but what an ordeal it was!

'Very well, I will give it you,' said Modest Alexeich, 'but I warn you that in future I shall not help you until you stop drinking. For a man who is in the service of the government, it is a disgraceful failing. I cannot refrain from reminding you of the well-known fact that many capable individuals have been ruined by this passion, whereas had they been abstinent, they might well, with time, have attained very high rank.'

The long periods went rolling on; 'inasmuch as . . .', 'arising out of that assumption . . .', 'in view of what has just been stated...', while poor Peter Leontyich suffered agonies of humiliation and experienced a strong desire for a drink.

The boys, when they came to visit Anya, usually in shabby trousers and with holes in their boots, also had to listen to long sermons.

'Every man ought to have his obligations!' Modest Alexeich told them.

He never parted with money. On the other hand, he gave Anya rings, bracelets, and brooches, remarking that these were good things to possess against a rainy day. He often opened her drawers and carried out an inspection to see that all the things were safe.

II

Meanwhile winter set in. Long before Christmas there was an announcement in the local paper that the usual winter ball was to take place in the Assembly Rooms on 29 December. Every evening, after his game of cards, Modest Alexeich talked in excited whispers with the wives of his colleagues, throwing anxious glances at Anya, and then spent a long time thoughtfully pacing the room. At last, late one evening, he stopped in front of Anya and said,

'You must get a ball-dress. Do you understand? Only please ask the advice of Maria Grigoryevna and Natalya Kuzminishna.'

And he gave her a hundred roubles. She took them; but when she ordered her ball-dress she did not consult anybody, only talked to her father and tried to imagine how her mother would have dressed for the ball. Her dead mother had always dressed in the latest fashion and always taken pains with Anya and dressed her exquisitely, like a doll; and she had taught her to speak French and to dance the mazurka superlatively well (before her marriage she had been a governess for five years). Like her mother, Anya knew how to make a new dress out of an old one, clean gloves with benzine, and hire *bijoux*; and, like her mother again, she could half close her eyes, lisp, adopt elegant poses, go into raptures when necessary, or look sad and enigmatic. From her father she had inherited dark eyes and hair, highly strung nerves, and his way of always making the best of his appearance.

When, half an hour before they left for the ball, Modest Alexeich came into her room without his frock-coat, in order to put his order round his neck in front of her long mirror, he was enchanted by her beauty and the brilliant freshness and airiness of her dress, stroked his whiskers in a self-satisfied manner and said,

'How nice you look . . . how very nice! Anyuta!' he went on, with sudden solemnity, 'I have made you happy, and today you can make me happy. I beg you to introduce yourself to his Excellency's good lady. In God's name! Through her I might receive the senior secretaryship!'

They went to the ball. Here were the Assembly Rooms, the porter at the entrance, the ante-room with its coat pegs, fur coats, scurrying lackeys, ladies in low-necked gowns shielding themselves from the draught with their fans, and smell of gas and soldiers. As Anya mounted the stairs on her husband's arm, the sight of her own reflection, full length and brightly illuminated by a multitude of lights, in an enormous mirror, awakened in her heart a feeling of gladness and the same anticipation of happiness as she had experienced at the railway halt that moonlit night. She walked proudly and confidently, conscious for the first time that she was a lady and not a little girl, and involuntarily imitating her dead mother in her gait and carriage. For the first time in her life she felt rich and free. Even the presence of her husband did not embarrass her, since from the moment she crossed the threshold she had instinctively sensed that the proximity of her elderly husband in no way detracted from her but on the contrary invested her with the piquant mystery men like so much. In the great ballroom the orchestra was already in full swing and dancing had begun. Plunged, after their official flat, into all the impressions of bright lights, colour, music and noise, Anya threw a glance round the room, and thought, 'Oh, how splendid!' and at once picked out in the crowd all her acquaintances, everybody she had met at evening parties or out walking, all the officers, schoolmasters, lawyers, officials, landowners, his Excellency, Artynov, the great ladies, beautiful or plain, elaborately dressed and extremely *decolletées*, who had already taken up their positions among the stalls of the charity bazaar, ready to begin trading for the benefit of the poor. An enormous officer, wearing epaulettes—she had met him in Old Kiev Street when she was a schoolgirl and now could not remember his name—sprang up as if out of the ground in front of her and asked her for a waltz, and she whirled away from her husband, feeling as though she were in a sailing-boat in a violent storm and he was left behind on the distant shore . . . With passionate enthusiasm she danced the waltz, and a polka, and a quadrille, passing from partner to partner, dizzy with the music and the noise, mixing French and Russian words, lisping, laughing, and thinking neither of her husband nor of anybody or anything else. She was a success with the men, that was clear, and indeed it was inevitable; she was breathless with excitement, feverishly clutched her fan, and felt very thirsty. Her father, Peter Leontyich, in crumpled tails that smelt of benzine, came up to her, holding out a saucer of pink ice-cream.

'You are charming tonight,' he said, gazing at her with immense pleasure, 'and I have never been so sorry that you were in such a hurry to get married . . . Why? I know you did it for our sakes, but . . .' With shaking hands he pulled out a packet of notes and said, 'I was paid for some lessons today, and I can settle my debt to your husband.'

She thrust the saucer into his hands and was pounced on and swept away by somebody else, catching a glimpse over her cavalier's shoulder of her father gliding over the polished floor, putting his arm round a lady, and dashing off round the room with her.

'How nice he is when he's sober!' she thought.

She danced the mazurka with the enormous officer; solemnly and heavily, like a carcase in uniform, he walked along, twisted his shoulders and chest, stamped almost imperceptibly—he was terribly unwilling to dance, but she fluttered by his side, teasing him with her beauty and her bare neck; her eyes blazed with enthusiasm, her movements were full of passion, while he grew steadily more indifferent, and proffered his arm with the gracious condescension of a king.

'Bravo, bravo!' said the spectators.

Little by little even the enormous officer was carried away; he grew animated and excited, yielded to the spell, let himself go and began to move lightly and youthfully, while she only twisted her shoulders and looked arch, as if she was a queen and he a slave, and then it seemed to her that the whole room was watching them, and all these people were spell-bound and full of envy. The enormous officer had hardly had time to thank her before the spectators moved aside and the men drew themselves up rather oddly, with their arms by their sides. It was his Excellency, wearing two stars on his coat, who was coming towards her. Yes, his Excellency was indeed coming to her, since he was staring straight at her and smiling sweetly, and at the same time mumbling his lips, as he always did when he saw a pretty woman.

'Delighted, delighted . . .,' he began. 'I shall have your husband placed under arrest for concealing such a treasure from us until now. I am the bearer of a message from my wife,' he continued, offering her his arm. 'You must come and help us . . . Mm, yes . . . We shall have to give you a beauty-prize . . . as they do in America . . . Mm . . . yes. The Americans . . . My wife is waiting impatiently for you.'

He led her into a stall in the shape of a little peasant hut and up to an elderly lady, the lower part of whose face was disproportionately big, so that she looked as if she was holding a large stone in her mouth.

'Come and help,' she said in a drawling nasal voice. 'All the pretty ladies are working in the charity bazaar, and you are the only one who is idle, for some reason. Why won't you help us?'

She went away and Anya took her place beside a silver samovar and some cups. She began to do a brisk trade at once. She would not accept less than a rouble for a cup of tea, and she made the enormous officer drink three cups. Artynov, the rich man with the protruding eyes, approached, wheezing asthmatically and wearing not the strange costume in which Anya had seen him in the summer, but tails like everybody else. Without taking his eyes off her, he drank a glass of champagne, for which he paid a hundred roubles, and then had a cup of tea and gave another hundred—and all without a word, wheezing with asthma . . . Anya invited customers in and took money from them, and was already profoundly certain that her smiles and glances afforded them nothing but the greatest pleasure. She now understood that she was created exclusively for this noisy, brilliant, laughing life with its music, dances, and admirers, and her long-standing terror of some power advancing upon and threatening to crush her seemed ridiculous; she no longer feared anybody, and her only regret was that her mother was not there to rejoice with her in her success.

Peter Leontyich, pale by now but still firm on his feet, came up to the stall and asked for a glass of cognac. Anya blushed, expecting him to say something unsuitable (she was already ashamed that her father was so poor and so ordinary), but he drank his cognac, threw down ten roubles out of his packet, and walked sedately away without saying a word. A little later she saw him dancing the *grand rond* with his partner, and this time he was staggering and shouting, to the great confusion of his lady, and Anya remembered that three years ago at the ball he had staggered and shouted in the same way—and ended by being taken home to bed by a police officer; and the following day the headmaster had threatened him with dismissal. How untimely these memories seemed!

When the samovars on the stalls were extinguished and the weary charitable ladies handed their takings to the elderly lady with a stone in her mouth, Artynov took Anya on his arm to the room where supper was served for all those who had taken part in the bazaar. There were about twenty people, not more, having supper, but it was very lively. His Excellency proposed a toast: 'In this luxurious dining-room it is fitting that we should drink to the success of the cheap dining-rooms which were the object of our bazaar today.' A brigadier-general proposed a toast 'to the power before which even the artillery quails', and everybody clinked glasses with the ladies. It was all very gay.

When somebody took Anya home, it was already growing light and cooks were on their way to market. Gay, intoxicated, full of new impressions and extremely weary, she undressed, fell into bed and was instantly asleep.

At one o'clock in the afternoon the maid wakened her and announced that Mr. Artynov had called. She dressed quickly and went into the drawing-room. Soon after Artynov left, his Excellency arrived to thank her for helping with the bazaar. Casting saccharine looks at her and mumbling his lips, he kissed her hand, asked permission to call again, and departed, and she stood in the middle of the room, amazed and enchanted, unable to believe that this change in her life, an astonishing change, could have happened so quickly; and at that moment her husband, Modest Alexeich, walked in . . . He stood before her with exactly the same ingratiating, sugary, slavishly deferential expression that she was accustomed to seeing on his face in the presence of the powerful and distinguished; and triumphantly, indignantly, contemptuously, sure that nothing would happen to her for it, she said, pronouncing every word with great distinctness,

'Go away, stupid!'

After this, Anya never had a free day, since she was always going out to picnics, or walking, or to the play. She returned home every day towards morning, and went to bed on the floor of the drawing-room, afterwards movingly telling everybody how she slept under the flowers. She needed a great deal of money, but she was no longer afraid of Modest Alexeich and spent his money as if it were her own; she did not ask him for any, or demand it, merely sent him her bills, or notes saying 'Give the bearer of this 200 roubles,' or '100 roubles; settle immediately.'

At Easter Modest Alexeich received the Order of St. Anne, second class. When he went to express his thanks, his Excellency laid aside his newspaper and settled back in his armchair.

'Well, now you have three Annas,' he said, studying his white hands with their pink nails, 'one in your button-hole and two round your neck.'

Modest Alexeich laid two fingers to his lips, for fear of laughing too loud, and said,

'Now we must expect the appearance in the world of a little Vladimir. May I venture to ask your Excellency to be godfather?'

He was referring to the Order of St. Vladimir, fourth class, and he had already begun to imagine himself repeating his witty remark, so successful in its resourcefulness and audacity, everywhere he went; he intended to make another, equally successful, but his Excellency was once more buried in his newspaper and only nodded his head . . .

And Anya went on driving behind troikas, hunting with Artynov, taking part in one-act plays, and going out to supper, and was less and less frequently with her family. Now they always dined alone. Peter Leontyich drank more heavily than before, there was no money, and the harmonium had long ago been sold for debt. The boys no longer allowed him out alone, and always followed him to see that he did not fall; and when, among the carriages parading on Old Kiev Street, they met Anya in a showy turn-out with Artynov on the box instead of the coachman, Peter Leontyich took off his top-hat and seemed about to call out something, but Petya and Andryusha took his arms and said imploringly,

'Papa, don't . . . Stop, papa . . .'

THE HOUSE WITH A MEZZANINE

An Artist's Story

1896

I

SIX or seven years ago I was living in the Province of T., on the estate of Belokurov, a young country gentleman, who got up very early, wore a long sleeveless under-coat like a merchant or a peasant, drank beer in the evenings, and was always complaining to me that he nowhere met with any sympathy in anything he did. He lived in a pavilion in the garden, and I in the old house itself, in the enormous colonnaded ballroom, where there was no furniture except a wide sofa on which I slept, and a table on which I laid out my patience. Here, even in calm weather, there was always a droning noise from the ancient pneumatic stoves, and when there were thunderstorms the whole house shuddered and seemed to be splitting up, and it was a little frightening, especially at night, when all ten of the large windows were suddenly lit up by a flash of lightning.

Condemned by fate to perpetual idleness, I did absolutely nothing. For hours together I contemplated through my windows the sky, the birds and the avenues of trees, read everything that was brought back from the post office for me, and slept. Sometimes I would leave the house and wander about until late at night.

Once, as I returned home, I strayed by chance into a small estate I did not know. The sun was already going down, and evening shadows lengthened over the flowering rye. Two close-planted ranks of very tall old firs, like two walls, formed a dark and beautiful avenue. I climbed easily over the fence and walked along this avenue, sliding over the fir-needles which here covered the ground to a depth of two inches. It was still and dark, and only high in the tree-tops a clear golden light quivered here and there, or was transformed by a spider's web into a rainbow. There was a strong, almost suffocating, smell of fir-needles. Then I turned into a long lime-tree walk. Here also all was neglect and antiquity; last year's leaves rustled mournfully underfoot and shadows lurked between the trees in the twilight. To the right, in an old orchard, an oriole, itself probably ancient, piped feebly and reluctantly. But now the lime trees, too, came to an end; I passed a white house with a terrace and a mezzanine story in the roof, and in front of me there unexpectedly opened up the prospect of the courtyard and of a wide pond, with a bathing hut, a crowd of green willows and, on the far bank, a village with a tall, narrow belfry on which a cross glowed with the reflection of the setting sun. For an instant there breathed on me the charm of something dear and familiar, as though I had known that same panorama in my childhood.

Near the white stone gates leading out of the courtyard, the ancient massive gates with their stone lions, stood two girls. One, the elder, thin, pale, and very beautiful, with a great shock of chestnut-coloured hair piled on her head, a small, stubborn mouth and a severe expression, hardly paid any attention to me; but the other, who was still very young—she was seventeen or eighteen, nor more—and equally thin and pale, with a big mouth, large eyes, and a shy look, gazed at me in surprise as I walked past and said something in English, and it seemed to me that these two charming faces had also been known to me for a long time. I returned home with the feeling that I had had a pleasant dream.

Soon after this, early one afternoon, when Belokurov and I were walking near the house, we were surprised to see a well sprung carriage drive into the courtyard, swishing through the long grass. It was the elder of the two girls; she had come with a subscription list to help the victims of a fire. Without looking at us, she told us very seriously and circumstantially how many houses in the village of Siyanovo had been destroyed by the fire, how many men, women, and children had been left without a roof over their heads and what immediate steps the Fire Committee, of which she was a member, proposed to take. When we had added our names to the list, she put it away and immediately began to take her leave.

'You have quite forgotten us, Peter Petrovich,' she said to Belokurov, offering him her hand. 'Come and see us, and if Monsieur N' (she mentioned my name) 'cares to see how some admirers of his work live, and is kind enough to call on us, Mama and I will be very pleased.'

I bowed.

When she had gone Peter Petrovich began to tell me about her. The young lady, he said, came of a good family, her name was Lydia Volchaninova, the estate on which she lived with her mother and sister was called Shelkovka, and so was the village on the other side of the pond. Her father had once held a prominent post in Moscow, and had died with the very high rank of Privy Councillor. In spite of their comfortable circumstances the Volchaninovs spent all their time in the country, summer and winter alike, and Lydia taught in their own village school at Shelkovka at a salary of twenty-five roubles a month. This was all she spent on herself, and she was proud of the fact that she earned her own living.

'An interesting family,' said Belokurov. 'Perhaps we might call on them some time. They will be very pleased to see you.'

One holiday afternoon after dinner we remembered the Volchaninovs and went to Shelkovka to see them. They were all, the mother and both her daughters, at home. The mother, Ekaterina Pavlovna, once evidently beautiful, but now prematurely grey, asthmatic, melancholy, and absent-minded, tried to engage me in conversation about painting. When she heard from her daughter that I might perhaps call at Shelkovka, she hastily recalled two or three of my landscapes which she had seen in exhibitions in Moscow, and now questioned me about what I had intended to express by them. Lydia, or Lida, as they called her at home, talked more to Belokurov than to me. Serious and unsmiling, she cross-questioned him about why he did not serve on the local District Council, and why he had never even been to a single one of its annual sessions.

'It is wrong of you, Peter Petrovich,' she said reproachfully. 'It's wrong. You ought to be ashamed.'

'True, Lida, true,' her mother agreed. 'It's a bad thing.'

'Our whole District is in Balagin's hands,' continued Lida, turning to me. 'He himself is chairman of the Executive Board, and he has distributed all the posts in the District among his nephews and sons-in-law and does what he likes. He must be fought. The young people ought to form a strong party, but you see what our young people are like. You should be ashamed, Peter Petrovich!'

The younger sister, Zhenya, was silent while they talked of the *zemstvo*. She never took any part in serious conversation, and her family thought of her as not yet grown up, and called her 'Meess', as if she was a little girl, because that is what she had called her English governess as a child. She watched me curiously all the time, and when I looked at an album of photographs, she explained them to me: 'That's uncle . . . That's my godfather . . .', and passed her small finger over the pictured faces, leaning her shoulder against me like a child, so that her slight, undeveloped bust, narrow shoulders, plait of hair, and thin waist, tightly drawn in by a belt, were all close before my eyes.

We played croquet and lawn tennis, walked in the garden, drank tea, and afterwards had a long, leisurely supper. After my huge columned ballroom I somehow felt at home in this small, comfortable house, where there were no oleographs on the walls, where the maid-servants were politely addressed as 'you' instead of 'thou', where everything seemed young and pure, thanks to the presence of Lida and Meess, and everything spoke of respectability. At supper, Lida talked to Belokurov again about the *zemstvo* and Balagin, and about school libraries. She was a vivid, sincere young woman with convictions, and interesting to listen to, although she talked a great deal and rather loud—perhaps because she was used to talking in school. My Peter Petrovich, on the other hand, who had preserved from his student days the habit of turning every conversation into an argument, talked boringly, slowly, and at great length, with an obvious desire to appear clever and progressive. His gesticulations overturned a sauce-boat and a big pool formed on the table-cloth, but nobody except me seemed to notice it.

As we returned home, the night was dark and still.

'Good breeding consists not in not spilling sauce on the table-cloth, but in not noticing when somebody else does so', said Belokurov with a sigh. 'Yes, a fine and cultured family. I have got out of touch with nice people, very much out of touch. Nothing but business, business all the time! Business!'

He spoke of how much work one must do if one wished to become a model farmer. I thought, 'What a dull and lazy fellow he is!' When he talked about something serious he stumbled laboriously along with long-drawn-out 'er-er-er's' and he worked in exactly the same way—slowly, always falling behind and missing the right moment. I had little faith in his practical abilities, if only because he used to carry around in his pocket for weeks the letters I entrusted to him to post for me.

'The worst of it is,' he muttered, walking beside me, 'the worst of it is that you work and work and never get any sympathy! No sympathy at all!'

II

I became a frequent visitor at the Volchaninovs'. Usually I sat on the lowest step of the terrace; I was depressed by dissatisfaction with myself and regret that my life was running away so fast and uninterestingly, and I was always thinking how much I should like to tear out of my breast the heart which had grown so heavy. Meanwhile, there was the sound of people on the terrace talking, dresses rustling, somebody leafing through a book. I soon became used to the fact that in the day-time Lida received sick people, distributed library books, and frequently walked off to the village, bare-headed and carrying a sunshade; in the evenings she talked loudly about the *zemstvo* and the schools. Whenever the talk began to deal with practical matters, this thin, handsome, unfailingly severe young woman with the small, delicately defined mouth, would say drily to me,

'This won't interest you.'

She did not care for me. She did not like me because I painted landscapes instead of depicting the people's hardships and because she thought I was indifferent to all that she believed in so firmly. I remember that once, when I was on the shores of Lake Baikal, I met a Buryat girl in a shirt and trousers of dark blue Chinese cotton, riding a horse; I asked her whether she would sell me her pipe, and while we talked, she looked contemptuously at my European face and hat; in one minute she had grown bored with talking to me, whooped and galloped away. In exactly the same way Lida despised what was alien to her in me. Outwardly she never expressed her dislike of me, but I was conscious of it and, sitting on the lowest step of the terrace, I felt irritated and would proclaim that treating sick peasants without being a doctor meant cheating them, and that it was easy to be charitable when you had five thousand acres.

Her sister, Meess, had no cares and lived a life of complete idleness, like me. As soon as she got up in the morning she took up a book and began to read, sitting on the terrace in a chair so deep that her feet barely reached the ground, or taking refuge with her book in the lime-tree avenue, or going out of the gates into the open country. She read all day long, greedily absorbed in her book, and it was only because her eyes sometimes looked tired and dazed and her face very pale that it was possible to guess how much her reading wearied her brain. When she saw me arrive she would blush slightly, leave her book and, looking into my face with her big eyes, begin a lively account of all that had been happening: how the soot had caught fire in the kitchen or one of the labourers had hooked a big fish in the pond. On weekdays she usually wore a light-coloured blouse with a navy-blue skirt. We went for walks together, picked cherries for jam, or rowed on the pond, and when she jumped to reach a cherry or struggled with the oars, her slight, thin arms showed through her white sleeves. Sometimes I sketched, while she stood beside me and watched admiringly.

One Sunday morning, at the end of July, I went to the Volchaninovs' early, about nine o'clock. I walked through the park, keeping at a distance from the house, looking for the white mushrooms which were very plentiful that summer, and leaving marks near them, so as to pick them later with Zhenya. There was a warm breeze blowing. I saw Zhenya and her mother, both in bright Sunday dresses, coming home from church, and Zhenya holding on to her hat because of the wind. Afterwards I could hear them having tea on the terrace.

These summer Sunday mornings on our two estates always had an uncommon attraction for me, a man without responsibilities, looking for excuses for his perpetual idleness. When the green garden, still wet with dew, was all sparkling and happy in the sunshine, when the scent of mignonette and oleanders was all round the house, when the young people, just back from church, were having their morning tea in the garden, and when everybody was so nicely dressed and carefree, and you knew that all these healthy, well-fed, handsome people were going to do nothing all the livelong day, you wished that life could always be the same. These were the thoughts I was thinking now as I wandered about the garden, prepared to wander in the same way, unoccupied and aimless, all day long, all summer long.

Zhenya came out to me with a basket; she looked as though she had known or had a feeling that she would find me in the garden. We gathered mushrooms and talked, and when she asked me a question she would walk in front so that she could see my face.

'A miracle happened in the village yesterday,' she said. 'Lame Pelagia has been ill for a whole year, and no doctors or medicines did her any good, but yesterday an old woman whispered a spell and she got better at once.'

'That isn't important,' I said. 'You mustn't look for miracles only among sick people and old women. Isn't health a miracle? And life itself? Whatever can't be comprehended is a miracle.'

'But aren't you afraid of what you can't understand?'

'No. If I meet with phenomena I don't understand, I approach them boldly and refuse to be intimidated. I am above them. A man ought to be conscious of his superiority to lions, tigers, stars, and everything else in nature, even what is incomprehensible and seems miraculous, otherwise he is not a man but a mouse, afraid of everything.'

Zhenya thought that I, as an artist, must know a great deal and be able to make a good guess at what I did not know. She wanted me to lead her into the realm of the beautiful and the eternal, that higher realm in which, she thought, I was at home, and she talked to me about God, eternal life, and the miraculous. And I, refusing to accept that I and my imagination would perish for ever when I died, answered, 'Yes, men are immortal'; 'Yes, eternal life awaits us.' She listened, believed, and did not ask for proof.

As we returned to the house, she stopped suddenly and said,

'Our Lida is a wonderful person. Isn't she? I love her

terribly much, and I could sacrifice my life for her at any time. But tell me'—Zhenya touched my sleeve with her finger—'tell me, why do you always argue with her? Why do you get angry?'

'Because she is wrong.'

Zhenya shook her head in denial, and tears appeared in her eyes.

'I can't understand it,' she said.

At this moment Lida, who had just come back from some errand, was standing near the porch with a whip in her hand, and giving a labourer some orders. Hurriedly, still talking loudly, she saw two or three sick people, then with a look of busy preoccupation walked through the rooms, opening first one cupboard and then another, and afterwards went up to the mezzanine floor; they looked for her for a long time, to summon her to dinner, and when she came we had already eaten our soup. For some reason I still remember and enjoy all these trifling details, and indeed I have a vivid memory of that whole day, although nothing particular happened. After dinner, Zhenya read, lying in the deep armchair, and I sat on the lowest step of the terrace. We said nothing. The sky clouded over and a few drops of thin fine rain began to fall. It was hot, the breeze had died away long before, and it seemed the day would never end. Ekaterina Pavlovna, flushed with sleep and carrying a fan, came out to us.

'Oh, mama,' said Zhenya, kissing her hand, 'it is bad for you to sleep in the day-time.'

They adored one another. When one of them went out into the garden, the other was instantly on the terrace, calling, 'Ah-ooooh, Zhenya!' or 'Mama, where are you?' They always said their prayers together, they had the same religious beliefs, and each understood the other without the need of speech. They had the same attitude to people, too. Ekaterina Pavlovna also had quickly grown used to and fond of me, and when I did not appear for two or three days would send to find out if I was well. She also admired my sketches, chattered to me as openly as Meess about everything that had happened, and often confided domestic secrets to me.

Her elder daughter inspired her with awe. Lida was never demonstrative and talked only of serious things; she lived her own life and was for her mother and sister exactly the same kind of sacrosanct and somewhat enigmatic personage as an admiral, always immured in his cabin, is for sailors.

'Our Lida is a remarkable person,' her mother often remarked. 'Isn't she?'

Now, while the rain drizzled, we talked about Lida.

'She is a remarkable person,' said her mother, and added in hushed conspiratorial tones, looking round apprehensively, 'People like her are few and far between, although, do you know, I am beginning to get a little worried. The school and the dispensary and the books are all very well, but why go to extremes? After all, she is twenty-three now, it is time she thought seriously about herself. All this running about after books and medicine chests, and you don't see how your life is passing . . . She ought to get married.'

Zhenya, pale with reading, her hair ruffled, raised her head and said, looking at her mother but as though speaking to herself,

'It is all in God's hands, *mamochka*.'

Then she buried herself once more in her book.

Belokurov arrived in his sleeveless coat and an embroidered shirt. We played croquet and lawn tennis and then, when it grew dark, had a long and leisurely supper, and again Lida talked about schools and about Balagin, who had got the whole District into his hands. Walking away from the Volchaninovs' that evening, I carried with me the impression of a long, long indolent day and the mournful reflection that everything on this earth, however long it may last, must come to an end. Zhenya saw us to the gates, and perhaps because she had spent the whole day, from morning until evening, with me, I felt that without her things were somehow tedious, and that all this nice family was very near to me; and for the first time in the whole summer I felt the urge to paint.

'Tell me, why do you lead such a dreary, boring kind of life?' I asked Belokurov, as we went home. 'My life is boring, dull, monotonous, because I am an artist, I am a strange person, eaten up with envy, dissatisfaction with myself, and disbelief in my work, ever since I was a child. I am always poor, I am a wanderer, but you, you are a healthy, normal person, a landowner, a gentleman—why do you live so uninterestingly, why do you take so little from life? Why, for example, have you not fallen in love with Lida or Zhenya before this?'

'You forget that I love another woman,' answered Belokurov.

He was talking about his friend, Lyubov Ivanovna, who lived in the garden pavilion with him. Every day I saw this lady, very heavy, plump and haughty, like a fat goose, walking in the garden in Russian costume with strings of beads, and always carrying a sunshade; every now and then servants called her in to a meal or for tea. About three years earlier she had rented one of the pavilions as a summer villa, and had simply gone on living there with Belokurov, apparently for ever. She was some ten years older than he and ruled him strictly, so that when he absented himself from the house he had to ask her permission. I often heard her sobbing in a gruff masculine voice, and then I sent her a message that if she did not stop, I would leave; and she stopped.

When we reached home Belokurov sat down on the sofa, frowning thoughtfully, and I walked about the room, filled with quiet agitation, as though I were in love. I wanted to talk about the Volchaninovs.

'Lida could only fall in love with a member of the *zemstvo* as enthusiastic as she is herself about hospitals and schools,' I said. 'Oh, for such a girl one could not only become a member of the *zemstvo*, but wear out iron shoes, like the hero of the fairy-tale. And Meess! How charming Meess is!'

Belokurov, with his drawling 'er-er-er', began to talk slowly about the disease of the age, pessimism. He spoke with assurance, and as if I was arguing with him. Hundreds of versts of desolate, monotonous, burnt-up steppe cannot cause as much depression as one man, when he sits and talks and one has no idea when he will go.

'It's not a question of pessimism or optimism,' I said irritated, 'but of the fact that ninety-nine out of a hundred people have no sense.'

Belokurov took this as referring to himself, was offended, and went away.

III

'The prince is staying in Malozemovo and sends you his regards,' said Lida to her mother as she took off her gloves on returning home from somewhere. 'He told me a lot of interesting things . . . He promised to raise the question of a medical centre for Malozemovo again at the next meeting of the Provincial Council, but he says there isn't much hope.' Turning to me she added,

'Excuse me, I am always forgetting that this can't have any interest for you.'

I felt annoyed.

'Why not?' I said, shrugging my shoulders. 'You do not want to know my opinion, but I assure you I am keenly interested in the question.'

'Really?'

'Yes. In my opinion, a medical centre is not needed at all in Malozemovo.'

My irritation had communicated itself to her; she looked at me out of half-closed eyes and asked,

'What *is* needed? Landscapes?'

'Not landscapes either. They don't need anything there.'

She finished taking off her gloves and opened a newspaper which had just been brought from the post; after a moment she said quietly, evidently trying to control herself,

'Last week Anna died in childbirth, and if there had been a medical centre near at hand she would still be alive. I think even landscape artists ought to have some convictions on the subject.'

'I have very definite convictions on the subject, I assure you,' I answered, while she screened herself with the newspaper, as if she did not want to hear. 'It seems to me that medical centres, schools, libraries, and dispensaries, in existing conditions, can only serve the cause of enslavement. The people are shackled in a great chain and you are not cutting through that chain, but only adding new links—there's my conviction for you.'

She raised her eyes to me with a derisive smile, but I went on, trying to seize my main point,

'What is important is not that Anna died in childbirth, but that all their lives all the Annas, Mavras, and Pelagias make themselves ill doing back-breaking work that is beyond their strength from morning till night, all their lives they tremble with anxiety for their sick and hungry children, all their lives they are afraid of dying or being ill, and all their lives they are never really well; they lose their looks too early, grow old before their time, and die in stench and filth; when their children grow up it's the same story all over again, and it goes on like that for hundreds of years, and countless millions of people live worse than animals, and in perpetual fear, all for the sake of a crust of bread. The whole horror of their situation is that they have no time to think of their souls, no time to remember that God created them in His own image and likeness; hunger, cold, animal fear, a great burden of labour, have shut them off like avalanches from every approach to spiritual activity, that is from precisely what distinguishes men from animals and is the only thing that makes life worth living. You go to their aid with hospitals and schools, but you are not freeing them from their chains with these things; on the contrary, you are enslaving them still further, because when you introduce new fads into their lives you multiply their wants, not to mention the fact that they have to pay the *zemstvo* for their books and mustard plasters, and that means they must work even harder.'

'I'm not going to argue with you,' said Lida, putting down the paper. 'I've heard it all before. I will only say one thing: one can't sit by with folded hands. It's true we're not saving humanity, and perhaps we are making many mistakes, but we do what we can, and we are right. The highest and most sacred duty of a civilized person is to serve his neighbour, and we try to serve as well as we can. You may not approve, but after all one can't please everybody.'

'True, Lida, true,' said her mother.

In Lida's presence she was always timorous, watching her anxiously while she talked, fearful of saying something superfluous or out of place; she never contradicted her but always expressed her agreement with 'true, Lida, true'.

'Peasant literacy, books full of wretched little sermons and anecdotes, and medical centres, cannot diminish either ignorance or mortality, any more than the light from your windows can illuminate this enormous garden,' I said. 'You give nothing with your interference in the lives of these people, you merely create new demands and new reasons for working.'

'But good God, one must do something, after all!' said Lida, annoyed, and her tone plainly showed that she considered my arguments worthless and despised them.

'Men must be freed from heavy physical labour,' I said. 'Their yoke must be lightened and they must be given breathing space, so that they need not spend all their lives over stoves and wash-tubs and in the fields, but may have time to think of the soul as well, and of God, and develop their spiritual possibilities more fully. The duty of every man lies in spiritual activity, the constant search for truth and the meaning of life. Make their rough, animal labour unnecessary, let them feel that they are free, and then you will see how much of a mockery your books and dispensaries are. Once a man recognizes his true mission in life, he will be satisfied only with religion, science, and art, not with all that nonsense.'

'Free them from labour!' mocked Lida. 'Do you suppose that's possible?'

'Yes. Take a part of their labour on yourself. If all of us, without exception, whether we live in the town or the country, agreed to share between us the labour expended by mankind as a whole on the satisfaction of physical needs, it would demand no more, perhaps, than two or three hours a day from each of us. Imagine all of us, rich and poor alike, working only three hours a day, and having the rest of our time free. Imagine further that, in order to be still less dependent on our bodies and have less work to do, we invent machines to do the work in our place and try to reduce our demands to the minimum. We harden ourselves and our children so that they shall not fear hunger and cold and we shall not tremble perpetually for their health, as Anna, Mavra, and Pelagia do now. Imagine that we don't support doctors, chemists, tobacco factories or distilleries—what a lot of free time we shall be left with in the end! We will jointly devote this leisure to the arts and sciences. Just as the peasants sometimes mend roads as a community enterprise, all of us jointly, like a village community, would seek truth and the meaning of life and—I am convinced of this—the truth would very soon be revealed and mankind be freed from the constant, agonizing, and oppressive fear of death, and even from death itself.'

'But you are contradicting yourself,' said Lida. 'You keep saying "science, science" and yet you won't have literacy.'

'Literacy, when all a man has to read is tavern signboards and an occasional little book he doesn't understand—literacy of that kind has existed among us since the time of Rurik, and Gogol's Petrushka has known how to read for a long time—and meanwhile what the village was in Rurik's time it still remains to this day. It is not literacy we want, but freedom for the broad development of our spiritual capacities. We must have not schools but universities.'

'You reject medicine as well.'

'Yes. It would be wanted only for the study of disease as a natural phenomenon, not for its cure. If a cure is needed, it is not for diseases but for their cause. Remove the principal cause, physical labour, and there will be no illness. I do not recognize a science of healing,' I went on excitedly. 'Learning and art, when they are genuine, aim not at temporary or partial ends, but at the eternal and universal, they search for the truth and meaning of life, for God and for the soul; and when they are applied to the needs and evils of the day, to dispensaries and libraries, they only complicate and encumber life. We have lots of doctors, chemists, and lawyers, a great many literate people, but we have no biologists, mathematicians, philosophers, or poets. All our intellect, all our mental energy, has gone on the satisfaction of temporary and transient needs . . . Scholars, writers, and artists work with a will, and thanks to them the amenities of life grow with every day and physical demands multiply, but the truth is still far beyond our reach and man remains as before the most rapacious and unclean of animals, and the tendency is for the majority of mankind to degenerate and lose for ever all capacity for living. In such conditions the life of an artist is without sense, and the more talented he is, the stranger and less comprehensible is his role, since he turns out to be working for the amusement of an unclean, rapacious animal and upholding the existing order of things. And I don't wish to work, and I won't . . . Nothing is needed, the world can go to hell!'

'Go away, Meess,' said Lida, evidently finding what I had to say bad for so young a girl.

Zhenya looked forlornly from her sister to her mother and went out.

'Those are the sort of charming things people usually say when they want to justify their indifference,' said Lida. 'It is easier to give up hospitals and schools than to heal and to teach.'

'True, Lida, true,' agreed her mother.

'You threaten to give up working,' went on Lida. 'Evidently you value your work highly. Let us stop arguing, then; we shall never agree, since I put the most imperfect of the libraries and dispensaries for which you have just expressed so much scorn higher than all the landscapes in the world.' Turning to her mother, she immediately continued in a different tone, 'The prince has got very thin and changed a great deal since he was here. They are sending him to Vichy.'

She told her mother about the prince so that she need not talk to me. Her face was flushed and to hide her agitation she stooped low over the table, as though she was short-sighted, and pretended to be reading the paper. My presence was unwelcome. I excused myself and went home.

IV

Outside all was quiet; the village on the other side of the pond was already asleep and there was not a light to be seen, except that in the pond the pale reflection of the stars was dimly visible. Standing motionless by the gates with their lions, Zhenya was waiting to see me out.

'Everybody in the village is asleep,' I said to her, trying to make out her face in the night shadows, and seeing her mournful dark eyes fixed on me. 'The innkeeper and the horse thieves are sleeping peacefully while we, decent respectable people, get on each other's nerves and quarrel.'

It was a melancholy August night—melancholy because the smell of autumn was already in the air; the moon was rising, shrouded in blood-red clouds, but it cast only the barest glimmer of light on the road and the dark fields of winter corn beside it. There were many stars. Zhenya walked beside me along the road and tried not to look at the sky, so that she should not see the falling stars, which for some reason frightened her.

'I think you are right,' she said, shivering with the nocturnal damp. 'If people, all acting together, could give themselves up to spiritual activity, they would soon come to know everything.'

'Of course. We are superior beings, and if we really recognized the full power of human genius and lived only for the highest aims, in the end we should become as gods. But that will never be; mankind will degenerate and there will be no trace of genius remaining.'

When the gates were out of sight Zhenya stopped and hastily shook my hand.

'Good night,' she said shivering; her shoulders had no covering but a thin little blouse and she was shrinking with the cold. 'Come tomorrow.'

I dreaded being left alone in my mood of irritation and dissatisfaction with myself and other people; by now I was myself trying not to look at the falling stars.

'Stay with me a moment longer,' I said. 'I beg you.'

I loved Zhenya. I must have loved her for meeting me and seeing me off, and for looking at me with affection and admiration. How touchingly beautiful were her pale face, slender neck, and thin arms, her weakness, her idleness, and her books. And her mind? I suspected that her mind was out of the ordinary, and I was delighted with the breadth of her views, perhaps because she thought differently from the stern, beautiful Lida, who did not like me. Zhenya liked me as a painter, I had captured her heart with my talent, I longed passionately to paint only for her, and I dreamed of her as my little queen, who would reign with me over these trees, fields, clouds, and sunsets, this world of nature which was so wonderful and enchanting, but in the midst of which I had until now felt hopelessly alone and unwanted.

'Stay a moment longer, I implore you,' I begged.

I took off my overcoat and covered her chilly shoulders; afraid of appearing ridiculous and ugly in a man's coat, she laughed and threw it off, and at the same moment I put my arms round her and began showering her face, shoulders, and arms with kisses.

'Until tomorrow!' she whispered and cautiously, as though afraid of disturbing the stillness of the night, embraced me. 'We have no secrets from one another, I shall have to tell my mother and sister at once . . . It is so terrible! Mama is all right, mama likes you, but Lida!'

She ran to the gates.

'Good-bye!' she called.

Then for a minute or two I could hear her running. I did not want to go home, and there was no reason to do so. I stood pondering for a short time and then quietly turned back, to look once more at the house she lived in, the dear, naïve old house which seemed to look down at me through the eyes of its mezzanine windows, and understand everything. I walked past the terrace, sat down on a garden seat in the dark shadows under an old elm near the tennis-court, and gazed at the house from there. In the windows of the upper floor, where

Meess had her room, a bright light shone out, turning green as the shade was lowered over the lamp. Shadows began to flit about . . . I was full of tenderness, peace, and satisfaction with myself, satisfaction that I had been able to allow myself to be carried away and fall in love, and yet at the same time I felt uncomfortable at the thought that at that very moment, a few steps away from me, Lida was living in one of the rooms in that house, Lida who did not like and perhaps even hated me. I sat there, wondering all the time if Zhenya would come out, and listened; I thought somebody was talking upstairs.

An hour passed. The green light was extinguished, and the shadows ceased to be visible. The moon was now riding high above the house and lighting up the sleeping garden and the paths; the dahlias and roses in the bed in front of the house were clearly visible, and all looked the same colour. It was growing very cold. I left the garden, picked up my coat on the road, and made my leisurely way home.

When I arrived at the Volchaninovs' the next day after dinner, the glass door into the garden stood wide open. I sat for a while on the terrace, expecting at any moment to see Zhenya appear from beyond the border on the tennis-court or in one of the avenues, or to hear her voice from the house, and then went into the drawing-room and the dining-room. There was not a soul there. From the dining-room I walked down the long corridor into the hall, and then back again. There were several doors in the corridor, and behind one of them Lida's voice sounded.

'A crow . . . had found somewhere . . .,' she was saying loudly and slowly, evidently dictating Krylov's fable, 'somewhere a piece of cheese . . . A crow . . . had found . . . Who's there?' she called suddenly, at the sound of my footsteps.

'It's me.'

'Oh! Excuse me, I can't come out to you just now, I am busy with Dasha.'

'Is Ekaterina Pavlovna in the garden?'

'No, she and my sister went away this morning to my aunt's in the Province of Penza. They will probably be going abroad this winter,' she added after a short silence. 'A crow . . . had . . . found . . . some . . . where . . . a piece . . . of cheese . . . Have you got that?'

I went out into the hall and stood there looking out at the pond and the village, not thinking of anything, and I could still hear,

'A piece . . . of cheese. A crow had found somewhere a piece of cheese . . .'

I left the grounds by the same way as I had come the first time, only in the opposite direction: first from the courtyard into the garden, past the house, then along the avenue of lime-trees . . . Here a little boy came running after me and gave me a note. 'I have told my sister everything, and she insists on my parting from you,' I read. 'I could never bring myself to distress her by disobedience. God will give you happiness; forgive me. If you knew how bitterly mama and I are crying!' Then the dark avenue of fir-trees, the tumble-down fence . . . Over the field where the rye had been in bloom and the quails had called, cows and hobbled horses now strayed. Here and there slopes of winter wheat shone brightly green. A sober workaday mood took possession of me and I was ashamed of all I had said at the Volchaninovs', and as bored with life as I had been before. When I got home I packed my things and in the evening left for St. Petersburg.

I never saw the Volchaninovs again. Not very long ago, travelling to the Crimea, I met Belokurov in the train. As before, he wore his long-skirted sleeveless coat and an embroidered shirt, and when I asked how he was, answered with an old-fashioned, 'Very well, thanks to your prayers.' We talked. He had sold his estate and bought a smaller one in Lyubov Ivanovna's name. He could not tell me much about the Volchaninovs. Lida, according to him, was still living at Shelkovka and teaching in the school; little by little she had managed to collect round her a small circle of sympathizers and they formed a party strong enough at the last elections to the *zemstvo* to 'turn out' Balagin, who until then had still held the whole District in his hands. About Zhenya Belokurov could only tell me that she did not live at home, and he did not know where she was.

I have begun to forget about the house with the mezzanine floor, and only occasionally, when I am writing or reading, I am suddenly reminded, for no reason, now of the green light in the window, now of the echoing sound of my own footsteps as I walked home through the field that night, in love and rubbing my hands with the cold. Even more rarely, at times when I am weighed down by loneliness, full of sadness, and dimly remembering these things, little by little it begins to seem to me that somebody is remembering me too, and waiting for me, and that we shall meet again . . .

Meess, where are you?

THE PEASANTS

1897

I

One of the waiters at the Moscow hotel called the Slav Bazaar, Nikolay Chikildeev, fell ill. His illness made his legs numb and affected his gait, so that on one occasion, as he was going along a corridor, he stumbled and fell with the tray of ham and peas he was carrying. He had to leave his job. What money he and his wife had went on treatment for him, they had nothing left to live on, everything was tedious without a job, and he decided that he ought probably to go back home to the country. At home being ill is easier and living is cheaper; it is not for nothing they say there's no place like home.

He arrived in his *Zhukovo* towards evening. In his childhood memories he saw his home as light, roomy, and comfortable, but now he was dismayed when he went into the hut, it was so dark, overcrowded, and dirty. His wife Olga, and his daughter Sasha, who had come with him, gazed in bewilderment at the big filthy stove, black with smoke and flies, which took up practically half the hut. There were so many flies! The stove was askew, the beams in the wall lay crooked, and the whole hut seemed on the point of collapse. In the corner near the door, by the icons, labels from bottles and pieces of newspaper were pasted up by way of pictures. Poverty, poverty everywhere! None of the grown-ups were at home, they were all helping with the harvest. On the stove sat a little girl of about eight, fair-haired, unwashed, and too uninterested even to glance at the new-comers. On the floor beneath, a white cat was busily playing with a black beetle.

'Puss, puss!' coaxed Sasha. 'Pussy!'

'She can't hear,' said the little girl. 'She's gone deaf.'

'Why?'

'She just did. Somebody hit her.'

At the first glance Nikolay and Olga had known the kind of life people led here, but they said nothing to one another; silently they set down the bundles they were carrying, and still silently went out into the street. Their hut was the third from the edge of the village, and looked the poorest and oldest; the second was not much better, but the first had a corrugated iron roof and curtains at the windows. This hut, which opened straight on to the street, stood alone, and part of it was an ale-house. All the huts formed a single row, and the whole quiet, sleepy little village, with willows, elderberries and rowan-trees visible in the yards, looked a pleasant spot.

Beyond the peasant huts began a steep and abrupt descent towards the river, with great boulders here and there in the clay bank. Narrow tracks wound down the slope, among the boulders and the pits dug by the potters, here and there broken pottery had been piled in heaps, some red, some brown, and down at the bottom was a bright green meadow, already mown, where the peasants' herd now wandered. The river, winding between beautiful banks overgrown with bushes, was almost three-quarters of a mile from the hamlet, and beyond it lay another wide green meadow, with straying animals and long strings of white geese, and beyond again, just as on the near side, a steep uphill slope and on the hill above it a large village, a church with a cluster of five cupolas, and, a little apart, a gentleman's house.

'It's nice here in your parts,' said Olga, making the sign of the cross as she turned towards the church. 'Lord, what a view!'

At exactly that moment the bell rang for the evening service (it was Saturday evening). Two little girls who were struggling with a pail of water at the bottom of the slope looked round towards the church to listen to the sound.

'Just about now they will be serving dinners in the Slav Bazaar,' said Nikolay pensively.

Sitting on the edge of the precipitous slope, Nikolay and Olga watched the setting sun and saw the gold and crimson sky reflected in the river, the windows of the church, and all through the air, tender, tranquil and inexpressibly pure, as it never is in Moscow. When the sun had gone down, the herd, lowing and bleating, made its way over the meadow, the geese flew across from the far side of the river, and everything became quiet; the tranquil light faded from the air and the evening shadows began their swift advance.

Meanwhile the old people, Nikolay's father and mother, both the same height, both stooped, toothless and emaciated, had returned home. The women had arrived too—Nikolay's sisters-in-law, Marya and Fekla, who had been working at the squire's across the river. Marya, his brother Cyriac's wife, had six children, and Fekla, whose husband had gone away into the army, two; and when Nikolay, coming into the hut, saw the whole family, all those bodies large and small, swarming on the sleeping-shelves above the stove, in cradles, and in every corner of the hut, and saw how greedily the old man and women ate black bread sopped in water, he realized that it had been useless to come here, ill, without money, and burdened with a family besides—useless!

'But where is brother Cyriac?' he asked, when greetings had been exchanged.

'Living in the forest as watchman for a merchant,' answered his father. 'The lad would be all right, but he's got such a terrible thirst.'

'He'll come to no good!' said the old woman tearfully. 'Our menfolk are a sad lot, they don't bring anything in, they only take it out. Cyriac drinks, and the old man knows his way to the ale-house as well, there's no denying. The Blessed Virgin is annoyed with us.'

Because there were visitors they brought out the samovar. The tea smelt of fish, the sugar was grey and nibbled, and there were black beetles running about on the bread and the cups; the tea was disgusting to drink and the talk was disgusting to listen to—all about poverty and sickness. They had not had time to drink more than a cupful each when a loud, prolonged drunken cry resounded from the yard:

'Ma-arya!'

'Seems as if Cyriac's coming,' said the old man. 'Talk of the devil.'

A silence fell. A little later the same cry came again, harsh and prolonged, sounding as if it came from underground:

'Ma-arya!'

Marya, the older sister-in-law, had gone white, and was standing pressed close to the stove, and it was strange to see the expression of fright on the face of this plain, broad-shouldered, powerful woman. Her daughter, the little girl who had been sitting on the stove and appeared so indifferent, broke into noisy weeping.

'What are *you* yelling about, you little pest?' shouted Fekla, a handsome woman, also very strong and broad in the shoulders. 'He won't kill her, I don't suppose!'

From the old man Nikolay learnt that Marya was afraid to live in the forest with Cyriac, and that whenever he was drunk, he always used to come for her, create an uproar, and beat her unmercifully.

'Ma-arya!' The cry sounded from close to the door.

'Good people, for Christ's sake, don't let him,' stammered Marya, gasping as though she had been lowered into icy water; 'help me, my darlings . . .'

The whole lot of children in the hut began to cry and Sasha, seeing them, began to cry too. A drunken cough sounded outside, and into the hut came a tall, black-bearded peasant wearing a fur hat; because his face was invisible in the dim light of the little lamp he was terrifying. This was Cyriac. Going up to his wife, he swung his arm and crashed his fist into her face; she made not a sound but, stunned by the blow, sank into a crouching position, and blood immediately began to flow from her nose.

'Shameful it is, shameful,' muttered the old man, climbing on to the stove, 'and in front of visitors, too! Sinful!'

The old women sat huddled together, occupied with their thoughts, saying nothing; Fekla rocked the cradle . . . Visibly conscious of the terror he inspired, and pleased by it, Cyriac seized Marya's arm and dragged her towards the door, roaring like a wild beast to make himself more terrible still, but at that moment he saw the visitors and stopped. 'Ah, so you've come,' he said, letting go of his wife. 'My own dear brother and his family . . .'

Swaying and opening wide his red, drunken eyes, he paused to say a prayer before the icon and continued,

'My dear brother and his family have come to the home of his parents . . . from Moscow, I mean. From the great capital city of Moscow, I mean, the mother of cities . . . Excuse me . . .'

He lowered himself to the bench near the samovar and began to drink tea, noisily sucking it up from the saucer, amid the general silence . . . He drank ten cups or so and then lay down on the bench and snored.

They began going to bed. Nikolay, as a sick man, was given a place on top of the stove with the old man; Sasha lay on the floor, and Olga went with the other women into the shed.

'No-ow, my little beauty,' she said, lying down on the hay beside Marya, 'tears don't do any good! You must be patient, that's all. The scripture says, "Whosoever shall smite thee on thy right cheek, turn to him the other also . . ." No-ow, my little beauty!'

Then in a low sing-song voice she talked about Moscow and about her life there and how she had been a chamber-maid in cheap hotels.

'In Moscow there are big houses, made of stone,' she said, 'and churches, lots and lots, seventy times seven, my little beauty, and all gentlefolk in the houses, and so handsome and so fine!'

Marya told her that she had never been, not merely to Moscow, but even to the District town; she was illiterate and did not know any prayers, not even 'Our Father'. She and the other sister-in-law, Fekla, who was now sitting at a little distance and listening, were both extremely backward and incapable of understanding any-thing. Neither loved her husband; Marya was afraid of Cyriac, and when he stayed with her she shook with fear and felt suffocated by his side because he smelt so strongly of vodka and tobacco. Fekla, in answer to the question whether she was not dull without her husband, said crossly,

'To hell with him!'

They talked for a while and fell silent . . .

It was chilly, and a cock crowing near the shed at the top of his voice prevented sleep. When the bluish light of morning was already penetrating through all the cracks in the walls, Fekla very quietly got up and went out, and afterwards her bare feet could be heard pounding the earth as she ran off somewhere.

II

Olga went to church, taking Marya with her. As they made their way down one of the paths towards the meadow, both were in good spirits. Olga liked the wide expanses of the landscape and Marya felt that in her sister-in-law she had found someone who would be near and dear to her. Below them a sleepy hawk glided over the meadow, the river was dark, mist drifted here and there, but a long stripe of sunlight lay on the hill on the opposite side, the church shone, and the rooks cawed furiously in the garden of the big house.

'The old man is all right,' Marya was saying, 'but granny is strict and she's always fighting. Our own corn only lasted till Shrovetide, now we have to buy flour at the ale-house—well, she's annoyed: says we all eat too much.'

'No-ow, my little beauty! You must be patient, that's all. It says: "Come unto me, all ye that labour and are heavy laden."'

Olga spoke deliberately, in a sort of chant, and she walked in a quick, bustling kind of way, like a poor pilgrim. She read the gospels every day, reading aloud like a parish clerk; there was much that she did not understand, but the sacred words touched her to the point of tears, and she pronounced words like 'behold' and 'verily' with a sweet sinking of the heart. She believed in God, in the Mother of God and in the saints; she believed that one must not offend anybody on the face of the earth—neither simple people, nor Germans, nor gipsies, nor Jews, and that woe will befall even those who are not kind to animals; she believed that all this was written in the scriptures and therefore when she said words from the bible, even those she did not understand, her face became compassionate, bright, and full of emotion.

'Where do you come from?' Marya asked her.

'From Vladimir. Only I was taken to Moscow a very long time ago, when I wasn't more than about eight.'

They came close to the river. On the further bank, at the water's edge, a woman stood taking off her clothes.

'That's our Fekla,' Marya informed her, 'she's been going to the gentleman's on the other side of the river. To the estate clerks. She's so bold and shameless and she uses such awful language—shocking!'

The black-browed Fekla, with her hair loose, still young and as sturdy as a girl, threw herself from the bank and began thrashing the water with her legs, making waves all round herself.

'Shameless—shocking!' repeated Marya.

A shaky foot-bridge of timber had been laid across the river, and directly below it, in the pure transparent water, were shoals of broad-headed mullet. Dew sparkled on the green bushes looking down at their reflections in the water. The breeze that had sprung up was comfortably warm. What a beautiful morning! And how beautiful life on this earth would probably be if it were not for poverty, grinding, irremediable poverty, from which there is no refuge anywhere. Only to look back at the village sufficed to recall all the preceding day—and the happy enchantment which had seemed to be everywhere vanished in an instant.

They went into the church. Marya stopped near the entrance, not daring to go any farther. She dared not sit down either, although they did not begin to ring for mass until nine o'clock. She just went on standing the whole time.

While the gospel was being read the people suddenly moved aside to make way for the family from the big house; two young ladies in white dresses and wide-brimmed hats came in with a round, rosy little boy in a sailor suit. Their appearance touched Olga's heart; she decided at first glance that they were nice, well-educated, and handsome people. Marya, however, looked at them askance, dismally and morosely, as if there had entered not people but a monster which might crush her if she did not get out of its way.

Whenever the deacon's bass voice rang out, she seemed to hear a cry of 'Ma-arya!' and she shuddered.

III

The village had heard of the arrival of the visitors, and by the time mass was over many people had gathered in the hut. The Leonyches, the Matveichevs, and the Ilyiches had all come to hear about their relatives who were working in Moscow. All the youngsters from Zhukovo who had learnt to read and write were sent off to Moscow and apprenticed as waiters or boots (just as those from the village on the other side of the river all went as bakers), and this had been going on for a very long time, ever since before the emancipation of the serfs, when a certain Luka Ivanych, a now legendary peasant from Zhukovo, who had been head waiter in one of the Moscow clubs, had employed under himself only men from his native place and these, becoming established, sent for their relatives and placed them in taverns and restaurants; and from that time the people round about never called Zhukovo anything but Servantville or Lackeydom. Nikolay had been sent to Moscow when he was eleven, and Ivan Makarych, one of the Matveichevs, who was at that time an attendant at the Hermitage Gardens, had found him a situation. Now, addressing the Matveichevs, Nikolay instructively informed them,

'Ivan Makarych was my benefactor, and it is my duty to pray for him day and night, because it was through him I got to be a respectable man.'

'You dear good soul!' tearfully exclaimed a tall old woman, Ivan Makarych's sister; 'and never a word do we hear of him, the dear man.'

'He was working at Omon's during the winter, and this season I heard he was somewhere out of town, in some pleasure gardens . . . He's getting old! Before, in the summer-time he sometimes used to bring home as much as ten roubles a day, but now everything's very quiet everywhere, and the old man's hard put to it.'

All the women looked at Nikolay's feet, shod with felt boots, and at his pale face, and said commiseratingly,

'You're not a very good provider, Nikolay Osipych, are you? How could you be?'

They all caressed Sasha too. She was ten years old, but small and very thin and from her appearance she might have been taken for about seven, not more. Among the other little girls, sunburnt, with roughly cropped hair and long, washed-out smocks, she with her white skin, big dark eyes, and a red ribbon in her hair, seemed an amusing plaything, like a little wild animal caught in the fields and brought into the hut.

'She can read!' boasted Olga, looking fondly at her

daughter. 'Read something, my little girl!' she said, bringing out a New Testament from the corner. 'You read, and these good Christians will listen.'

The Testament was old and heavy, bound in leather, and with thumbed margins, and gave out a smell as though monks had come into the hut. Sasha raised her eyebrows and began in a loud, sing-song voice,

'And when they were departed, behold, the angel of the Lord . . . appeareth to Joseph in a dream, saying, Arise, and take the young child and his mother . . .'

'The young child and his mother,' repeated Olga, red with emotion.

'And flee into Egypt . . . and be thou there until I bring thee word . . .'

At this point Olga could contain herself no longer and burst into tears. First Marya and then Ivan Makarych's sister looked at her and sobbed. The old man coughed and busied himself with trying to find a gift for his granddaughter, but found nothing and gave up with a wave of the hand. When the reading was finished the neighbours went off home much moved and very pleased with Olga and Sasha.

Because it was Sunday the family remained at home all day. The old woman, who was called Granny by her husband, her daughters-in-law, and her grandchildren alike, tried to do everything herself; she stoked the stove, set up the samovar, even did the milking, and afterwards grumbled that she was worn out with work. She was always worrying lest somebody should eat a bite too much, or her husband and daughters-in-law sit and do nothing. Now she thought she could hear the geese from the ale-house getting into her vegetable plot through the back yards, and she ran out with a long stick, and afterwards spent half an hour uttering strident yells among her cabbages, which were as lean and wizened as she was herself; now she imagined that a crow was after her chickens, and she rushed out scolding to drive it away. She stormed and grumbled from morning till night, and often made so much noise that passers-by stopped in the street.

She treated her husband without affection, and abused him as a lazy worthless nuisance. He was a shiftless, unreliable, ignorant man and if it had not been for her continual nagging would perhaps never have done any work at all, but only sat on the stove and talked. He told his son at great length all about some fancied enemies and complained of the slights which were apparently put upon him every day, and it was tiresome to have to listen to him.

'Yes,' he was saying, clutching his sides. 'Yes . . . About a week after the Exaltation of the Cross, it was, and I'd sold my hay for thirty copecks a pood, nice and easy . . . Yes . . . All right . . . Only, you see, I was carting the hay one morning, all nice and easy, not interfering with nobody; but my luck's out, I look and there's the elder just coming out of the pub, Antip Sedelnikov. "Where are you taking that off to, you old so-and-so?"—and he fetches me one on the ear.'

As a result of the excesses of the previous day Cyriac was suffering from a severe headache and was ashamed to face his brother.

'What vodka does for you! Oh, my God!' he muttered, shaking his aching head. 'Brother and sister, my dears, please forgive me, for Christ's sake; I'm very sorry.'

Because it was Sunday they had bought soused herring at the tavern and made soup with the heads. At noon they all sat down to drink tea, and they went on drinking it for a long time, until they were sweating and seemed swollen with tea, and only then began to eat the soup, all from one pot. Granny had hidden the herrings themselves.

In the evening a potter was firing pots on the slope. Below in the meadow girls were dancing in a ring and singing. An accordion was playing. On the other side of the river another kiln was burning and girls were singing, and the singing sounded soft and harmonious in the distance. The peasants in and round the tavern were making a great deal of noise, singing discordantly in drunken voices and swearing so violently that Olga could only shudder and repeat,

'Oh, heavens! . . .'

She was amazed that the swearing went on without a pause, and that those who swore loudest and longest were the old men, for whom the time had come to die. The children and young girls heard all the bad language and were not at all disturbed, and it was evident that they had been used to it since the cradle.

It was past midnight, the kilns on both the near and the farther bank had gone out, but people were still about on the meadow and in the tavern. The old man and Cyriac, drunk, arm-in-arm, and bumping their shoulders together, came up to the shed where Olga and Marya were lying.

'Let her alone,' pleaded the old man, 'let her be . . . She's a good woman . . . It's a sin . . .'

'Ma-arya!' shouted Cyriac.

'Let her be . . . A sin . . . The woman's all right.'

They stood for a minute near the barn and then went on.

'I lo-ove the pretty flowers!' the old man suddenly struck up in a high piercing tenor. 'I lo-ove to pick them in the field!'

Then he spat, swore horribly, and went into the hut.

IV

Granny had stationed Sasha near her vegetable plot and told her to watch that the geese did not get in. It was a hot August day. The tavern geese could reach the plot round the backs of the houses, but at the moment they were busy picking up oats near the tavern and peacefully conversing together, and only the gander was craning his neck as if trying to see whether the old woman was coming with her stick; there were other geese that might come from down the bank, but these were now feeding a long way away on the other side of the river, stretching in a long white garland over the meadow. Sasha stood there for a short time, grew bored and, seeing that the geese were not coming, went away to the steep slopes down to the river.

There she saw Marya's eldest daughter Motka, standing motionless on top of a big boulder and looking towards the church. Marya had had thirteen children, but only six were left and they were all girls, not one boy; the eldest was eight years old. The barefooted Motka was standing in her long smock in the full glare of the sun, which beat down on the top of her head, but she took no notice of this and stood as if turned to stone. Sasha placed herself beside her and said, looking at the church,

'God lives in the church. In people's houses they have lamps and candles, but God has little lamps that are red and green and blue, like little eyes. At night God walks about in the church, and the holy blessed Virgin with him, and St. Nicholas, bump, bump, bump . . . And the watchman is frightened, he's very frightened! No-ow, my little beauty,' she added, in imitation of her mother. 'And when the end of the world comes, all the churches will fly away into heaven.'

'And the bells as well?' asked Motka in her deep voice, drawing out every syllable.

'Yes, all the bells as well. And when it's the end of the world, all the good people will go to heaven and the bad ones will go into the everlasting fire, my little beauty. God will say to my mother, and to Marya too, "You have never done anybody any harm, so you go to the right, into heaven;" and he will say to Cyriac and Granny, "Go to the left, into the fire." And if anybody has eaten meat in Lent he will send them to the fire too.'

She looked up at the sky, opening her eyes wide, and said:

'Look at the sky without blinking and you will see the angels.'

Motka also looked at the sky, and a minute passed in silence.

'Can you see them?' asked Sasha.

'No, I can't,' said Motka gruffly.

'I can. The little angels are flying all over the sky and their little wings go twinkle, twinkle, like gnats.'

Motka thought for a little, still looking at the sky, and then asked,

'Will Granny burn?'

'Yes, she will, my little beauty.'

From their boulder to the very bottom ran a smooth, steep slope, covered with soft green grass that made you want to touch it with your hand or lie down on it for a time. Sasha lay down and rolled to the bottom. Motka, her face solemn and severe, drew a deep breath and followed her example, and her smock rolled up to her shoulder in the process.

'How funny it makes you feel!' said Sasha delighted.

They both climbed up to roll down again, but at that moment the shrill familiar voice rang out. Oh, how terrible! Granny, toothless, bony, stooping, her short grey hair straggling in the wind, was driving the geese out of her kitchen-plot with a long stick, shouting as she did so,

'Breaking down all my cabbages, you damned pestilential birds, curses on you!'

She saw the little girls, dropped the stick, picked up a switch, and seizing Sasha's neck in fingers as dry and hard as wood, began to whip her. Sasha wept with pain and fear, and at the same time the gander, stretching his neck and waddling from foot to foot, went up to the old woman and gave her a nip; returning to his flock he was greeted by all the geese with approving cackles. Then Granny set about thrashing Motka, whose smock was rolled up once again. Heartbroken and crying loudly, Sasha went into the hut to complain; behind her came Motka, also crying, but in a deep-toned roar, and, as she did not wipe away her tears, with a face as wet as though she had dipped it in water.

'Good gracious!' exclaimed Olga in amazement, when the two entered the hut. 'Blessed Virgin!'

Sasha began to tell her story, and at that moment Granny came in, uttering piercing shrieks of abuse, Fekla flew into a rage, and the hut was filled with noise.

'Never mind, never mind!' White and upset, Olga stroked Sasha's head, trying to comfort her. 'She is your grandmother, and it is wrong to be cross with her. Never mind, my little one.'

Nikolay, who was already exhausted by the constant uproar, the hunger, fumes, and stench, who hated and despised poverty, and who felt ashamed of his father and mother before his wife and daughter, swung his legs off the stove and addressed his mother in a plaintive and irritable voice.

'You can't whip her! You have no right whatever to whip her!'

'You're a poor sort of creature, dying up there on the stove,' Fekla yelled at him spitefully. 'It was an ill wind that brought you all here to sponge on us!'

Sasha, Motka, and the other little girls had hidden in a corner on the stove behind Nikolay's back, listening to everything in terrified silence, and their little hearts could be heard thumping. In a family containing a sick person, who has been hopelessly ill for a long time, there occur dreadful moments like this, when all those near to him timidly and secretly, in the depths of their hearts, wish for his death; it is only the children who always fear the death of a loved one and are filled with dismay at the thought of it. Now the little girls held their breath and gazed at Nikolay with woebegone expressions, thinking that he was soon going to die, and they wanted to cry and to say something kind and sympathetic to him.

He clung to Olga, as though seeking her protection, and said to her in a quiet, unsteady voice,

'Olga, my dear, I can't stay here any longer. It is too much for me. For God's sake, for the sake of Christ in heaven, write to your sister Claudia Abramovna, let her sell or pawn everything she's got, and send us the money, and we will go away from here. Oh Lord,' he went on with anguished longing, 'if only I could catch a glimpse of Moscow again! If only I could see it, even in dreams, my own dear Moscow!'

When evening fell and the hut grew dark, the atmosphere became so dismal that it was difficult to speak at all. Granny, still angry, steeped her crusts of rye-bread in water and sat mumbling them for a long time, a whole hour. Marya milked the cow, brought the pail of milk into the hut and stood it on the bench; then Granny poured it slowly and carefully into jugs, evidently pleased that now, during the fast before the Assumption, nobody would be able to have milk, and it would all be left. She only poured a very little, no more than a drop, into a saucer for Fekla's baby. When she and Marya carried away the jugs to the cellar, Motka jumped up, clambered down from the stove, went to the bench where the wooden bowl of crusts stood, and splashed some milk into it from the saucer.

Granny, returning to the hut, applied herself to her crusts again, while Sasha and Motka, sitting on the stove, watched her and were glad that she had broken the fast and now would certainly go to hell. They cheered up and went to bed, and Sasha, as she fell asleep, imagined the Day of Judgement: there was a blazing furnace like the potter's, and the Evil One, with horns like a cow's, and black all over, was driving Granny into the fire with a long stick, just as she herself had driven the geese a little time ago.

V

On the Feast of the Assumption, at eleven o'clock at night, the lads and girls who had been strolling in the meadow at the foot of the bank suddenly raised a hue and cry and began to run towards the village; those who were sitting at the top, on the edge of the bank, could not for a moment understand why.

'Fire! Fire!' came a desperate cry from below. 'We're on fire!'

Those who were sitting above looked round and saw a terrible and extraordinary sight. Over the thatched roof of one of the end huts stood a whirling seven-foot-high column of fire, scattering sparks all around like a splashing fountain. On the instant all the roof blazed up brightly, and the loud crackling of the fire became audible.

The moonlight was obscured, and the whole village was now bathed in flickering red light; black shadows coursed over the ground, and there was a smell of burning; those who had run up the steep slope, out of breath and too shaken to speak, jostled and fell, and could not recognize one another with eyes unaccustomed to the glare. It was a dreadful spectacle. Especially dreadful was the fact that pigeons were flying in the smoke above the flames, and that in the ale-house, where they did not yet know of the fire, the singing and the sound of the accordion still went on as though nothing had happened.

'Uncle Simon's burning!' shouted somebody in a loud harsh voice.

Marya rushed about round their hut, weeping and wringing her hands, her teeth chattering, although the fire was far away, at the other end of the village; Nikolay emerged in his felt boots and the children flocked out in their little smocks. Near the policeman's hut somebody was beating a sheet of iron. The air resounded with the clang, clang, clang . . . . and the incessant, clamorous noise squeezed the heart and made the blood run cold. Old women stood with icons in their hands. Sheep, calves, and cows had been driven from the yards into the street, and chests, sheepskins, and tubs had been carried out. The black stallion, who was not allowed with the other horses because he kicked and bit them, had been set at liberty, and galloped, snorting and stamping, through the village and back again, then stopped by a cart and began lashing out at it with his hind feet.

The church bells on the other side of the river began to ring the alarm.

It was hot near the burning hut and so light that every blade of grass was clearly visible. On one of the boxes they had managed to drag out sat Simon, a red-haired peasant with a big nose, wearing a jacket and a cap pulled down to his ears; his distracted wife lay face downwards, groaning. A little old man of about eighty, with a big beard, looking like a gnome, not one of the villagers but evidently connected with the fire, wandered about near by, bare-headed and with a white bundle in his arms; the fire was reflected in his bald head. The village elder, Antip Sedelnikov, as swarthy and black-haired as a gipsy, approached the hut with an axe in his hands, smashed the windows one after another, for some unknown reason, and then began to chop at the porch.

'Women, water!' he shouted. 'Get the fire-engine! Look alive!'

The peasants who had been drinking in the ale-house dragged along the fire-engine. They were all drunk, staggering and falling about, and they all had helpless expressions and tears in their eyes.

'Girls, water!' shouted the elder, who was also drunk. 'Run, run!'

The women and girls ran down to where the spring was, struggled up the hill with full pails and tubs, emptied them into the engine, and ran off again. Olga, Marya, Sasha, and Motka were all bringing water. Women and little boys pumped the water, the hose began to hiss and the elder, pointing it now at the door, now at a window, constricted the jet with his finger, so that its hissing became still sharper.

'That's it, Antip!' came an approving chorus. 'Go it!'

Antip crawled into the entrance passage, where the fire was, and shouted,

'Pump! Put your backs into it, good Christians, in this catastrophe!'

The men stood in a crowd and watched the fire without doing anything. Nobody knew where to begin, nobody knew what to do, yet all round there were stacks of hay and corn, sheds, and heaps of dry brushwood. Cyriac and old Osip, his father, both somewhat tipsy, stood among the others. The old man, as though trying to justify his inactivity, turned to the woman lying on the ground and said,

'Don't take on so, neighbour! The house is done for—so what's the use?'

Simon, addressing now one of the bystanders, now another, was giving an account of the reason for the fire.

'That little old man there, with the bundle, is an old servant of General Zhukov's . . . He was one of our general's cooks, God rest his soul. He comes to us this evening and says, "Let me stay the night" . . . Well, we had a drink or two, you know what it's like . . . My old woman was fussing round with the samovar, to get the old man some tea, and by bad luck she had put the samovar in the passage, and so the flame shot out of the chimney straight into the roof, right in the straw, and that was that. We were all but burnt ourselves. The old man's cap did get burnt up, more's the pity.'

The insistent alarum of the iron sheet and the clamour of the church bell across the river went on unendingly. Olga, bathed in the glare, panting, throwing frightened glances at the red sheep and the rose-tinted pigeons flying through the smoke, went on running first downhill and then up. She felt as though the din was piercing through her like a sharp stake, she thought the fire would go on for ever, she thought Sasha had got lost . . . When the roof fell in with a roar, the thought that now the whole village must inevitably burn down deprived her of all her strength, so that she could no longer carry water, but sat on the edge of the bank with her pail by her side; beside her and lower down the slope other women sat keening as if at a wake.

At this point two carts arrived bringing the clerks and workmen from the estate on the other side of the river, who had their own fire-engine with them. A very young student, his white jacket unbuttoned, came on horseback. Axes were wielded, a ladder was raised against the framework of the burning hut, and five men at one time clambered on to it, first among them the student, red in the face and shouting commands in a shrill hoarse voice, as though extinguishing fires was an everyday affair for him. They began to drag the beams out of the hut; they pulled apart the cow-shed, the fence, and the nearest stack.

'Don't let them tear things down,' various harsh voices said from among the crowd. 'Don't let them do it!'

Cyriac moved towards the hut with a resolute look, as though he meant to stop the new-comers from pulling things down, but one of the workmen turned him back and gave him a blow on the back of the neck. This raised a laugh, the workman struck Cyriac again, and he fell and crawled back into the crowd on all fours.

Two pretty girls wearing hats—the student's sisters, apparently—had also arrived from the other side of the river. They stood watching the fire from a distance. The beams that had been pulled out were no longer flaming, but gave off a great deal of smoke; the student, working with the hose, turned the jet now on the beams, now on the peasants, now on the women who were bringing water.

'Georges!' the girls called, reproachfully and anxiously. *'Georges!'*

The fire was over. It was only when people began to

disperse that they noticed that it was already dawn, and that everybody looked pale and rather smudgy, as they always do in the early morning when the last stars go out in the sky. As they left the scene the peasants were already laughing and joking about General Zhukov's cook and the fur cap that got burnt; they already felt the desire to treat the fire as a joke and were almost sorry that it was over so quickly.

'You were a good fireman, sir,' said Olga to the student. 'You ought to come to Moscow: we have fires there every day, if you can believe me.'

'Are you really from Moscow?' asked one of the young ladies.

'Yes, I am. My husband worked at the Slav Bazaar, miss. And this is my daughter,' she went on, indicating Sasha, who felt chilly and was clinging to her. 'She comes from Moscow too, miss.'

The two girls said something to the student in French and he gave Sasha a twenty-copeck piece. Old Osip saw this, and hope suddenly shone in his face.

'Thank God, your honour, there was no wind,' he said to the student, 'or else the whole place would have burnt down in no time. Your honour, good people,' he added sheepishly in a lower tone, 'it's a cold morning, we could do with a warm . . . spare enough for a half-bottle.'

He got nothing and, sighing, made his way slowly home. Olga, standing on the edge of the slope, saw the two carts crossing the river by a ford, and the ladies walking across the meadow; a carriage was waiting for them on the other side. Coming into the hut, she told her husband enthusiastically,

'So good! And so handsome! And the young ladies are like little cherubs.'

'Plague take them!' said the sleepy Fekla ill-naturedly.

VI

Marya considered herself unhappy and often said she wished she was dead; Fekla, on the other hand, found everything about their life to her taste: the poverty and the dirt and the everlasting brawling. She ate what she was given, without question; made her bed anywhere with anything handy, threw out her slops from the porch, shook her hair loose as soon as she entered the house, and walked barefoot in the meadow. From the first day she had detested Olga and Nikolay purely because they did not like the life.

'We'll see what you fine Moscow gentlefolk will get to eat here!' she said with spiteful enjoyment. 'We'll see!'

One morning—by now it was the beginning of September—Fekla, pink with the cold, healthy and handsome, carried up from the spring two pails of water; Marya and Olga were sitting at the table drinking tea.

'Tea with sugar!' said Fekla derisively. 'Fine ladies!' she added, putting down the pails, 'it's the fashion with you to drink tea every day, is it? Mind you don't get all swelled up with it!' she went on, looking venomously at Olga. 'You got used to feeding up your big fat mug in Moscow, fatty!'

As she swung round the yoke, it struck Olga on the shoulder, making both sisters-in-law clasp their hands and exclaim,

'Oh heavens!'

Then Fekla went down to the river to wash clothes, scolding so loudly all the way that she could be heard in the hut.

The day passed. The long autumn evening set in. In the hut they were winding silk; everybody was busy with it except Fekla: she had gone across the river. The silk came from a neighbouring factory and the whole family together earned only a little—about twenty copecks a week.

'It was better under the masters,' said the old man, as he wound the silk. 'You worked and ate and slept all in their proper turn. You got cabbage soup and buckwheat porridge for dinner and for supper as well. As much cucumber and cabbage as you liked: you could eat to your heart's content, as much as ever you wanted. Things were stricter, too. Everybody behaved themselves.'

The only light was from one small lamp, which burned dimly and smoked. When anybody tilted the lamp and a great shadow fell over the window, the bright moonlight could be seen. Old Osip went on with his leisurely tale of how people lived before the emancipation, how in those very places where life was now so dull and poverty-stricken there had been hunting with greyhounds and borzois, and the beaters were treated to vodka, and whole trains of carts full of game went to Moscow for the young gentlemen, and bad peasants were punished by being flogged or sent away to the family estate in Tver Province, and good ones were rewarded. Granny told them some stories as well. She could remember everything, absolutely everything. She talked about her mistress, who was a God-fearing woman with a debauched and dissipated husband, and all of whose daughters made disastrous marriages: one married a drunkard, another a tradesman, the third eloped (Granny herself, at that time a young girl, had helped in the elopement); and they all, like their mother, died young of broken hearts. Recalling all this, Granny even shed a few tears.

Suddenly there was a knock at the door that made them all start.

'Uncle Osip, let me spend the night!'

There entered a little bald old man, General Zhukov's cook, the same whose cap had been burnt. He squatted down and listened, and then he also began to remember and tell various stories. Nikolay, sitting on the stove and dangling his feet over the edge, listened and asked questions all the time about the food they prepared for the masters. They talked of various meat dishes and soups and sauces, and the cook, who also had a very good memory, named dishes that are now unknown; there was, for example, a dish made of bulls' eyes and called 'Early-morning Pick-me-up'.

'Did you make *côtelettes maréchale*, too?' asked Nikolay.

'No.'

'Dear me, call yourselves cooks!'

The little girls, sitting or lying on the stove, looked down at them unblinkingly; there seemed to be a very large number of them, like cherubs in the clouds. They liked the stories, sighing, shuddering, and paling now with delight, now with fear, and they listened to Granny's stories, which were the most interesting of all, with bated breath, afraid to move a muscle.

They went to bed in silence and the old people, a little disturbed and agitated by their own stories, thought of how good youth is; of how when it is gone, whatever it has been like, there remains in the memory only what was lively, joyful, and touching; and of the coldness of death when it no longer lies beyond the horizon—best not to think of that! The lamp went out. The dark shadows, and the two little windows bright with moonlight, and the stillness, and the creaking of the cradle, all served only as reminders that life was over, and there was no way of calling it back . . . You doze off and forget yourself for a moment, but suddenly somebody brushes against your shoulder or breathes on your cheek—and sleep vanishes, your body feels numb with lying, and nothing comes into your head but thoughts of death; turn over on the other side, and you forget about death, but the same old tiresome, depressing thoughts go round and round, thoughts of want, and food, and the increased price of bread; and a little later you remember again that life is over and there is no way to call it back . . .

'Oh, Lord!' sighed the cook.

Somebody knocked very softly at the window. It must be Fekla coming back. Olga got up, yawning and whispering a prayer, unlocked the door, and then unfastened the bolts in the passage. But nobody came in; it only blew cold from the street and bright moonlight suddenly shone inside. Through the open door Olga could see the street, quiet and empty, and the moon riding through the sky.

'Who's there?' she called.

'Me,' came the answer. 'It's me.'

By the door, pressed back against the wall, stood Fekla, completely naked. She was trembling with cold, her teeth were chattering, and in the clear moonlight she looked very pale, beautiful, and strange. The shadows and the lustre of the moonlight on her skin made her sharply visible and brought out especially clearly her dark brows and her firm young breasts.

'Those brutes on the other side stripped me and turned me loose like this,' she said. 'I came home without my clothes . . . as naked as the day I was born. Bring me something to put on.'

'Come inside!' Olga, who was also beginning to shiver, said softly.

'I don't want the old man and woman to see me.'

Indeed, Granny was already restless and muttering,

and the old man was asking 'Who's there?' Olga brought her own skirt and blouse and put them on Fekla, and then they both crept quietly into the hut, trying not to make a noise with the doors.

'Is that you, you sleek hussy?' grumbled Granny angrily, guessing who it was. 'Ugh, be damned to you, fly-by-night! Somebody ought to wring your neck!'

'It's all right, it's all right,' whispered Olga, as she covered Fekla up, 'it's all right, my little beauty.'

Once again everything was quiet. Nobody ever slept well in the hut, everybody was kept awake by something persistent and inescapable: the old man by the pain in his back, Granny by her worries and ill humour, Marya by fear, and the children by itching and hunger. Now too their sleep was disturbed; they turned from side to side, muttered, got up for a drink.

Suddenly Fekla gave a loud harsh bellow, but immediately controlled herself and her occasional sobs grew gradually softer and more muffled until they ceased altogether. From time to time the sound of a clock striking was borne from the other side, across the river; but there was something odd about the clock; it struck five and afterwards three.

'Oh Lord!' sighed the cook.

Looking at the window it was difficult to know whether the moon was still shining or it was already dawn. Marya got up and went out, and she could be heard milking the cow in the yard and telling it to 'Stand sti-ill!' Granny also went out. It was still dark inside the hut, but objects were now visible.

Nikolay, who had not slept all night, climbed down from the stove. From a small green chest he took out his tail-coat, put it on and, going over to the window, smoothed down the sleeves, stood for a moment with his hands under the tails—and smiled. Then he carefully took it off, laid it away in the chest, and lay down again.

Marya returned and began to kindle the stove. She was still evidently half asleep and waking up as she moved about. She seemed to have been dreaming, or perhaps yesterday's stories had come into her mind, for she stretched luxuriously in front of the stove and said, 'No, freedom is best!'

VII

The gentleman—that was what they called the rural police chief in the village—had come. The time and reason of his arrival had been known for a week. There were only forty households in Zhukov, but arrears of state and *zemstvo* taxes amounted to more than two thousand roubles.

The policeman had stopped at the inn; he 'partook' of two glasses of tea and then went on foot to the village elder's hut, near which there was already a crowd of defaulters waiting. The elder, Antip Sedelnikov, in spite of his youth—he was only a little over thirty years old—was strict and always took the authorities' side, although he was poor himself and paid his taxes irregularly. He evidently enjoyed being the elder and liked the sense of power, which he could not exercise in any other form than strictness. At meetings he was feared and obeyed; he had been known to pounce on a drunken man in the street or near the inn, tie his hands behind his back and put him in the lock-up; he had once even put Granny there and kept her there for twenty-four hours because, coming to the meeting instead of Osip, she had started to scold. He had never lived in a town or read a book, but had acquired a few learned words from somewhere or other and loved to use them in conversation, and for this he was respected, if not always understood.

When Osip came into the elder's hut with his redemption book, the police chief, a spare old man with grey whiskers, wearing a grey plain-clothes jacket, was sitting at a table near the door, making notes. The hut was clean, and all its walls adorned with pictures cut from magazines; in the most conspicuous position, near the icon, hung a portrait of Alexander of Battenberg, the former Prince of Bulgaria. Antip Sedelnikov stood by the table with folded arms.

'Your Honour, he owes a hundred and nineteen roubles,' he said when Osip's turn came. 'He paid a rouble before Easter, but not a copeck since.'

The police chief raised his eyes to Osip and asked, 'Why is that, my man?'

'Show God's mercy, your Honour,' began Osip, getting agitated, 'and allow me to say, last summer the gentleman from Lyutoretsk says, "Osip," he says, "sell me your hay . . . Sell it me," he says. Why not? I had more than a ton and a half I could sell, the women had mowed every bit they could. Well, we made a bargain . . . Everything's all right, all nice and easy . . .'

He began to complain about the elder, turning every now and then to the other peasants as though inviting them to bear witness for him; his face grew red and sweaty and his eyes sharp and malicious.

'I don't understand why you are telling me all this', said the policeman. 'I am asking you . . . I want to know from you why you don't pay your arrears. You all keep on not paying; do you expect me to answer for you?'

'I haven't got it!'

'These remarks are inconsequential, your Honour,'

said the elder. 'Factually, the Chikildeevs are of the impecunious class, but if you would care to ask the others, the whole cause is vodka, and they are very dissipated. Quite without intelligence.'

The police chief made a note and said to Osip in calm, even tones, as if he was asking for a drink of water,

'Get out!'

He left very soon; and when he got into his cheap tarantass, coughing, it was plain even from the look of his long thin back that he had already forgotten about Osip, the elder, and the *Zhukovo* arrears, and was thinking of his personal concerns. Before he had had time to cover three-quarters of a mile, Antip Sedelnikov had removed the samovar from the Chikildeevs' hut, and Granny was following him shrieking at the top of her voice,

'I won't give it up! You can't have it, you devil!'

He walked quickly, with long strides, and she came panting along behind him, all but falling, hunched and furiously angry; the kerchief had slipped from her head to her shoulders and her grey hair, with a greenish tinge, blew untidily about. All at once she stopped and, like a real insurrectionist, began beating her breast with her fists and shouting even louder, in a kind of wailing chant,

'Good Christians, believers in God! Friends, we have been wronged! Brothers, we are oppressed! Oh, oh, my dears, come to our aid!'

'Granny, Granny,' said the elder sternly, 'have some sense!'

Without the samovar the Chikildeevs' hut was quite desolate. There was something shocking and humiliating about the deprivation, as though the hut had been dishonoured. It would have been better if the elder had seized and carried off the table, all the benches, and all the cooking pots; the place would not have seemed so empty. Granny shouted, Marya wept, and the little girls, seeing her, wept too. The old man, feeling guilty, sat glum and silent in a corner. Nikolay was silent, too. Granny loved and pitied him, but now she forgot her pity and turned on him with shrewish reproaches, thrusting her fists almost into his face. She shouted that it was all his fault: really, why had he sent them so little when his letters had boasted that he was earning fifty roubles a month at the Slav Bazaar? Why had he come there, and with his family into the bargain? . . . If he died, what was there to bury him with? . . . Nikolay, Olga, and Sasha were a pitiful sight.

The old man heaved a sigh, took his cap and went to see the elder. It was already dark. Antip Sedelnikov was soldering something near the stove, blowing out his cheeks; there was a smell of burning. His children, thin and unwashed, no better than the Chikildeevs', were playing on the floor; his wife, a plain freckled woman with a big stomach, was winding silk. It was a wretched, poverty-stricken family and only Antip himself looked young and handsome. Five samovars stood in a row on a bench. The old man crossed himself before the portrait of Prince Battenberg and said,

'Antip, show God's mercy, give me back the samovar! For Christ's sake!'

'Bring three roubles and then you can have it.'

'I haven't got it!'

Antip puffed out his cheeks, the fire hummed and hissed, and the samovars reflected its light. The old man twisted the cap in his hands and said, after a moment's thought,

'Give it back!'

The swarthy elder now seemed quite black and looked

like a sorcerer; he turned towards Osip and said, speaking harshly and rapidly,

'The whole matter depends on the chairman of the *zemstvo*. At the administrative session on the twenty-sixth you may testify to the cause of your dissatisfaction either orally or in writing.'

Osip did not understand a word of all this, but was satisfied with it and went home.

Some ten days later the rural police chief again came to the village, stayed about an hour, and departed. The weather just then was windy and cold; the river had frozen long before but there was still no snow, people were worn out because the road could not be used. Late one Sunday afternoon neighbours came in to sit and talk for a time with Osip. They talked in the dark, since it would have been sinful to work and so the lamp had not been lighted. There was some news, rather disagreeable. Thus in two or three houses hens had been seized and sent off to the canton, and there they had died because nobody fed them; sheep had been seized, carted off with their feet bound, and transferred to fresh carts at every village, and on the way one had died. Now they were trying to settle who was to blame.

'The *zemstvo*!' said Osip. 'Who else?'

'The *zemstvo*, of course.'

They blamed the *zemstvo* for everything—arrears of quit-rents and taxes, persecutions, bad harvests—although not one of them knew what was meant by *zemstvo*. This went back to the days when the rich peasants, owning their own factories, shops or inns, had been for a time members of the *zemstvos*, been dissatisfied with them and then begun to abuse them in their factories and taverns.

They talked of the fact that God had not sent the

snow: firewood had to be carted, and it was impossible either to walk or to drive a cart over the hummocky ground. In earlier days, fifteen or twenty years before or longer, conversations in Zhukovo had been much more interesting. Then every old man looked as though he was keeping a secret, knew something, and was expecting something; they talked of documents with gold seals, the division of property, new territories, talked in hints and allusions; but now the people of Zhukovo had no secrets, their whole life was like an open book for anybody to read, and they could talk only of hardship, or fodder, or the absence of snow . . .

They fell silent. Then they remembered the chickens and the sheep again and began to discuss who was to blame.

'The *zemstvo*!' said Osip gloomily. 'Who else?'

VIII

The parish church was six versts away, in Kosogorovo, and people went there only when they were obliged to, for christenings, weddings, and funerals; they went to the other side of the river to pray. On Sundays, in fine weather, the girls dressed themselves up and went to mass in a body, and it was a joyful sight to see them walking across the meadow in their red and green and yellow dresses; in bad weather, however, they all stayed at home. For communion they went to the parish church. From each of those who had not made their Easter preparations during Lent the priest took fifteen copecks when he carried the cross in procession round the huts at Easter.

The old man did not believe in God because he hardly ever thought of him; he recognized the supernatural, but thought it concerned only women, and when people talked in his presence of religion or miracles and asked what he thought, he would answer reluctantly, scratching his head:

'How should I know?'

Granny believed, but rather hazily; everything was mixed up in her memory, and she had hardly begun to think of sin and death and the salvation of souls before wants and worries seized hold of her mind and she immediately forgot what she had been thinking of. She could not remember any prayers and in the evening at bedtime she usually stationed herself before the icons and whispered,

'Holy Virgin of Kazan, Holy Virgin of Smolensk, Holy Virgin with the three hands . . .'

Marya and Fekla crossed themselves, and went to communion once a year, but had no understanding of religion. They did not teach their children to pray or speak to them of God or inculcate any rules of conduct, only forbade them to eat certain foods during fasts. In the other families it was almost the same: very few believed, very few understood. At the same time everybody loved the holy scriptures, loved them tenderly and reverently, but they had neither bibles nor anybody to read and explain them, and because Olga sometimes read the gospels to them they respected her, and everybody addressed her and Sasha politely as 'you' instead of 'thou'.

Olga often went to church festivals and special services in the neighbouring villages and the District town, where there were two monasteries and twenty-seven churches. She was an absent-minded woman and while she was engaged in one of these pilgrimages would forget all about her family, and only when she returned home make the joyful discovery that she had a husband and a daughter, and then she would say, smiling and radiant,

'God has blessed me!'

The things that went on in the village pained and disgusted her. There was drinking on St. Elias's Day, drinking on the Feast of the Assumption, drinking on Holy Cross Day. The Feast of the Intercession was a parish holiday in Zhukovo and on that occasion the peasants drank for three days; they drank fifty roubles of village communal funds and afterwards collected more money for vodka from every household. The Chikildeevs killed a sheep on the first day and ate great quantities of mutton in the morning, at dinner-time and in the evening, and then the children got up during the night to eat more. Cyriac was terribly drunk the whole three days, drinking everything he possessed, even his fur cap and his boots, and beat Marya so violently that she had to be brought round by pouring water over her. Afterwards everybody felt ashamed and disgusted.

Even in Lackeydom, in Zhukovo, however, there was one genuine religious ceremonial. This was in August, when the icon of the Blessed Virgin was carried round the whole District, from village to village. On that day, while she was waited for in Zhukovo, the weather was calm and overcast. The girls in their bright Sunday dresses had gone out to meet the icon in the morning, and they brought her into the village late in the afternoon, with singing and a procession, while the bells pealed across the river. A great throng of people from the village and elsewhere blocked the street; there was noise, dust, and jostling . . . The old man, Granny, and Cyriac all stretched out their hands towards the icon, their eyes eagerly fixed on it, and said, weeping,

'Holy Mother of God, pray for us!'

It was as though they had suddenly understood that there was no empty abyss between earth and heaven, that the rich and powerful had not yet got their hands on everything, that there still remained one protection against insult, slavish bondage, oppressive, intolerable poverty, and the terrible vodka.

'Mother of God, pray for us!' sobbed Marya. 'Pray for us!'

The service was over, the icon was carried away, everything went on as before, and once again coarse, drunken voices were raised in the tavern.

It was only the rich peasants who feared death; the richer they grew, the less they believed in God and the salvation of souls, and they dedicated candles and attended services only from fear of their earthly end or as a precaution. The poorer peasants, however, were not afraid of death. The old man and Granny were told to their faces that they had had their day and the time had come for them to die, and they did not mind. Nobody hesitated to say to Fekla in Nikolay's presence that when he died it would mean that Denis, her husband, would get his discharge and be sent home. Marya, indeed, not only did not fear death, but wished it was not so long in coming, and was glad when her children died.

They did not fear death, but on the other hand they had an exaggerated terror of any kind of illness. The merest trifle—a disordered stomach or a slight chill—was enough to make Granny lie down on the stove, well covered up and groaning loudly and continuously, 'I'm dy-ing!' The old man would hurry away for the priest and Granny would receive the last sacraments. They were always talking about colds, and worms, and tumours wandering about in the body and striking up to the heart. They were most afraid of catching cold and so even in summer wrapped up well and kept warm on the stove. Granny loved taking medicine and often went to the hospital, where she used to tell them that she was fifty-eight, not seventy; she supposed that if the doctor knew her real age he would refuse to treat her and say it was time for her to die, instead of trying to get well. She usually left for the hospital early in the morning, taking two or three of the little girls with her, and returned in the evening, cross and hungry, with drops for herself and ointments for the little girls. Once she took Nikolay as well, and for about two weeks afterwards he was taking drops, which he said did him good.

Granny knew all the doctors, medical orderlies, and quacks for thirty versts around, and did not like any of them. At the Feast of the Intercession, when the priest went round the huts with the cross, the parish clerk told her of an old man living near the prison in the town, whose cures were very successful, and advised her to consult him. Granny followed the advice. When the first snow fell she paid a visit to the town and brought back a bearded little old man, a converted Jew, whose whole face was a network of little blue veins. There happened to be some jobbing craftsmen working in the hut at the time: a tailor, an old man in fearsome spectacles, cutting a waistcoat out of bits and pieces of cloth, and two lads twisting wool for felt boots; Cyriac, who had been dismissed for drunkenness and was now living at home, was sitting beside the tailor mending a yoke. The hut felt crowded, stuffy, and smelly. The Jew looked at Nikolay and said that he would have to apply cupping-glasses.

He applied them, while the old tailor, Cyriac, and the little girls stood watching, and imagined they could see the illness coming out of Nikolay. Nikolay too watched the cups clinging to his chest and gradually filling with dark blood, and felt that something was indeed being drawn out of his body, and he smiled with pleasure.

'They are a good thing,' said the tailor. 'God grant you may feel the benefit!'

The Jew applied twelve cups and then twelve more, drank some tea, and departed. Nikolay began to shiver; his cheeks fell in, his face shrank, as the women said, into a fist, his hands turned blue. He rolled himself in a blanket and a sheepskin, but felt colder and colder. Towards evening he became very low-spirited; he asked them to lay him on the floor, asked the tailor not to smoke, then grew quiet under the sheepskin and died before morning.

IX

Oh, how harsh and long the winter was!

They had used up all their own grain by Christmas and had to buy flour. Cyriac, now living at home, created an uproar in the evenings, frightening everybody, and in the mornings suffered from headache and shame, a pitiful spectacle.

The lowing of the hungry cow in the shed, heart-breaking to Marya and Granny, could be heard day and night. As if by design, hard frosts continued all through the winter, and the snow piled into deep drifts. The winter was prolonged, too: Lady Day brought a real winter snow-storm, and there was snow at Easter.

The winter, however, did come to an end. At the beginning of April the days were warm and the nights frosty; winter had not yielded, but one warm day it was conquered at last—streams flowed and birds began to sing. The whole meadow and the bushes near the river were drowned in the spring floods and all the expanse between Zhukovo and the farther bank was covered with one vast sheet of water from which flocks of wild duck took wing. Every evening the fiery spring sunset with its gorgeous clouds produced something new, extraordinary, and improbable, precisely the sort of thing that one does not believe in, seeing the same colours and the same clouds in a picture.

The cranes flew swiftly overhead, calling mournfully, as though inviting you to go with them. Standing on the edge of the steep bank, Olga gazed for a long time at the floods, the sun, the church shining as if with a renewal of youth; her tears flowed and her breath caught with her passionate longing to go right away somewhere, anywhere, even to the ends of the earth. It had already been settled that she should go back to Moscow as a housemaid, and that Cyriac should go with her, to find employment as a house-porter or the like. Oh, only to get away soon!

When the ground was dry and the weather warm, they prepared to set out. Olga and Sasha, with packs on their backs, both in bast shoes, left the house as soon as it was light; Marya went out too to see them on their way. Cyriac was not well and was staying at home for another week. Olga prayed for the last time with her face turned towards the church, thinking of her husband, but she did not weep; only her face grew wrinkled and ugly, like an old woman's. During the winter she had become thinner, paler, and a little greyer, and now instead of its former comeliness and pleasant smile her face bore the resigned, melancholy expression of bereavement, and there was something slow and stupid in her look, as though she were deaf. She was sorry to part from the village and the peasants. She remembered how they had carried Nikolay through the village, how a requiem mass was said at each hut, and how everybody had wept in sympathy with her sorrow. During the summer and winter there had been days and hours when it had seemed that these people lived worse than cattle, and that it was terrible to live among them: they were coarse, dishonest, dirty, and drunken; they could not get on with one another, but quarrelled constantly, because they did not respect but feared and distrusted each other. Who kept the tavern and tempted the people to drink? The peasant. Who squandered and drank the money that belonged to the village community, the school, and the church? The peasant. Who stole from his neighbour and set fire to his property or bore false witness in court for a bottle of vodka? The peasant. Who attacked the peasant in *zemstvo* and other meetings? The peasant. Yes, living with them had been terrible, but all the same they were human beings, they suffered and wept as human beings, and there was nothing in their lives for which some excuse could not be found. Back-breaking labour, which made the whole body ache at night, cruel winters, scanty harvests, overcrowding—and there was no help, and nowhere to expect help from. Those who were richer and stronger could not help, since they were themselves coarse, dishonest, and drunken, and wrangled just as insufferably; the pettiest official or clerk treated the peasants like tramps, said 'thou' even to elected village leaders and churchwardens, and considered he had a right to do so. Was it indeed possible to look for help or a good example from greedy, grasping, dissolute, lazy people who went into the villages only to abuse, plunder, and intimidate? Olga remembered the pitiful, crushed faces of the old people once during the winter, when Cyriac was taken off to be flogged for some offence . . . And now she was sorry for all these people, terribly sorry, and as she walked, she kept turning to look at the huts.

When they had gone about three versts, Marya said good-bye, then she knelt down and began to wail, falling face downward,

'I'm all alone again, poor unhappy me, wretch that I am . . .'

She lamented for a long time, and for even longer Olga and Sasha could see her, still on her knees, repeatedly bowing down to the ground, with her hands clutching her head, and the rooks flying over her.

The sun rose high, it grew warm. Zhukovo was a long way behind them. Walking was a pleasure, and Olga and Sasha soon forgot both Marya and the village; they were in good spirits and everything diverted them. Now it was a tumulus, now a line of telegraph poles striding one after another to an unknown destination and disappearing over the horizon, their wires humming mysteriously; now a little farm-house visible some way off, buried in greenery, smelling of moisture and hemp and somehow seeming to be lived in by happy people; now the skeleton of a horse whitening alone in the fields. Larks sang indefatigably, quails piped, and the cry of a corncrake sounded like the creaking of an old iron hinge.

At midday Olga and Sasha came to a large village. There in the wide street they met the little old man, General Zhukov's cook. He was hot, and his red, sweating, bald head shone in the sun. Olga and he did not know one another, then they both looked round at the same moment, recognized each other, and went their separate ways without a word. Stopping before the open windows of a hut that seemed richer and newer than the others, Olga bowed and said in a loud, shrill chant,

'Good Orthodox Christians, alms for the love of

Christ, whatever you can spare, God rest the souls of your parents and grant them the kingdom of heaven.'

'Good Orthodox Christians,' struck up Sasha, 'for the love of Christ, whatever you can spare, the kingdom of heaven . . .'

THE CART

1897

THEY left the town at half-past eight in the morning.

The road was dry, the beautiful April sun shone warmly, but there was still snow in the ditches and among the trees. The long, dark, bitter winter had lasted until recently, and the spring had come suddenly, but to Marya Vasilyevna, who was sitting in the cart, there seemed nothing new or interesting in the warmth, the weary translucent woods, warmed by the breath of spring, the black flocks of birds flying over the enormous pools, like lakes, in the fields, or that wonderful fathomless sky, into which it would seem such joy to disappear. For thirteen years now she had been a teacher, and it was impossible to count the number of times during those years that she had travelled to the town for her salary; and whether it was spring, as now, or a wet autumn evening, or winter, it was all the same to her, and she had only one invariable wish: to get the journey over as soon as possible.

She felt as though she had lived in these parts for a very long time, about a hundred years, and it seemed to her that she knew every stone and every tree on the way from the town to her school. Her past and her present were both here, and she could conceive of no other future than the school, the road to the town and back, the school again, and then the road once more . . .

She had grown unused to recalling her past before she became a schoolmistress—and had almost entirely forgotten it. Once she had had a father and mother; they had lived in a big flat near the Red Gate in Moscow, but of all that life there remained in her memory only something confused and hazy, like a dream. Her father had died when she was ten years old, and her mother soon afterwards . . . She had a brother, an officer, and at first they had corresponded, but then her brother stopped answering her letters, he had got out of the habit. Of her former possessions there remained only a photograph of her mother, but the damp in the schoolhouse had faded it, and now nothing could be seen but the hair and forehead.

When they had gone about three versts, old Simon, who was driving the horse, turned round and said,

'There's been an official arrested in the town. He's been sent away. Seems, people say, he killed Alexeev, the mayor, with some Germans.'

'Who told you that?'

'At Ivan Ionov's inn they saw it in the papers.'

They said nothing more for a long time. Marya Vasilyevna was thinking of her school and of the fact that it would soon be the examination, and she was sending in four boys and one girl.

Just as she was thinking about the examination they were overtaken by Khanov, the landowner, in his carriage and four; it was he who had conducted the examination at her school the year before. As he drew level he recognized her and bowed.

'Good morning!' he said. 'Are you going home?'

This Khanov, a man of about forty, with a worn face and an indolent look, was already beginning to show his age, but he was still handsome and women found him attractive. He lived alone on his big estate, had never entered the government service, and was said to do nothing at home but walk about whistling from place to place, or play chess with his old manservant. He was also said to drink a great deal. It was certainly true that at the examination the year before even the papers he brought with him smelt of scent and spirits. On that occasion he had been wearing new clothes, and Marya Vasilyevna had found him very charming and felt shy sitting beside him. The examiners she was used to were cold and judicious, but this one could not remember a single prayer, had no idea what questions to ask, was very polite and considerate, and gave nothing but top marks.

'I am going to see Bakvist,' he continued, addressing Marya Vasilyevna, 'but I'm told he's not at home.'

From the highway they had turned into a by-road, Khanov in front and Simon following. The four horses plodded straight along the road, dragging the heavy carriage through the mud with great effort. Simon zig-zagged about, driving off the road, now over a bit of higher ground, now on the grass, and frequently jumping down to help the horses. Marya Vasilyevna went on thinking about the school, and about whether the examination would be easy or difficult. She was annoyed with the *zemstvo* office, where she had not been able to find anybody on the previous day. How inefficient! For two years now she had been asking for the dismissal of the caretaker, who never did any work, spoke roughly to her pupils, and often struck them, but nobody would listen to her. It was difficult to find the chairman in the office, and if you did find him, he would complain, with tears in his eyes, that he had not a moment to spare; the inspector visited the school once in three years and understood nothing about his job, since he had been an excise officer and had only got his present post through influence; the school governors met extremely rarely, nobody knew where; the superintendent was a semi-illiterate peasant, who owned a tannery, unintelligent, coarse, and a close friend of the caretaker's—and God knew where she could go with her complaints for redress . . .

'He really is very handsome,' she thought with a glance at Khanov.

The road got worse and worse . . . They drove into the forest. Here there was nowhere to turn aside, the ruts were deep, and murmuring streams of water flowed along them. Prickly branches whipped into one's face.

'What sort of road would you call this?' asked Khanov laughing.

The schoolmistress looked at him and wondered why he was eccentric enough to live here. What was the use of his money, his attractive appearance, and his civilized tastes in the mud and boredom of this wilderness? Life here gave him no privileges; he had to travel at a walking pace along abominable roads, like Simon, and suffer the same discomforts. Why should anybody who could live in St. Petersburg or abroad live here? What harm would it do him, a rich man, she wondered, to make this bad road into a good one, so that he need not be so acutely inconvenienced or see the look of despair on the faces of his coachman and Simon? But he only laughed, and evidently it did not matter to him, he did not want a better life. He was kind, gentle, and naïve, did not understand this coarse kind of life and knew no more about it than he had about the prayers at the examination. The only things he ever gave the school were globes, and he sincerely believed he was being helpful, a notable worker for the cause of the people's education. But what use were his globes here?

'Hold tight, Vasilyevna!' said Simon.

The cart gave a violent lurch and seemed on the point of toppling over; something heavy slid on to Marya Vasilyevna's legs—it was the things she had bought in the town. There was a steep slope up a bank of clay, where streams of water ran noisily down in sinuous courses and seemed to have eaten the road away—how could any vehicle be expected to get through? The horses snorted. Khanov climbed down from his carriage and walked in his long overcoat by the side of the road. He was very hot.

'What sort of road would you call this?' he asked again, with a laugh. 'At this rate it won't take long to wreck the carriage.'

'You're not obliged to travel in weather like this, are you?' said Simon sharply. 'You ought to have stayed at home.'

'It's dull at home, grandad. I don't like staying at home.'

By the side of old Simon he looked graceful and vigorous, but there was a something barely perceptible in his walk that betrayed a creature already poisoned, enfeebled, and on the verge of destruction. The forest seemed suddenly to smell of vodka. Marya Vasilyevna felt a touch of fear and grief for this man who was ruining himself for unknown reasons, and the idea came to her that if she was his wife or his sister she would be prepared to sacrifice her whole life to save him from shipwreck. His wife? Life was so arranged that, while he lived alone on his big estate and she lived alone in her benighted village, somehow the very idea that they could be equals or familiars seemed impossible and absurd. In fact, it was painful and discouraging to think how incomprehensibly life and complex human relationships were arranged.

'I can't understand either,' she thought, 'why God gives good looks, a charming manner, and kind, sad eyes to weak, unhappy, futile people, or why they are so attractive.'

'We go to the right here,' said Khanov, getting into his carriage. 'Good-bye and good luck!'

She thought again of her pupils, the examination, the caretaker, the school governors, but when the sounds of the retreating carriage came to them on the wind these thoughts mingled with others. Her mind involuntarily dwelt on a fine pair of eyes, love, a happiness that could never be . . .

She marry? The mornings were cold, and there was nobody to light the stove, since the caretaker had always disappeared somewhere; her pupils began to arrive almost before it was light, bringing in mud and snow and making a noise; everything was inconvenient and uncomfortable. Her flat was one small room and a kitchen. Every day when work was over her head ached, and after dinner she had indigestion. Money had to be collected from the children for firewood and to pay the caretaker, and given to the superintendent, and even then this well-fed, insolent peasant had to be begged for the love of God to send the wood. At night she dreamed of examinations, peasants, and snow-drifts. This kind of life had aged and coarsened her, she had grown plain, angular and awkward, as though she was cased in lead; she was afraid of everything; in the presence of any of the governors or the superintendent she stood all the time, not daring to sit down, and when she spoke of one of them, she used deferential expressions like an inferior. Nobody liked her, and her life ran on monotonously, without affection, friendly sympathy, or interesting acquaintances. How dreadful it would be if she, in her situation, were to fall in love!

'Hold tight, Vasilyevna!'

Another steep climb uphill.

She had gone into teaching out of necessity, without feeling any vocation for it; she never thought about having a mission or the value of education, and the most important thing in her profession always seemed to her to be not the pupils or education but examinations. Indeed, what time was there to think about her vocation or the benefits of education? Teachers, poor doctors, and unqualified medical assistants, with the enormous amount of work they must do, have not even the consolation of thinking that they are serving an idea, or the community, since their heads are stuffed all the time with thoughts about the next meal, firewood, bad roads, and illness. It is a hard, uninteresting life, and the only people who will put up with it for very long are uncomplaining cart-horses like Marya Vasilyevna; the lively, active, impressionable people who talk of their vocation and of service to an idea soon grow weary and abandon the whole thing.

To find the shortest and dryest route Simon tried to go now across a meadow, now by back ways; but in one place peasants refused to let him proceed, in another there was no through road because it was church land, and somewhere else Ivan Ionov had bought a plot of ground from the gentleman who owned it and dug a ditch all round. They kept having to turn back.

They came to Lower Gorodishche. Near the inn, on

ground that had been spread with dung, underneath which the snow still lingered, stood carts carrying carboys of sulphuric acid. Inside the inn there were a great many people, mostly carters, and a smell of vodka, tobacco, and sheepskins. The place was noisy with talk and the continual slamming of a door; in the shop which occupied the next room an accordion played without a moment's pause. Marya Vasilyevna sat drinking tea; at the next table some peasants, steaming with tea and the heat of the inn, drank vodka and beer.

There was a confusion of voices: 'Listen Kuzma! What are you laughing at over there? God bless us! I can tell you one thing, Ivan Dementyich! A matchmaker, see?'

A short, black-bearded, pockmarked peasant, startled by something, suddenly began to swear abominably.

'What are you using such language for? You over there!' Simon, who was sitting away to one side, called out angrily. 'Can't you see the lady?'

'The lady . . .' mocked somebody from the other corner.

'You stuck pig!'

'We didn't mean no harm . . .' said the little peasant, embarrassed. 'Excuse us. We pay our money, I mean, and the lady pays hers . . . Good morning!'

'Good morning,' answered the teacher.

'Thank you kindly.'

Marya Vasilyevna was enjoying her tea, and growing as red as the peasants; her thoughts were again occupied with firewood and the caretaker . . .

'Wait a bit, matchmaker!' came a voice from the next table. 'That's the school-teacher from Vyazovye—we know her! The lady's looks are all right.'

'Not so bad!'

The door went on slamming as people went out and others came in. Marya Vasilyevna still thought about the same things, and in the next room the accordion played on and on. There had been spots of sunlight on the floor, then they had moved on to the counter and up the wall and disappeared entirely; that meant the sun had already declined from its noon. The peasants at the next table were getting ready to leave. The little man, swaying slightly, walked over to Marya Vasilyevna and offered her his hand; seeing him, the others also shook hands with her; they went out one by one and the door creaked and banged nine times.

'Vasilyevna, come on!' called Simon.

They set out again. Once again their pace was slow.

'A little while back they were putting up a school here, in their Lower Gorodishche,' said Simon, turning round. 'Shocking goings-on there were!'

'Oh, what?'

'Seems the chairman put a thousand in his own pocket, and so did the superintendent, and the teacher five hundred.'

'The whole school is only costing a thousand. It's wrong to slander people like that, grandad. It's all rubbish.'

'I don't know anything about that . . . I'm only saying what other folks do.'

It was plain, however, that Simon did not believe her. The peasants had no trust in her; they thought she received too large a salary—twenty-one roubles a month (five would have been enough)—and that she kept for herself the biggest part of the money she collected from her pupils for firewood and the caretaker. The superintendent thought the same as the rest of them, and he himself made something out of the wood and, unknown to the authorities, received a salary as superintendent from the peasants. The forest, thank God, was at an end, and now there was nothing but level open country all the way to Vyazovye. There was not much farther to go: across the river, and then the railway line, and there was Vyazovye.

'Where on earth are you going?' Marya Vasilyevna asked Simon. 'Take the right-hand road to the bridge.'

'Why? We can get across here. It's not so very deep.'

'Mind you don't drown the horse.'

'What?'

'Khanov has gone by the bridge, look,' said Marya Vasilyevna, who had just seen the four-in-hand far away to the right. 'I think that's him, isn't it?'

'Ye-es. He can't have found Bakvist. What a fool, God have mercy, he's gone that way, and what for? This is quicker by a good three versts.'

They had come to the river. In summer it was not much more than a stream, easily crossed by the ford and usually drying up in August, but now, after the spring floods, it was a river some forty feet wide, swift flowing, muddy, and cold; on the bank and close to the water there were fresh ruts, which showed that somebody had gone across at this point.

'Gee up!' shouted Simon with anxious irritation, pulling hard on the reins and flapping his elbows as though they were wings. 'Gee up!'

The horse waded in until the water reached its belly and then stopped, but immediately went on again, pulling hard, and Marya Vasilyevna felt a sensation of piercing cold in her feet.

'Gee up!' she cried also, standing up. 'Gee up!'

They emerged on the other bank.

'What a state to let things get into!' grumbled Simon,

straightening the harness. 'Nothing but a damned pest, that there *zemstvo* . . .'

Her shoes and galoshes were full of water, the lower part of her dress and coat soaked and dripping; the packets of sugar and tea had got wet—and this was the most annoying of all; Marya Vasilyevna could only wring her hands in despair and say,

'Oh, Simon, Simon! . . . Really, what possessed you? . . .'

At the railway crossing the barrier was down: an express train was leaving the little station. Marya Vasilyevna stood by the crossing and waited for it to pass, trembling all over with cold. Vyazovye was already in sight—the school with its green roof and the church, its crosses on fire with the reflections of the evening sun; the station windows were on fire too, and the engine puffed out rose-coloured smoke . . . It seemed to her that everything was shaking with cold.

Here was the train; the windows gave back a blinding light, like the church crosses, so that it hurt to look at them. On the platform of one of the first-class coaches stood a lady. Marya Vasilyevna glanced at her for an instant: her mother! How strong the likeness was! Her mother had had just such luxuriant hair, just such a forehead and tilt of the head. Vividly, with startling clarity, for the first time in all those thirteen years she saw her mother, her father, her brother, the flat in Moscow, the fishes in the aquarium, everything down to the smallest detail, heard the sound of the piano and her father's voice, felt herself to be, as she had been then, young, handsome, and well-dressed, in a bright, warm room, in her family circle; she was seized with a feeling of joy and happiness, she pressed her hands rapturously to her temples and called tenderly and imploringly,

'Mama!'

And without knowing why, she burst into tears. At that very moment Khanov drove up in his carriage, and seeing him she imagined a happiness that never had been and smiled, nodding to him like a friend and equal, and it seemed to her that it was her happiness and triumph that shone in the sky and in all the windows and on the trees. Yes, her father and mother had never died, she had never been a teacher, that was a long, strange, painful dream, and now she had awakened . . .

'Get in, Vasilyevna!'

In an instant it had all disappeared. The barrier lifted slowly. Marya Vasilyevna, numb and shaking with cold, got into the cart. The carriage and four crossed the line, and Simon followed. The keeper on the crossing took off his cap.

'Here's Vyazovye. We've arrived.'

A VISIT TO FRIENDS

1898

THE letter arrived one morning:

Kuzminki, 7 June

Dear Misha,

You have quite forgotten us. We should like to see you; do come as soon as you can. We implore you on our bended knees, come today, let us see your bright eyes again!

In impatient expectation,

Ta and Va.

The letter was from Tatyana Alexeevna Loseva who, ten or twelve years ago when Podgorin was living in Kuzminki, had been called Ta for short. But who was Va? Podgorin remembered long talks, happy laughter, novels, evening walks, and a whole flower-garden of girls and young women living in and around Kuzminki, and recalled a simple, lively, intelligent face, with freckles that suited the dark chestnut hair so well—that was Varya, or Varvara Pavlovna, Tatyana's great friend. She had passed her medical examinations and was practising somewhere on the other side of Tula in a factory, and now was evidently on a visit to Kuzminki.

'Dear Va!' thought Podgorin, giving himself up to his memories. 'What a delightful person she is!'

Tatyana, Varya, and he were almost the same age; but at that time he was a student and they were already grown-up young ladies and regarded him as a boy. And now, although he was a lawyer and beginning to go grey, they still called him Misha, thought of him as young, and said that he had had no experience of life yet.

He was very fond of them but, it seemed, fonder in recollection than in real life. For him reality was something little known, incomprehensible, and alien. Alien, too, was this short, playful letter, which had probably taken a long time to compose; Tatyana's husband, Sergey Sergeich, was probably standing behind her while she wrote it . . . Kuzminki had become part of her dowry only six years before, but that same Sergey Sergeich had already ruined it and now every time money had to be paid into the bank or off the mortgage they turned to Podgorin, as a lawyer, for advice; moreover, they had twice asked him for loans. Evidently they wanted either advice or money from him this time as well.

Kuzminki was no longer as attractive as it had been. It was melancholy there. The laughter and noise, the happy, care-free people, the assignations on quiet moon-lit nights, had all gone, and most important of all, youth had gone too; besides, it was probably only in memory that it had all been so enchanting . . . Besides Ta and Va there had been Na as well, Tatyana's sister Nadezhda, who used to be called, half in jest and half in earnest, his sweetheart; he had watched her grow up, he was expected to marry her, and at one time he was in love with her and ready to fulfil the expectation, but now she had reached the age of twenty-three and he was still unmarried.

'How oddly things have all turned out, though,' he thought now, re-reading the letter with a troubled mind. 'But I can't not go; they would be hurt . . .'

The fact that he had not been to see the Losevs for a long time lay on his conscience like a stone. He thought it over, pacing about the room, and decided with an effort to discharge his obligations by going to them for two or three days; and then he would feel free and his mind would be easy, at least until the next summer. Leaving for the Brest Station after luncheon, he told his servants that he would return in three days.

The journey from Moscow to Kuzminki took two hours, and the drive from the station another twenty minutes. From the station itself one could see Tatyana's wood and three tall narrow summer villas, begun and never finished by Losev, who had lashed out in various speculative enterprises during the first years after his marriage. These villas had contributed to his ruin, together with various agricultural undertakings and his frequent excursions to Moscow, where he lunched at the Slav Bazaar, dined at the Hermitage, and ended the day in Little Bronnaya Street or the Zhivoderka with the gipsies (he called this 'shaking up his system'). Podgorin also drank, sometimes heavily, and was not particular about the women he consorted with, but he did it all indolently and coldly, without experiencing any pleasure, was thoroughly sickened when others in his presence yielded to such temptations with passionate enjoyment, and could neither understand nor like people who felt freer in the Zhivoderka than at home among respectable women; they seemed to him to be covered with every kind of defilement, clinging to them like burrs. He disliked Losev, considered him an uninteresting, incompetent young idler, and had often felt sickened in his company.

Sergey Sergeich and Nadezhda met him just beyond the wood.

'My dear fellow, why have you forgotten us like this?' said Sergey Sergeich, kissing him three times on the cheeks and then holding him by the waist with both hands. 'You have quite fallen out with us, my dear friend.'

He had large coarse features, a thick nose, and a scanty reddish beard; he combed his hair down flat to one side, like a merchant, to make himself seem simple and very Russian. When he talked he sent his breath straight into his companion's face, and when he was silent he breathed heavily through his nose. His well-nourished body and superfluous weight were a handicap to him and in order to breathe more easily he was always sticking out his chest, which made him look overbearing. His sister-in-law, Nadezhda, looked ethereal beside him. She was a light blonde with a pale skin, kind affectionate eyes, and a good figure; Podgorin had no idea whether she was beautiful or not, because he had known her since she was a child and grown too used to her appearance. Now she was wearing a white dress with an open neck and the sight of that long white bare neck was new and not altogether pleasant to him.

'My sister and I have been expecting you since the morning,' she said. 'Varya is with us and she expects you too.'

She took his arm with a sudden smile and uttered a joyful little cry as though struck by an enchanting idea. The field of flowering rye, motionless in the calm air, and the sunlit wood, were beautiful, and it seemed as though Nadezhda had noticed them only now, as she walked with Podgorin.

'I have come for three days,' he said. 'You must forgive me; I could not get away from Moscow any sooner.'

'It's too bad, you've forgotten us completely,' said Sergey Sergeich with good-humoured reproach. '*Jamais de ma vie!*' he exclaimed suddenly, snapping his fingers.

He had a trick of startling his hearer by ejaculating some phrase quite unconnected with the subject of conversation, snapping his fingers as he did so. He was always imitating somebody, too; if he rolled his eyes or carelessly tossed back his hair or dropped into a pathetic vein, it meant that the day before he had been to a theatre or a formal dinner, with speeches. Today he was shuffling along with stiff knees like somebody with gout—this also must have been an imitation.

'You know, Tanya didn't believe you would come,' said Nadezhda. 'But Varya and I had a presentiment that you would; I somehow knew you would arrive by that very train.'

'*Jamais de ma vie!*' repeated Sergey Sergeich.

The ladies were waiting in the garden, on the terrace. Ten years before, Podgorin, then a poor student, had taught Nadezhda mathematics and history in return for his board and lodging; and Varya, who was attending Higher Educational Courses for Women seized the opportunity of taking Latin lessons. Tanya, already a grown-up and beautiful girl, thought of nothing but love, desired nothing but love and happiness, passionately desired them, and waited for the lover who filled her dreams day and night. Now, when she was already past thirty, as stately and beautiful as ever in her loose tea gown, with her round white arms, she thought only of her husband and her two little girls, and her expression revealed that even while she was talking and smiling now, those same thoughts were hidden behind the façade, she was constantly on the alert to guard her love and her right to that love, and ready at any moment to throw herself on any enemy who wished to take her husband or children from her. She loved intensely and believed herself to be loved in return, but jealousy and fear for her children were a constant torment to her and prevented her from being happy.

After noisy greetings on the terrace, all of them except Sergey Sergeich went into Tatyana's room. Here the sun did not penetrate through the lowered blinds and the light was dusky, so that all the roses in the big bouquet in the room seemed the same colour. Podgorin was installed in an old armchair by the window. Nadezhda sat down at his feet on a low stool. He knew that besides the affectionate reproaches, the jokes and laughter that were proceeding now and that so reminded him of the past, there would be another, unpleasant, conversation about notes of hand and mortgages—it was not to be avoided—and thought it might be better to talk of business at once, without postponement; to get it out of the way as soon as possible and—then into the garden and the fresh air . . .

'Wouldn't it be best for us to begin with business?' he said. 'What is the news with you here in Kuzminki? Does everything prosper in the state of Denmark?'

'Things are not going well with us,' answered Tatyana with a mournful sigh. 'Our affairs are in a bad way, so bad that it seems impossible for it to be worse,' she said, beginning to pace the room in agitation. 'Our estate is being sold, the auction is fixed for the seventh of August, it has been advertised everywhere and buyers come here and look through the rooms . . . Anybody has the right now to come into my room and look at it. Legally, perhaps, it is right, but to me it is humiliating and outrageous. We have nothing to pay our debts with and nowhere left to borrow from. In short, it is terrible, terrible! I swear,' she went on, stopping in the middle of the room, her voice shaking and tears springing to her eyes, 'I swear by everything that is holy, by my children's happiness, that without Kuzminki I can't go on! I was born here, it is my home, and if they take it away from me I can't go on living, I shall die of despair.'

'I think you are taking too dark a view,' said Podgorin. 'You will get over it. Your husband will take a post, you will start again on fresh lines, begin a new life.'

'How can you say that?' exclaimed Tatyana; now she seemed very beautiful and strong, and the fact that she was ready to fall on the enemy who wanted to take away her husband, her children, and her home was expressed in her face and her whole figure with peculiar sharpness. 'What sort of new life would that be? Sergey is looking for something, and he has been promised the position of Tax Assessor somewhere in the wilds of Ufa or Perm, and I'm ready to go anywhere at all, Siberia if necessary, and live there ten or twenty years, but I must know that sooner or later I shall come back to Kuzminki. Without

Kuzminki I can't go on. I can't and won't. I won't!' she cried, stamping her foot.

'You're a lawyer, Misha,' said Varya, 'you know all the dodges, and it is your job to advise people what to do.'

There was only one answer that was both true and sensible: 'You can't do anything', but Podgorin hesitated to say it bluntly and murmured vaguely:

'It needs thought . . . I'll think about it.'

There were two different people inside him. As a lawyer he knew how to drive hard bargains, in court and with his clients he was uncompromising and expressed his opinion bluntly and decisively, with casual friends he allowed himself occasional coarse indulgences, but in his intimate personal life, with people he knew very well or had known for a long time, he displayed extraordinary delicacy, was shy and sensitive and seemed unable to speak out. A single tear, an oblique glance, a lie or even an ugly gesture, were enough to make him shrink into himself and lose all his will-power. Now, with Nadezhda sitting at his feet, his dislike of her bare neck disturbed him and even made him feel like going back home. Once, a year ago, he had met Sergey Sergeich at a certain establishment in Bronnaya Street, and now he felt awkward with Tatyana, as though he himself had had a hand in deceiving her. The talk about Kuzminki, too, put him in a great difficulty. He was used to ticklish or unpleasant problems being settled by judges or juries, or simply by some statutory provision; when they were put to him personally, for his decision, he was at a loss.

'Misha, you are a friend, we all love you like one of the family,' went on Tatyana, 'and I won't try to conceal that you are our only hope. For God's sake tell us what we can do. Perhaps we ought to send a petition somewhere? Perhaps it isn't too late to transfer the estate to Nadya's name, or Varya's? . . . What are we to do?'

'Come to the rescue, Misha,' said Varya, lighting a cigarette. 'You were always clever. You haven't seen much or had any experience of life yet, but you have a good head on your shoulders . . . I know you will help Tanya.'

'I must think . . . Perhaps I shall think of something.'

They went for a stroll in the garden, then into the fields. Sergey Sergeich came as well. He took Podgorin's arm and kept drawing him on ahead, plainly intending to talk to him about something, probably the bad state of his affairs. Walking and talking with Sergey Sergeich was painful, though. From time to time he would kiss you, always three times, he would take your arm, put his own arm round your waist, breathe in your face, and you felt as though he were covered with something sweet and sticky, and would stick to you at any moment; and that expression in his eyes that said he wanted something from you and was going to ask for it, produced a distressing effect, as though he was pointing a revolver at you.

The sun went down, it began to grow dark. Here and there along the line of the railway, lights came on, green and red . . . Varya stopped and, looking at the lights, began to recite:

> Straight runs the line between narrow embankments,
> With mile-posts and bridges and rails,
> And all down its length lie the bones of the Russians . . .
> So many! . . .

'How does it go on? Oh, Lord, I forget everything!'

> We toiled in the heat of the sun, and in winter;
> Eternally stooping . . .

She recited in a magnificent chest-voice, with much feeling; her face glowed with lively colour and tears stood in her eyes. This was the old Varya, Varya the student, and Podgorin, listening to her, thought of the past and remembered that he too, when he was a student, knew many fine poems by heart and liked to recite them aloud.

> His back is still bent as of old with his labours,
> As of old he is stubbornly mute . . .

Varya could not remember any more. She stopped, with a faint, indolent smile, and the green and red lights seemed suddenly pathetic after her recitation . . .

'Ah, I've forgotten!'

Podgorin, on the other hand, had just remembered—it had somehow survived intact in his memory from his student days—and quietly continued the recitation under his breath:

> The people of Russia has toiled and endured
> This highway of iron was built on its suffering;
> Willing endurance will go now to fashion
> A broad road, a bright road its own feet may travel . . .
> The only regret . . .

Varya had remembered the rest. 'The only regret,' she interrupted him, 'the only regret is that neither you nor I will still be alive when that great day comes!'

She laughed and clapped him on the shoulder.

They returned home and sat down to supper. Sergey Sergeich, imitating somebody, carelessly tucked a corner of his napkin under his collar.

'Let's drink a toast,' he said, pouring out vodka for Podgorin and himself. 'We old students once knew both how to drink and make fine speeches, and how to act. I drink to your health, old friend, and do you drink to the health of an old fool of an idealist, and wish him the luck to die still the same idealist. What's bred in the bone . . .!'

All through supper Tatyana watched her husband with jealous tenderness, anxious lest he should eat or drink something that was not good for him. She thought of him as a man much spoilt by women, jaded and world-weary—and this both pleased her and made her suffer. Varya and Nadya were also affectionate with him and watched him anxiously as though they were afraid he might take it into his head to get up and go away. When he wanted to pour another glass of vodka for himself, Varya pulled a stern face and said,

'You are poisoning yourself, Sergey Sergeich. You are a person of sensitive nerves and might easily become an alcoholic. Tanya, tell them to remove the vodka.'

Generally speaking Sergey Sergeich had a great success with women. They liked his height and strong build, his big features, his idleness, and his misfortunes. They said he was very kind, and that was why he was extravagant; he was an idealist, and therefore impractical; he was honest and pure-hearted and could not adapt himself to people and circumstances, that was why he never had anything and could not find himself a settled occupation. They respected and had profound faith in him and spoilt him with their adoration, so that he himself began to believe that he was idealistic, impractical, honest, pure-hearted, and head and shoulders above them.

'Why don't you say something nice about my little girls?' said Tatyana, gazing fondly at her two healthy, well-fed, roly-poly little girls as she put full plates of rice pudding in front of them. 'Just look at them! They say every mother praises her own children, but I assure you I am quite impartial, they really are remarkable children. Especially the elder.'

Podgorin smiled at her and at the little girls, but he thought it strange that this young, healthy, and far from stupid woman, an organism essentially so big and complex, should expend all her energy and vital strength on such a small and uncomplicated task as the organization of this home, which was sufficiently well organized without her help.

'It may perhaps be necessary,' he thought, 'but it is neither interesting nor intelligent.'

'Before he could say knife, the bear was on him,' said Sergey Sergeich, snapping his fingers.

They finished supper. Tatyana and Varya seated Podgorin on a sofa in the drawing-room, and again began talking to him in low voices about business matters.

'We must save Sergey Sergeich,' said Varya, 'it is our moral duty. He has his weaknesses, he is improvident and never thinks of a rainy day, but that is because he is very kind and generous. His heart is just like a child's. If you gave him a million he would have none of it left in a month's time, he would have given it all away.'

'True, true,' said Tatyana, with tears running down her face. 'I have had a lot to suffer with him, but I must confess he is a marvellous person.'

Neither of them could restrain herself from the small cruelty of saying reproachfully to Podgorin,

'Your generation isn't like that, Misha!'

'What have generations got to do with it?' thought Podgorin. 'After all, Losev is only about six years older than me, not more.'

'Life isn't easy in this world,' said Varya with a sigh. 'There is always the threat of some loss hanging over you. Now they try to take your estate away, now somebody falls ill and you are afraid they will die—and so on all the time. But there is nothing to be done about it, my friends.

We must submit to a higher will without repining, we must remember that nothing in this world is accidental, everything has an ultimate aim. Misha, you haven't lived or suffered much yet, and you will laugh at me; laugh if you like, but all the same I tell you that several times when I was in the most acute trouble I had a clairvoyant experience which completely changed my outlook, and now I know that nothing ever occurs by chance and that everything that happens in the course of our lives is fore-ordained.'

How little this Varya, grey-haired, tightly corseted, wearing a fashionable dress with puffed sleeves, this Varya twisting a cigarette in long thin fingers that for some reason were trembling, this Varya easily lapsing into mysticism, and talking in a languid monotone—how little this Varya resembled Varya the student, auburn-haired, gay, noisy, and daring . . .

'What has become of all that?' he thought, bored with listening to her.

'Sing something for us, Va,' he said, to cut short this talk about clairvoyance. 'You used to sing well once.'

'Ah, Misha, that's an old story now.'

'Well, recite some Nekrasov.'

'I've forgotten it all. That bit just now came out quite unexpectedly.'

In spite of the corset and the puff sleeves it was obvious that she was badly off, and went hungry at that mill on the other side of Tula. It was very obvious, too, that she was overworked; hard, monotonous work, her constant intervention in other people's affairs, and her worries about other people had aged and wearied her, and Podgorin, looking now at her sad, faded face, thought that help was really needed not for Kuzminki or Sergey Sergeich, on whose behalf she was taking so much trouble, but for herself.

Higher education and the fact that she had become a doctor did not seem to have touched the woman in her. In exactly the same way as Tatyana she loved weddings, births, christenings, long talks about children, and love-stories with happy endings, and read nothing in the newspapers but accounts of fires, floods, and ceremonial occasions; she was very anxious that Podgorin should propose to Nadezhda, and if it had happened would have wept with emotion.

He did not know whether it was by chance or through Varya's contrivance that he was left alone with Nadezhda, but the mere suspicion that he was being watched and that something was wanted from him disturbed and embarrassed him, and in Nadezhda's company he felt as though he had been put into a cage with her.

'Let's go into the garden,' she said.

They went into the garden, he dissatisfied, annoyed, and not knowing what to talk about, and she proud and happy to have him near her, evidently pleased that he would be staying another three days, and perhaps full of sweet dreams and hopes. He did not know whether she loved him, but he did know that she had grown used to and fond of him long ago and still saw him as her tutor, and that there was now going on inside her the same process as had gone on previously in her sister Tatyana; that is that she thought of nothing but love, getting married as soon as possible, and having a husband, children, and home of her own. She still kept the emotions of friendship, which children feel so strongly, and it was altogether possible that she simply respected Podgorin and was fond of him as a friend, but was in love not with him but with her dreams of a husband and children.

'It is getting dark,' he said.

'Yes. The moon rises late now.'

Their walk was confined to one path round the house. Podgorin did not want to go deeper into the garden: it was darker there and he would have had to take Nadezhda's arm and come very close to her. There were shadows moving on the terrace, and it seemed to him that these were Tatyana and Varya and that they were watching him.

'I want to ask your advice,' said Nadezhda, standing still. 'If Kuzminki is sold Sergey Sergeich will go away to work, and then our lives will be completely altered. I shall not go with my sister, I shall leave her, because I don't want to be a burden to her family. I shall have to work. I shall go somewhere in Moscow, earn some money, and help my sister and her husband. You will give me some advice, won't you?'

Altogether unacquainted with hard work, she was now inspired by the idea of an independent life of labour and, as could be read in her face, full of plans for the future; and that life, in which she would work and help others, seemed to her fine and romantic. He could see her pale face and dark eyebrows close to him, and he remembered what an apt and intelligent pupil she had been, how full of natural promise, and what a pleasure it had been to teach her. And now she was probably not just a young lady looking for a husband, but an intelligent, noble young girl of unusual goodness, with a meek, gentle heart, who might be moulded like wax into any shape you chose, and who, if she found the right environment, might become a superb woman.

'Why not marry her, after all?' thought Podgorin, but the idea alarmed him and he began to walk towards the house.

Tatyana was sitting at the piano in the drawing-room, and her playing vividly brought back the old days when they used to play, sing, and dance in that drawing-room far into the night, with the windows open and the birds singing in the garden and down by the river. He became more cheerful and indeed high-spirited, danced with Nadezhda and Varya, and afterwards sang. A corn on his foot became painful and he asked permission to put on a pair of Sergey Sergeich's slippers; it was strange, but wearing the slippers he felt at home, one of the family ('like a brother-in-law' flashed through his mind), and was even more cheerful. Seeing him, they all grew livelier and more cheerful, as though they had become younger; all their faces shone with the hope that Kuzminki would be saved. After all it was simple: all that was needed was for somebody to think of something, or ferret through a few law-books, or for Nadya to marry Podgorin . . . That business, moreover, was evidently progressing very well. Nadya, pink-cheeked and happy, with eyes full of tears in expectation of something wonderful, whirled through the dances, and her white dress floated out, showing her slender, beautiful legs in flesh-coloured stockings . . . Varya, very pleased, took Podgorin's arm and said softly, with a meaningful expression:

'Don't run away from your happiness, Misha. Take it now when it has come of its own accord within your grasp, or else you will have to run after it; but by then it will be too late, you will never catch up with it.'

Podgorin felt inclined to make promises and raise hopes, and even to believe that Kuzminki would be saved and that it was quite a simple matter.

'And thou shalt be the empress of the world . . .' he sang, striking an attitude, but suddenly he remembered that there was nothing, absolutely nothing he could do for these people, and he lapsed into silence as though it was his fault. Afterwards he sat silently in a corner, keeping his feet, shod in somebody else's slippers, well out of sight.

Seeing him like this the others also understood that it was no longer possible to do anything, and became silent. The piano was closed. Everybody noticed that it was getting late, time to go to bed, and Tatyana turned out the big lamp in the drawing-room.

A bed had been made up for Podgorin in the pavilion in which he had once lived. Sergey Sergeich saw him there, holding a candle high above his head, although the moon was up and it was light. They walked along a path between lilac-trees, with the gravel grating under their feet.

'Before he could say knife, the bear was on him,' said Sergey Sergeich.

Podgorin felt as though he had heard that line a thousand times. How tired he was of it! When they came into the pavilion Sergey Sergeich took out of his roomy jacket a bottle and two glasses, and put them on the table.

'This is cognac,' he said. 'Number nought-nought. Varya's in the house, and one can't drink while she's there, she immediately begins to go on about alcoholism, but here we are free. It's a magnificent cognac.'

They sat down. The cognac did indeed appear to be a good one.

'Let's really drown our sorrows tonight,' went on Sergey Sergeich, nibbling a slice of lemon. 'I was a student in Germany in the old days, and I still like to shake up my system occasionally. I can't do without it.'

In his eyes there was again the expression that said he wanted something from Podgorin and was on the point of asking for it.

'Drink, my dear fellow,' he went on, sighing; 'otherwise

things get too much for us. The end has come for oddities like me, we're finished. Idealism is out of fashion nowadays. The rouble is supreme now, and if you don't want to be shoved on one side, you must bow down and worship the rouble. But I can't. It revolts me!'

'When is the auction to be?' asked Podgorin, to change the subject.

'On the seventh of August. But I'm not counting on being able to save Kuzminki, my dear fellow. There's an enormous accumulation of arrears, and the estate doesn't bring in any income, only losses every year. It's not worth it . . . Tanya's sorry, of course, it's her family home, but I confess I am even partly glad. I'm no country-dweller. My sphere is the big noisy town, my element is strife!'

He went on talking, but still without coming to the point, and always watching Podgorin vigilantly, as if waiting for the right moment. Suddenly Podgorin saw his eyes very near and felt his breath on his cheek . . .

'Come to the rescue, my dear chap!' said Sergey Sergeich, breathing heavily, 'Let me have two hundred roubles! I beseech you!'

Podgorin intended to say that he himself was pressed for money, and he thought he would rather give the two hundred roubles to some beggar or simply lose it at cards, but he grew terribly confused and, feeling in that little room with its one candle as though he were caught in a trap, and anxious to be rid as soon as possible of that heavy breathing and the soft clinging hands holding him by the waist, began hastily looking through his pockets for the wallet in which his money was.

'Here you are,' he muttered, taking out a hundred roubles. 'The rest later. I haven't any more with me. You see, I don't know how to say no,' he continued irritably, beginning to grow angry. 'I have an intolerably weak character. Only please give me the money back later. I am hard pressed myself.'

'Thank you, thank you, dear friend!'

'And for God's sake stop imagining you're an idealist. If you're an idealist, I'm a Dutchman. You're simply a frivolous idler and nothing more.'

Sergey Sergeich sighed deeply and sat down on the sofa.

'You're angry, my dear chap,' he said, 'but if you only knew how difficult things are with me just now! I am having a dreadful time. I swear to you, my dear chap, I'm not sorry for myself. No, I'm sorry for my wife and children. If it wasn't for my wife and the children I should have put an end to myself long ago.'

His head and shoulders suddenly began to shake and he sobbed.

'That's all we needed,' said Podgorin, filled with annoyance and walking restlessly about the room. 'Really, what can you do with a man who does such an enormous amount of harm and then weeps? Your tears leave me helpless, I can't say anything to you. You are crying, so you must be in the right.'

'I've done a lot of harm? Oh, how little you know me! how little you understand me!'

'Fine, we'll say I don't understand you, only please don't cry. It's disgusting.'

'Oh, how little you know me!' repeated Losev with the utmost sincerity. 'How little you know me!'

'Look at yourself in the glass,' Podgorin went on. 'You are no longer a young man, and soon you will be old. The time has come at last for you to stop and think, to give yourself some sort of account, at any rate, of who and what you are. A whole life spent in doing nothing, a whole life of empty childish chattering, posturing, and grimacing—doesn't it make your own head dizzy, aren't you bored stiff with that kind of life? Difficult with you! Things are tedious enough with you to drive anybody crazy!'

Having said all this he went out of the pavilion and slammed the door behind him. It was probably the first time in his life he had been sincere enough to say exactly what was in his mind.

A little later he was already sorry he had been so harsh. What was the use of talking seriously to or arguing with a man who was always lying, who ate too much, drank too much, spent a great deal of other people's money, and at the same time was convinced that he was an idealist and a martyr? Here one was dealing with sheer stupidity or with inveterate bad habits that had corroded the whole organism like a disease and could no longer be cured. In any case, indignation and bitter reproaches did no good, and one ought rather to have laughed; one good burst of mockery would do much more than ten sermons!

'It would have been simpler to take no notice at all,' thought Podgorin, 'and, most important, not give him the money.'

A little later still he had forgotten all about both Sergey Sergeich and his hundred roubles. It was a quiet pensive night, very bright and clear. When Podgorin gazed at the sky on moonlit nights it always seemed to him that only he and the moon were wide awake and everything else was asleep or drowsy; neither people nor money had any place in his mind, and his mood grew gradually quieter and more peaceful; he felt alone on the earth, and in the nocturnal stillness the sound of his own footsteps had a mournful ring.

The garden was surrounded by a white stone wall. At the right-hand corner of the side facing the open country stood a tower, built long ago, in the days of serfdom. The lower part was of stone and the upper story of wood, with a platform, a conical roof, and a tall spire on which showed the black silhouette of a weathercock. There were two doors at the bottom of the tower, so that it was possible to go through from the garden to the fields, and steps which creaked underfoot led up to the platform. Old, broken armchairs had been thrown under the stairs and the moonlight coming in through the door lit them up, so that with their crooked legs cocked upwards they seemed to have come to life in the night and to be lying in wait for somebody here in the stillness.

Podgorin went up the steps to the platform and sat down. Immediately beyond the garden wall was an embanked ditch which formed the estate boundary and beyond again a wide expanse of open country bathed in moonlight. Podgorin knew that the forest lay directly in front, about two versts from the house, and now he thought he could see its dark line in the distance. Quails and corncrakes were calling and from time to time the cry of a cuckoo, also still awake, came from the direction of the forest.

There was a sound of footsteps. Somebody was walking in the garden and coming towards the tower.

A dog began to bark.

'Zhuk!' called a woman's voice softly. 'Come here, Zhuk!'

He heard somebody enter the tower below him and a moment later a black dog, an old friend of his, appeared on the embankment of the ditch. It stopped, looking up towards where Podgorin was sitting, and amicably wagged its tail. A little later a white figure rose like a ghost from the blackness of the ditch and also stopped on the embankment. It was Nadezhda.

'What can you see there?' she asked the dog, looking upwards.

She did not see Podgorin, but probably felt his nearness, for she smiled and her pale face, lit up by the moon, looked happy. The black shadow of the tower, stretching for a long way over the surface of the field, the motionless white figure with a blissful smile on the pale face, the black dog, the shadows of both—the whole scene was like a dream . . .

'There is somebody there . . .' said Nadezhda softly.

She stood expecting him to go down or call her to him and, at last, speak out and make them both happy on this beautiful, peaceful night. White, pale, and slender, very beautiful in the moonlight, she waited for caresses; her constant dream of love and happiness had exhausted her, it was no longer in her power to conceal her feelings, and her whole figure, her shining eyes, and the happy smile now congealed on her features betrayed her secret thoughts; he, though, was uncomfortable, shrank into himself and became very quiet, not knowing whether he ought to speak and try to turn the whole thing into a jest in his usual manner, or to remain silent. His chief feeling was of chagrin and his thoughts were confined to the fact that here in the country, on a moonlit night, near a girl who was in love and full of romantic dreams, he was just as indifferent as in Little Bronnaya Street—evidently because this poetry no longer had any more meaning for him than that crude prose. Meetings by moonlight were equally meaningless, and so were slender-waisted white figures, mysterious shadows, towers, country houses, and 'types' like Sergey Sergeich or himself, Podgorin, with his cold indifference, his constant disillusionment, his inability to adapt himself to real life or accept what it could give, and his anguished, aching longing for what did not and could not exist on the earth. Now, sitting here, in this tower, he would have preferred a good firework display, or a procession by the light of the moon, or Varya, who would have recited 'The Railway' again, or some other woman, who, standing on the embankment where Nadezhda was standing now, would have talked about something new and interesting, unconnected with love or happiness, or if she did talk about love, it would be only as a summons to new forms of life, higher and more sensible, on the eve of which we are now perhaps living, and of which we sometimes have a presentiment . . .

'There's nobody there,' said Nadezhda.

She stood for another moment and then quietly, with drooping head, set out in the direction of the wood. The dog ran ahead. For a long time Podgorin could still see the patch of white.

'How oddly things have all turned out, though . . .' he repeated to himself as he returned to his lodge.

He could not imagine what he should talk about to Sergey Sergeich and Tatyana, or how he should behave towards Nadezhda, the next day, and the day after that—and he felt embarrassment, fear, and boredom in anticipation. How could he fill the three long days he had promised to spend there? He remembered the talk about clairvoyance and Sergey Sergeich's quotation, 'Before he could say knife, the bear was on him,' remembered that on the next day, for Tatyana's benefit, he would have to smile at her two chubby, well-fed little girls—and decided to leave.

At half-past five Sergey Sergeich appeared on the terrace of the big house in a Bokhara dressing-gown and a tasselled fez. Without losing a minute, Podgorin went to him and began to take his leave.

'It is essential for me to be in Moscow by ten o'clock,' he said, without looking at him. 'I had completely forgotten that I am expected at the notary public's office. Please let me go. When your wife and sister-in-law get up, tell them I apologize, I am terribly sorry . . .'

He did not listen to what Sergey Sergeich said, but hurried away, his eyes constantly seeking the windows of the big house, for fear the ladies would wake up and detain him. He was ashamed of being so nervous. He felt that he was at Kuzminki for the last time and would never come there again, and as the carriage took him away, he looked round several times at the lodge in which he had once spent so many happy days, but his heart was cold and he felt no regrets . . .

The first thing he saw on his table at home was the note he had received the previous day. 'Dear Misha,' he read. 'You have quite forgotten us . . . Come as soon as you can . . .' For some reason he remembered Nadezhda whirling in the dance, her dress floating up and showing her legs in their flesh-coloured stockings . . .

Ten minutes later he was sitting at his desk working, and had already forgotten all about Kuzminki.

ON LOVE

1898

[This is one of a series of stories planned by Chekhov, of which he wrote only three; all are concerned with Ivan Ivanych, a veterinary surgeon, and his friend the schoolmaster Burkin. The preceding story in the series tells how the two, overtaken by rain on a hunting expedition, spent the night on a near-by estate owned by one Pavel Constantinych Alekhin.]

THE next day they had very good patties, crayfish, and mutton chops for breakfast, and during the meal the cook, Nikanor, came upstairs to ask what the visitors would like for dinner. He was a man of medium height, with a puffy face, and small eyes; he was clean-shaven and looked as though his whiskers had been not shaved off but plucked out.

Alekhin told them that his beautiful maid Pelagia was in love with the cook. Since he was a drunkard and had a violent temper, she would not marry him, but was prepared to live with him without marriage. He was very pious, and his religious convictions would not permit him to live in this way; he demanded that she should marry him, he would not have it otherwise, and he scolded her when he was drunk and even struck her. When he was drunk she hid upstairs, sobbing, and then Alekhin and the other servants did not leave the house, so that they could protect her in case of need.

They began talking of love.

'How love is born,' said Alekhin, 'why Pelagia did not fall in love with somebody who was a better match for her in mind and body, instead of that ugly customer Nikanor—everybody here calls him the ugly customer—

and how much questions of personal happiness count for in love—all these are unanswered questions that you may discuss to your heart's content. To this day only one indisputably true thing has ever been said about love, that "these things are a great mystery"; everything else that has been said or written about it does not answer but merely poses problems, and they remain unsolved. The explanation which seems to fit one case has no bearing on ten others; and the best thing, in my opinion, is to explain each instance in isolation, without attempting to generalize. We must, as the doctors say, individualize each separate case.'

'Very true,' Burkin agreed.

'We ordinary educated Russians have a passion for problems with no solution. The usual thing is to make love poetic, and adorn it with roses and nightingales, but we Russians beautify our love with these portentous questions, and what is more, we always choose the dullest of them for discussion. In Moscow, while I was still a student, I had a mistress, a charming lady who, when I held her in my arms, was always thinking about how much money I would give her that month, and about the price of beef. So we, when we are in love, never stop asking ourselves, is this honourable or dishonourable, wise or foolish? what will this love lead to? and so on. I don't know whether this is a good thing or not, but I do know that it is a nuisance, an irritation, and a cause of discontent.'

It seemed probable that he wanted to tell a story. People who live alone always have something on their minds that they would be glad to talk about. Bachelors in towns go to baths and restaurants simply on purpose to talk, and sometimes tell bath attendants or waiters very interesting stories, but in the country they pour out their hearts to their visitors. Now the sky outside the windows was grey and the trees dripping with rain, there was nowhere they could go in such weather, and nothing remained to do but talk and listen.

'I have lived and farmed at Sofyino for a long time now,' began Alekhin, 'ever since I left the university. I was brought up to do nothing, and by inclination I am studious, but when I came here the estate carried a big debt, and as my father owed money partly because he had spent a great deal on my education, I decided to remain here and work until I had paid the debt off. I made my decision and began work, I confess, not without some repugnance. The land here is not very fruitful and to farm it without loss needs either serf labour or hired farm-hands, which is almost the same thing, or running one's farm like a peasant and working on the land oneself, with one's family. There is no middle course. But at that time I didn't give my mind to such subtleties. I did not leave one square foot of land undisturbed, I rounded up all the men and women from the neighbouring villages, and this whole place seethed with activity; I myself ploughed and sowed and reaped, tasks which wearied me and made me scowl with distaste, like a village cat driven by hunger to eat cucumbers in the vegetable plot; my whole body ached and I fell asleep as I walked. At first I thought I could easily reconcile this hard-working life with my civilized habits; I need only, I thought, observe certain external rules. I lived here upstairs in the formal apartments and established the custom of having coffee and liqueurs served after luncheon and dinner, and at night I used to read the *European Messenger* in bed. But Father Ivan, our parish priest, called on me once and drank all my liqueurs at one sitting; and the *European Messenger* got sent to his daughters, because in the summer, especially at hay-time, I didn't even manage to get as far as my bed, but slept in a sleigh in the shed, or in a watchman's hut somewhere in the forest—what chance was there of doing any reading? Little by little I moved downstairs and began to dine in the kitchen; nothing remained of the luxury of my former style of living but all those servants, who had been my father's before me and from whom it would have been painful for me to part.

'Soon after the New Year I was elected an honorary Justice of the Peace. This meant that sometimes I had to go to the town sessions of the District Court, and this was a welcome break for me. When you live here for two or three months without getting away, especially in winter, you finally get to the point of positively yearning for the sight of a black frock-coat. And at the assizes there were frock-coats and uniforms and tail-coats; it was all lawyers, people who had all had the same sort of education, and there was somebody to talk to. After sleeping in the sleigh and eating in the kitchen, to sit in an armchair, in clean linen and light shoes and with a chain round one's neck, was such luxury! I was made cordially welcome in the town and I was very glad to meet people. And of all my new friendships the most stable and, to tell the truth, the one I most enjoyed, was with the Vice-Chairman of the District Court, Luganovich. You both know him: the nicest of men. It began immediately after a famous arson case; the judicial examination had lasted two days and we were tired out. Luganovich looked at me and said,

' "I tell you what! Come and have dinner with us."

'This was unexpected, since I didn't know him well, only officially, and had never been to his house. I only called at my hotel to change my dress before going on to dinner. And then I had the pleasure of meeting Luganovich's wife, Anna Alexeevna. At that time she was still very young, not more than twenty-two, and her first child had been born six months earlier. It is all in the past, and I should be hard put to it now to define exactly what was so unusual about her, and what I found so attractive, although then, at dinner, it was all so irresistibly obvious to me; I saw a woman who was young, beautiful, kind, cultured, charming, a woman of a kind I had never met before; and I instantly felt that here was somebody dear and already familiar, as though I had seen that face and those wise, friendly eyes in my childhood, in the album which lay on my mother's chest of drawers.

'In the arson case the accused were four Jews who were supposed, quite unjustifiably in my opinion, to be a gang. At dinner I was very agitated and distressed, and I can't remember what I said, but Anna Alexeevna kept shaking her head and saying to her husband,

' "Dmitri, how can that happen?"

'Luganovich is a good soul, one of those simple-hearted people who are firmly of the opinion that if a man has been accused that means he is guilty, and that you can't express any doubt of the justice of the verdict except on paper, in legal form, and certainly not at table or in a private conversation.

' "You and I are not fire-raisers," he said gently, "and we are not being tried or put in prison."

'And both husband and wife tried to make me eat and drink more; and from various little things, the way, for example, they made the coffee together, or the way they understood one another with half a word, I was able to deduce that their life was peaceful and happy and that they liked having visitors. After dinner they played duets on the piano, then it grew dark and I went back to my room. This was at the beginning of spring. After that I spent the whole summer without leaving Sofyino, and I had no time even to think of the town, but the memory of the graceful, white-skinned woman remained with me every day of that time; I did not think about her, but it was if her light shadow lay across my mind.

'In the late autumn there was a charity performance at the theatre in the town. I entered the Governor's box (I had been invited there during the interval), looked round and saw Anna Alexeevna sitting beside the Governor's wife, and again I had that same irresistible, conquering impression of beauty and kind, charming eyes, and the same feeling of nearness.

'We sat together, and afterwards strolled in the foyer.

' "You are thinner," she said. "Have you been ill?"

' "Yes. I caught cold in my shoulder, and I sleep badly when the weather is wet."

' "You look tired. In the spring, when you came to dinner with us, you were younger and livelier. You were full of enthusiasm and had a lot to say; you were very interesting, and I own I was just a little attracted to you. For some reason I have often thought of you during the summer, and today, when I was getting ready for the theatre, I felt sure I should see you."

'She laughed.

' "But today you look tired," she repeated. "It ages you."

'The next day I lunched with the Luganoviches; after luncheon they drove out to their *dacha* to shut it up for the winter, and I went with them. I returned with them to town and at midnight drank tea with them in a quiet family fashion, with a fire burning on the hearth and the young mother running in and out to see that her little girl was asleep. After that I went to the Luganoviches' every time I was in the town. They got used to me, and I to them. Usually I went in without being announced, as if I were at home.

' "Who's there?" I would hear from the further rooms in that slow voice that seemed to me so beautiful.

' "It's Paul Constantinych," the housemaid or the nurse would answer.

'Anna Alexeevna would come out to me with a pre-occupied face, and she always asked,

' "Why have you stayed away so long? Has something happened?"

'Her look, the elegant, aristocratic hand she offered me, her simple dress, the way she did her hair, her voice, her walk—produced on me every time the same impression of something new and unusual in my life, and something important. We talked for long periods and sat silent for long periods, or she played the piano for me. If there was nobody at home I would sit and wait, talk to the nurse, and play with the little girl, or lie on the Turkish divan reading the newspaper, and when Anna Alexeevna returned I would meet her in the hall and take her parcels, and for some reason I carried them every time with such love and pride, as though I were a boy.

'There is a proverb "The good wife had no troubles, so she bought a pig." The Luganoviches had no troubles, so they made friends with me. If I didn't go into the town for a long time, it meant I must be ill, or something had happened to me, and they both got very worried. They worried because I, an educated man, who knew languages, instead of employing myself with science or literature, lived in the country and went round and round like a squirrel in a cage, working very hard and never having a copeck. They thought I must be suffering, and if I talked and laughed and ate, it was only to hide my sufferings, and even when I was feeling cheerful and happy I could feel their inquiring glances. They were especially touching when things really were going badly for me, when some creditor was pressing me or I could not find the money for a payment that was due; the two of them, husband and wife, would whisper together by the window, and then he came to me with a solemn face and said,

' "If you are in need of money just now, Pavel Constantinovich, my wife and I hope you will not hesitate to borrow from us."

'And his ears grew crimson with emotion. Sometimes, after the same whispering at the window, he came up to me, his ears all red, and said,

' "My wife and I beg you to accept this little present from us."

'And he would give me some studs or a cigarette-case or a lamp; and in return I would send them game, butter, and flowers from the country. They were both well off, by the way. In those early days I often borrowed money, and I was not very particular but borrowed it wherever I could, but no power on earth would have made me borrow from the Luganoviches. But why talk about that?

'I was unhappy. Whether I was in the house or the fields or the shed, I thought about her and tried to understand the mystery of a beautiful and intelligent young woman who had married a dull fellow, almost an old man (her husband was past forty) and borne his children—tried to understand the mystery of that dull fellow himself, a good-natured simpleton, who reasoned with such boring sagacity, hung about at balls and parties, indolent and useless, among the dull solid citizens, with a resigned apathetic air as though he had been brought there for sale, and yet believed in his own right to happiness and to have children by her; and I was always trying to understand why it should have been him she happened to meet instead of me, and why it had been necessary for such a terrible mistake to occur in our lives.

'Every time I went to the town I could see from her eyes that she had been expecting me; and she herself would admit that she had had a certain special feeling all day and had guessed that I would come. We sat together for long periods, talking or silent, and never admitted our love to each other, but hid it timidly and jealously. We were afraid of everything that might reveal our secret even to ourselves. My love was deep and tender, but I used my common sense, I asked myself what our love might lead to if we had not enough strength to fight against it; it seemed to me incredible that my sad quiet love might suddenly and rudely interrupt the peaceful current of the lives of her husband, her children, and the whole household where I was so loved and trusted. Was it honourable? She would have gone with me, but where to? Where could I have taken her? It would have been a different matter if I had had a splendid, interesting life, if I had been fighting for the liberation of my country, for example, or been a famous scholar or actor or artist, but this after all would have meant enticing her away from one set of ordinary, everyday surroundings to another just as commonplace, and perhaps even more so. And how long would our happiness have lasted? What would have happened to her if I had fallen ill or died, or if we had simply fallen out of love?

'She evidently reasoned in a similar way. She thought of her husband and children and of her mother, who loved her husband like a son. If she had given way to her emotions she would have had either to lie or to tell the truth, and in her position both the one and the other would have been equally inappropriate and terrible. And she was tormented by the question of whether her love would bring me happiness, or simply further complicate a life already hard enough and full of every kind of misfortune. She thought she was not young enough for me, not sufficiently energetic and hard-working to begin a new life, and she often told her husband that I ought to marry some good, sensible girl who would be a good housewife and a helpmeet for me—and immediately added that it was doubtful if such a girl was to be found in the whole town.

'Meanwhile the years passed. Anna Alexeevna already had two children. When I went to the Luganoviches' the servants smiled a greeting, and the children shouted that Uncle Paul Constantinych had come, and hung on my neck; everybody was glad. They did not understand what was going on in my heart and thought I, too, was glad to be there. They all saw in me a noble-hearted creature. Both grown-ups and children felt the presence of a noble-hearted creature in the house, and this brought a special charm into their relations with me, as though their lives also were purer and nobler for my presence. Anna Alexeevna and I went to the theatre together, always on foot; we sat side by side in the stalls and I silently took the opera-glasses from her hands—and then I felt that she was near me, that she was mine, and that we could not do without one another, but, by some odd misunderstanding, we always said good-bye and parted like strangers as soon as we came out of the theatre. God knows what talk there already was about us in the town, but there was not a word of truth in anything that was said.

'In later years Anna Alexeevna began to go more frequently to stay with her mother or her sister; she was liable to black moods, and began to have moments when the consciousness of her unsatisfactory, wasted life made her unwilling to see her husband and children. She was being treated for disordered nerves.

'We remained silent, everybody else remained silent, but among strangers she experienced a strange kind of irritation with me; whatever I said she disagreed with, and if I was involved in an argument she took the side of my opponents. Whenever I dropped anything she said coldly, "Congratulations!"

'If I forgot the opera-glasses when I went to the theatre with her, she always said afterwards, "I knew you would forget them."

'Fortunately or unfortunately, everything in our lives comes to an end sooner or later. The time for us to part came when Luganovich was appointed Chairman of the District Court in one of the western provinces. They had to sell their furniture and horses and *dacha*. When we drove to the *dacha* and then, as we were returning, looked round for a last sight of the garden and the green roof, everybody felt sad and knew that the time had come to say good-bye to more than just the *dacha*. It had been decided that at the end of August we should see Anna Alexeevna off to the Crimea, where she had been ordered to go by her doctors, and that a little later Luganovich and the children would leave for his western province.

'There was quite a big crowd to see Anna Alexeevna off at the station. When she had already said good-bye to her husband and the children, and only a moment was left before the third bell rang, I hurried into her carriage to put one of her baskets, which she had almost left behind, on the rack; and we had to say good-bye. When our glances met, there in the carriage, our strength failed us, I took her in my arms, she pressed her face against my breast, and the tears came from our eyes; kissing her face, her shoulders, her hands, wet with tears—oh, how unhappy we were!—I confessed my love, and with a burning pain in my heart I realized how futile, petty, and illusory all the obstacles to our love had been. I realized that when you love, your judgement of that love must arise from something higher and more important than happiness or unhappiness, sin or virtue, in their current meanings, or else you must not try to judge at all.

'I kissed her for the last time, and pressed her hand, and we parted—for ever. The train was already moving. I sat down in the next carriage—it was empty—and stayed there in tears until the next station. Then I went home to Sofyino on foot . . .'

While Alekhin had been talking the rain had stopped and the sun had come out. Burkin and Ivan Ivanych went out on to the balcony; there was a beautiful view from it over the garden and the long reach of river now shining in the sun like a mirror. Their admiration of the view was mingled with compassionate regret that the man with the wise, kind eyes who had told them his story with such simple candour, really did turn round and round here on his enormous estate like a squirrel in a cage, and had not engaged in science or something else which might have made his life more agreeable: they thought, too, of the grief-stricken face the young woman must have had when he said good-bye to her in the train and kissed her face and shoulders. Both of them had seen her in the town, and Burkin even knew her slightly and thought her beautiful.

FROM A CASE-BOOK

1898

THE professor had received a telegram from the Lyalikov factory asking him to go there at once. The daughter of a Mrs. Lyalikov, evidently the owner of the factory, was ill, but more than that it was impossible to learn from the long, clumsily worded telegram. The professor did not go himself, but sent his house-surgeon, Korolev.

From Moscow one had to go two stations down the line and then drive about four versts. A troika had been sent to the station for Korolev; the coachman wore a peacock feather in his hat and answered all questions with a loud soldierly 'Yes sir!', 'No sir!' It was a Saturday evening and the sun was setting. Crowds of work-people walking from the factory towards the station bowed to the horses behind which Korolev rode. He was captivated by the evening, and the gentlemen's houses, and the summer villas beside the road, and the birch-trees, and the quiet mood of everything around, now on the eve of the holiday, when it seemed that the country-side and the woods and the sun were all, like the work-people, preparing to rest—to rest and perhaps to pray . . .

He had been born in Moscow and grew up there, did not know the country, was not interested in country factories, and never went near them. But he had read about them, visited factory-owners and talked to them, and when he saw a factory in the distance or close at hand always thought that although everything was quiet and peaceful enough on the outside, within there must be the impenetrable ignorance and stupid selfishness of the masters, the dreary, unhealthy labour of the workers, wrangling, vodka, and insects. Now, when the work-people respectfully and fearfully moved out of the way of the carriage, he sensed physical uncleanness, drunkenness, nervous tension, and distraction in their faces, their caps, their way of walking.

They entered the factory gates. On both sides the workers' little houses, women's faces, washing, and blankets hung out on the porches, slid quickly past. 'Look out!' shouted the coachman without checking the horses. Here was a wide, grassless yard which held five enormous, fairly widely separated groups of buildings, with factory chimneys, warehouses, and barracks for the workers, all covered with a grey, dusty-looking deposit. Here and there, like oases in the desert, were pitiful little gardens, and the green or red roofs of the houses in which the administrative staff lived. The coachman pulled up the horses sharply and the carriage stopped at a house, freshly painted in grey; in front of it was a small garden with a lilac-tree covered in dust, and the yellow steps smelt strongly of paint.

'Please come in, doctor,' said women's voices in the porch and the hall, and there was the sound of sighs and whispering. 'Please come in, we've been waiting . . . absolute misery. This way please.'

Mrs. Lyalikov, a plump elderly woman in a black silk dress with fashionable sleeves, but simple and not well educated, to judge by her face, looked anxiously at the doctor and could not make up her mind to offer him her hand, she was so timid. Beside her stood another person, lean and no longer young, with short hair and pince-nez, wearing a brightly patterned blouse. The servants called her Christina Dmitrievna and Korolev guessed that she was the governess. She, as the best-educated person in the house, had probably been entrusted with the task of meeting and welcoming the doctor, because she at once began to give him a hasty account, full of trivial and tiresome detail, of the causes of the illness, but without saying who was ill or what was the matter.

While the doctor and the governess sat and talked the mistress of the house stood waiting quietly by the door. From what they said Korolev understood that it was Liza, a girl of twenty, the only child and heiress of Mrs. Lyalikov, who was ill; she had been ill for a long time and had been treated by various doctors, but on the previous night she had had such palpitations that nobody in the house had slept; they were afraid she would die.

'One might say that she has been delicate since her childhood,' said Christina Dmitrievna in a sing-song voice, wiping her lips from time to time with her hand. 'The doctors say it's nerves, but when she was little the doctors drove her scrofula inwards, so I think it may come from that.'

They went to see the patient. Quite grown up, big and tall, not pretty, but like her mother, with a wide, disproportionately developed lower jaw, covered up to the chin and with uncombed hair, she gave Korolev the impression in the first moment of a poor unfortunate creature who had been given warmth and shelter out of pity, and it seemed impossible to believe that she was the heiress to five enormous factory buildings.

'Well, we've come to have a look at you,' began Korolev, 'and make you well. Good evening.'

He introduced himself and shook her hand—a large, cold, ugly hand. She sat up, and it was plain that she had long been used to doctors as, indifferent to her uncovered shoulders and chest, she allowed herself to be examined.

'I have palpitations,' she said. 'All night I was so frightened . . . I almost died of fright! Give me something to take.'

'Yes, yes, very well! don't excite yourself.'

Korolev examined her and shrugged his shoulders.

'There is nothing wrong with the heart,' he said, 'everything is functioning properly, everything is in order. Your nerves must have been playing you up a little, but that is very usual. We must suppose that the attack is over; lie down and go to sleep.'

Just then a lamp was brought into the bedroom. His patient screwed up her eyes against the light and then suddenly grasped her head in her hands and burst into sobs. The impression of an ugly wretched creature vanished and Korolev no longer noticed the small eyes and the coarsely developed lower part of the face; he saw an expression of gentle suffering which was intelligent and very touching, she seemed to him to be all grace, femininity, and simplicity, and he wanted to soothe her not with medicines or advice but with simple words of kindness. The mother put her arms round her daughter's head and clasped her to herself. What grief and despair was in the old woman's face! She had brought up her daughter, grudging nothing, devoting her whole life to having her taught languages, dancing, music, bringing to the house dozens of tutors and the very best doctors, and keeping a governess, and now could not understand the cause of those tears and all that suffering; she was uncomprehending and at a loss, and her expression was guilty, anxious, desperate, as though there was something terribly important she had omitted, something she had left undone, somebody she had not got hold of—but she did not know what or who.

'Lizanka, you . . . again . . .' she said, pressing her

daughter to her. 'My darling, my dearest, my little daughter, tell me what is the matter. Have pity on me, tell me.'

Both were weeping bitterly. Korolev sat down on the edge of the bed and took Liza's hand.

'Come, stop crying, what good does it do?' he said gently. 'After all, nothing on earth would be worth all those tears. Come, we won't cry, we mustn't . . .'

To himself he said, 'It is time she was married . . .'

'Our doctor at the factory has been giving her potassium bromide,' said the governess, 'but I notice that it only makes her worse. In my opinion, if the heart is to be prescribed for, then it should be . . . I forget what the drops are called . . . Convallamarin, would it be?'

Another recital of details followed. She kept interrupting the doctor, prevented him from speaking, and, from the earnest endeavour depicted in her face, seemed to assume that, as the most highly educated woman in the house, she was obliged to carry on an uninterrupted conversation with the doctor, exclusively on medical subjects.

Korolev found this a bore.

'I don't find anything very special,' he said, leaving the bedroom and addressing his remarks to the mother. 'If the factory doctor has been treating your daughter, let him continue to do so. The treatment has been correct up to now, and I cannot see any necessity to change your doctor. What purpose would it serve? The illness is so ordinary, nothing serious . . .'

He spoke without haste, as he pulled on his gloves, while Mrs. Lyalikov stood motionless, gazing at him with eyes red from weeping.

'There is still half an hour before the ten o'clock train,' he said. 'I hope I shan't miss it.'

'Can't you stay with us?' she asked, with tears again streaming down her cheeks. 'I am ashamed to trouble you, but if you will be so kind . . . For God's sake,' she continued in a low voice, glancing round at the door, 'stay the night with us. She is all I have . . . my only daughter . . . I was frightened last night, I can't get over it . . . Don't go, for God's sake! . . .'

He wanted to tell her that he had a great deal to do in Moscow, and that his family was expecting him home; it was tiresome to spend the evening and all night in a strange house without necessity, but he looked at her face, sighed, and silently began to remove his gloves.

All the lamps and candles were lit in both drawing-rooms for his benefit. He sat at the piano turning over the music, and then looked at the portraits and other pictures on the walls. The pictures, painted in oils and hung in gilt frames, showed views of the Crimea, a stormy sea with a little boat, a Roman Catholic monk holding a glass of wine, all very cold and dull and uninspired . . . In the portraits there was not a single beautiful or interesting face, nothing but high cheek-bones and staring eyes; Lyalikov, Liza's father, had a low, narrow forehead and a self-satisfied expression; his uniform, with a medal and a Red Cross badge on the breast, fitted his big, plebeian body like a sack. Poor taste, haphazard, unintelligent luxury, as uncomfortable as that uniform; the floors were irritating with their high polish, so were the chandeliers, one was reminded of the merchant who wore his medal round his neck in the baths . . .

There was a sound of whispering from the hall, and somebody was snoring softly. From outside there suddenly came a harsh broken metallic clamour, such as Korolev had never heard before, and which he did not understand now; it aroused strange unpleasant echoes in his heart.

'I don't think I would live here for anything on earth . . .' he thought, beginning to look through the music again.

'Doctor, please come and have something to eat,' called the governess in a low voice.

He went in to supper. The table was large, and bore a great deal of food and wine, but there were only two people for supper, himself and Christina Dmitrievna. She drank Madeira, ate rapidly, and glanced at him through her pince-nez as she talked.

'Our work-people are very contented. In winter we have plays at the factory, in which they take part themselves, and magic-lantern lectures, and there is a marvellous tea room, and I don't know what more they could ask. They are very devoted to us, and when they knew that Liza was worse, they had prayers said for her. They are not educated, but they have their feelings too.'

'It looks as though you hadn't any men in the house at all,' said Korolev.

'Not one. Peter Nikanorych died eighteen months ago, and we were left alone. So we three live together. Here in summer, and in winter in Moscow, in the Polyanka. I have been with them for over ten years. Like one of the family.'

They were served with sturgeon, chicken rissoles, and fruit *compote*; the wines were French and expensive.

'Please, doctor, don't stand on ceremony,' said Christina Dmitrievna, eating away, and wiping her mouth with her fist; it was evident that she lived on the fat of the land here. 'Please do have something.'

After supper the doctor was taken to a room where a bed had been prepared for him. But he did not feel like sleep, the air was close and the room smelt of paint; he put on his overcoat and went out.

It was cool outside; enough light lingered to make the outlines of all five blocks of buildings with their chimneys, barracks, and warehouses clear in the grey air. Because of the holiday they were not working, the windows were dark; only in one of the blocks a furnace was still burning, two windows glowed red, and from time to time the chimney emitted flame as well as smoke. Outside the enclosure frogs were croaking and a nightingale singing a long way off.

As he looked at the factory buildings and the barracks where the work-people were sleeping, his thoughts were the same as on every occasion when he saw factories. Granted the theatrical shows for the workers, the magic lanterns, the factory doctors, the various improvements in conditions, all the same the work-people whom he had met today on the way from the station were completely indistinguishable in appearance from those he had seen long ago in his childhood, when there were no plays for factories and no improved conditions. He, as a doctor, who had correctly diagnosed chronic conditions the root cause of which was unknown and incurable, regarded the factory also as a baffling phenomenon, the cause of which was also obscure and incurable, and considered all attempts to ameliorate factory life not unnecessary but equivalent to the treatment of an incurable disease.

'There is something insoluble here, of course,' he thought, looking at the crimson windows. 'Fifteen hundred or two thousand mill-hands work incessantly in unhealthy conditions making bad cotton prints, live on the edge of starvation and only occasionally, in the taverns, wake up from the nightmare; hundreds of people supervise the work, and the whole lives of these hundreds are spent in recording fines, in abuse and injustice, and only two or three individuals, the so-called bosses, reap the benefits, although they do no work at all and despise the prints. But what are the benefits, and how do they reap them? Mrs. Lyalikova and her daughter are unhappy, they are a pitiful sight, and the only person to get any enjoyment out of life is Christina Dmitrievna, an elderly, rather silly old maid in pince-nez. That means the net result of the work of those five factories and the sale of their bad cotton prints in the markets of the East is that Christina Dmitrievna can eat sturgeon and drink Madeira.'

Suddenly the same strange noises that Korolev had heard before supper rang out again. Near one of the buildings somebody was beating a sheet of metal, immediately damping down the reverberations after each stroke, so that the result was a series of short, harsh, blurred sounds, like 'bray . . . bray . . . bray . . .' Then there was half a minute of silence, and from another building noises just as abrupt and unpleasant but much lower in pitch, bass notes, re-echoed—'drun . . . drun . . . drun . . .' Eleven times. Evidently it was the watchman sounding eleven o'clock.

From near a third block: 'dack . . . dack . . . dack . . .' And so on round all the blocks and then behind the barracks and beyond the gates. It was as if the sounds were emitted in the quiet of the night by this monster itself, with its blood-red eyes, this devil that owned the masters and the men here, and cheated both alike.

Korolev went out of the enclosure into the fields.

'Who goes there?' a rough voice shouted near the gate.

'Like a prison, . . .' he thought, not answering.

Here the nightingales and the frogs were more audible

and one was conscious of the May night. From the station came the sound of a train; sleepy cocks were crowing somewhere, but for all that the night was quiet and the world slept peacefully. In a field not far from the factory stood the framework of a building, and the materials for its construction had been piled up beside it. Korolev sat down on some boards and went on with his thoughts.

'Only the governess feels satisfied here, and the factory works for her pleasure. But it only seems so, she is a mere figurehead. The principal personage, for whom everything here is done, is the devil.'

He thought about the devil, in whom he did not believe, and looked at the two windows where the fire glowed. It seemed to him that the devil himself was looking at him out of those two blood-red eyes, the unknown power that had created the relations between the weak and strong, that gross mistake that nothing could now rectify. The strong must be an impediment to the life of the weak, it is a law of nature, but it can be understood and easily fitted into a system of ideas only in newspaper articles and textbooks, whereas in the chaotic muddle of everyday life, the tangle of trivialities from which human relationships are woven, it is no longer a law but a logical absurdity, when both strong and weak alike fall victims to their mutual relationships, involuntarily submitting to some directing power, unknown, standing outside life, and alien to man. Such were Korolev's thoughts as he sat on the pile of boards, and little by little he became possessed by the feeling that the unknown, mysterious power was in fact close at hand and watching him. Meanwhile the east grew steadily paler and time passed swiftly. Against the grey background of the dawn, when everything around was as empty as though all life was extinct, the five mill blocks and their chimneys had a special aspect, different from that they wore in the daylight; the mind quite lost sight of the fact that there were telephones, steam engines, and electricity inside them, and somehow turned involuntarily to thoughts of pile-dwellings and the Stone Age, and felt the presence of primitive mindless forces . . .

Once again, 'bray . . . bray . . . bray . . . bray . . .'

Twelve times. Then a deep stillness for half a minute and, from the other end of the enclosure, 'drun . . . drun . . . drun . . .'

'Terribly unpleasant!' thought Korolev.

'Dack . . . dack ... .' resounded from a third place, broken and harsh as if with annoyance, 'dack . . . dack ...'

It took four minutes to strike twelve o'clock. Then all was quiet; and again it felt as if everything around was dead.

Korolev sat for a little longer before returning to the house, but it was a long time before he went to bed. There was whispering and the shuffling of slippers and bare feet in the neighbouring rooms.

'Has she had another attack?' thought Korolev.

He went out to look at his patient. It was already quite light indoors and in the drawing-room faint sunlight, penetrating through the morning mist, quivered on the walls and floor. Liza's door was open, and she herself was sitting in an arm-chair by the bed, wrapped in a dressing-gown and a shawl and with her hair loose. The blinds were drawn.

'How do you feel?' asked Korolev.

'All right, thank you.'

He felt her pulse and then straightened the hair which had fallen over her forehead.

'You are not sleeping,' he said. 'It is wonderful weather

outside, spring, the nightingales are singing, and you sit here in the dark, thinking.'

She listened, looking into his face; her eyes were intelligent and sad, and it was plain that she wanted to say something to him.

'Does this often happen with you?' he asked.

Her lips moved and she answered, 'Yes. I find almost every night difficult.'

At that moment the watchman began to strike two o'clock in the yard. The 'bray . . . bray . . .' resounded again and she shuddered.

'Do these noises disturb you?' he asked.

'I don't know. Everything here disturbs me,' she answered, beginning to ponder. 'Everything disturbs me. I can hear sympathy in your voice, and from the moment I saw you I somehow felt that I could talk to you about anything.'

'Talk then. I should like you to.'

'I want to tell you what I think. I don't think I am ill, but I am worried and frightened, because I must be, I can't help it. Even the healthiest person can't help being alarmed if, for example, a robber is prowling under his window. I am often in the doctors' hands,' she went on, looking down at her knees and smiling shyly, 'and of course I am very grateful and I don't deny the usefulness of their treatment, but I should like to be able to talk not with a doctor but with somebody near to me, a friend who would understand me and convince me that I am right, or wrong.'

'Have you no friends?' asked Korolev.

'I am lonely. I have my mother, and I love her, but all the same I am lonely. It is the way things have turned out . . . Lonely people read a lot, but they don't talk much or hear much talk, and life is mysterious to them; they are mystics and can even see the devil where he isn't. Lermontov's Tamara was lonely, and she saw the devil.'

'Do you read much?'

'Yes. After all, all my time is free, from morning till night. I read in the day-time, but at night—my head is empty, nothing but shadows instead of thoughts.'

'Do you see things at night?' asked Korolev.

'No, but I feel . . .'

She smiled again and raised her eyes to the doctor with a look so sad and so intelligent; she seemed to trust him, to wish to be sincere with him, and to think as he did. But she said nothing and was perhaps waiting for him to speak.

He knew what to say to her; it was clear to him that she must leave her five mills and her million, if she had one, as soon as possible, leave this devil that watched at night; it was also clear to him that she thought this herself and was only waiting for somebody she trusted to confirm it.

But he did not know how to say it. How? When people have been sentenced, it is uncomfortable to ask them what they were guilty of; so with very rich people it is awkward to ask why they want so much money, why they manage their riches so badly, or why they don't give it up when they can see it is the cause of their unhappiness; and if one begins to talk about these things, the result is usually shamefaced, uncomfortable, and tedious.

'How can I say it?' Korolev wondered. 'Besides, is it necessary to say it?'

He said what he wished to express, therefore, not directly but in a roundabout fashion.

'In your position as the owner of a factory and a rich heiress you are dissatisfied, you don't believe in your right to such things and here you are, unable to sleep;

and of course that is better than if you were satisfied, slept soundly, and thought that all was well. Your insomnia is honourable; at all events, it is a good sign. Really, a conversation such as we are having now would have been unthinkable to our parents; they didn't hold conversations in the middle of the night, they slept soundly, but we, our generation, sleep badly, we worry, we talk a lot and we are always trying to decide if we are right or wrong. But for our children or grandchildren that question—whether they are right or wrong—will have been settled. Things will be clearer to them. Life will be good about fifty years from now, the only trouble is that we shan't last till then. It would be interesting to see.'

'What will our children and grandchildren do?' asked Liza.

'I don't know . . . Probably drop everything and go away.'

'Where will they go?'

'Where? Where they like,' said Korolev laughing. 'There are plenty of places for a good, clever man to go.'

He looked at his watch.

'But the sun is up by now,' he said. 'It is time you went to sleep. Get undressed and sleep yourself into health. I am very pleased to have met you,' he went on, shaking hands with her. 'You are a fine, interesting person. Good night!'

He went to his room and to bed.

The next morning when the carriage came round for him, everybody went out to the porch to see him off. Liza was dressed for Sunday in a white dress, with a flower in her hair, pale and languid; she looked at him as she had done the day before, sadly and wisely, smiled, talked, and did everything with an expression of wanting to say something special and important to him—to him alone. They could hear the larks singing and the church bells ringing. The mill windows all shone brightly, and as he drove to the station Korolev had forgotten about the work-people, and the pile dwellings, and the devil, and thought of the time, perhaps already near, when life would be as bright and joyful as this peaceful Sunday morning; and of how pleasant it was to drive in a good carriage, behind a troika, on a fine spring morning like this, and warm oneself in the sunshine.

THE DARLING

1898

OLENKA, the daughter of Collegiate Assessor Plemyannikov, retired, sat in a thoughtful mood on the veranda in her own courtyard. It was hot; the flies were annoyingly persistent, and it was pleasant to think that it would soon be evening. Dark rain-clouds were moving up from the east, and every now and then a breath of moisture was wafted from that quarter.

Kukin, the proprietor and manager of the Tivoli pleasure gardens, who lived here in a lodge in the courtyard, was standing in the middle of it looking up at the sky.

'Rain again!' he said in despair. 'It's going to rain again! Rain every day, every blessed day—it might be doing it on purpose! It's disastrous, you know. It's ruin! Terrible losses every day!'

He clasped his hands and went on, addressing Olenka: 'What a life, Olga Semenovna! I could cry! You work, you try hard, you wear yourself out, you don't sleep at nights, you're always thinking what's the best thing to do—and what happens? On one side there's the public—everyone knows they're a lot of ignorant savages. I give them the very best of musical comedies with charming scenic effects and marvellous comedians for topical songs, but do they want that? Do they understand any of it? They want cheap fair-ground rubbish. Give them vulgarity! On the other hand, just look at the weather! Rain almost every evening. From the time it set in, on the tenth of May, and all through May and June—absolutely frightful! The public doesn't come, but I have to pay the rent, don't I? And the artists?'

The next day the clouds gathered again towards evening, and Kukin said with an hysterical laugh, 'Well, what does it matter? Let it rain! Let it flood the whole garden, and me with it! Take away all my happiness in this world and the next! Let the artists take me to court! What's a court? Let them send me to penal servitude in Siberia! Or to the scaffold! Ha, ha, ha!'

And the next day the same thing again . . .

Olenka listened to Kukin silently and seriously, and once or twice tears came into her eyes. In the end, his misfortunes touched her heart and she fell in love with him. He was short and skinny, with a yellow face, and he combed back the hair on his temples and spoke in a thin tenor voice, with much twisting of the lips; his face always wore a despairing expression, but all the same he had awakened real and profound emotion within her. She was always in love with somebody or other; she could not live without it. Earlier she had loved her dear papa, who was now a sick man, sitting in an arm-chair in a darkened room and breathing laboriously; she loved the aunt who sometimes, once or twice a year, came from Bryansk to see them; and earlier still, when she was at school, she had been in love with her French master. She was a gentle, good-humoured, soft-hearted young lady, blooming with health, and with a meek soft glance. Looking at her plump pink cheeks, the dark mole on her soft white neck, and the good-natured artless smile with which she listened to anything pleasant, the men thought, 'Yes, not bad . . .', and smiled too, and lady visitors could not refrain from suddenly grasping her hand in the middle of a conversation and saying in a gush of delight, 'Darling!'

The house in which she had lived since she was born, and which was secured to her by her father's will, was in the Gipsy Quarter on the outskirts of the town, not far from the Tivoli Gardens; in the evening she could hear the music playing and the rockets bursting in the gardens, and it seemed to her that Kukin was battling with his fate and taking his chief enemy—the indifferent public—by storm; she felt a sweet sinking of the heart, she had no wish for sleep, and when he returned home in the early hours, she knocked softly at her bedroom window and, showing him only her face and one shoulder through the curtain, smiled warmly . . .

He proposed and they were married. When he had a proper view of her neck and full healthy shoulders, he clasped his hands and said, 'Darling!'

He was happy, but as it rained on the wedding day and afterwards during the night, his face did not lose its expression of despair.

After the wedding they lived pleasantly enough. She sat in the box-office, looked after the arrangements in the gardens, made notes of the expenses, and distributed the wages and salaries, and her rosy cheeks and good-natured, artless, almost radiant smile appeared now in the box-office window, now in the wings, now in the bar. She had already begun telling her acquaintances that the most notable, the most important and necessary thing in the whole world was the theatre, and that only in the theatre could one find true enjoyment and become civilized and cultured.

'But does the public understand that?' she would say. 'They want fair-ground rubbish. Yesterday we gave *Faust Inside-Out*, and almost all the boxes were empty, but if Vanechka and I had put on some insipid trifle, the theatre would have been full to the doors, believe me. Tomorrow Vanechka and I are presenting *Orpheus in the Underworld*; do come!'

Whatever Kukin said about the theatre and the actors, she said as well. Like him she despised the public for its indifference to art and its boorish ignorance; she interfered in rehearsals, corrected the actors, kept an eye on the musicians' conduct, and when there was an unfavourable notice of the theatre in the local newspaper, she wept and then went round to the editorial offices to clear the matter up.

The actors liked her and called her 'Vanechka and I' or 'the darling'; she was sorry for them and lent them small sums of money, and if they occasionally cheated her, she only wept in secret, but did not complain to her husband.

They did quite well in the winter, too. They took the theatre in the town for the whole winter and let it for short periods, now to a Ukrainian troupe, now to a conjuror, now to local amateurs. Olenka grew plumper and was radiant with satisfaction, and Kukin grew thinner and yellower and complained of frightful losses, although business was fairly prosperous all the winter. At night he coughed, and she plied him with raspberry and lime-flower tea, rubbed him with eau-de-Cologne and swathed him in her own soft shawls.

'What a dear sweet person you are!' she would say with complete sincerity, smoothing his hair. 'You are so handsome!'

In Lent he went to Moscow to collect a company, and without him she could not sleep, but spent all the time sitting by the window and looking at the stars. She compared herself at this time to the hens, which also feel restless and are sleepless all night when there is no cock in the hen-house. Kukin was detained in Moscow, wrote that he would return by Easter, and began to make arrangements for the Tivoli Gardens in his letters. But very late on the evening of Palm Sunday a sudden ominous knocking was heard at the gates; somebody was thumping out boom! boom! boom! on the wicket-gate, as though it were a barrel. The sleepy cook, splashing with her bare feet through the puddles, hurried to open it.

'Open up, please!' said a muffled bass voice from outside. 'A telegram for you!'

Olenka had had telegrams from her husband before, but now for some reason she felt numb with apprehension. With shaking hands she unfastened the telegram and read these words:

'Ivan Petrovich passed away today suddenly nycally await instructions fuferal Tuesday.'

Those were the words printed in the telegram, 'fuferal' and the still more incomprehensible 'nycally'; the signature was that of the operetta company's stage manager.

'My darling!' sobbed Olenka. 'Vanechka my dearest,

my own darling! Why did I ever meet you? Why did I get to know you and fall in love with you? Why have you left me all alone, your poor Olenka, your poor unhappy Olenka? . . .'

Kukin was buried on the Tuesday in Moscow, in the Vagankov cemetery; Olenka returned home on Wednesday and as soon as she entered the house flung herself down on her bed, sobbing so loudly that she could be heard outside in the street and in the neighbours' courtyards.

'The poor darling!' said the neighbours' wives, crossing themselves. 'Darling Olga Semenovna, how she suffers, my dear!'

Three months later the sorrowful Olenka, in deep mourning, was returning from mass. One of her neighbours, Vasili Andreich Pustovalov, manager of the merchant Babakaev's timber warehouse, who was also on his way home from church, happened to walk beside her. He was wearing a straw hat and a white waistcoat with a gold chain across it, and looked more like a landowner than a tradesman.

'There is order in everything, Olga Semenovna,' he said gravely, in a sympathetic voice, 'and if one of our dear ones dies, it means that God wills it so, and if that is the case we ought to control ourselves and bear it with resignation.'

He accompanied Olenka to the gate, said good-bye and continued on his way. After this she could hear his grave voice all day long, and hardly had she closed her eyes than his dark beard appeared before them. She had taken a great liking to him. She had evidently produced an effect on him also, because a little later an elderly lady whom she hardly knew called to take coffee with her, and had no sooner sat down at the table than she began to talk without delay about Pustovalov, what a good, sound man he was and how any young lady would be pleased to marry him. Three days later Pustovalov himself called; he did not stay long, about ten minutes, and said little, but Olenka fell in love with him, so much in love that she did not sleep all night, felt burning hot, as though she had a fever, and in the morning sent for the elderly lady. The match was soon made, and the wedding followed.

When they were married Pustovalov and Olenka lived happily. He usually stayed at the warehouse until dinner-time, and then went out on business and was replaced by Olenka, who sat in the office until evening, writing up the accounts and sending out the orders.

'The price of wood rises by twenty per cent. every year now,' she told the customers and her friends. 'Good gracious, we used to deal in local timber, but now Vasechka has to travel to the Province of Mogilev for it every year. And what a tariff!' she would say, covering both cheeks with her hands in alarm. 'What a tariff!'

It seemed to her that she had been dealing in wood for a long, long time and that wood was the most important and necessary thing in life; she heard something dear and touching in words like baulk, tie-beam, laths, joists, and purlins . . . At night she dreamt of mountains of planks and deals and endlessly long trains of wagons carrying timber far out beyond the town; she dreamt of a whole regiment of timbers thirty feet long and ten inches wide, standing on end, advancing to attack the warehouse, and of planks and deals clashing together with the hollow resonance of seasoned wood, falling down and then rising again as they piled one on top of the other. Olenka would scream in her sleep and Pustovalov would say tenderly, 'Olenka, what is the matter, my dear? Cross yourself!'

Whatever her husband thought, she thought too. If he thought that the room was too hot or that business was quiet at the moment, she was of the same opinion. Her husband did not care for any form of amusement or recreation, and stayed at home on Sundays and holidays, and so did she.

'You're always at home or else in the office,' said her friends. 'You ought to go to the theatre darling, or the circus.'

'Vasechka and I have no time for theatre-going,' she answered gravely. 'We are working people, we have no use for trivialities. What good can one find in your theatres?'

On Saturdays she and Pustovalov went to the evening service, and on Sundays to early mass, and walked back side by side from church, their faces full of emotion, both of them sweet-smelling, and her silken clothes rustling pleasantly; at home they drank tea with fine white bread and all kinds of jam, and then ate pasties. Every day at midday the courtyard and the street outside were pervaded by an appetizing smell of *borshch*, roast lamb or duck, or fish, and nobody could go past the gates without feeling hungry. In the office the samovar was always boiling, and customers were regaled with tea and cracknels. Once a week the couple went to the bath-house and returned, red in the face, side by side.

'We are all right,' Olenka said to her acquaintances, 'we are happy, thank God. God grant everybody may live like Vasechka and me.'

When Pustovalov went away to Mogilev Province for wood, she sadly missed him, could not sleep at night, and wept. Smirnin, the young regimental veterinary surgeon who lived in the lodge, sometimes called on her in the evening. He would talk or play cards with her, and this cheered her up. His stories about his own family were especially interesting; he was married and had a son, but he and his wife had parted because she had been unfaithful, and now he hated her and sent her forty roubles a month for his son's keep. When she heard about this Olenka sighed and shook her head, and felt sorry for him.

'Well, God bless you,' she would say, as she lighted him to the stairs with a candle. 'Thank you for sharing my boredom; God keep you, and the Blessed Virgin . . .'

She always expressed herself very gravely and soberly in imitation of her husband; when the vet had already disappeared through the door downstairs she would call after him,

'You know, Vladimir Platonych, you ought to make it up with your wife. You should forgive her, if only for your son's sake! . . . I suppose the little boy understands everything.'

When Pustovalov returned she would tell him in a low voice all about the vet and his unhappy family history, and both sighed and shook their heads and talked about the boy, who was probably pining for his father; and then, by some strange association of ideas, they both knelt down before the icons, bowed to the ground, and prayed that God would send them children.

And so the Pustovalovs lived quietly and peacefully together in love and complete harmony for six years. But then one winter day at the warehouse Vasili Andreich, after drinking hot tea, went out without his fur cap to dispatch some timber, caught cold, and fell ill. He was attended by the best doctors, but his illness ran its course and he died after being ill for four months. Olenka was a widow once more.

'Why have you forsaken me and left me all alone, my

darling?' she sobbed, after her husband's funeral. 'How shall I be able to live without you, poor unhappy me? Good people, pity me, left all alone . . .'

She wore black, with crape weepers, renounced hats and gloves for ever, rarely went out of the house, and then only to church or her husband's grave, and at home lived like a nun. And only after six months had passed did she take off her black veil and open the shutters. Sometimes she could be seen in the mornings going to market with her cook, but how she lived now and what went on in the house could only be conjectured. People made guesses, for example, from the fact that they saw her drinking tea in her little garden with the vet while he read the newspaper aloud to her, or that, meeting a lady of her acquaintance at the post office, she said,

'We have no proper veterinary inspections in the town, and this causes a great deal of illness. You keep hearing of people being infected by milk or catching diseases from horses and cows. We ought to take as much care of domestic animals' health as of people's.'

She echoed the vet's ideas and was now of the same opinion as he about everything. It was plain that she could not live a single year without an attachment, and that she had found her new happiness in her own lodge. Anybody else would have been condemned, but nobody could think ill of Olenka, and everything in her life was so understandable. She and the vet did not mention the change that had taken place in their relationship, and indeed tried to conceal it, but in this they were not successful, because Olenka was not capable of having a secret. When his regimental colleagues came to visit him she would begin, as she poured tea or offered them supper, to talk about cattle plague, tuberculosis in domestic animals, or municipal slaughter-houses, and he would be terribly embarrassed and when the visitors had gone would seize her hand and hiss angrily,

'I've asked you not to say anything about things you don't understand! When we vets are talking among ourselves, please don't interfere. It ends by being a nuisance!'

She used to look at him in consternation and alarm and ask,

'What can I talk about then, Volodechka?'

With tears in her eyes she would throw her arms round him and beg him not to be angry, and they were both happy.

This happiness did not last for very long, however. The veterinary surgeon went away with his regiment for ever, since the regiment was being transferred to a very distant post, almost in Siberia. And Olenka was left alone.

This time she was really alone. Her father had been dead a long time and his chair lay in the attic, covered with dust and minus a leg. She grew thin and plain, and in the street passers-by no longer looked at her as they used to, or smiled at her; her best years were evidently past and left behind, and now a new kind of life, unknown and best not thought about, was beginning. In the evening Olenka sat on the veranda and heard the band playing and rockets bursting in the Tivoli Gardens, but this no longer brought any ideas into her mind. She gazed indifferently at her empty courtyard, thinking of nothing, desirous of nothing, and afterwards, when it was dark, went to bed and dreamed of her empty courtyard. She ate and drank like an automaton.

The chief thing, and the worst of all, was that she no longer had any opinions. She saw objects around her and understood all that was going on, but she could not form an opinion about anything and did not know what to talk about. And how terrible it is not to have any opinions! You see, for example, a bottle standing on the table, or the rain coming down, or a peasant driving a cart, but what the bottle or the rain or the peasant is for, what sense there is in them, you can't say, and you wouldn't speak about them even for a thousand roubles. In Kukin's and Pustovalov's day, and afterwards in the vet's, Olenka could explain anything and would have expressed an opinion on anything you liked, but now her mind and her heart were as empty as her courtyard, and she was as uneasy and bitter as though she had eaten an enormous quantity of wormwood.

Little by little the town expanded on all sides; the Gipsy Quarter was already called a street, and where the Tivoli Gardens and the timber yard had been, houses had sprung up and a network of side streets was taking shape. How quickly the time flies! Olenka's house had darkened, the roof was rusty, the cart-shed was warped out of shape, and the whole courtyard was overgrown with tall grass and stinging nettles. Olenka herself had grown old and plain; in summer she sat on her veranda and her soul, as before, was empty and dull and tasted of wormwood, and in winter she sat by the window and looked at the snow. With the first breath of spring, or the sound of church bells borne on the wind, memories of the past would rush in upon her, she would feel a sweet contraction of the heart and abundant tears would flow from her eyes, but it was only for a minute, and then everything was empty again and it was impossible to find a reason for living. Bryska the black cat would rub up against her and purr softly, but these feline endearments left Olenka unmoved. That was not what she needed! She needed a love which would possess her whole being, all her mind and soul, furnish her with ideas and her life with purpose and warm her ageing blood. And she would shake black Bryska off her lap and say irritably,

'Go away, go away! . . . You're not wanted here!'

So day followed day and year followed year—with never a joy, never an opinion. Whatever Mavra, the cook, said was good enough.

Late one warm July afternoon, when the town cattle were being driven along the street and the whole courtyard was full of clouds of dust, somebody suddenly knocked at the wicket-gate. Olenka herself went to open it and was thunderstruck when she looked out: outside the gate stood Smirnin, the vet, now grey-haired and in civilian dress. All her memories were revived on the instant and she lost her self-control, burst into tears and, without a word, laid her head on his shoulder, so deeply moved that she did not notice how they went into the house together and sat down to drink tea.

'My darling!', she murmured, shaking with joy. 'Vladimir Platonych! What good angel has brought you here?'

'I want to settle down here for good,' he told her. 'I have resigned and now here I am, come to try my luck as a free man, and live a settled life. Besides, it is time to put my son into a school. He's grown. I've made it up with my wife, you know.'

'Where is she?' asked Olenka.

'She's with the boy at the hotel, while I am going round looking for somewhere to live.'

'Good Lord, my dear, take my house! What is wrong with it as somewhere to live? Good gracious, I won't take any rent for it, either,' and Olenka, becoming excited, again burst into tears. 'Live here; the lodge is quite big enough for me. Oh Lord, what joy!'

The next day the roof of the house was already being painted and the walls whitewashed, and Olenka, arms akimbo, was walking about the courtyard giving orders. The old smile lighted her face and she had become livelier and fresher, as though she had awakened from a long sleep. The vet's wife, a thin plain woman with short hair and a petulant expression, had come, bringing with her the little boy Sasha, small for his age (he was nine years old) and chubby, with bright blue eyes and dimpled cheeks. Hardly had the little boy entered the courtyard than he was chasing the cat, and his cheerful, happy laughter rang out.

'Is it your cat, auntie?' he asked Olenka. 'When it has kittens, please give us one. Mama is very frightened of mice.'

Olenka talked to him and gave him tea, and felt a sudden warmth and a sweet faintness at her heart, as though he were her own son. In the evening, when he sat in the dining-room learning his lessons, she watched him warmly and compassionately and whispered,

'My darling, my little beauty . . . My dear child, you are so clever and so fair.'

'An island,' he read out, 'is a piece of land entirely surrounded by water.'

'An island is a piece of land,' she repeated, and it was the first statement she had made with conviction after so many years of silence and emptiness of ideas.

She already had her own opinions, and at supper talked to Sasha's parents of how difficult it is for children to be educated in a high school, but how all the same a classical education is better than a modern one, since from a high school all roads are open: you can be a doctor, if you like, or an engineer, if that is what you want.

Sasha began going to the high school. His mother went away to her sister's in Kharkov and did not return; his father went off every day to inspect herds of cattle, and sometimes was away from home for two or three days, and it seemed to Olenka that Sasha was completely neglected, that he was not wanted in the house, and that he was dying of starvation; and she took him into the lodge and established him in a little room there.

Now Sasha has been living with her in the lodge for six whole months. Every morning Olenka goes into his room; he is sound asleep with his hand under his cheek, his breathing imperceptible. She is sorry to have to wake him.

'Sashenka', she says sorrowfully, 'get up, darling! It's time for school.'

He gets up, dresses, and says his prayers, then sits down to breakfast; he drinks three glasses of tea and eats two big cracknels and half a French loaf with butter. He is still not quite awake, and therefore out of humour.

'You haven't learnt your fable properly, Sashenka,' says Olenka, looking at him as though she were seeing him off on a long journey. 'What a lot of trouble you give me! You must try, darling, and study hard . . . Do what your teachers tell you.'

'Oh, drop it, please!' says Sasha.

Then he walks along the road to school, very small, but wearing a big cap, with his satchel on his back. Olenka walks silently behind him.

'Sashenka-a-a!' she calls.

He looks round and she thrusts a date or a caramel into his hand. When they turn into the street where the school stands he is ashamed to be seen being followed by a tall stout woman; he looks round and says,

'You go home, auntie; I can get there by myself now.'

She stands and watches him without taking her eyes off him until he vanishes under the school entrance. Oh, how much she loves him! Of all her previous attachments not one was so profound, never before has she surrendered her whole heart and soul so defencelessly and unselfishly, or with such consolation, as now, when her maternal feeling goes on burning brighter and brighter. For this child who belongs to somebody else, for the dimples in his cheeks and his school cap, she would give her whole life, and give it gladly, with tears of tenderness. Why? Who knows why?

When she has taken Sasha to school, she goes quietly home, happy, peaceful, and overflowing with love; her face has grown younger in the past half-year and is radiant and smiling; it gives pleasure to the passers-by to look at her and they say,

'Good morning, darling Olga Semenovna! How are you getting on, darling?'

'They have to work very hard at school now', she tells people at the market. 'Seriously, yesterday in the lowest form they were given a fable to learn by heart, and a Latin translation, and an exercise . . . How can a little boy do all that?'

And she begins to talk about the teachers and the lessons and the textbooks—the very same things that Sasha says about them.

At three o'clock they dine together, and afterwards they do the homework together and weep over it together. When she puts him to bed she spends a long time making the sign of the cross over him and whispering prayers, and then, when she goes to bed, lies dreaming of the distant and hazy future when Sasha has finished his education and becomes a doctor or an engineer and owns his own big house, horses and a carriage, gets married and has children . . . She falls asleep still dwelling on the same thought, and tears trickle from her closed eyes down her cheeks. The black cat lies close to her side and purrs, 'Prr . . . prr . . . prr . . .'

Suddenly there is a loud knock at the wicket-gate. Olenka wakes up, breathless with fright and with her heart beating heavily. Half a minute passes, and there is another knock.

'It's a telegram from Kharkov,' she thinks, her whole body beginning to tremble. 'His mother wants Sasha to go to her in Kharkov . . . Oh, God!'

She is in despair; her head, hands, and feet grow cold, and she thinks there is no more unhappy creature in the whole world. But another minute passes, and the sound of voices tells her that it is only the vet returning home from the club.

'Oh, thank God!' she thinks.

Little by little the load lifts from her heart and she feels easy again; she lies down and thinks of Sasha, fast asleep in the next room and occasionally saying in his sleep,

'I'll show you! Get away! Stop scrapping!'

THE LADY WITH THE LITTLE DOG

1899

I

THERE was a rumour that somebody new had appeared on the Esplanade: a lady with a little dog. Dmitri Dmitrich Gurov, who had been staying in Yalta for two weeks and grown used to the place, had begun to be interested in new people himself. Sitting on the covered terrace at Vernet's, he saw a young lady in a fashionable beret, fair-haired and not very tall, walking along the Esplanade; behind her trotted a white Pomeranian.

Afterwards he met her several times a day in the municipal park and in the square. She took her walks alone, always in the same beret and with the white pom; nobody knew who she was, and she was simply called the lady with the little dog.

'If she has no husband or acquaintances here,' Gurov pondered, 'it might be a good idea to get to know her.'

He was not yet forty, but he already had a twelve-year-old daughter and two schoolboy sons. A marriage had been arranged for him while he was still in his second year at the university, and now his wife seemed to be half as old again as he. She was tall and dark-browed, an outspoken, serious, stolid and, as she said herself, thinking woman. She read a great deal, believed in spelling reform, and called her husband not Dmitri but Dimitri, and he privately considered her unintelligent, narrow-minded and inelegant, was afraid of her, and disliked being at home. He had begun to be unfaithful to her long before, and he had been unfaithful many times, and probably for that reason almost always expressed a low opinion of women, and when they were discussed in his presence referred to them as an inferior race.

It seemed to him that he had learnt enough about them by bitter experience to call them what he pleased, but all the same he could not have lived even a few days without the 'inferior race'. In the company of men he was bored, ill at ease, monosyllabic and cold, but among women he felt free and knew what to talk about and how to behave; he even found it easy to be silent with them. In his appearance, his character, and his whole being there was something charming and elusive that disposed women in his favour and attracted them; and he knew this, and in turn felt some power drawing him to them.

Repeated experiences, bitter indeed, had long since taught him that every intimate relationship, although at first lending so pleasing a variety to life and appearing in the guise of an easy and delightful adventure, inevitably developed, between people leading well-ordered lives, and especially irresolute and unenterprising Muscovites, into an extraordinarily complicated problem, and that in the end the situation always became tiresome. But at every new encounter with an attractive woman the experience somehow slipped his mind, he was filled with the desire to live, and everything seemed extremely simple and amusing.

Late one afternoon, then, he was dining in an open-air restaurant when the lady in the beret drifted up to occupy the next table. Her expression, the way she walked, her clothes, the way she did her hair, all told him that she came from a respectable section of society, was married, and in Yalta for the first time, alone, and bored . . . There is much untruth in the stories of the impurity of local morals, and he despised them, knowing that for the most part they were invented by people who would themselves have been willing to transgress if they had known how; but when the lady sat down at the next table, three paces away from him, he remembered those stories of easy conquests and trips into the mountains, and was suddenly captivated by the alluring idea of a quick, transitory attachment, a romance with an unknown woman of whose very name he was ignorant.

He made friendly overtures to the pom and then, when it approached, shook his finger threateningly at it. The pom growled. Gurov shook his finger again.

The lady glanced at him and immediately lowered her eyes.

'He doesn't bite,' she said, blushing.

'May I give him a bone?' he asked, and when she nodded her head, went on politely, 'Have you been long in Yalta?'

'About five days.'

'And I've endured it almost to the end of my second week.'

There was a short silence.

'The time goes quickly, and yet it is so boring here!' she said, not looking at him.

'It's the fashion to say it's boring here. The native of Belev or Zhizdra lives his life there without being bored, but let him come here and it is, "Oh, what boredom! And the dust!" You would think he came from Granada.'

She laughed. Then both continued their dinners in silence, like strangers; but afterwards they walked away side by side, striking up the light playful conversation of people who are contented and at leisure and do not mind where they go or what they talk about. They strolled along talking of the strange light on the sea; the water was a soft, warm lilac colour, and the moon made a golden stripe across it. They talked of how airless it was after the hot day. Gurov told her that he was a native of Moscow, educated as a philologist but working in a bank, had once trained to sing in a private opera company but later gave it up, and had two houses in Moscow . . . From her he learned that she had grown up in St. Petersburg but married in a provincial town, where she had been living for two years, that she would be staying in Yalta about a month longer, and that her husband, who also needed a rest, would perhaps come to fetch her. She was quite unable to say whether her husband worked for the Provincial Administration or the Board of the Provincial *Zemstvo*, and she herself found this very amusing. Gurov learnt also that she was called Anna Sergeevna.

Afterwards, in his hotel room, he thought about her and about the fact that they would probably meet the next day. They must. Getting into bed, he remembered that not so very long ago she had still been at school being educated, just as his daughter was now, and remembered too how much shyness and stiffness there still was in her laughter and her conversation with a stranger—this must be the first time in her life she had been alone in circumstances where she could be followed and watched and talked to, all with one secret end in view, at which she could not help but guess. He remembered her thin frail neck and beautiful grey eyes.

'There is something pathetic about her, all the same,' he thought as he fell asleep.

II

A week had passed since their first meeting. It was a holiday. It was stuffy indoors, and outside the wind raised whirling clouds of dust and blew people's hats off. It was a thirsty day, and Gurov made frequent calls at the café terrace, offering Anna Sergeevna now fruit drinks and now ice-cream. There was no escaping from the heat.

In the evening, when the wind had died down a little, they went to the mole to see the steamer come in. There were many people waiting about on the landing-stage; they had come to meet steamer passengers and were holding bunches of flowers. Here two characteristics of the Yalta holiday crowds were extremely obvious: the elderly ladies dressed like young ones, and the great number of generals.

Because of the rough sea the steamer arrived late, after

sunset, and then spent a long time manœuvring about before putting in at the mole. Anna Sergeevna watched the boat and the passengers through her lorgnette, as if looking for somebody she knew, and when she turned to Gurov her eyes were shining. She talked a great deal, asking disjointed questions and immediately forgetting what it was she had asked; then she dropped her lorgnette in the crowd and lost it.

The gaily-dressed crowd had dispersed, people's faces could no longer be seen, the wind had dropped altogether, and still Gurov and Anna Sergeevna stood as if waiting for somebody else to leave the steamer. Anna Sergeevna had stopped talking and was smelling her flowers, not looking at Gurov.

'The weather has improved now it is evening,' he said. 'Where shall we go now? Shall we take a drive somewhere?'

She did not answer.

Then he looked hard at her, suddenly embraced her and kissed her on the mouth, and the scent and dampness of the flowers enveloped him; then he immediately glanced round, fearful that somebody had seen them.

'Let us go to your room . . .' he said softly.

They walked quickly away.

Her room was close and smelt of the scent she bought at a Japanese shop. Gurov, looking at her now, thought, 'How many different kinds of encounter there are in life!' From the past he retained memories of good-natured, carefree women, gay with love and grateful to him for their happiness, however short-lived; and of others, like his wife, for example, who made love without sincerity, with unnecessary talk, affectedly, hysterically, with an expression that said this was not love, not passion, but something more significant; and of two or three others, extremely beautiful and cold, over whose faces suddenly passed a rapacious expression, a look of obstinate desire to take, to snatch from life more than it could give; these last were women no longer in their first youth, capricious, unreasonable, despotic, and stupid, and when Gurov cooled towards them, their beauty roused him to hatred and the lace on their underclothes seemed to him like fishes' scales.

But this time there was an awkward consciousness of the stiff timidity of inexperienced youth and an impression of panic, as though somebody had suddenly knocked at the door. Anna Sergeevna, it appeared, 'the lady with the little dog', had her own peculiar attitude to what had happened, very serious, as though it spelt disaster and ruin, and this seemed strange and inappropriate. Her features grew slack and lifeless, her long hair drooped miserably on either side of her face, and her pose of dejected meditation was like that of the woman taken in adultery in some old picture.

'This is wrong,' she said. 'You will be the first to lose your respect for me now.'

There was a water-melon on the table. Gurov cut himself a slice and began to eat it in a leisurely fashion. At least half an hour passed in silence.

Anna Sergeevna was pathetic; she exhaled the innocence of a respectable, naïve woman who knew little of life. The single candle burning on the table hardly lighted her face, but it was evident that something was very wrong in her soul.

'Why might I cease to respect you?' asked Gurov. 'You don't know what you're saying.'

'May God forgive me!' she said, and her eyes filled with tears. 'This is terrible.'

'You seem to be trying to find excuses for yourself.'

'What excuse can there be for me? I am a low, wicked woman, I despise myself and have no thought of excusing myself. It is not my husband I have deceived, but myself. And not only now—I have been deceiving myself for a long time. My husband is perhaps a good, honourable man, but, you know, he is a lackey! I don't know what he does, or what his position is, I only know he is a lackey. When I married him I was twenty years old and tormented by curiosity; afterwards I wanted something better. After all, I told myself, another kind of life does exist. I wanted to live! To live and live . . . I was devoured by curiosity . . . you won't understand this, but I swear I could no longer control myself, something had happened to me, I could not help myself, and I told my husband I was ill and came here . . . And here I walked about in a sort of daze the whole time, like somebody crazy . . . and now I'm a wicked, common woman and anybody can look down on me.'

It bored Gurov to listen to her; that naïve tone and that penitence, so unlooked-for and inappropriate, irritated him; if it had not been for the tears in her eyes, one might have supposed she was joking or playing a part on the stage.

'I don't understand,' he said softly; 'What is it you want?'

She hid her face on his breast and clung to him.

'Believe me, believe me, I implore you . . .' she said. 'I love a pure, honest life, and sin revolts me, I don't know myself what I'm doing. Simple people say the devil tempted them. And I can say now the devil tempted me.'

'Stop it, stop it . . .' he murmured.

He looked into her fixed, frightened eyes, kissed her, talked to her quietly and gently, and little by little she grew calm and her gaiety returned; they both began to laugh.

Later, when they went out, there was not a soul on the Esplanade and the town with its cypresses looked quite dead, but the sea still beat noisily against the shore and one small boat rocked on the waves, its lantern blinking drowsily.

They found a carriage and drove out to Oreanda.

'I've only just found out your surname, downstairs in your hotel: it said von Diederitz on the board,' said Gurov. 'Is you husband a German?'

'No, I think his grandfather was, but he is Russian Orthodox himself.'

In Oreanda they sat on a bench not far from the church and looked silently down at the sea. Yalta was barely visible through the morning mists, and white clouds hung motionless over the mountain tops. Not a leaf stirred on the trees, the cicadas chirped shrilly and the monotonous, muffled roar of the sea, borne from below, spoke of peace and the eternal sleep that awaits us. That same roar resounded before Yalta or Oreanda existed, it resounds now and will continue to resound with the same dull resonance and the same unconcern when we are no more. In this constancy and this complete indifference to the life or death of each one of us there lies concealed the pledge of our eternal salvation, of the unbroken progress of life on earth and of perpetual fulfilment. Sitting side by side with a young woman who seemed so beautiful in the light of dawn, lulled and enchanted by the contemplation of his fabulous surroundings—the sea, the mountains, the clouds, the wide expanse of sky—Gurov pondered that when you come to think about it everything on this earth is beautiful, everything except what we think and do when we forget the higher aims of existence and our human dignity.

Some man or other—he must have been a night watchman—came up, looked at them, and went away. Even this little incident seemed mysterious and beautiful, too. They could see the steamer from Theodosia arriving, lit by the dawn and with its lanterns already extinguished.

'There is dew on the grass,' said Anna Sergeevna after a silence.

'Yes. It's time we went home.'

They returned to the town.

After this they met at noon every day on the Esplanade, had luncheon together, walked, dined, and gazed enraptured at the sea. She complained of sleeping badly and of palpitations, asked the same questions over and over again, was agitated now by jealousy, now by the fear that he did not sufficiently respect her. Often, in the Square or the Gardens, when nobody was near them, he drew her suddenly to him and kissed her passionately. The complete idleness, these kisses in broad daylight, glancing round in fear lest somebody had seen, the heat, the smell of the sea, and the constant passing before their eyes of idle, well-dressed, well-fed people, seemed to have revitalized him; he talked to Anna Sergeevna of how beautiful and attractive she was, was impatiently passionate, and never left her side, while she was often pensive and was always asking him to confess that he neither loved nor respected her, but saw her simply as an ordinary woman. Very late almost every evening they drove out of the town, to Oreanda or the waterfall, and the expeditions were an invariable success, yielding impressions every time of beauty and majesty.

They had been expecting the arrival of her husband. Instead, a letter came in which he informed her that there was something wrong with his eyes and begged her to go back as soon as possible. Anna Sergeevna left hurriedly.

'It is right that I should go away,' she said to Gurov. 'It is destiny.'

She left by carriage, and he went with her. This part of the journey took all day. When she was sitting in the express train and the second bell had rung, she said,

'Let me look at you again . . . One more look. That's right.'

She did not weep, but she was sad and seemed ill, and her features trembled.

'I shall think of you . . . remember you,' she said. 'God bless you and keep you; go on living. Don't think ill of me. We are parting for ever, we must, because we ought never to have met at all. God bless you.'

The train left quickly, its lights soon disappeared, and after a minute it could no longer be heard; it was as if everything had conspired to put a speedy end to that sweet dream, that madness. Left alone on the platform gazing into the dark distance, Gurov heard the chirping of the grasshoppers and the hum of the telegraph wires with a feeling that he had just woken up. He reflected that this had been one more adventure or incident in his life, and that it was already over and only memories remained . . . He was troubled and sad and slightly penitent; after all, this young woman whom he would never see again had not been happy with him; he had been kindly and sincere with her, nevertheless through his attitude, his tone of voice, and his caresses glimmered a slight tinge of irony and the rather crude conceit of the conquering male, one who was almost twice her age into the bargain. She had always called him kind, noble, and out of the ordinary; evidently he appeared different to her from the reality, which meant that he had involuntarily deceived her . . .

Here at the station there was already a hint of autumn in the air and the evening was chilly.

'It's time for me to go north, too,' thought Gurov as he left the platform. 'Quite time!'

III

At home in Moscow it already seemed like winter; stoves were lighted and it was dark in the morning when the children were having breakfast and getting ready for school, and their nurse made a light for a short time. The frosts had begun. When the first snow comes and the first day of going about in sledges, it is pleasant to see the white earth and the white roofs, the air is fresh and exhilarating to breathe, and one remembers one's young days. The old lime trees and birches, white with frost, have a kindly look; they are nearer to the heart than palms and cypresses, and among them one no longer hankers for the mountains and the sea.

Gurov was a native of Moscow, he got back to Moscow on a fine frosty day, and when he put on his fur coat and warm gloves and walked along Petrovka Street, and on Saturday evening heard the sound of church bells, his recent travels and the places where he had been lost all their charm for him. Little by little he was absorbed into the life of Moscow, eagerly read three newspapers a day, and at the same time declared that it was a matter of principle with him never to read any Moscow papers. He already felt the pull of restaurants, clubs, dinner-parties, and ceremonial occasions, and was flattered by the fact that well-known lawyers and actors visited him and that at the Doctors' Club he played cards with a professor. Nor was he daunted by a full-sized portion of Moscow *selyanka* . . .

He had thought that when a month or so had passed,

Anna Sergeevna would have faded into the mists of memory and he would dream of her and her touching smile only occasionally, as he did of all the others. But more than a month had passed, real winter had set in, and everything was as clear in his memory as though he had parted from Anna Sergeevna only the day before. And his memories burned ever more brightly. When the voices of the children penetrated into his study in the evening quiet, after they had finished their homework, when he heard a sentimental song or a mechanical organ in a restaurant, or when a snow-storm howled in the chimney, suddenly everything came alive in his memory once more: what had happened on the mole, the early morning cloud on the mountains, the boat from Theodosia, and the kisses. He would pace about the room for a long time, remembering and smiling, and then the memories were gradually transformed into day-dreams and in his imagination what had been merged into what would yet be. Anna Sergeevna did not appear in his dreams, but went with him everywhere like a shadow, following him about. If he closed his eyes he saw her before him as if she were alive, and she seemed even more beautiful, younger and more tender than she really was; he too now seemed to himself a better person than he had been then in Yalta. In the evenings he saw her looking at him from the book-case, the hearth, the corner of the room, and heard her breathing and the caressing rustle of her clothes. In the street he followed women with his eyes, searching for someone who looked like her . . .

He was nagged by a powerful desire to share his memories with somebody. But it was impossible to speak of his love in his own home, and outside it there was nobody he could talk to, either among the other tenants in the house, or at the bank. And what was there to say? Had he really been in love then? Had there been there anything beautiful, poetic, instructive or even interesting in his relations with Anna Sergeevna? He had to confine himself to vague hints about love and women, and nobody guessed what he was driving at, only his wife raised her dark eyebrows and said,

'It doesn't suit you at all to play the vain young man, Dimitri.'

One night, as he left the Doctors' Club with his partner, a civil servant, he could not help saying,

'If you only knew what a charming woman I met in Yalta!'

The civil servant got into his sledge and drove off, but suddenly turned round and called,

'Dmitri Dmitrich!'

'What?'

'You were right just now: that sturgeon was a bit off!'

Suddenly, for some reason, these very ordinary words made Gurov angry; they seemed to him gross and disparaging. What barbarous manners, what people! What stupid nights, what dull, featureless days! Frenzied card-playing, drunkenness, greed, constant chatter, always about the same thing! Unnecessary activities, and talk round and round the same topic, usurped most of one's time and one's best energies, and in the end what remained was a stunted and wingless life, a conglomeration of trivialities, from which it was as impossible to escape as if one were in a madhouse or a prison.

Gurov fumed and fretted through a sleepless night and had a headache all the next day. He slept badly during the following nights too, spending much time sitting up in bed and thinking, or pacing the room from corner to corner. His children bored him, the bank bored him, there was nowhere he wanted to go, nothing he wanted to talk about. During the Christmas holidays he made preparations for a journey and told his wife he was going to St. Petersburg to use his influence on behalf of a certain young man—and went to the provincial capital where Anna Sergeevna lived. With what purpose? He himself hardly knew. He wanted to see Anna Sergeevna, talk to her, and if possible arrange a rendezvous.

He arrived in the town in the morning, and engaged the best room in the hotel; the floor was carpeted with thick grey army cloth, and on the table stood an inkwell, grey with dust, in the shape of a rider with his hat in his raised hand and his head broken off. The hotel porter gave him the information he needed: von Diederitz lived in his own house in Old Goncharnaya Street, not far from the hotel; he lived in a very handsome style, kept his own horses, and was known to everybody in the town. The porter pronounced his name 'Dridiritz'.

Gurov made his leisurely way to Old Goncharnaya Street and looked for the house. Immediately in front of it stretched a long, grey fence topped with sharp spikes.

'That's the sort of fence to run away from', thought Gurov, glancing from it to the windows and back again.

He pondered: the government offices were not open today, and the husband was probably at home. In any case it would be tactless and disconcerting to go to the house. If, on the other hand, he sent a note, it might perhaps fall into the husband's hands and ruin everything. The best thing would be to trust to chance. He went on walking backwards and forwards along the street near the fence and waited for an opportunity. He saw a begger entering the gates and being set upon by the dogs, and then an hour later heard the faint, muffled sound of a piano. It must be Anna Sergeevna playing. Suddenly the front door opened and from it emerged an old woman with the familiar white Pomeranian at her heels. Gurov wanted to call to the dog, but his heart suddenly began to pound and in his excitement he could not remember the pom's name.

He went on walking about, hating the grey fence more and more, and beginning to think, with growing annoyance, that Anna Sergeevna had forgotten him and was perhaps already amusing herself with somebody else, so natural a development in the situation of a young woman compelled to look at that confounded fence from morning till night. He returned to his room and sat there on the sofa, not knowing what else to do, and then dined, and then dozed for a long time.

'How stupid and upsetting all this is,' he thought when he woke up and saw the dark windows: it was already evening. 'Now I've had all the sleep I need. What am I going to do in the night?'

He sat on the bed, which was covered with a cheap grey hospital blanket, and jeered angrily at himself,

'Well, that's your lady with the little dog . . . That's your adventure for you . . . Here you are, sitting here!'

At the station in the morning a poster in very large type had caught his eye: *The Geisha* was having its first local performance. He remembered this and went to the theatre.

'Very likely she goes to first nights,' he thought.

The theatre was full. As usual in provincial theatres, a mist hung over the chandeliers and the gallery was restless and noisy; in the front row, before the performance began, the local dandies stood with their hands behind their backs; and there in the Governor's box his daughter sat in the front wearing a boa, while the

Governor modestly concealed himself behind the curtains, and only his hands were visible; the lowered curtain swayed, the orchestra spent a long time tuning up. All the time the audience were arriving and looking for their seats Gurov was searching avidly among them with his eyes.

Anna Sergeevna came in. She sat down in the third row, and when Gurov saw her his heart contracted and he realized clearly that the whole world now held for him nobody nearer, dearer or more important; this little woman lost in the provincial crowd, with nothing striking about her, holding a vulgar lorgnette in her hand, now filled his whole life, was his joy and his sorrow and the only happiness he now desired for himself; and to the accompaniment of the bad orchestra with its cheap, trashy fiddles, he thought of how pretty she was. Thought and dreamed.

A very tall, round-shouldered young man with small side-whiskers had come in with her and sat down by her side; he nodded his head at every step he took and seemed to be perpetually bowing. This was probably the husband whom in an outburst of bitter feeling that time in Yalta she had called a lackey. There was in fact something of the discreet menial in his long figure, his side-whiskers and his small bald patch, his smile was ingratiating and in his button-hole the badge of a learned society shone like a hotel servant's number.

During the first interval her husband went out to smoke and she remained in her seat. Gurov, who was also sitting in the stalls, went up to her and said in a trembling voice and with a forced smile,

'Good evening.'

She looked at him and turned pale, looked again in terror, unable to believe her eyes, and crushed her fan and her lorgnette together in her hands, evidently struggling not to swoon. Neither spoke. She remained seated and he stood, alarmed by her agitation, not venturing to sit beside her. The flutes and fiddles of the orchestra began tuning up, and suddenly he felt afraid and it seemed as though people were watching from all the boxes. Now she stood up and went swiftly towards the exit; he followed her, and they walked aimlessly along corridors and up and down stairways, and before their eyes passed a succession of ladies, men in the uniforms of the courts, the schools and the ministries, all wearing badges, and winter coats hanging on pegs; and the draughts brought them the smell of cigar and cigarette ends. Gurov, whose heart was beating heavily, thought, 'Oh, God! Why are all these people, this orchestra, here? . . .'

In that instant he suddenly remembered how he had said to himself, on the station platform when he had seen Anna Sergeevna off, that everything was over and they would never see each other again. But how very far from over it all was!

On a dark narrow staircase where a notice said 'Entrance to Circle' she stopped.

'How you frightened me!' she said, breathing heavily and still pale and dazed. 'Oh, how you frightened me! I'm half dead. Why have you come? Why?'

'Anna, you must understand, you must . . .' he said in a hasty undertone. 'Try to understand, I beg you . . .'

She looked at him with fear, with entreaty, with love, her gaze fixed, the better to retain his features in her memory.

'I have suffered so much!' she went on, without listening to him. 'I have been thinking of you all the time, I have been living on my thoughts of you. I so much wanted to forget you, to forget; why, why did you come?'

On a landing higher up two schoolboys were smoking and looking downwards, but Gurov did not care, drew Anna Sergeevna to himself and began to kiss her face, her cheeks, her hands.

'What are you doing, what are you doing?' she said in alarm, pushing him away. 'We have both gone out of our minds. You must go away today, go away at once . . . In the name of all that is holy, I beg you . . . Somebody is coming!'

Somebody was coming up the stairs.

'You must go . . .' went on Anna Sergeevna in a whisper. 'Do you hear, Dmitri Dmitrich? I will come to you in Moscow. I have never been happy, I am wretched now, I shall never be happy, never! Don't make me suffer even more! I swear I will come to Moscow. Now we must part! My dear, my dear, my dearest, we must part!'

She pressed his hand and began to hurry down the stairs, looking back at him all the time, and he could see in her eyes that she had indeed not been happy . . . Gurov stood for a while listening, and when all was quiet looked for the peg on which he had hung his coat and left the theatre.

IV

So Anna Sergeevna began to come to Moscow to see him. Once every two or three months she left her home, telling her husband that she was going to consult a professor about her female ailments, and her husband both believed and disbelieved her. When she arrived in Moscow she stayed at the Slav Bazaar, and immediately sent a red-capped messenger to Gurov; Gurov went to the hotel to see her, and nobody in Moscow knew anything about it.

On one occasion he was going there in this way on a winter morning (the messenger had been at his house the previous evening but had not found him there). His daughter was with him because he wanted to walk with her as far as the school, which was on his way. Snow was falling in big soft flakes.

'It is three degrees above freezing now, and yet it is snowing,' said Gurov to his daughter. 'But it is only warm on the surface of the ground, you know, the temperature in the upper layers of the atmosphere is quite different.'

'Why are there no thunderstorms in winter, papa?'

He explained this also. While he talked he was thinking that here he was, going to an assignation, and not a living soul knew about it or probably ever would. He had two lives: one open, which everybody who needed to could see and know about, full of conventional truth and conventional lies, resembling in every way the lives of his friends and acquaintances—and the other passing in secret. And by some strange and perhaps accidental conjunction of circumstances, everything that was important, interesting, and essential to him, everything in which he was sincere and true to himself, everything that formed the kernel of his existence, went on in secret, while all his falsehood, the cover under which he hid to conceal the truth, like for example his work in the bank, the arguments in the club, his references to the 'inferior race', his attendance at formal parties with his wife—all this was in the open. And he judged others by himself, distrusted what he could see and always supposed that every man's real and most interesting life went on under cover of secrecy as if under cover of night. Every personal existence was kept hidden, and perhaps that was partly the reason why civilized people were so nervously concerned about respect for personal privacy.

When he had left his daughter at the school, Gurov went to the Slav Bazaar. He took off his winter overcoat in the lobby, went upstairs and knocked softly at the door. Anna Sergeevna, dressed in his favourite grey dress, and fatigued with the journey and with waiting, had been expecting him since the evening before; she was pale, looked at him without smiling, and hardly let him get into the room before falling on his neck. Their kiss was as long and lingering as though they had not met for two years.

'Well, how are things with you?' he asked. 'Is there any news?'

'Wait a bit, I'll tell you presently . . . . I can't now.'

She could not speak because she was weeping. She turned away from him and put her handkerchief to her eyes.

'Well, let her cry for a little, I will just sit here,' he thought as he sat down in an arm-chair.

Then he rang the bell and ordered tea for himself, and while he was drinking it she still stood, turned away towards the window . . . She was crying with excitement and the painful consciousness that sadness was inherent in the very structure of their lives; they could see each other only in secret and must hide from other people like thieves. Were their lives not lying in ruins?

'Stop crying!' he said.

It was evident to him that the time when this love of theirs would end, unknown as it was, was still far distant. Anna Sergeevna was growing more and more strongly attached to him, she adored him, and it was unthinkable to tell her that everything must come to an end some day; besides, she would not have believed it.

He went to her and laid his hands on her shoulders, intending to soothe her with kindly raillery, and at that moment he caught sight of himself in the glass.

His hair was already beginning to turn grey. It seemed strange to him that he should have aged so much in the last few years and grown so ugly. The shoulders on which his hands rested were warm and quivering. He felt compassionate towards that life, still so warm and beautiful but probably not far from beginning to fade and wither like his own. Why did she love him so? He always seemed different to women from his real self, and what they loved in him was not him but a man created by their own imaginations, whom they had been eagerly seeking all their lives; afterwards, when they found out their mistake, they continued to love him all the same. And not one of them had been happy with him. Time had passed; he had made new acquaintances, become intimate with them, parted from them, but never once loved; he had known anything you like, but never love.

And only now, when his head was already grey, had he fallen really and truly in love, for the first time in his life.

Anna Sergeevna and he loved each other in a very close and intimate way, like husband and wife or very dear friends; it seemed to them that fate had destined them for each other, and they could not understand how they each came to be married to somebody else; they were like two migrant birds, a male and a female, who had been caught and put in different cages. They had forgiven each other for everything shameful in their pasts, they forgave everything in the present, and they felt that their love had transformed them both.

Before, in moments of depression, he had tried to

comfort himself with any kind of argument that came into his head, but now he had no use for arguments, he felt profoundly sympathetic and wanted only to be tender and sincere . . .

'Stop crying, my beautiful,' he said; 'you've had your cry—it's over now. Now let's talk and we will think of something.'

Then they had a long and serious talk about how they might avoid the necessity of hiding, deceiving, living in different places, being parted for long periods. How could they free themselves from these intolerable shackles?

'How, how?' he asked himself, clutching his head. 'How?'

It seemed to him that it only required a little more thought and a solution would be found, and then a wonderful new life would begin; and to both of them it was clear that it was still a long, long way to the end, and that the most difficult and complicated part was only just beginning.

IN THE RAVINE

1900

I

THE village of Ukleevo lay at the bottom of a ravine, so that from the high road and the railway station only the church belfry and the chimneys of the calico-printing works were visible. When passers-by asked what village it was, they were told,

'That's where the sexton ate all the caviare at the funeral.'

Once after a funeral at the industrialist Kostyukov's house, the old sexton saw some caviare among the other good things to eat and eagerly began devouring it; they nudged him and pulled at his sleeve but he seemed bemused with enjoyment: he noticed nothing, only went on eating. He ate all the caviare, and the jar had held about four pounds. Much time had passed since then, the sexton had long been dead, but the caviare was still remembered. Whether it was because of the poverty of the life there, or because people were too unobservant to have noticed anything but this trivial incident of ten years earlier, no other story was ever told about the village of Ukleevo.

The place was never free from fever, and it was muddy even in summer, especially close to the fences in the wide shade of the old willows leaning over them. There was always a smell of waste from the works and of the acetic acid that was used in dressing the prints. The works—three calico-printers and a tannery—were not situated in the village itself but on its outskirts or at a little distance. They were not very large and between them employed no more than about four hundred hands. The tannery often made the water in the stream stink; its waste poisoned the meadow, the peasants' cattle got anthrax, and the tannery was ordered to close down. It was now supposed to be shut, but work went on in secret, with the connivance of the Inspector of Rural Police and the District Medical Officer, to each of whom the owner paid ten roubles a month. In the whole village there were only two decent buildings, made of brick and roofed with iron; one housed the administration of the group of villages which formed the *Volost*, and in the other, which had two stories and stood opposite the church, lived Gregory Petrovich Tsybukin, a shopkeeper from Epiphano.

Gregory kept a grocer's shop, but only as a cover for his real trade in vodka, cattle, skins, grain, pigs, and anything else that came along; when, for example, there was a demand from abroad for magpies for trimming ladies' hats, he made a profit of thirty copecks a pair on them; he bought standing timber, lent money at interest, and was in general an old man with an eye for business.

He had two sons. The elder, Anisim, was a policeman, in the detective branch, and was rarely at home. Stepan, the younger, had stuck to trade and helped his father, but real assistance was not expected of him, as he was deaf and not strong; his wife, Aksinya, a beautiful, graceful woman, who wore a hat and carried a sunshade on Sundays, rose early, went to bed late, and spent the whole day bustling about, with her skirts tucked up and her keys rattling, between the warehouse, the cellar, and the shop. It was a pleasure for Old Tsybukin to look at her, his eyes lighted up when he saw her, and his only regret was that she was not married to his elder son but to the younger, who was deaf and evidently no connoisseur of feminine beauty.

The old man had always enjoyed family life, and he loved his family better than anything else on earth, especially his cherished elder son, the detective, and his daughter-in-law. Hardly had Aksinya married the deaf son than she began to display an unusual head for business, and already knew who could be allowed credit and who not. She always kept the keys in her own possession, not trusting even her husband with them, rattled away at the abacus, looked horses in the mouth like a mujik and was always either laughing or shouting;

and whatever she did or said the old man only looked at her fondly and murmured,

'That's my daughter-in-law! That's my beauty, my darling . . .'

He was a widower, but a year after his son's marriage he could bear it no longer and married again himself. Thirty versts from Ukleevo a girl of good family, Varvara Nikolaevna, no longer in her first youth, but handsome and attractive, was found for him. Hardly had she settled in the little room on the first floor than the whole house seemed to grow lighter, as though new glass had been put in all the windows. Lamps burned before the icons, the tables were covered with table-cloths as white as snow, red-flowered plants appeared on the window-sills and in the garden, and at dinner they no longer all ate from one bowl, but a plate was laid at each place. Varvara Nikolaevna had a warm and friendly smile, and everything in the house seemed to smile too. All kinds of beggars and pilgrims found their way into the yard, a thing that had never happened before; the dismal wailing voices of poor women from the village and the apologetic coughing of thin, sickly peasants dismissed from the works for drunkenness were heard under the windows of the house. Varvara gave them help with money, food, and old clothes and later, when she was used to the place, began to take a few things from the shop as well. Once the deaf man saw her carrying two two-ounce packets of tea and this worried him.

'Mamasha has taken two packets of tea,' he told his father. 'Who shall I charge it to?'

The old man did not answer, but stood for a moment thinking, his eyebrows twitching, and then went upstairs to his wife.

'Varvarushka, my dear, whenever you want anything

from the shop, just take it,' he said affectionately. 'Take it and welcome; don't hesitate.'

Next day the deaf man shouted to her as he ran across the yard,

'If you need anything, mamasha, take it.'

The fact that she was charitable to the poor was something new and bright and cheerful, like the icon-lamps and the red flowers. Just before fasts or during the festival of the patron saint of the parish, which lasted three days, when they palmed off on the peasants putrid salt beef with such an overpowering smell that it was almost impossible to stay near the tubs, or accepted scythes, fur caps, and women's clothes in pawn from drunken men, and when factory workers, stupefied by bad vodka, sprawled in the mud, and sin seemed to hang in the air like a thick fog, there was some relief in the idea that there, in the house, there was a neat, quiet woman who had nothing to do with tainted beef or vodka; at such oppressive, gloomy times her charity acted as a kind of safety valve.

The days in the Tsybukin house were one long bustle. Before sunrise Aksinya was puffing and panting as she washed herself in the passage, while the samovar boiled in the kitchen and hummed like a prophet of doom. Old Gregory Petrovich, dressed in a long black frock-coat and nankeen trousers tucked into high shining boots, and looking small and clean, walked about the room with his heels drumming on the floors like the father-in-law in the well-known song. The shop was opened. When it grew light the racing droshky was brought round to the front steps and the old man got briskly into it, pulling his big cap down over his ears, and to look at him nobody would have said that he was fifty-six. His wife and daughter-in-law saw him off, and at these times, when he was wearing his good clean frock-coat, and the great black stallion which had cost three hundred roubles was harnessed to the droshky, the old man did not like to be approached by rough peasants with their requests and complaints; he hated and was disgusted by them, and if he saw one waiting for him by the gate would shout angrily,

'What are you doing there? Move on!'

Or, if it was a beggar,

'God will provide.'

He used to drive round the country-side on business; his wife, dressed in dark clothes and wearing a black apron, tidied the rooms and helped in the kitchen. Aksinya served in the shop and from the yard one might hear the ringing of bottles and coins, her laughter and shouts and the angry retorts of the customers she had been rude to; it was apparent all the time that the clandestine trade in vodka was already in full swing there in the shop. Her deaf husband also sat in the shop, or walked bare-headed up and down the street, with his hands in his pockets, looking absent-mindedly at the peasants' huts or up at the sky. In the house they drank tea about six times a day, and sat down to meals about four times. In the evening they counted the receipts and entered them in the accounts, then slept soundly.

In Ukleevo the three print-works and the homes of the owners, the Old Khrymins, the Young Khrymins, and Kostyukov, were all linked by telephone. The telephone had been connected to the *Volost* Administration as well, but there it soon ceased to function because bugs and cockroaches got into the wooden base. The Chairman was semi-literate and wrote every word in official documents with a capital letter, but when the telephone was out of order he said,

'Yes, being without a telephone will make it a bit difficult for us.'

Litigation was always going on between the Old Khrymins and the Young Khrymins, and sometimes the Young Khrymins quarrelled among themselves and went to law, and then their works stood idle for a month or two until the quarrel was made up again, and this provided entertainment for the Ukleevo villagers, since there was much talk and gossip about every dispute. On Sundays Kostyukov and the Young Khrymins would go out driving, dashing through Ukleevo and running down calves. Aksinya, dressed in her best, her starched skirts rustling, would be strolling in the street near the shop and they would swoop down on her and carry her off, pretending to be abducting her by force. Then Old Tsybukin would go out, too, to show off his new horse, and take Varvara with him.

In the evening after the drive, when people were going to bed, there would be the sound of somebody playing an expensive accordion in the Young Khrymins' courtyard, and when there was a moon the music stirred and gladdened the heart, so that Ukleevo no longer seemed a hole.

II

Tsybukin's elder son Anisim came home very rarely, only on major holidays; on the other hand, if anybody was returning to the village he would often send presents or letters by them, the letters written by somebody else in a beautiful handwriting on paper of good quality and looking like petitions. They were full of expressions Anisim never used in speech: 'Dearest Papasha and Mamasha, I sent you a pound of herbal tea for the satisfaction of your physical requirements.'

At the bottom of every letter was scratched, as if with a cross-nibbed pen, 'Anisim Tsybukin', and under that again, in the first excellent handwriting, 'Agent'.

The letters were read aloud several times, and the old man, much affected, and scarlet with emotion, would say,

'You see, he didn't want to stop at home, he wanted to be a scholar. Well, he can please himself. Everybody must go their own way.'

One day just before the beginning of Lent there was heavy rain and sleet; the old man and Varvara went to the window to look out, and there was Anisim driving up in a sledge from the station. He had not been expected. When he came into the room he seemed restless and disturbed about something, and he remained so all the time; yet his bearing was somehow jaunty. He seemed in no hurry to leave, and it began to look as though he might have been dismissed from his post. Varvara was glad of his coming; she would watch him with a kind of archness, sighing and shaking her head.

'How's this, my dear?' she would say. 'Well, well, a lad that's twenty-eight already and still a bachelor, dear me yes . . .'

From the next room the murmur of her quiet, even tones always sounded like 'dear me yes, dear me no'. She began holding whispered conversations with the old man and Aksinya, and their faces also took on arch and mysterious expressions, as though they were conspirators.

They had decided to get Anisim married.

'Dear me, yes! . . . Your young brother's been married for a long time now,' said Varvara, 'and you're still without a mate, like a cock at the market. How does that come about? Well, well, you must get married, God willing, and then you must please yourself, go back to your work if you like, and your wife can stay at home and help us. Dear me yes, you've been getting into bad ways, my lad, and you've forgotten what it is to live properly, I can see. Dear me yes, you're a shocking lot, you people in the town.'

When Tsybukins got married, only the best-looking brides were chosen for them, just as if they were rich people. A beauty was found for Anisim, too. He himself was dull and unremarkable in appearance; with his feeble and unhealthy constitution and small stature, he had full, swollen cheeks that looked as though he was puffing them out, sharp unblinking eyes and a thin reddish beard, the ends of which he chewed in thoughtful moods; he was addicted to drink besides, and this showed in his face and walk. But when he was told that a pretty wife had been found for him, he said,

'Well, I'm not so bad myself. We Tsybukins are a good-looking family, I must say.'

The village of Torguevo lay very close to the town. One end of it had recently been incorporated in the town, the other still remained a village. In the town part, in her own little house, lived a certain widow; she had a sister who was very poor and went out to work by the day, and this sister had a daughter, Lipa, also working by the day. Everybody in Torguevo was already talking about Lipa's beauty, and the only trouble was her frightful poverty; it was argued that some elderly man or widower might marry her and not mind her being destitute, or take her to live with him 'as she was', and that through her her mother would be provided for also. Varvara heard of Lipa from a matchmaker and went to Torguevo to see her.

Then the usual 'bride-showing' was arranged at the aunt's house in a fitting manner, with food and wine;

Lipa wore a new pink dress specially made for the occasion, and a scarlet ribbon shone like a flame in her hair. She was rather thin and frail, with fine delicate features, brown from working in the open air; a timid melancholy smile was always on her lips and her eyes were like a child's, trusting and curious.

She was young, no more than a girl, with breasts still hardly developed, but she had reached the legal age of marriage. She really was beautiful, and only one thing about her was not entirely pleasing—her large masculine hands, now hanging idly like two great lobster-claws.

'She hasn't a dowry, but we'll pay no heed to that,' said the old man to the girl's aunt; 'we took a wife for our Stepan out of a poor family too, and now we're as pleased as could be. She's got golden hands, in the house and in the business as well.'

Lipa stood near the door, seeming to be trying to say, 'Do as you will with me; I trust you,' but Praskovya the day-labourer, her mother, overwhelmed with shyness, stayed hidden in the kitchen. Once in her youth the merchant in whose house she was washing floors had flown into a rage and stamped his foot at her; she was so terrified that she fainted, and the effect remained with her for the rest of her life. Her arms and legs were always shaking with fear, and her cheeks quivered. Sitting in the kitchen, she strained to overhear what the visitors said, and kept crossing herself, pressing her fingers to her forehead and gazing at the icon. Anisim, slightly drunk, kept opening the kitchen door and saying in an easy manner,

'Why are you sitting here, dearest mamasha? We miss you.'

Praskovya shrank, clasping her hands to her gaunt emaciated bosom, and answered,

'Oh no, sir, don't . . . It is very good of you, sir.'

After the bride-showing the wedding-day was named. When they got home Anisim spent all his time walking round the house whistling or, suddenly reminded of something, became thoughtful and stood gazing with motionless fixity at the floor, as though trying to probe the depths of the ground with his eyes. He expressed neither pleasure at the fact that he was going to be married, and that very soon, on the Monday after Easter week, nor desire to see his bride again, but only whistled. It was evident that he was marrying only because his father and stepmother wished it and because it was the custom; in the country a son gets married so that there shall be another woman to help in the house. When he went away again he seemed in no hurry, and in general his behaviour was unlike what it had been on his former visits—he seemed peculiarly detached, and what he said was not to the point.

III

In the little village of Shikalovo lived two sisters, dressmakers, who belonged to the Flagellant sect. New clothes for the wedding had been ordered from them and they frequently came for fittings and always sat a long time drinking tea. For Varvara they made a brown dress trimmed with black lace and bugles, and Aksinya's was light green with a yellow plastron and a train. When they had finished their work, Tsybukin paid the dressmakers not in money but in goods from the shop, and they went away sadly with their arms full of parcels of stearin candles and sardines, which were of no use to them, and when they came out of the village into the open country they sat down on a little mound and began to cry.

Anisim arrived three days before the wedding, all in new clothes. He was wearing shiny rubber galoshes and a red cord with beads at the ends instead of a tie; his overcoat, also new, hung from his shoulders like a cloak.

He soberly said a prayer before the icon, then greeted his father and gave him ten silver roubles and ten fifty-copeck pieces; he gave the same amount to Varvara and twenty quarter-roubles to Aksinya. The great charm of these gifts was that all the carefully selected coins were new and glittered in the sunlight. Anisim pulled a long face and puffed out his cheeks, trying to appear staid and serious; he smelt of vodka and had probably made a dash for the refreshment room at every station. There was again a kind of overdone ease and detachment about his manner. Then Anisim and the old man drank tea and had something to eat, while Varvara kept running her hands through all the bright new roubles and asked after villagers who were living in the town.

'They're all right, God be praised, they are getting on well,' said Anisim. 'Only something has happened in Ivan Egorov's family: his old woman, Sonia Nikiphorovna, is dead. Consumption. The memorial dinner for the repose of her soul cost two and a half roubles a head from the pastry-cook's. They had wine too. There were some of the peasants from the village there, and it was two and a half roubles apiece for them as well. They didn't eat a thing. What do peasants know about sauces?'

'Two and a half roubles!' said the old man, shaking his head.

'Well, what about it? It's not the country there. You can go into a restaurant for a bite to eat, you order something, a few other people turn up, you have a drink—and before you know where you are, it's dawn and you've got a bill for three or four roubles apiece. And if Samorodov's there, he likes to finish up with coffee and brandy, and brandy costs sixty copecks a glass.'

'What a liar!' said the old man with delighted admiration. 'What a marvellous liar!'

'I spend all my time with Samorodov now. He's the one who writes my letters to you for me. He writes a marvellous hand. And if I was to tell you what sort of man Samorodov is, mamasha,' he went on cheerfully, addressing Varvara, 'you wouldn't believe me. We all call him Mukhtar, because he's just like an Armenian to look at—all black. I can see right through him, I know as much about his business as I do about my own, mamasha, and he knows it and goes everywhere I go, he won't leave me alone; we're inseparable. He seems a bit uneasy, but he can't live without me now. Wherever I go, he goes too. My instinct is sound and reliable, mamasha. Say you take a look at a street market, and there's a peasant selling a shirt. "Stop, that shirt's stolen!" And it turns out I'm right; the shirt is stolen.'

'But how do you know?' asked Varvara.

'I don't, it's just instinct. I don't know anything about the shirt, only somehow it seems to draw me: it's been stolen, and that's all about it. In our department they always say, "Oh, Anisim's gone snipe-shooting!"—that means looking for stolen goods. Yes . . . Anybody can steal things, it's holding on to them that's the difficulty. As big as the world is, there's nowhere you can hide stolen property in it!'

'Somebody stole a ram and two ewes from the Guntorevs here in the village last week,' said Varvara with a sigh. 'And there's nobody here to investigate . . . Dear me no! . . .'

'What? Well, I might look into it. I wouldn't mind.'

The wedding day came. Although chilly, it was a brisk

bright April day. From early morning the village was full of the coming and going of troikas and pairs of horses with bright-coloured ribbons on the arched yokes and in their manes, their harness bells jingling. The rooks, disturbed by the bustle, cawed in the willows, and the starlings, as though rejoicing over the wedding at the Tsybukins', burst their lungs with incessant chattering.

In the house the tables were already covered with hams, enormous whole fish, stuffed birds, tins of sprats, all kinds of pickled and salted meats and fish, and a multitude of bottles of vodka and home-made wines, and there was a smell of smoked sausage and tinned lobster gone sour. The old man trotted round the tables, drumming his heels on the floor and rattling knives together. From time to time somebody shouted a demand to Varvara and she, panting and looking distracted, ran into the kitchen, where Kostyukov's chef and the Young Khrymins' cook had been busy since dawn. Aksinya, with her hair curled, and wearing her corsets but no dress, whirled about the yard in her squeaky new boots, affording occasional flashing glimpses of her bare knees and neck. There was a lot of clatter, argument and shouting; passers-by stopped to watch through the open gates, and there was a general feeling of something extraordinary afoot.

'They've gone to fetch the bride!'

Harness-bells jangled loudly and died away far beyond the village . . . Soon after two o'clock people came hurrying up: the bells were audible again, they were bringing the bride! The church was full, the chandeliers were blazing, the choristers, at Old Tsybukin's insistence, were singing from music. The brilliant lights and bright dresses dazzled Lipa, the loud voices of the choir beat in her head like hammers, both her boots and the corsets she was wearing for the first time in her life pinched her, and she looked like somebody who has just recovered from a swoon and is gazing about in bewilderment. Anisim in his black frock-coat, with the red cord instead of a tie, seemed moody, staring intently at one spot and crossing himself hastily whenever the choir shouted very loud. His heart was violently moved and he wanted to cry. This church had been familiar to him from his earliest childhood; his dead mother had carried him here to receive the sacraments, he had sung in the choir with the other boys; he remembered every corner and every icon. Now he was being married in it, he was marrying because it was right and proper, but his thoughts were elsewhere, he seemed almost to have forgotten about his wedding. He could not see the icons for tears, there was a weight at his heart; he prayed that God would somehow avert the imminent disaster that threatened to crash down on him at any moment, as thunder-clouds in time of drought sometimes pass over a village without shedding a single drop of rain. He was irretrievably trapped in the morass of his past sins, so many and so irreparable that it seemed incongruous to ask for forgiveness. He asked for it, nevertheless, and even sobbed aloud, but nobody took any notice; they thought he had been drinking.

A child's frightened crying sounded in the crowd,

'Mummy, mummy, take me out of here, please, mummy!'

'Quiet, please!' called the priest.

As they returned from church a crowd ran after them; there were more crowds round the shop, by the gates, and in the yard under the windows of the house. These last were peasant women who had come to sing songs in the young couple's honour. They had hardly stepped over the threshold before the choir, who were already standing inside in the passage with their music, began singing at the top of their voices and a band of musicians, specially ordered from the town, struck up. Long-stemmed champagne glasses of sparkling Don wine were brought to them and Elizarov the carpenter, who was in business for himself, a tall, lean old man with eyebrows so bushy that his eyes were scarcely visible, addressed the bride and bridegroom,

'Anisim, and you, my child, love one another, lead godly lives, my children, and the blessed Queen of Heaven will not forsake you.' He fell on the old man's shoulder and sobbed. 'Gregory Petrovich, let us weep, let us weep tears of joy!' he said in a shrill wail, and immediately burst into guffaws and boomed in a deep bass, 'Ho, ho, ho! You've got another pretty daughter-in-law here! Every part of her is in its rightful place, I mean, all nice and smooth, no rattles, all the machinery in working order, plenty of screws.'

He was a native of the Egoryev District, but had worked in the Ukleevo mills since he was a young man, and felt at home there. He had been as old and long and lean as he was now ever since people could remember, and had borne his nickname, Old Crutch, for a very long time. Perhaps because for forty years he had confined himself to maintenance work in the mills, he judged any person or thing solely from the point of view of working order: were repairs necessary? Before sitting down now at table, he tested several chairs for soundness, and even touched the smoked fish in the same spirit. After the sparkling wine, everybody sat down to table. The guests talked as they moved chairs about, the choir sang in the passage, the band played, and meanwhile the peasant women went on with their songs, all in unison—and there was such a terrible, barbarous mixture of noises that it made the head reel.

Old Crutch kept turning from side to side in his place, bumping his neighbours with his elbows, interrupting their conversation and himself alternating between weeping and loud laughter.

'My children, my children, my children . . .' he said in a rapid mutter. 'Aksinyushka, my dear, Varvarushka, my darling little adzes, let us always live in peace and harmony . . .'

He was not a great drinker, and now he was tipsy from one glass of English bitters. This horrible liquor, made of God knows what, stunned everybody who drank it as if they had been pole-axed. Tongues began to get into tangles.

All the parish clergy were present, with the clerks from the works and their wives, and traders and pot-house keepers from other villages. The Chairman of the *Volost* and his clerk, who had worked together for fourteen years, and in all that time had never signed a single document or let a soul leave the office without cheating or insulting somebody, now sat side by side, both equally fat and well-fed and both by now so steeped in deceit that the very skin of their faces seemed somehow peculiar and fraudulent. The clerk's wife, a scrawny woman with a squint, had brought all her children with her; squinting at the plates like a bird of prey, she swooped on everything that came within her reach and hid it in her own and the children's pockets.

Lipa sat like a statue, still with the same expression she had worn in the church. Anisim had not exchanged a word with her since their first meeting, and still did not know what her voice sounded like; now, sitting beside her, he drank English bitters, still without a word, and when he was tipsy said to Lipa's aunt, who was sitting opposite him,

'I have a friend called Samorodov. A remarkable man. An honorary citizen, and he knows how to talk. But I can read him like a book, aunty, and he knows it. Do me the honour of drinking Samorodov's health with me, aunty!'

Varvara hovered round the tables, pressing the guests to eat, weary, flustered, and yet evidently pleased that there were so many dishes and that everything was so grand—now nobody could criticize. The sun sank, but the meal still went on; by now nobody knew what they were eating or drinking, and nobody could make out what anybody else was saying; only occasionally, when the band was quiet, some woman would be heard shouting in the yard,

'Bloodsuckers, grinding the faces of the poor, may the devil carry you off!'

In the evening there was dancing to the band. The Young Khrymins arrived, bringing their own wine, and when a quadrille was being danced, one of them held a bottle in each hand and a glass in his mouth, and this amused everybody. In the very middle of the quadrille some of the men suddenly squatted down on their haunches and began doing folk-dance steps; Aksinya's green figure darted about so fast that her train raised a draught. Somebody stepped on one of her flounces and Old Crutch shouted,

'Hi, your skirting-board's come loose! Children!'

Aksinya had artless grey eyes which seldom blinked, and an ingenuous smile played constantly over her face. In those unblinking eyes, that little head on the long neck and that lithe figure there was something snakelike; all green, with a yellow breast and that smile on her face, she seemed on her guard, like an adder watching a passer-by from among the young rye in the spring, tense and with head raised ready to strike. The Khrymins treated her with easy familiarity and it was evident that she had long been on intimate terms with the eldest of them. Her deaf husband noticed nothing, and did not even look at her; he sat with his legs crossed, eating nuts, which he cracked so loudly with his teeth that it sounded like pistol shots.

Now Old Tsybukin abruptly advanced to the middle of the floor, waving a handkerchief as a sign that he also wanted to dance a Russian dance, and a roar of approval ran through the house and the yard,

'*Himself* has stepped out! *Himself*!'

Varvara danced, but the old man only waved his handkerchief and shuffled his heels; but the people in the yard, hanging on to one another to get a look through the windows, were delighted, and for a moment forgave him everything—both his riches and his insolence.

'That's the boy, Gregory Petrovich! That's right, keep it up! You see you're still good for something! Ha, ha!'

It was very late before it was all over, after one o'clock in the morning. Anisim, staggering, went round all the singers and the band and gave each a new half-rouble as a parting gift. The old man, not staggering, but producing the impression of hopping on one foot, saw his guests off and told each of them,

'The wedding has cost me two thousand.'

As they went away, somebody left behind his old coat in place of the Shikalovo innkeeper's good one, and Anisim's temper suddenly flared up. He began shouting,

'Stop! I'll make a search at once! I know who stole it! Stop!'

He ran out into the street in pursuit of somebody, but was caught, dragged back to the house, pushed, sweating, drunk and still crimson with rage, into the room where her aunt had already undressed Lipa, and locked in.

IV

Five days had passed. Anisim, getting ready to leave, went upstairs to say good-bye to Varvara. All the icon-lamps were lit, there was a smell of incense, and she was sitting by her window knitting a red woollen stocking.

'You haven't spent much time with us,' she said. 'I suppose it's too dull for you here? Dear me, yes . . . We live well, we've plenty of everything, and we gave you a proper big wedding; the old man's been saying he spent two thousand on it. In short we live like rich merchants, only it's dull here . . . We treat the poor people very badly. It makes my heart ache, my dear, to see how badly; and, my God, if we barter a horse or buy anything or hire a workman, we cheat everybody. Cheating, nothing but cheating. The vegetable oil in the shop is bitter and rancid, people would be better off with tar. Well, why can't we sell good oil?—tell me that.'

'It's none of my business, mamasha.'

'But, after all, we all have to die, don't we? Dear me, dear me, really you ought to say something to your father . . .'

'Why don't you talk to him yourself?'

'Well! If I told him what I think, he'd only tell me to mind my own business, like you. In the next world they'll want to know whose business it is! God's judgements are righteous.'

'Of course they won't want to know,' said Anisim,

sighing. 'After all, there isn't any God, mamasha. Who is there to want to know?'

Varvara looked at him with amazement and flung up her hands with a laugh. The fact that she was so sincerely surprised at what he said, and looked at him as if he was mad, troubled him.

'Perhaps God does exist, only I can't believe in him,' he said. 'During my wedding I had a very queer feeling. You know if you take an egg out from under a hen and the chick is cheeping inside it, well, my conscience suddenly began cheeping inside me, and all the while during the service I was thinking, God does exist! But when I came out of the church—it was gone. Anyway, how should I know whether there is a God or not? That's not what they taught us about when we were little; even before a baby is weaned he is taught only one thing, to know his place. Papasha doesn't believe in God either, you know. You were telling me about some sheep that had been stolen from the Guntorevs . . . Well, I found out that it was a peasant from Shikalovo who stole them, but Papasha has the skins . . . That's faith in God for you!'

Anisim winked and nodded his head.

'The Chairman of the *Volost* doesn't believe in God either,' he went on, 'nor the clerk, nor the sexton either. If they go to church, and fast in Lent, it's only so that people shan't say anything against them, and just in case there is a Day of Judgement after all. Now they say the end of the world has come because people have got slack, they don't honour their fathers and mothers, and things like that. That's rubbish. The way I see it is this, mamasha, what causes all the grief is that people haven't enough conscience. I can see through them, mamasha, and I know. If a man has a stolen shirt, I can see it.

A man is sitting in an inn, and you think he's drinking tea, and that's all about it, but for me, the tea's all right, but I see something else as well—he hasn't got a conscience. You can go all day without seeing one man with a conscience. And the whole reason is because they don't know whether there's a God or not . . . Well, good-bye, mamasha. Keep well and happy, and remember me kindly.'

Anisim bowed down to the ground at Varvara's feet.

'Thank you for everything, mamasha,' he said. 'You are a great help to our family. You are a very good woman and I like you very much.'

He went out, deeply moved, then turned back and said,

'Samorodov has got me involved in a certain business: I shall be rich, or else I shall be finished. If anything happens you must comfort my father, mamasha.'

'Oh come, what's all this about? Dear me, yes . . . God is merciful. Well, well, Anisim, you ought to be nice to your wife; as it is, you both look at one another all sulky; you might at least smile a bit, really.'

'Yes, she's a bit strange . . .' said Anisim, sighing. 'She doesn't know anything and she's got nothing to say. She's very young, wait till she grows up.'

The tall sleek black stallion already stood by the front steps, harnessed to a dog-cart.

Old Tsybukin took a run, jumped nimbly up on the seat and took the reins. Anisim kissed Varvara, Aksinya, and his brother. Lipa was standing on the steps too, motionless and looking away, as though she had not come out to see him off but by chance, for no particular reason. Anisim went up to her and brushed her cheek very lightly with his lips.

'Good-bye,' he said.

Without looking at him she gave a rather strange smile; her face quivered, and somehow everybody felt sorry for her. Anisim also took a leap into the dog-cart, and sat with his arms akimbo, as though he thought himself handsome.

While they were driving up out of the ravine Anisim kept looking back at the village. It was a bright warm day. The village herd was being driven out for the first time, and the women and girls walked with the cattle, dressed in their best. The brown bull bellowed, rejoicing in his freedom, and pawed the ground with his front feet. Larks were singing everywhere, above them and below. Anisim looked round at the neat white church—it had just been whitewashed—and remembered how he had prayed in it five days before; he looked at the school-house with its green roof and at the stream where he once used to bathe and catch fish, and a stormy joy welled up in his heart; he wished a wall would rise up out of the ground to stop him from going any farther, so that he would be left here with nothing but the past.

At the station they went into the refreshment room and drank a glass of sherry each. The old man felt in his pocket for his purse.

'It's my treat!' said Anisim.

The old man, touched, clapped him on the shoulder and winked at the waiter, as much as to say, 'You see what a fine son I've got!'

'You ought to stop at home, with the business,' he said; 'you'd be invaluable. I'd gild you from head to foot, son!'

'It simply can't be done, papasha.'

The sherry was rather sour and smelt of sealing-wax, but they had another glass each.

When the old man got back from the station he did not recognize his younger daughter-in-law for the first few minutes. As soon as her husband had driven out of the yard, Lipa had changed, becoming suddenly gay. Barefooted, wearing an old worn skirt, and with her sleeves rolled up to the shoulder, she was in the passage washing the stairs and singing in a thin silvery voice, and when she carried out her big tub of dirty water and looked at the sunshine, smiling like a child, she might have been a lark herself.

An old workman who was passing the front door shook his head and heaved a sigh.

'Yes, fine daughters-in-law you have, Gregory Petrovich, sent by God!' he said. 'Not women, but absolute treasures!'

V

On the eighth of July Elizarov, nicknamed Old Crutch, and Lipa were returning from the village of Kazanskoe, to which they had made a pilgrimage on the occasion of the church festival—that of the Virgin of Kazan. A long way behind walked Lipa's mother Praskovya, who always lagged behind, because she was ill and short of breath. It was late in the afternoon.

'A-a-ah!' said Old Crutch in astonishment, as he listened to Lipa. 'A-ah! . . . Well?'

'I'm very fond of jam, Ilya Makarych,' said Lipa. 'I sit down by myself in a corner and drink tea and eat jam with it. Or else I have it with Varvara Nikolaevna and she tells me a sad story. They have lots of jam—four jars. "Eat it, Lipa," they say, "don't be afraid." '

'A-ah! Four jars!'

'They're rich. Tea with white bread, and as much meat as you like as well. They're rich, only it frightens me there, Ilya Makarych. Ooh, I'm so frightened!'

'What are you frightened of, my child?' asked Old Crutch, looking round to see whether Praskovya was far behind.

'At first, after the wedding, I was frightened of Anisim Grigoryich. He was all right, he didn't do me any harm, only when he came near me I felt frozen all over, right in my bones. And I couldn't sleep a single night, I was shaking and saying my prayers all the time. But now I'm frightened of Aksinya, Ilya Makarych. She's all right, she's always laughing, only sometimes she looks out of the window, and her eyes look so cross, and they are green and shining like a sheep's in the shed. The Young Khrymins are always on at her; "Your old man's got a bit of land, Butekino, about a hundred acres it is, this bit of land," they say, "and it's got sand and water, so you build a brickworks on it, Aksyusha," they say, "and we'll go shares with you." Bricks are twenty roubles a thousand now. The profits are good. Well, yesterday at dinner Aksinya said to the old man, "I want to put a brickworks at Butekino," she said, "and go into business for myself." That's what she said, and then she laughed. But Gregory Petrovich looked as black as thunder, you could see he didn't like it. He said, "While I'm alive nobody's going to do anything on their own, it's all got to be together." Well, she gave him a look, and she ground her teeth . . . We had pancakes, and she wouldn't eat them!'

'A-ah! . . .' said Old Crutch, amazed. 'Wouldn't eat them!'

'And I wish you'd tell me when she sleeps!' went on Lipa. 'She'll sleep for about half an hour, and then she gets up and walks about all over, and looks to see if the peasants have stolen something or set something on fire . . . I'm frightened of her, Ilya Makarych! And after the wedding the Young Khrymins never went to bed, but went straight off to the town and had the law on one another; and people say that was all through Aksinya. Two of the brothers promised to build her the works, but the other was annoyed, and the mill was shut for a month and my uncle Prokhor was out of work and had to go round to all the houses asking for scraps. I told him, "You ought to go ploughing or sawing wood, uncle; what do you want to disgrace yourself for?" But he said, "I've got out of the way of peasant's work, Lipynka. I can't do anything."

By a copse of young aspens they stopped to rest and wait for Praskovya. Elizarov had been his own master for a long time, but he did not own a horse and went everywhere about the district on foot, with a little sack in which he carried bread and an onion, and he walked with long strides, swinging his arms. It was difficult to keep up with him.

At the entrance to the copse was a mile-post. Elizarov felt it to see if it was solid. Praskovya came up panting. Her wrinkled face with its constant expression of fear was beaming with happiness: she had been to church today, like other people, then she had walked round the fair and drunk pear-kvass there! This was a rare thing with her, and it even seemed to her now that today she had really enjoyed herself for the first time in her life. After a rest all three went on together. The sun was setting and its rays struck through the wood and shone on the tree-trunks. In front of them they could hear a murmur of voices. The girls from Ukleevo had long since gone ahead, but they had lingered here in the wood: probably they were picking mushrooms.

'Hoy, lasses!' shouted Elizarov. 'Hoy, my beauties!'

There was a sound of laughter in reply.

'Old Crutch is coming! Old Crutch! Silly old man!'

The echoes laughed too. Now they had left the copse behind. They could see the tops of mill chimneys, and the cross on a bell-tower flashed: it was the village, 'where the sexton ate all the caviare at the funeral'. They were almost home; they had only to go down into that great ravine. Lipa and Praskovya, who were barefooted, sat down on the grass to put on their shoes; the carpenter sat down with them. Looked at from above, Ukleevo with its willow-trees, its white church and its stream looked pretty and peaceful, except for the mill roofs, painted a dark ugly colour for the sake of economy. On the farther slope rye was visible, some in cocks and sheaves dotted here and there, as though scattered by a storm, and some newly cut, in long swathes; the oats, too, were ripe and now shone in the sun like mother-of-pearl. It was harvest-time. Today was a holiday, but tomorrow, Saturday, they would be gathering the rye and loading the hay, and then Sunday was another holiday; every day thunder rumbled in the distance; it was sultry and looked like rain; and, looking now at the fields, all of them wondered whether God would allow the grain to be gathered in time, and their hearts were filled with mingled emotions of cheerfulness and anxiety.

'Mowers come dear nowadays,' said Praskovya. 'A rouble forty a day!'

People were still pouring in from the fair at Kazanskoe; peasant women, mill-hands in new caps, beggars, children . . . Now a cart passed, stirring up the dust, with an unsold horse running behind it and seeming pleased that it had not been bought, now a reluctant cow was dragged along by the horns, then came another cart with drunken peasants dangling their legs over the side. One old woman led by the hand a little boy in a hat and boots too big for him; the child was exhausted by the heat and the heavy boots which did not allow his legs to bend at the knees, but all the same he was blowing a toy trumpet with all the power of his lungs and without a pause; now they had gone down the hill and turned into the street, but the sound of the trumpet could still be heard.

'Our mill-owners seem to be in a shocking bad temper lately, somehow,' said Elizarov. 'Awful! Kostyukov's been getting annoyed with me. "You've used too many boards on the cornices," he says. Too many, how? "I used as many as I needed to, Vasili Danilych," I said, "and no more," I said. "I don't eat them with my porridge, boards," I said. "How dare you speak to me like that?" he said. "You so-and-so blockhead! Remember who you are! It was me," he shouts, "that made you your own master!" "Well," I said, "that's a fine thing, that is! When I worked for wages," I said, "I had tea to drink every day just the same." "You're all a lot of swindlers!" he says. I didn't say anything, but I thought, you can call us swindlers in this world, but in the next world it's you that'll be the swindlers. Ho, ho, ho! Next day he climbed down a bit. "You mustn't take offence at what I said, Makarych," he said. "If I said more than I should, there's this about it, after all, I'm a merchant of the First Guild, and superior to you, and you oughtn't to answer me back," he said. "Well, you may be a merchant of the First Guild," I said, "and I'm a carpenter, that's true. Saint Joseph was a carpenter as well" I said. "It's an honourable trade, ours, and pleasing to God," I said, "and if you want to be superior to me, Vasili Danilych, you're welcome," I said. But afterwards, after this talk, I mean, I thought, "Which is the superior really? A merchant of the First Guild or a carpenter?" The carpenter, of course, children!'

Old Crutch thought a moment and added,

'I'll tell you what it is, children. The one who works hard and is patient, he's the superior!'

The sun had gone down, and over the stream, in the churchyard and in the meadow a thick mist was rising, as white as milk. Now, as darkness advanced rapidly, lights twinkled down below and the mist seemed to hide a bottomless abyss. Lipa and her mother, who had been born beggars and were ready to remain so to the end, giving away to others everything they had except their meek, fearful souls—perhaps for a brief moment they dreamed that in this enormous mysterious world, in the infinite hierarchy of lives, even they had importance, even they were superior to somebody; sitting here now above the village they were content, smiled happily and forgot that all the same they must return below.

At last they went back home. By the yard gates and round the shop reapers were sitting on the ground. The villagers of Ukleevo usually refused to work for Tsybukin, and he had to hire strangers; now in the half-light they all seemed to be men with long black beards. The shop was open, and through the door the deaf man could be seen playing draughts with the boy. The reapers were singing softly, so that they could scarcely be heard, or loudly demanding their money for the previous day's work, but they were not paid for fear they might leave before the morning. Old Tsybukin, in his shirt-sleeves, sat with Aksinya under a birch tree by the porch, drinking tea; a lamp was burning on the table.

'Gra-andad!' said one of the mowers outside the gate in a teasing drawl. 'Give us half, anyhow! Gra-a-andad!'

There was a burst of laughter, and then the almost inaudible singing began again . . . Old Crutch sat down for a glass of tea too.

'Well, so we've been at the fair,' he began. 'We've had a day out, my children, a very good day, praise be. But there was something else that wasn't so good: Sashka the smith bought some tobacco, and so he gave the man a half-rouble piece. And it was a bad one,' went on Old Crutch, glancing round; he was trying to whisper, but speaking in a hoarse strangled voice that was audible to everybody. 'The half-rouble turns out to be a bad one. So they ask him, "Where did you get it?". And he says, "I got it from Anisim Tsybukin. He gave it me when I was at his wedding," he says. So they called the policeman and took him away . . . You'd better look out that nothing happens, Petrovich, no sort of talk . . .'

'Gra-andad!' the same teasing voice called from outside the gates. 'Gra-andad!'

There was a silence.

'Ah, my children, my children, my children . . .' murmured Old Crutch rapidly, getting up; he was overcome by sleepiness. 'Well, thank you for the tea and sugar, children. It's time for bed. I'm getting a bit tumbledown, my beams are rotten. Ho, ho, ho!'

As he walked away he said with a sob,

'It must be getting time for me to die!'

Old Tsybukin did not finish his tea, but he sat a little longer, thinking; from his expression he seemed to be listening hard to the footsteps of Old Crutch, now far down the street.

'Perhaps Sashka the smith was telling lies,' said Aksinya, guessing what he was thinking.

He went into the house and a little later returned with a small bundle; when he unwrapped it brand-new roubles flashed in the lamplight. He took one, tried it with his teeth, threw it down on the tray, then took another . . .

'The roubles really are false . . .' he said, looking at

Aksinya as though he could not understand. 'These are the ones . . . Anisim brought them, they're his present. You take them, daughter,' he whispered, thrusting the bundle into her hands, 'take them and throw them into the well . . . Blast them! And see there's no talking. Whatever happens . . . Take the samovar away, put the light out . . .'

Lipa and Praskovya, sitting in the shed, saw the lights go out one after the other; but upstairs in Varvara's room the blue and red icon-lamps still shone, shedding peace, contentment, and ignorance. Praskovya could not get used to her daughter's having married a rich man and when she came to the house cowered timidly in the passage with an imploring smile; tea and sugar were sent out to her there. Lipa could not get used to it either, and after her husband went away she slept not in her bed but wherever she happened to be—in the kitchen or in the shed, and every day she scrubbed floors or washed clothes and felt as though she was still going out to work. This time, returning from their pilgrimage, they drank tea in the kitchen with the cook, then went into the shed and lay down on the floor between the sledge and the inner wall. It was dark there and smelt of harness. The lights went out all round the house, then they heard the deaf man locking up the shop and the reapers disposing themselves for sleep in the yard. Far away at the Young Khrymins' somebody was playing the accordion . . . Praskovya and Lipa fell asleep.

There was bright moonlight when they were awakened by the sound of footsteps; Aksinya stood by the entrance with a bundle of bedding in her arms.

'Perhaps it is cooler here . . .' she said, then came in and lay down almost on the threshold, with the moonlight falling full on her.

She did not sleep but lay sighing heavily, tossing and turning with the heat, and throwing off almost all the clothes—and what a proud handsome animal she was in the magical light of the moon! A short time passed and then the sound of footsteps came again: in the doorway appeared the white figure of the old man.

'Aksinya!' he called. 'Are you here?'

'Well?' she answered angrily.

'I told you just now to throw that money in the well. Did you do it?'

'What an idea, throwing money into the water! I gave it to the reapers . . .'

'Oh my God!' said the old man in fear and amazement. 'You obstinate woman! . . . Oh my God!'

He went away, clasping his hands and talking to himself as he walked. A little later Aksinya sat up, sighed heavily with annoyance, then got up, gathered her bedding into a heap and went out.

'Why did you marry me into this house, mamenka?' said Lipa.

'People have to get married, daughter. We didn't make the world.'

They were ready to give way to feelings of inconsolable distress. But somebody seemed to look down on them from the height of heaven, from the blue sky up there among the stars, seeing everything that happened in Ukleevo and keeping watch. However great the evil, the night was peaceful and beautiful, and the truth, equally quiet and beautiful, still existed and would continue to exist in God's world, and everything on earth was only waiting to be merged into that truth, as the moonlight merged into the night.

They both fell asleep, comforted and clinging together.

VI

The news that Anisim was being held in prison on a charge of counterfeiting and circulating coins had reached Ukleevo some time before. Months had passed, more than half a year, the long winter was over, the spring had come, and both in the house and in the village people had got used to the fact. When anybody passed the house or shop at night they would remember where he was, and for some reason the tolling of the parish-church bell also reminded people that Anisim was in prison awaiting his trial.

A shadow seemed to lie over the yard and its buildings. The colour of the house had darkened, the roof was rusty, the green paint on the heavy iron-bound shop door had gone blackish, dry and wrinkled or, as the deaf man said, 'corky'; Old Tsybukin himself seemed somehow dingy. He had given up trimming his hair and beard and looked shaggy; he no longer took a running jump into the tarantass or shouted 'God will provide' to the beggars. His powers were failing, as was evident in everything about him. People were no longer so afraid of him; the village constable had sent in an official report on the shop, although he still received his proper bribe, as before; the old man had been summoned to the town three times to be tried for illicit trading in vodka, but the case was always being postponed because of the non-appearance of witnesses, and he was worn out.

He visited his son often, hired lawyers, submitted petitions, and presented churches with banners. To the Superintendent of the prison where Anisim was confined he had given a silver holder for a tea-glass, with an enamelled inscription, 'There is measure in all things', and a long spoon.

'There's nobody to speak up for us, nobody at all,' Varvara would say. 'Oh dear dear . . . You ought to ask some gentleman to write to the top authorities . . . If they would only let him out until the trial! Why should the poor lad be kept pining away there?'

She, too, was much distressed, but she had grown stouter and whiter-skinned; she kept the lamps burning before the icons as before, saw that everything in the house was kept clean, and offered her visitors jam and apple preserve. The deaf man and Aksinya looked after the shop. A new business had been started—the brick-yard at Butekino, and Aksinya went there in the trap almost every day; she drove herself and when she met anybody she knew would stretch out her neck like a snake in the young rye and smile her artless and enigmatic smile. Lipa spent all her time playing with her baby, who had been born just before Lent. He was a very small baby, thin and ailing, and it seemed strange that he could see and cry, was counted as a person and even had a name, Nikiphor. When he was lying in his cradle Lipa would walk away to the door, bow and say, 'Good morning, Nikiphor Anisimych!'

Then she rushed headlong to him and kissed him, and again retreated to the door, bowed and said,

'Good morning, Nikiphor Anisimych!'

He would kick up his little red legs, and his wails would be mingled with chuckles, as if he were Elizarov the carpenter.

The day of the trial was appointed at last. The old man left five days before it. They heard that the peasants who had been called as witnesses had been sent for; the old workman, who had also been summoned, left too.

The trial was on Thursday. But Sunday passed, the old man did not return, and there was no news. Late on

Tuesday afternoon Varvara was sitting by the open window, listening for the old man's return. In the next room Lipa was playing with her baby. She tossed him in her arms and exclaimed gleefully,

'You'll grow up so-o big, so-o big! You will be a big peasant and we will go out to work in the fields together! We'll go out working together!'

'Come, come!' said Varvara, offended. 'What's this you're making up about being a day labourer, little silly? We're going to make a merchant of him! . . .'

Lipa began to sing softly, but a little later she had forgotten again and was saying,

'You'll grow up into a bi-ig, bi-ig peasant, and we'll go out to work together!'

'Now! You're doing it again!'

With Nikiphor in her arms, Lipa stopped by the door and asked,

'Why do I love him so much, mamenka? Why am I so wrapped up in him?' she went on, her voice trembling and her eyes glistening with tears. 'Who is he? What sort of person is he? He's so light, like a little feather, like a crumb, but I love him, I love him like a real person. He can't do anything, look, he can't talk, and yet I know everything he wants to say with his dear little eyes.'

Varvara strained her ears as they heard the sound of the evening train approaching the station. Had the old man come? She no longer heard or understood what Lipa was saying, she did not notice how time was passing, but only trembled all over, not with fear but with eager curiosity. She saw a cart full of peasants rattling swiftly past. It was the witnesses coming from the station. As it passed the shop the old workman jumped down and came into the yard. People there could be heard greeting him and asking questions . . .

'Deprived of all rights and property,' he said loudly, 'and Siberia for six years with hard labour.'

Aksinya could be seen coming out of the back door of the shop; she had been serving somebody with paraffin, had a bottle in one hand and a funnel in the other, and was holding some silver coins in her mouth.

'Where is papasha?' she mumbled.

'At the station,' answered the workman. 'He says he'll come when it gets a bit darker.'

When it was known that Anisim had been condemned to hard labour, the cook, thinking that the proprieties demanded it, began keening in the kitchen as though over a death,

'You have left us all alone, Anisim Grigoryich, our bright falcon . . .'

The dogs, alarmed, began to bark. Varvara ran to the window and, straining her voice to the utmost and rocking from side to side in her distress, shouted to the cook,

'Stop, Stepanida, stop! Don't torture us, for Christ's sake!'

Nobody remembered to set out the samovar, they could not give their minds to anything. Lipa alone did not seem able to grasp what it was all about and continued to occupy herself with the baby.

When the old man arrived from the station nobody asked him any questions. He greeted them and then walked silently through all the rooms; he would not have any supper.

'We have nobody to speak up for us . . .' began Varvara, when they were alone. 'I told you to ask some of the gentlemen, but you wouldn't listen to me . . . Perhaps a petition would . . .'

'I did all I could!' said the old man with a wave of his hand. 'When Anisim was condemned I went to the gentleman that was defending him and he said, "There's nothing to be done now, it's too late." And Anisim says just the same, it's too late. All the same, when I came away from the court I talked to a lawyer; I gave him something in advance . . . I'll wait just a bit longer and then I'll go again. God's will be done.'

Once more he walked silently through the rooms, and when he returned to Varvara said,

'I think I must be ill. My head . . . it's all cloudy. I can't think straight.'

He closed the door so that Lipa should not hear and went on softly,

'I'm worried about my money. You remember Anisim brought me some new roubles and half-roubles on Low Sunday, before the wedding? I hid one of the packets, but some of the other coins got mixed up with my own money . . . Once, when my uncle Dmitri Philatych, rest his soul, was alive, he was always going away to Moscow or the Crimea for goods to sell. He had a wife and his wife, while he was away on his travels, I mean, had her fun with other men. She had six children. Well now, when uncle was drunk he used to laugh and say, "I've got no way of telling," he said, "which are my own and which are somebody else's." He was an easy-going sort, you see. Well, I'm like that now. I can't tell which is my real money and which is bad. It seems to me it's all bad.'

'Well, well, God bless you!'

'When I bought my ticket at the station in the town and paid with three roubles, I couldn't help thinking all the time they were bad ones. And I'm afraid. I must be ill.'

'No use talking, we are all in God's hands . . . Dear me yes . . .' said Varvara, shaking her head. 'You ought to think of this, Petrovich . . . Suppose something happens to you, by bad luck, you're not a young man. If you die, you ought to see to it that your little grandson isn't wronged after you've gone. Oh dear, I'm afraid they'll not do right by Nikiphor, that they won't! He's got no father, you might say, and his mother is young and silly . . . You ought to put him down, the little boy, if it's only for a bit of land, that Butekino, Petrovich, you really ought! Think about it!' Varvara went on trying to persuade him. 'He's a nice baby, it's a shame! You go tomorrow and write it down on paper. What is there to wait for?'

'I forgot about my grandson . . .' said Tsybukin. 'I must say hello to him. So you say the boy's all right? Well, well, let him grow. Bless him!'

He opened the door and beckoned with his finger for Lipa to come to him. She came up with the child in her arms.

'If you want anything, Lipynka, you must ask for it,' he said. 'And you must eat whatever you like, we don't grudge you anything, only keep well . . .' He made the sign of the cross over the child. 'And look after my grandson. My son is gone, so only my little grandson is left.'

The tears ran down his cheeks; he sobbed and walked away. A little later he went to bed and, after seven sleepless nights, slept soundly.

VII

The old man was going to the town for a short time. Somebody told Aksinya that he was going to a lawyer to make a will and that he was leaving Butekino, the very place where her brick-kilns were, to his grandson Nikiphor. She heard about this when the old man and Varvara were sitting under the birch tree by the steps one morning, drinking tea. She locked the shop doors, from the street and from the yard, collected up all the keys she had, and flung them at the old man's feet.

'I won't work for you any more!' she shouted, bursting into sobs. 'It seems I'm not your daughter-in-law but a servant! Everybody's laughing; "Look," they say, "see who the Tsybukins have found to be their servant!" You haven't hired me! I'm not a beggar, I'm not some kind of slave, I have a father and mother!' Without wiping away her tears she fixed the old man with swimming eyes full of malice and squinting with rage; her face and neck were red and strained as she shouted at the top of her voice.

'I won't work for you any more!' she continued. 'I'm sick to death of it! When it comes to work and sitting in the shop day in and day out, and slipping out to fetch vodka at night—I can do that, but when it's giving away land, then it's for that jail-bird's woman and her brat! She's the mistress here, the fine lady, and I'm her servant! Give her the lot, the convict's wife, and may it choke her! I'm going home. Find yourselves another fool, you damned tyrants!'

The old man had never brawled in his life, or punished his children, and he could not admit the idea that any of the family could be rude to him or behave disrespectfully; now he was terrified and fled into the house, where he hid behind a cupboard. Varvara was so panic-stricken that she could not get up from her chair, but only waved both her arms about as though trying to drive away a bee.

'Oh dear, oh good heavens, what is it all about?' she murmured in terror. 'Why must she shout like that? Oh dear me . . . People will hear! Not so loud . . . Oh dear, not so loud!'

'You've given the convict's wife Butekino,' Aksinya

went on shouting, 'give her everything now, I don't want anything from you! Go to hell! You're all a gang of thieves here! I've seen enough, I've finished with you! You've been robbing everybody that came your way, rich and poor, old and young, you bandits! Who sold vodka without a licence? And what about the false money? You've got your chests stuffed full of bad money, so now you don't need me any more!'

A crowd had already gathered by the open gates and was gazing into the yard.

'Let them look!' shouted Aksinya. 'I'll shame you! I'll make you burn with shame! I'll make you crawl at my feet! Hi, Stepan!' she called to her deaf husband. 'We're going home this instant! We'll go to my father and mother, I'm not going to live with jail-birds! Get ready!'

Washing was hanging on lines in the yard; she tore down her petticoats and blouses and threw them, still damp, into the deaf man's arms. Then, beside herself with fury, she dashed along the lines of clean clothes, tore them all down, flung everything that did not belong to her on the ground and trampled on it.

'Oh heavens, get her away!' groaned Varvara. 'What is she doing? Give her Butekino, give it her for the sake of Christ in heaven!'

'We-ell! What a woman!' they were saying at the gates. 'What a woman for you! She's run wild—terrible!'

Aksinya ran into the kitchen, where the washing was being done. Lipa was working there alone, the cook had gone down to the stream to do some rinsing. Steam was rising in clouds from the tub and the boiler near the hearth, and the kitchen was stuffy and dark with it. There was a pile of still unwashed clothes on the floor, and near it, so that he should not come to any harm if he fell, Nikiphor lay on the bench, kicking up his little red legs. At the moment when Aksinya rushed in Lipa had just taken her shift from the pile and put it in the tub, and was stretching out her hand to a big ladle full of boiling water which stood on the table . . .

'Give that here!' said Aksinya, glaring at her with hatred and snatching the shift out of the tub. 'You've no business touching my things! You're a convict's wife, you ought to know your place!'

Lipa looked at her, panic-stricken and not understanding, but then suddenly she caught the look Aksinya threw at the baby and knew at once; she turned as pale as death . . .

'You took my land, now take that!'

With these words Aksinya snatched up the ladle and threw the boiling water over Nikiphor.

There followed a shriek such as had never been heard in Ukleevo before, and it was unbelievable that so small and weak a creature as Lipa could scream so wildly. A sudden silence fell on the whole place. Aksinya went into the house without a word and with her old artless smile . . . The deaf man was still in the yard with his arms full of washing; silently and without haste he began to hang it up again. Until the cook came back from the stream nobody dared go into the kitchen and see what was there.

VIII

Nikiphor was taken to the local hospital and there before the evening he died. Lipa would not wait until they came to fetch her but wrapped him in a little blanket and set off for home carrying him in her arms.

The hospital, newly built, with big windows, stood

high up on a hill; it shone in the light of the setting sun, looking as if it was on fire inside. There was a small village at the foot of the hill. Lipa walked along the road and sat down by a little pond before she came to the village. A woman had brought a horse to the pond, but the horse was not drinking.

'What more do you want?' said the perplexed woman softly. 'What do you want?'

A boy in a red shirt sat at the edge of the water washing his father's boots. Not another soul was in sight either in the village or on the hill.

'He's not drinking,' said Lipa, looking at the horse.

Then the woman and the boy with the boots went away and there was nobody to be seen anywhere. The sun had gone to bed, hidden under a counterpane of purple and gold brocade, and the long red- and lilac-coloured clouds watching over its sleep stretched across the sky. Lost somewhere in the far distance a bittern was booming with a muffled, melancholy sound like a cow shut up in a shed. The cry of this mysterious bird was heard here every spring, but nobody knew what it was or where it lived. Up the hill by the hospital, among the bushes close to the pond, beyond the village, and in the fields all round, the nightingales were in full song. A cuckoo, reckoning up somebody's age, kept losing count and going back again to the beginning. In the pond frogs quarrelled angrily, bursting their sides, and it was even possible to make out the words, 'You're another! You're another!' What a din there was! Every creature seemed to be calling or singing on purpose to prevent anybody from sleeping on this spring night, and so that everybody, even the angry frogs, should value and enjoy every moment: after all, we have only one life!

A silvery half-moon shone in the sky, and there were

many stars. Lipa could not remember how long she had been sitting by the pond, but when she got up to go everybody in the village was asleep and there was not a light anywhere. It was probably about twelve versts to the house, but her strength was failing and she had no idea of the way; the moon shone now in front, now on her right, and the same cuckoo, hoarse by now, was still calling with mocking laughter, 'Look out, look out, you're lost, you're lost!' Lipa walked quickly; she had lost the kerchief from her head . . . She looked at the sky and wondered where her child's soul was now: was he following her, or was he floating up there among the stars, no longer thinking of his mother? Oh, how lonely it was in the open country at night, among all the singing, when she herself could not sing, and among the incessant cries of joy, when she herself could not rejoice, while to the equally solitary moon looking down it was all the same whether it was spring or winter now, and whether people were living or dead . . . It is hard to have nobody near when the heart is full of sorrow. If only she had Praskovya, her mother, with her, or Old Crutch, or the cook, or some peasant!

Suddenly she distinctly heard the sound of human speech:

'Put the horses in, Vavila!'

In front of her a fire was burning by the roadside; the flames had died down and there was nothing left but glowing red embers. She could hear horses munching. Out of the darkness loomed up two carts—one with a barrel in it and a lower one loaded with sacks—and two men; one was leading a horse to put it in the shafts, the other stood motionless by the fire with his hands behind his back. A dog began to growl near one of the carts. The man who was leading the horse stopped and said,

'Seems to be somebody on the road.'

'Quiet, Sharik!' the other shouted to the dog.

It was evident from his voice that this other was an old man. Lipa stood still and said, 'God be with you!'

The old man came up to her and said after a pause, 'Good evening to you!'

'Your dog won't bite me, will he, grandad?'

'It's all right, go on. He won't touch you.'

'I've been to the hospital,' said Lipa after a short silence. 'My little son died there. Now I'm carrying him home.'

The old man must have disliked being told this, for he moved away and said hastily,

'Never mind, my dear. It's God's will. Don't loiter, lad!' he said to his companion. 'Look lively!'

'Your yoke isn't here,' said the young man. 'I can't see it.'

'You're a regular slowcoach!'

The old man picked up one of the embers and blew on it—but it lit up only his eyes and nose; then, when the yoke had been found, he went close to Lipa with the light and looked at her; his glance expressed sympathy and tenderness.

'You are a mother,' he said. 'Children are always dear to their mothers.'

He sighed as he said it and shook his head. Vavila threw something on the fire and trampled it down, and immediately it became very dark; the scene vanished and as before there was nothing but the open fields, the sky full of stars, and the noise of the birds preventing one another from sleeping. A corncrake's harsh cry came from what seemed to be the very spot where the fire had just been.

When a minute had passed the carts and the old man

and the tall Vavila were all visible again. The carts creaked as they came out on to the road.

'Are you holy men?' Lipa asked the old man.

'No, we're from Firsanovo.'

'When you looked at me just now it comforted my heart. The young man is gentle too. So I thought, these must be holy men.'

'Have you far to go?'

'To Ukleevo.'

'Get in, we'll take you as far as Kuzminki. There you go straight on and we turn left.'

Vavila got into the cart with the barrel, the old man and Lipa into the other. They went at a walk, Vavila in front.

'My little son was in awful pain all day,' said Lipa. 'He looked at me with his little eyes without a word, he wanted to tell me, but he couldn't. Oh Lord God, oh Blessed Virgin! I was so upset that I kept falling on the floor. I was standing by the bed and I kept falling down. Tell me, grandad, why should a baby suffer before it dies? When a big person, a man or woman, is in pain, their sins are forgiven, but why should a little child suffer, when it has no sins? Why?'

'Who can tell?' answered the old man.

They went on in silence for about half an hour.

'Nobody can know everything, all the whys and wherefores,' said the old man. 'A bird is made with two wings, not four, because two are enough to fly with; and so a person is not made to know everything, only a half or a quarter. He knows as much as he needs to for living.'

'I'd rather walk, grandad. I have a misery at my heart.'

'Never mind, sit still.'

The old man yawned and made the sign of the cross over his mouth.

'Never mind,' he repeated. 'Yours is only a small trouble. Life is long—there's good and bad both to come yet, there's everything to come. Great is Mother Russia!' he said, looking about him. 'I've been all over Russia and seen everything, my dear, so you can believe me. There will be good things and there will be bad things too. I was in Siberia as a village delegate, and on the Amur and in the Altai, and then I settled in Siberia, and I farmed there, then afterwards I got homesick for Mother Russia and came back home to my village. We came back home on foot, and I remember once we were on a ferry-boat, and there I was, as thin as thin, all ragged and barefoot and half frozen and sucking a crust, and a gentleman was going by and he looked at me and tears ran down his face, he was sorry for me. "Ah," says he, "your bread is black, and your days are black . . ." And I got back, as the saying goes, with neither hearth nor home; I did have a wife once, but I left her in Siberia, I buried her there. So then I got my living as a farm-labourer. And then what? I'll tell you: then there were good times and bad times both. And I've no wish to die now, my dear, I wouldn't mind living another twenty years; so there must have been more good than bad. Great is Mother Russia,' he said, and again gazed all about him

'Grandad,' asked Lipa, 'when a person dies, how many days does his soul wander about on the earth afterwards?'

'How do I know? We'll ask Vavila here—he went to school. Now they teach them everything. Vavila!' called out the old man.

'What?'

'Vavila, when a man dies, how many days does his soul walk on earth?'

Vavila stopped the horse and only then answered,

'Nine. But when my uncle Kirilla died his soul stayed in our hut for thirteen days after.'

'How do you know?'

'There was a rapping in the stove for thirteen days.'

'Well, all right. Drive on,' said the old man, but it was plain that he did not believe a word of it.

Near Kuzminki the carts turned on to the high road, and Lipa went straight on. It was growing light. When she was going down into the ravine the huts and church of Ukleevo were covered in mist. It was cold, and it seemed to her that the same cuckoo was still calling.

Lipa got home before the herd had been driven out into the fields: everybody was asleep. She sat down on the steps and waited. The old man came out first; as soon as he saw her, he understood what had happened and for a long time, unable to utter a word, could only mumble.

'Ah, Lipa,' he said at last, 'you didn't look after my grandson . . .'

They had waked Varvara. She clasped her hands and sobbed, and immediately began to lay out the child.

'Such a pretty baby he was,' she repeated time after time. 'Oh dear, dear . . . The only boy, and you couldn't even look after him, you little silly . . .'

They had a requiem mass in the morning and again in the evening, and the next day they buried him. After the funeral the guests and clergy ate a great deal, greedily, as though it was a long time since they had eaten. Lipa helped to wait at table and the priest, raising the fork on which he had impaled a salted mushroom, said to her,

'Don't grieve for the little one. Of such is the kingdom of heaven.'

It was only when everybody had gone home that Lipa fully realized that Nikiphor was gone, and that she would never see him again, and she burst into tears. She did not know where to go to weep, for she felt that after the little boy's death there was no place for her in that house, that she counted for nothing there and was only in the way. Others felt this also.

'What are you making that noise for?' shouted Aksinya, appearing suddenly in the doorway; she was wearing new clothes for the funeral and had powdered her face. 'Shut up!'

Lipa tried to stop but could not, and only sobbed louder than ever.

'Do you hear me?' shouted Aksinya, stamping her foot with rage. 'I'm talking to you! Get out of this house, and don't set foot here again, jail-bird. Get out!'

'Come, come, come!' fussed the old man. 'Aksyuta, my dear, don't be so harsh . . . If she is crying it's understandable enough . . . the child is dead . . .'

'Understandable . . .' mocked Aksinya. 'She can stay here tonight, but tomorrow she can clear out, bag and baggage! Understandable! . . .' she repeated tauntingly, gave a jeering laugh and went into the shop.

Early the next morning Lipa went away to her mother in Torguevo.

IX

Today the roof and door of the shop have been painted and shine like new, bright geraniums flower on the window-sills as of old, and what happened in Tsybukin's house and yard three years ago is almost forgotten.

Old Gregory Petrovich is still regarded as the master, but in actual fact everything has passed into Aksinya's hands; she does all the buying and selling and nothing is done without her consent. The brick-yard is doing well; because bricks are in demand for the railway the price has risen to twenty-four roubles a thousand; the village women and girls cart the bricks to the station and load them into wagons, and for this they get twenty-five copecks a day.

Aksinya has gone into partnership with the Khrymins, and their mill is now called 'Khrymin Sons and Co.' They have opened an inn near the station, and the expensive accordion is now played not at the mill but in this inn, which is frequented by the postmaster, who has also set up in some sort of business enterprise, and by the stationmaster. The Young Khrymins have given the deaf Stepan a gold watch which he takes out of his pocket every now and then and holds up to his ear.

People say in the village that Aksinya has seized great power; and indeed her great power is evident when she drives to her works in the morning, looking handsome and happy, with her artless smile, and afterwards when she is directing the business of the brick-yard. Everybody in the house is afraid of her, and so is everybody in the village and at the works. When she goes into the post office the postmaster jumps to his feet and says,

'Please be good enough to take a seat, Xenia Abramovna.'

A certain dandified landowner, no longer young, who always wears Russian dress, but made of the finest cloth, with high patent leather boots, was so captivated by her conversation once when he was selling her a horse that he gave her the reduction in price she was asking for. He held her hand for a long time, looking into her arch, merry, artless eyes, and said,

'For a woman like you, Xenia Abramovna, I'm ready to do anything she likes. Only tell me, when can we meet without fear of interruption?'

'Whenever you please!'

Ever since then the elderly dandy has driven to the shop almost every day for a glass of beer. The beer is atrocious, as bitter as wormwood. The landowner shakes his head, but he drinks it.

Old Tsybukin no longer takes any part in the business. He does not keep any money on him, because he cannot distinguish between real and counterfeit, but he keeps his own counsel and tells nobody of his weakness. He has grown somewhat forgetful, and if a meal is not set before him he does not ask for it himself; they have grown used to having dinner without him, and Varvara often says,

'He went to bed without supper again yesterday.'

She says it unconcernedly, because she has got used to it. For some reason he has been going about in a heavy overcoat winter and summer alike, and it is only on the very hottest days that he does not go out, but stays at home. Usually he wraps himself up well, puts on his overcoat and turns up the collar, and then goes for a walk through the village or along the road to the station, or sits from morning till evening on a bench by the church gates. He sits there without moving. The passers-by greet him, but he does not answer, because he dislikes peasants as much as ever. If anybody asks him a question he replies quite sensibly and politely, but shortly.

Rumours are current in the village that his daughter-in-law has turned him out of his own house and does not give him anything to eat, so that he has to live on charity: some people are glad about this, but others are sorry.

Varvara has grown even stouter and her complexion is still whiter, and she does good deeds as before; Aksinya does not interfere with her. They have so much jam now that there is not time to eat it before the new crop of fruit is ripe; it goes sugary and Varvara almost cries, not knowing what to do with it.

Anisim is beginning to be forgotten. Once a letter arrived from him, written in verse on a big sheet of paper, like a petition, and in the same beautiful handwriting as before. His friend Samorodov is evidently undergoing his punishment in the same place. Under the verses one short line had been added in an ugly, almost illegible writing: 'I am always ill here, I'm miserable, for Christ's sake help.'

Once—it was a bright autumn day, late in the afternoon—Old Tsybukin was sitting by the church gates, with his coat collar turned up so that only his nose and the peak of his cap were visible. At the other end of the long bench sat Elizarov the carpenter, and beside him the school caretaker Yakov, a toothless old man of about seventy. Old Crutch and the caretaker were talking.

'Children ought to keep their old folks and look after them . . . honour thy father and thy mother,' said Yakov angrily, 'but that daughter-in-law has turned her husband's father out of his own house. The old man's got nothing to eat or drink and where can he go? Three days without food.'

'Three days!' marvelled Old Crutch.

'There he sits and never says a word. Too weak. And why keep it quiet? She ought to be taken to court—nobody would praise her up there.'

'Who was praised in court?' asked Old Crutch, who had not heard properly.

'What?'

'The woman's all right, a hard worker. In their business you can't get on without it—sin, I mean . . .'

'Out of his own house,' Yakov went on angrily. 'When she gets a house of her own it'll be time enough to turn people out of it. Ha! a nice one she is, and no mistake! She's poi-oison!'

Tsybukin listened without moving.

'Your own house or somebody else's, it's all the same, so long as it's warm and there are no nagging women . . .' said Old Crutch with a laugh. 'When I was young I loved my Nastasya dearly. She was a nice quiet woman. But she always used to be on at me, "Buy a house, Makarych! Makarych, buy a house! Buy a horse, Makarych!" When she died she was still saying, "Makarych, buy yourself a racing droshky, so as not to have to walk". But all I ever bought for her was gingerbread, that's all.'

'That deaf husband of hers is a fool,' went on Yakov, not listening, 'nothing but a big fool, a regular goose. What does he understand? Hit a goose on the head with a stick—and even then it won't understand.'

Old Crutch got up to go back home to the mill. Yakov got up too, and they walked away together, still talking. When they had gone about fifty yards Old Tsybukin also got up and trailed after them with uncertain steps, as though walking on ice.

The village was already plunged in twilight, and the sunshine fell only on the upper part of the road that wound like a snake from top to bottom of the slope. The old women were returning from the wood, bringing the children with them; they carried baskets of brown and yellow mushrooms. A crowd of women and girls were walking from the station, where they had been loading wagons with bricks; their noses and their cheeks under the eyes were covered with red brick-dust. They were singing. In front of all the others came Lipa, singing in her thin voice, gazing up at the sky and carolling away as if exultant that the day was over, praise God, and they could rest. Among the crowd was her mother, Praskovya the day-worker, who was carrying a bundle in her hand and, as usual, panting.

'Good evening, Makarych!' said Lipa, when she saw Old Crutch. 'Good evening, my dear!'

'Good evening, Lipynka!' said the delighted Elizarov. 'My darling girls, all of you, be nice to your rich carpenter! Ho! ho! My children, my little children!' Old Crutch sobbed. 'My darling little adzes!'

Old Crutch and Yakov walked on, and they could be heard continuing their discussion. Behind them, Old Tsybukin met the crowd, and a sudden silence fell. Lipa and Praskovya had fallen a little behind, and when the old man came level with them, Lipa bowed low and said,

'Good evening, Gregory Petrovich!'

Her mother bowed too. The old man stopped and looked at them without a word; his lips were trembling and his eyes full of tears. Lipa took out of her mother's bundle a piece of buckwheat pasty and gave it to him. He took it and began to eat.

The sun had already set; its brightness had faded even from the road at the top of the ravine. It was growing dark and chilly. Lipa and Praskovya walked on, and for a long time afterwards they went on crossing themselves.

THE BISHOP

1902

I

On the eve of Palm Sunday there was an evening service in progress in the Old Petrovsky Convent. When the distribution of the palms began it was nearly ten o'clock; the candles needed snuffing and had grown dim, and a mist seemed to cover everything. In the dusk of the church the crowd swayed like a sea and to the Right Reverend Bishop Peter, who had been unwell for the past three days, all the faces—old and young, men's and women's—looked alike, and everybody who came up for palm seemed to have the same look in the eyes. The doors could not be seen through the mist, the crowd still moved forward, and it looked as if it had no end and never would have. There was a choir of women's voices, and a nun was doing the reading.

How stuffy it was, and how hot! How long the service went on! Bishop Peter was tired. His breathing was laboured, quick and harsh, his shoulders ached with weariness, his legs were trembling. He was unpleasantly disturbed by the presence of a religious maniac uttering an occasional shriek in the gallery. Suddenly, as if he was dreaming or delirious, the bishop thought he saw his mother, Maria Timofeevna, whom he had not seen for nine years, approaching him among the crowd and going away again when she had received a branch of palm from him, looking at him all the time with a bright, kind, happy smile, until she was lost in the crowd. For some reason tears began to trickle down his face. His heart was at peace, there was nothing wrong, but he gazed fixedly at the left-hand side of the choir, where the reading was going on, and where in the misty light it was impossible to recognize anybody, and wept. Tears glittered on his face and in his beard. Somebody close to him began to weep also, then somebody else farther away, then another and another, and little by little the church was filled with the sound of quiet weeping. In a short time, however—five minutes or so—the nuns' choir was singing, the weeping had ceased, and everything was as before.

Soon afterwards the service came to an end. When the bishop got into his carriage to go home, the whole convent garden, lit by the moon, was flooded with the gay, beautiful sound of heavy, costly bells. The white walls, the white crosses on the graves, the white birch trees and the black shadows, and the distant moon in the sky directly over the convent seemed now to be living their own private lives, incomprehensible, though near, to mankind. It was the beginning of April and the night was chilly after the warm spring day; there was a slight frost, and the soft cold air felt like the breath of spring. The road from the convent lay over heavy sandy ground and they had to travel at a walk; on both sides of the carriage pious women pilgrims trudged slowly through the sand in the bright peaceful moonlight. All were pensive and silent, and everything around was young and warm and near, everything—the trees and the sky and even the moon—and one longed to feel that it would always be so.

At last the carriage reached the town and rolled along the main street. The shops were all shuttered, except that at the millionaire merchant Erakin's they were experimenting with electric lighting, which flickered violently;

a crowd had gathered near. Then followed a succession of wide dark streets, then the highway beyond the town, the open country and the smell of pine-trees. Suddenly there rose before their eyes a white castellated wall, a tall bell-tower behind it, and a cluster of five large, shining golden domes; this was the Pankratievsky Monastery, where Bishop Peter lived. The same peaceful, contemplative moon rode high above the monastery. The carriage turned in at the gates, grating over the sand; here and there black monkish figures flitted through the moonlight, and there was the sound of footsteps on flagstones . . .

'Your mama arrived while you were out, my lord,' announced the lay brother when the bishop entered his quarters.

'Mamenka? When did she come?'

'Before the service. She inquired where you were and then went to the convent.'

'That means I did see her just now in the church! Good heavens!' The bishop laughed with joy.

'The lady asked me to inform you that she would come tomorrow, my lord,' went on the lay brother. 'She had a little girl with her, her granddaughter, I suppose. She is staying at Ovsyannikov's inn.'

'What time is it now?'

'Just after eleven.'

'Oh, what a pity!'

The bishop sat for a short time in the parlour, thoughtful and somehow unable to believe that it could be so late. His arms and legs ached and he had a pain in the back of his skull. He felt hot and uncomfortable. When he was a little rested he went into his bedroom and again sat for a time, still thinking of his mother. He heard the lay brother going away, and Father Sisoy coughing in the next room. The monastery clock struck the quarter.

The bishop changed his clothes and began to read the prayers before retiring. He read the old, long-familiar prayers attentively, and at the same time thought of his mother. She had nine children and about forty grandchildren. At one time she had lived in a poor village with her husband, who was a deacon, and she had been there a very long time, from the age of seventeen until she was sixty. The bishop remembered her from his early childhood, almost ever since he was three years old; how he had loved her! His dear, precious, unforgotten childhood! Why did those long-past days, gone beyond recall, seem brighter, richer, and more festive than they had been in reality? When he had been unwell in his childhood and youth, how tender and considerate his mother had been! Now his prayers mingled with his memories, which burned steadily brighter, like a flame, and the prayers did not interfere with his thoughts of his mother.

When he had finished he undressed and lay down, and immediately, as soon as darkness closed round him, he saw his dead father, his mother, his native village of Lesopolye . . . The creaking of wheels, the bleating of sheep, church bells on bright summer mornings, gipsies under the window—how sweet it was to think of these things! He remembered Father Simeon, the mild, gentle, warm-hearted priest at Lesopolye; he himself was short and spare, but his son, a seminary student, was enormously tall and spoke in a booming bass voice. Once, when he was in a rage with the cook, he called her 'You Jehudil's she-ass!' and Father Simeon, hearing it, said not a word, only felt deeply ashamed because he could not remember where such an ass was mentioned in holy scripture. His successor at Lesopolye was Father Damian, who was a heavy drinker, occasionally got to the stage of seeing green snakes, and even acquired the nickname of 'Snaky Damian'. The schoolmaster at Lesopolye was Matthew Nikolaich, who had been educated in a seminary and was a good man and far from stupid, but who also drank; he never beat his pupils, but for some reason always kept a bundle of birch-twigs hanging on his wall, with a completely nonsensical Latin inscription underneath: '*Betula kinderbalsamica flagellatica.*' He had a shaggy black dog which he called Syntax.

The bishop laughed: eight miles from Lesopolye was the village of Obnino, which had a miraculous icon. Every summer the icon was carried in procession through all the neighbouring villages, and the bells rang all day, now in one village and now in another; it used to seem to the bishop (he was known as Pavlusha then) that the air was trembling with happiness, and he followed the icon, bare-headed and barefooted, with innocent faith and an innocent smile, blissfully happy. In Obnino, he now remembered, there were always a great many people, and the priest there, Father Alexis, in order to save time during the preparation of the Eucharist, made his deaf nephew Hilarion read out the inscriptions written on bits of paper 'for the health' or 'for the repose of the soul' of various people; Hilarion read them, occasionally receiving five or ten copecks for his services, and once, when he was already grey-haired and growing bald, suddenly found written on one piece of paper, 'What a fool you are, Hilarion!' Until he was at least fifteen Pavlusha himself had been backward and so bad at his studies that it had been intended to take him away from the seminary and place him in a shop; once, coming into the post office at Obnino for letters he had gazed at the clerks for a long time and then said, 'May I ask how you are paid, monthly or daily?'

The bishop crossed himself and turned over on his other side, so that he might stop thinking and go to sleep.

'My mother has come . . .' he remembered, and laughed.

The moon was shining in at the window, the floor gleamed, and shadows lay across it. A cricket was chirping. Father Sisoy snored on the other side of the wall, in the next room, and in that elderly snore there was something reminiscent of a solitary, orphaned, even homeless, child. Sisoy had at one time been housekeeper to the diocesan bishop, and now he was called 'the former Father Housekeeper'; he was seventy years old and lived in a monastery sixteen versts from the town, or in the town itself, according to circumstances. He had come to visit the Pankratievsky Monastery three days before, and the bishop had kept him so that he might talk to him at leisure about business and questions of organization.

At half-past one the bell rang for matins. Father Sisoy could be heard coughing, muttering something in a dissatisfied tone, then rising and walking barefoot about the rooms.

'Father Sisoy!' called the bishop.

Sisoy went into his own room and a little later appeared wearing boots and with a candle in his hand; he had a cassock over his nightshirt and a discoloured old skull-cap on his head.

'I can't sleep,' said the bishop, sitting up. 'I must be ill. But what it is I don't know. I'm hot!'

'You must have caught cold, my lord. You should be rubbed with tallow.'

Sisoy stood for a moment and then yawned, 'Lord have mercy upon me, miserable sinner!'

'They have electric light at Erakin's now,' he said. 'I don't like it!'

Father Sisoy was old, wizened and bent, and always displeased with something, and his eyes were angry and protuberant like a crab's.

'I don't like it!' he repeated as he went away. 'I don't like it, confound them!'

II

On the following day, Palm Sunday, the bishop said mass at the cathedral in the town, then he called on the diocesan bishop and on a certain elderly general's wife, who was very ill, and finally returned home. At two o'clock he had two cherished guests for dinner, his old mother and his niece Katya, a little girl of eight. All through dinner the spring sunshine came in through the window that looked on the courtyard, and cheerfully lighted up the white table-cloth and Katya's red hair. They could hear through the double windows the rooks cawing and the starlings chattering in the garden.

'It is nine years since I saw you,' said the old woman, 'and yet when I looked at you in the convent—good Lord! you haven't changed the slightest bit, except perhaps you are a little thinner, and your beard is longer. Blessed Virgin, Mother of God! Yesterday at the service nobody could help crying. When I looked at you, all of a sudden I began to cry myself, but I couldn't tell why. His will be done!'

In spite of the affection with which she spoke, she was evidently embarrassed, as though she did not know whether to address him familiarly as 'thou' or more respectfully as 'you', and whether to permit herself to laugh or not, and she seemed to feel more like a deacon's wife than a mother. Katya gazed unblinkingly at her Right Reverend uncle as if trying to divine what kind of man he was. Her hair sprang up like an aureole behind the comb and velvet ribbon which held it, her nose was snub, her eyes clever. She had broken a glass before she sat down at table, and now her grandmother, while she was talking, moved first a tumbler and then a wineglass out of her reach. The bishop listened to his mother, remembering how once, a great many years ago, she had taken him and his brothers and sisters to see some relatives who were supposed to be rich; then it had been her children she fussed over, now it was her grandchildren, and here she had brought Katya . . .

'Your sister Varenka has four children,' she told him, 'and Katya here is the eldest, and my son-in-law Father Ivan, God knows why, fell ill and died three days before the Assumption. Now Varenka is left quite destitute.'

'And how is Nikanor?' asked the bishop, speaking of an elder brother.

'All right, praise God. He hasn't much, but God be thanked it's enough to live on. Only there is one thing: his son Nikolasha, my grandson, wouldn't go into the Church but went to the university to be a doctor. He thinks it's better, but I don't know. His will be done!'

'Nikolasha cuts up dead bodies,' said Katya, spilling water over her knees.

'Sit still, my little girl,' said her grandmother tranquilly, taking the glass from her hand. 'Say a prayer as you eat.'

'It is so long since we saw each other!' said the bishop, tenderly stroking his mother's arm and shoulder. 'I missed you when I was abroad, mamenka, I missed you very much.'

'Thank you.'

'I used to sit by the open window in the evenings, all by myself, and a band would begin to play, and all at once I would be so homesick for my own country, and I think I would have given anything only to be at home and to see you . . .'

His mother smiled a beaming smile, but immediately pulled a serious face and said again, 'Thank you.'

His mood had changed somewhat abruptly. He looked at his mother and could not understand what made her adopt that timid and deferential expression and tone of voice, and he did not recognize her. He began to feel depressed and annoyed. His head ached as it had the day before, his legs ached unbearably, the fish he was eating seemed tasteless and unappetizing, and he was thirsty all the time . . .

After dinner two rich gentlewomen came to see him, and sat for about an hour and a half in silence, with long faces; then the archimandrite, a silent and rather stupid man, called on business. Then the bell rang for the evening service, the sun went down behind the wood, and the day was over. Returning from the church, the bishop hastily said his prayers, lay down, and covered himself as warmly as he could.

He found the thought of the fish he had eaten at dinner unpleasant. The moonlight disturbed him, and later he heard talking. In one of the other rooms, probably the parlour, Father Sisoy was talking about politics.

'The Japanese are at war now. There is fighting going on. The Japanese, my dear, are the same as the Montenegrins, the same race. They were under the Turkish yoke together.'

Then he heard Maria Timofeevna's voice.

'So then, after we had prayed to God and had a cup of tea, we went to Novokhatnoe, to Father Egor, and then . . .'

Every now and then he heard 'a cup of tea' again, until

it seemed that her whole life consisted of nothing but cups of tea. Slowly and languidly the bishop was recalling the seminary and the theological college. He had been the Greek master in the seminary for about three years, and by that time he was unable to read without glasses; then he had become a monk and been appointed assistant head of the seminary. Then he took his doctor's degree. When he was thirty-two he was made rector of the seminary and superior of his monastery, and life then was so easy and pleasant, and seemed so long, so very long, as if it would go on for ever. Then he began to be ill, became very thin, went almost blind, and had to drop everything, on the doctors' orders, and go abroad.

'And then what?' asked Sisoy in the next room.

'Then we had a cup of tea . . .' answered Maria Timofeevna.

'Good gracious, your beard is green!' said Katya suddenly in amazement, and then she laughed.

The bishop remembered that Father Sisoy's beard really did have a greenish tinge, and laughed too.

'Good Lord, the child's a perfect pest!' said Sisoy loudly and angrily. 'How spoilt she is! Be quiet!'

The bishop was remembering the white church, quite new, in which the services were held abroad; he recalled the sound of that warm sea. He had had a flat of five high, light rooms, a new desk in the study, a library. He read and wrote a great deal. He remembered how he had pined for his own country, how every day below his windows a blind beggar woman had sung love songs and played a guitar, and how listening to her always for some reason made him think about the past. Eight years had passed, he had been summoned back to Russia, and now he was a suffragan bishop and all the past was somewhere very far away and hazy, as though it was a dream . . .

Father Sisoy came into the room with a candle.

'Oh!' he said in surprise. 'Are you asleep already, my lord?'

'What is it?'

'Well, after all it is still very early, ten o'clock or even earlier. I bought a candle today, and I should have liked to rub you with tallow.'

'I feel hot . . .' said the bishop, sitting up. 'I really must do something. My head is bad . . .'

Sisoy took off his shirt and began to rub his chest and back with the tallow.

'That's right . . . that's right . . .' he said. 'Jesus Christ our Lord . . . That's right. I went into the town today, and called on—what's his name?—archpriest Sidonsky . . . I had tea with him . . . I don't like him! Jesus Christ our Lord . . . That's right . . . I don't like him!'

III

The bishop of the diocese, who was old and very fat, was ill with rheumatism or gout and had not risen from his bed for the past month. The Right Reverend Bishop Peter visited him almost every day and received his petitioners for him. Now, when he was feeling ill himself, he was struck by the emptiness and pettiness of all the things they asked for or lamented over; their ignorance and timidity angered him; the cumulative weight of all this futility and triviality oppressed him, and he thought he could now understand the diocesan bishop, who had once, as a young man, written *The Doctrine of Free Will*, but now seemed to be absorbed in trifles to the exclusion of everything else, and to give no thought to God. The suffragan bishop had no doubt grown unused while he was abroad to Russian ways of life and now did not find them easy; he thought the common people coarse, the women petitioners tiresome and stupid, the seminarists and their instructors ill-educated and sometimes barbarous. The documents coming in and going out were reckoned in tens of thousands, and what documents! The ecclesiastical authorities of the diocese gave all the priests, young and old, and even their wives and children, marks for conduct—five, four, or sometimes only three, and there had to be discussions of all this and solemn reports had to be written and read. There was positively not a free moment, his soul was troubled all day long, and Bishop Peter knew peace only when he was in church.

He could not get used to the fear which, through no wish of his own, he inspired in people, in spite of his mild and modest disposition. All the people in the province, when he looked at them, seemed to be small, frightened, and apologetic. In his presence they were all abashed, even the old archpriests, they all bowed down to the ground before him and recently one petitioner, an old woman, the wife of a village priest, had been too frightened to utter a word, and had gone away empty handed. And he, who could never bring himself to speak ill of people in his sermons or reprove them, because of the compassion he felt for them—lost control of himself with petitioners, raged and threw the petitions on the floor. During the whole time he had been here not one person had spoken to him sincerely, in a simple human fashion; even his old mother seemed to have changed, completely changed! Why, he could not help asking, did she talk endlessly and laugh a great deal with Sisoy, when with him, her son, she was serious, mostly silent and stiff, which was not like her at all? The only person who behaved freely in his presence and said whatever he wished was old Sisoy, who had been in attendance on bishops all his life and outlasted eleven of them. For that reason it was easy to be with him, although he was no doubt an absurd and tedious old man.

On Tuesday after mass Bishop Peter was at the diocesan bishop's house, received petitioners there, and got excited and angry; then he went home. He still felt unwell, as before, and longed to be in bed; but he had hardly got in when he was informed that Erakin, a young merchant who gave largely to church charities, wished to see him on very important business. He had to be seen. Erakin stayed about an hour, talking very loudly, almost shouting, and it was difficult to grasp what he was saying.

'God grant it may!' he said as he went away. 'Most essential! It's all according to how things turn out, my lord. I hope it may!'

After him came the Mother Superior of a distant convent. As soon as she had gone the bell rang for the service and he had to go into church.

The monks' singing that evening was harmonious and inspired; a young priest with a black beard was officiating. As the bishop listened to the reading about the bridegroom coming at midnight and the chamber richly adorned, he felt not remorse for his sins, nor affliction, but peace of soul and serenity, and his thoughts carried him back to the distant past, to his childhood and youth, when they used to sing in the same way of the bridegroom and the richly adorned chamber, and that past seemed to him to be living, beautiful and joyful, as it probably never had been in reality. Perhaps in that other world, that other life, we shall remember the distant past and our lives here on earth with the same feeling. Who knows? The bishop was sitting in the sanctuary, where it was dark. Tears flowed down his cheeks. He thought that he had attained everything that was attainable by a man in his position, he believed in God, and yet not everything was clear, there was something lacking, and he did not want to die; it still seemed to him that he lacked the most essential thing, of which he had once dimly dreamed, and in the present he was still disturbed by the same hopes for the future as he had felt in his childhood, and at the college, and abroad.

'How well they are singing today,' he thought, listening to the choir. 'So very well!'

IV

On Thursday—it was Maundy Thursday—he said mass in the cathedral. When the service was over and people were going home, it was warm and sunny and gay; water gurgled in the ditches, and the sweet incessant singing of the larks in the fields outside the town was an invitation to repose. The trees had awakened from their winter sleep and smiled a welcome, and above them the fathomless immensity of the pale blue sky stretched away into the unknown.

When he arrived home the bishop drank great quantities of tea, then changed his clothes, lay down on his bed, and told the lay brother to close the shutters. The bedroom grew dim. But what weariness, what an ache in his arms and legs and back, a dull cold ache, what a noise in his ears! It was a long time since he had slept, it seemed to him, a very long time, and what prevented him from sleeping was always some triviality that began to haunt his mind as soon as he closed his eyes. From the neighbouring rooms the sound of voices and of clinking glasses and tea-spoons came to his ears, as they had done yesterday. Maria Timofeevna was telling Father Sisoy something in a cheerful voice, with many little jokes, and he replied in his surly, discontented voice, 'Well, really!' 'Never!' 'What next?' The bishop again felt first irritated and then hurt that with other people the old lady behaved in a simple, ordinary way, while with him, her son, she was timid, spoke little, and then did not say what she meant and, it seemed to him, even sought for pretexts to stand up whenever he was in the room, because she felt uncomfortable sitting in his presence. And his father? If he had been alive he would probably have been unable to utter one word while the bishop was there . . .

In the next room something fell to the floor and broke; Katya must have dropped a cup or saucer, because Father Sisoy spat and said angrily,

'The child's a perfect pest, Lord forgive me, miserable sinner! We'll soon have nothing left!'

Then it became quiet, except for noises from outside. When the bishop opened his eyes again he saw Katya standing motionless in the room, with her eyes fixed on him. As usual, her red hair stood up from behind her comb like a halo.

'Is that you, Katya?' he asked. 'Who is it that keeps opening and shutting a door downstairs?'

'I can't hear them,' said Katya, listening.

'There, somebody went through it just now.'

'But that's your stomach rumbling, uncle!'

He laughed and stroked her hair.

'So your cousin Nikolasha cuts up dead bodies, does he?' he asked after a pause.

'Yes. He's a student.'

'And is he nice?'

'Yes, he's all right. Only he drinks vodka an awful lot.'

'And what did your father die of?'

'Papasha was poorly and he was ever so thin, and all at once he got a bad throat. I had it as well, and my brother Fedya, we all had bad throats. Papasha died, uncle, but we got better.'

Her chin trembled and tears filled her eyes and trickled down her cheeks.

'My lord,' she said shrilly, crying bitterly now, 'we are very poor now, uncle, mamasha and all of us . . . Will you give us some money? . . . please . . . darling uncle!'

He was in tears now, too, and for a long time his emotion prevented him from speaking; then he stroked her cheek, patted her shoulder and said,

'It's all right, it's all right, my little girl. Holy Easter Sunday will be here soon, and then we will have a talk . . . I will help . . . I will help . . .'

His mother came in timidly and quietly, said a prayer before the icons and, seeing that he was not asleep, asked,

'Will you have a little drop of soup?'

'No, thank you . . .' he answered. 'I'm not hungry.'

'You don't seem very well . . . now I look at you . . . Well, how can you help being ill? All day on the go, the whole day—good God, it's distressing simply to look at you! Well, Easter isn't far off now, and then you can rest, please God, and we can talk, but I won't bother you with my talking now. Come along, Katechka, we'll let his lordship have a little sleep.'

He remembered her speaking to some church dignitary long ago, when he was a boy, in just that playfully deferential tone . . . It was only from the extraordinary kindness in her eyes and the timid anxiety of the quick glance she threw at him as she went out that it was possible to tell that she was his mother. He closed his eyes and seemed to sleep, but he heard the clock strike twice, and Father Sisoy coughing in the next room. His mother came in again and watched him timidly for a few minutes. He heard somebody drive up to the door in what sounded like a barouche or a closed carriage. There was a knock, the bedroom door opened and closed: the lay brother had come in.

'Your lordship!' he called.

'What?'

'The horses have been brought round, it is time for the Twelve Gospels.'

'What time is it?'

'A quarter past seven.'

He dressed and drove to the cathedral. All through the twelve gospels he had to stand in the middle of the church without moving, and the first gospel, the longest and most beautiful, he read himself. A lively and vigorous mood possessed him. He knew this first gospel, 'Now is the Son of man glorified', by heart; and as he read it, he raised his eyes from time to time and saw the sea of lights on either side of him and heard the sputtering of the candles, but the people, as in former years, were invisible, and it seemed to him that these were the same people as in his childhood and youth, and that they would be the same every year, until a day known only to God.

His father had been a deacon, his grandfather a priest, his great-grandfather a deacon, and perhaps his whole family had belonged to the priesthood ever since Russia had accepted Christianity, and his love for the church services, the priesthood and the sound of church bells was inborn, deep and ineradicable; in church, especially when he was taking part in the service, he always felt alive, active, and happy. So it was now. It was only after the reading of the eighth gospel that he realized his voice had failed, even his cough was inaudible, he had a violent headache, and he was worried by the fear that he might fall at any moment. Indeed, his legs grew completely numb, so that little by little he ceased to feel them at all, and he knew neither how he continued to stand, nor on what, nor why he did not fall . . .

When the service was over it was a quarter to twelve. As soon as he got home the bishop undressed and went to bed, without even saying his prayers. He could not speak, and felt that he could no longer stand. When he had covered himself with the blanket he felt a sudden unbearable longing to be abroad. He thought he would have given his life not to have to see these wretched cheap shutters and low ceilings, or smell this heavy monastic smell. If only there was one person to whom he could talk and open his heart!

For a long time he heard somebody's footsteps in the next room, and could not remember who it was. At last the door opened and Sisoy came in with a candle and a tea-cup in his hands.

'Have you gone to bed already, my lord?' he asked. 'And here I am wanting to rub you with vodka and vinegar. If you rub hard enough it is very beneficial. Jesus Christ our Lord . . . That's right . . . That's right . . . I've just been into our monastery . . . I don't like it! I shall leave tomorrow, my lord, I won't stay here any longer . . . Jesus Christ our Lord . . . That's right . . .'

Sisoy was incapable of staying long in one place, and he felt as though he had been in the Pankratievsky Monastery for a year. Listening to him it was difficult to make out where his home was, whether he liked anything or anybody or whether he believed in God . . . He himself did not know why he was a monk and never thought about it, and he had long forgotten the time when he became one; it was if he had been born a monk.

'I'll go tomorrow. I must get away from them all!'

'I should like to have a talk with you . . . But I can't collect my thoughts,' said the bishop softly, with a great effort. 'I don't know anything or anybody here, you know.'

'Well, I'll stay till Sunday if you like; so be it, but I won't stay any longer. I've had enough of them!'

'What sort of bishop am I?' went on the bishop softly. 'I ought to be a village priest, or a parish clerk . . . or a plain monk . . . I am crushed by all this . . . crushed . . .'

'What? Jesus Christ our Lord . . . There you are . . . Well, sleep well, my lord . . . What's the use of saying those things? What good is it? Good night!'

The bishop did not sleep all night. In the morning, about eight o'clock, he had an intestinal haemorrhage. The lay brother, alarmed, ran first to the archimandrite and then to the monastery doctor, Ivan Andreich, who lived in the town. The doctor, a stout old man with a long grey beard, spent a long time examining the bishop, shaking his head and frowning all the time, and then said,

'Do you know what, my lord? You have typhoid fever!'

In the space of about an hour the effect of the haemorrhage had been to make the bishop much thinner and very pale; he was shrunken, his face was wrinkled, his eyes looked enormous, and he appeared to have aged and grown less tall; to himself he seemed thinner, feebler, and more insignificant than anybody else in the world, and he felt that everything that had been had retreated very far away, and would neither continue to exist nor ever be repeated.

'How wonderful!' he thought. 'How wonderful!'

His old mother came. When she saw his wrinkled face and big eyes she was frightened, fell on her knees beside the bed and began to kiss his face, shoulders, and hands.

She too thought he seemed thinner, weaker, and less important than anybody else, and she no longer remembered that he was a bishop, but kissed him like a very dear and beloved child.

'Pavlusha, darling,' she said, 'my dearest! . . . My little son! . . . What has brought you to this? Pavlusha, answer me!'

Katya stood beside her, pale and stern, unable to understand what was the matter with her uncle or why her grandmother's face was so full of suffering and her words so sad and moving. The bishop could no longer speak at all, he knew nothing, and in his imagination he was a simple ordinary man, walking quickly and happily through the fields, tapping his stick on the ground, with the wide sky above him, flooded with sunshine; he was free now, as free as a bird, and could go where he liked!

'Pavlusha, my little son, answer me!' said the old woman. 'What is the matter? My dearest!'

'Don't bother his lordship,' said Sisoy angrily, as he passed through the room. 'Let him sleep a while . . . There's no need . . . what is the use?'

Three doctors arrived, held a consultation and went away again. The day was long, incredibly long, then night fell and moved slowly, slowly, until just before dawn on Saturday the lay brother went to the old woman, who was lying on the sofa in the parlour, and asked her to go into the bedroom: the bishop had died.

The next day was Easter Sunday. There were forty-two churches and six monasteries in the town, and the clamorous joyful noise of bells hung over it all day long, making the spring air turbulent; the birds sang, the sun shone brilliantly. The big market square was full of noise: swings rocked, barrel-organs played, accordions squealed, drunken voices shouted. In the afternoon the smart turn-outs paraded in the main street—in short, all was gaiety and well-being, just as it had been the year before and would, in all probability, be the year after.

A new suffragan bishop was appointed a month later, and nobody remembered Bishop Peter. Soon he was quite forgotten. Only the old woman, the dead man's mother, living with her son-in-law the deacon in a remote little provincial town, would talk, when she went out in the evenings to bring back her cow from the pasture, and met the other women there, about her children and grandchildren, and her son who had been a bishop, whom she would mention timidly, fearing that she would not be believed.

And indeed, not everybody did believe her.

PRINTED IN GREAT BRITAIN
AT THE UNIVERSITY PRESS, OXFORD
BY VIVIAN RIDLER
PRINTER TO THE UNIVERSITY